The War for Caelum

www.battlesofliolia.blogspot.com
battlesofliolia@gmail.com

The Battles of Liolia

The War for Caelum

WRITTEN & ILLUSTRATED
BY
WILL MATHISON

THIS BOOK IS DEDICATED
TO
ALL THOSE PERSONALLY AFFECTED BY CANCER.

Never give up hope, stay courageous, make new friends

along the way, and know that you are not alone.

TO SUPPORT THE BATTLE AGAINST CANCER AND
IN HONOR OF ALL THOSE WE'VE LOST,

ALL OF THE PROCEEDS FROM THE SALE OF THIS
BOOK WILL BE DONATED
TO
RELAY FOR LIFE
AND OTHER CHARITIES
DEVOTED TO FINDING A CURE FOR CANCER AND
SUPPORTING IMPACTED FAMILIES.

CONTENTS

Marenta Loras

Fangmaw Mountains

Great Feather
Peaks

Esphodale

Alsh

Bridge of Moraff

Sorrealis

Caelum

Lake Vascent

Arcanian Woods

erindor

Grain Fields

* Portal

Civitas Levi

Storx River

Grove of the Silver
Tree

THE DUNGEONS OF CIVITAS LEVI
~ 1 ~

"He's dead, mother."

Speilton saw the pain in Herdica's eyes as what she already knew to be true was confirmed, but her face remained calm and set. She beared the worn appearance of a warrior who has seen many battles , but she also possessed the vibrancy of a survivor.

"Were you there?" she asked steadily, but Speilton could tell tears were balanced on her eyelids, and her composure was fracturing. "Did you see him... see him go?"

"Yes," Speilton responded. "I was there. I was with him when it happened. He was protecting me when it...when he-"

"And that's what is important," she interrupted. "Your father...he hadn't expected to return here."

"What do you mean?" Speilton asked softly as he watched his mother blink back tears.

"He knew the danger of leaving. He knew what awaited all of you in Liolia. And, he also knew he wasn't what he used to be. Your father was a warrior at heart, but years here in Caelum made him a bit soft," she chuckled quietly in an attempt to ward off the sorrow.

"I didn't notice," Speilton smiled. "He still fought...well, much better than I had seen anyone fight before."

"So, he still had it?" Herdica asked, her eyes crinkling with that soft mixture of pride and loss.

1

"The way he fought, with such grace, I would have imagined he could have cut down any man in Liolia. If Retsinis hadn't had the Sword of Power, then-"

But the sudden clenching of his mother's jaw and a sudden dash of fear stopped him mid-sentence. "So it was Retsinis then, who killed him?"

Speilton nodded. "He found us, and Father dueled while I was engaged with this Warlock. I tried, Mother, to help him."

She reached across the small wooden table at which the two sat and clasped his hand. "There was nothing you could do. Retsinis…he can't be defeated. If your father fought him, it was to save you."

"I shouldn't have let him."

His mother laughed. "In all the years I was married to that man I could never keep him from doing something after his heart was set. He traveled with you for that very purpose – to protect you when the moment came."

"He didn't need to do that," Speilton protested.

"But he did. After everything we put you through, he knew he owed you that much. Speilton, you have no idea the guilt your father and I carried with us every day we lived here. We left you - and your brother and sister - alone to fight a war we were unable to end. We knew the pain we were putting you through, but we held on to that small assurance that one day the Order of the Bow would bring you all here with us."

"I know, Mother. I understand."

"And if he knew you were here, and you were safe, he would be overjoyed."

"Mother," Speilton dissented for the first time, "they have me in jail here. All of us have been jailed by the Phoenixes."

2

"Just give it time. Many of us are working for your release."

"But every moment we wait here, Liolians die. Retsinis is planning to end our world, and then he will come here."

"He cannot find us here," Herdica spoke resolutely. "It is impossible for him to discover the portals between our worlds without any help."

It was now that Speilton scanned the small, square room before speaking. The two Phoenix guards that had ushered him out of his cell deep beneath Civitas Levi to this meeting room to speak to his mother were still perched a few feet away beside the single door to the room, and Speilton eyed them as he leaned in and spoke softly. "But he's not alone."

His mother narrowed her eyes into a questioning expression. "Retsinis is not alone in this campaign. He has with him the Versipellis."

There was a moment's pause as his mother attempted to recall who the Versipellis were and what danger they posed, and then her eyes grew large with fright. "The spirits? The three harbingers of doom? I remember reading of them long ago."

"Yes, that's them."

"Have they just arrived? Who all knows about their presence?"

"Well," Speilton chose his words carefully. "They have been in Liolia for a few years now. And before recently, it was only a few of us that knew."

"So, you knew?" she asked pragmatically. "And who did you tell?"

"Well…no one."

"You kept this from Teews and Millites?"

3

"I wanted to tell them, many times, but it's complicated. If the word got out, there would be panic. The Wizards would leave – they abandon worlds where the Versipellis have appeared. And...well it wasn't their problem to deal with. You see, I was chosen by them."

"Chosen?" his mother asked. "Wait, I recall reading about that as well. They choose three people from each world. People they use to exert influence. People they manipulate to lead to the end."

"Pawns," Speilton simplified. "We're their pawns."

The pain returned to Herdica's eyes as she looked into the face of her son as if seeing for the first time he possessed a terminal disease. Still holding his hand, she turned Speilton's wrist showing the thin white scar in the shape of an eye on the back of her son's hand. "How long have you known?"

"Not too long now," Speilton admitted. "When I found out I went after them. Well, actually first they took Teews and lured me after her."

"Do you know who the others are?" she asked carefully.

"There are two others with the mark," Speilton nodded toward the scar. "A man named Ince who's with us here. And the other is a boy. Nigal. I think he is still in the Igniacan Underbelly in Liolia."

"So you think the three of you were supposed to have played some role in their attack on Liolia. You were the three...chosen?"

"The cursed, yes. And we must play some role, yet I do not know how. Not yet, at least."

"Perhaps they were wrong in choosing you three."

4

"No," Speilton shook his head. "No, they do not make mistakes like that. The three of us are still alive. And Ince and Nigal have not yet played any considerable role. So they must still be plotting, which means there is still a chance we can save Liolia."

But his mother was already shaking her head. "Speilton, you have seen Liolia. You have faced Retsinis. You know there is nothing left for you there."

"How can you say that?" Speilton pulled away from her grasp. "How can you turn your back on your people? On your world?"

His mother diverted her eyes and shook her head quietly. "I wish we could bring them all here."

"And why don't you? Why do the Phoenixes keep themselves hidden? This land has enough resources. The land spreads empty as far as the eye can see. We could bring everyone here, and they could travel far and wide in this land to settle."

"You know what would happen if the doors to Caelum were opened wide. If the forces of evil you speak of, Retsinis and the Versipellis and the Warlocks ever found out what existed here, they would march on this land and kill every last soul."

"And the longer you hide here, the longer they have to discover Caelum. I wouldn't be surprised if they are on their way as we speak."

"Even if they find out about this land, they need a Phoenix to let them enter," Herdica dismissed the idea.

"So, we just leave them to die then? The rest of the Liolians will die without us, that much I know."

His mother was quiet, and despite her tears' efforts to break forth, she retained her resolve and steady face. "Retsinis has the Drakon," Speilton added. "And

Ferrum Potestas, the Sword of Power. And with that sword he has turned thousands of Liolian men, women, and children to his side. His army of the turned, the Nuquamese, is vast, and they are all loyal slaves to him and the magic of his sword. And on top of it all, he has the Warlocks and the Daerds."

"Then what can you do to stop him?" his mother asked. "He cannot be defeated. If you go, there is nothing you can do but die along with the rest of them."

"We could unite Milwaria, all of the kingdoms of men and elves and giants and creatures of the forest. We already have the Calorians and the dwarves with us. And Onaclov has the ring…" His words stopped as he remembered what had occurred. "Actually Retsinis's troops have that as well now. Which means they also have the sea monster Cetus. But we do have two dragons. And the element wands."

"But you no longer have the Wizards?" his mother asked.

"Well, it is possible they still may not know about the Versipellis, which means they might still be willing to help."

"If others know, the Wizard Council will know soon enough."

"There is something else," Speilton broke in. "Something that may help us."

"What?" his mother asked quietly.

"I'm not sure exactly. It's more of a theory. Something I was told long ago. It's…well it's…"

"It's complicated," his mother finished.

Speilton nodded. "I believe there is something hidden away, in Liolia."

The austere look returned to Herdica's face at the mention of that world.

6

"Mother," Speilton continued, "I need your help."

As he spoke, Speilton reached again for his mother's hand, and his mind reached out across the room to the torches mounted on either side of the door. Just as he had in the endless hours he was confined to his small prison cell, he connected with the soft flames and called them forth. The slow burning suddenly erupted into a smokey blaze, drawing the attention of the two guards mounted next to them. As they fluttered their wings and backed away from the sudden roar, Speilton slipped a thin shaving of wood into his mother's hand and locked eyes with her. He could tell she was reluctant to take it, but she gave nothing away.

"I'm not giving up on Liolia," Speilton continued as his mother silently slipped the scrap of wood with scratched words across it into her robes. "It may not be your home anymore, but it's still mine. And I'll do whatever it takes to defend it."

His mother nodded, understanding his mind was decided. "You are so very like your father. But your father also knew when to fight and when to save his own life. And in the end, he gave his life so that you could live."

"This isn't just about me, Mother. During the last battle, the Versipellis showed me something. I…I don't know if they were just visions to lead me astray or draw me into a trap or if they were truly visions of things to come but…"

"What did you see?" his mother asked softly, her words and gaze all offering herself to share the weight of his pain.

7

"I saw people dying. Many people dying. Friends…family."

Speilton was glad she didn't press him any further, for she quickly understood what he meant.

"And you think you can stop these things from happening?" she asked. "If they really are visions of things to come?"

"I know I have to try," Speilton said firmly. "Maybe that is exactly what the Versipellis want me to do. Maybe it's all a trap after all. But I need to know. I can't just ignore what I've seen."

"I wouldn't expect you to," she said quietly. "However, for now you must remain in your cell, and I will work to arrange your freedom with the Order of the Bow."

But the look in her eyes showed she had guessed what the wood shred entailed, and for now she would keep it a secret.

Speilton gave his mother a slight smile and looked into her eyes that seemed so familiar yet so foreign; the eyes of a mother he had never been given the chance to know. But he needed her now, and now that she held his small message written on the thin film of wood he had chipped off of his bed, he could only wait and hope.

MIDNIGHT ESCAPE
~ 2 ~

Speilton waited the endless hours in his small room thinking over his plans for once he escaped the walls of Civitas Levi. Over the past two weeks while he had been confined to his room, Speilton had been plagued with an abundance of time to think, with very little idea of what to expect. He was holding onto an idea, borne more from hope than any substantial evidence, and his inability to find out the truth was torturous. He needed to return to Liolia, but he was a world away, locked within a simple white-stone cell below a city of gold and glass.

Two nights after the meeting he was allowed to have with his mother, he heard the slightest shuffling of someone outside the doors of his cell. Quickly, he shook off the first whispers of slumber that had begun to ease his body into sleep, and he rose to his feet. The scratch of a key against the door indicated someone was attempting to enter, then suddenly the door creaked ever so slightly open, and the round face of a young Phoenix poked into the room.

"King Speilton," the small Phoenix chirped, peering into the dim light of the cell. "Oh good! This is your room! I almost opened the wrong cell just a moment ago."

Speilton rushed to the open door and glanced both ways down the hall. "Did my mother send you?"

"She did," the Phoenix replied cheerily. "It's me, Beati! I bet you didn't recognize me now that my plume has grown on top of my head."

Turning back to observe the Phoenix again, Speilton said softly, "I nearly didn't. You have grown since I last saw you."

"I'm able to fly on my own now!" the Phoenix added proudly.

"That's great," Speilton whispered back, "but look Beati, I really need your help right now. I have to get out of the city tonight and make it to the portal by morning."

"That's what your mother told me. Do not worry! We have figured everything out. I've come to break you out of your prison, and now we must go find Prowl."

"Perfect," Speilton replied. "Now which way do we go?"

"Follow me," Beati announced, picking the jingling set of keys he'd used back off the ground with his beak and fluttering down the hallway on awkward wings.

They made their way quietly down winding hallways lined with cell doors. Speilton knew his men slept on the other side as he walked, and he struggled not to snatch the keys from Beati to free them. But where he was going, and under the circumstances, he would have to make the journey alone. This meant leaving even his brother Millites and his sister Teews, as well as his other close friends that had also sought refuge in Caelum after their retreat out of Nuquam. Finally, they emerged from the labyrinth into an entrance hall with two other Phoenixes unconscious on the ground.

"What happened?" Speilton asked as Beati led them through the room and out into the streets.

"Don't worry, they're okay. Aurum gave them a sleeping draught earlier today."

"Aurum?" Speilton asked, warmed by the mention of her name. "Is she here?"

"Of course! Who else do you think is going to retrieve Prowl?"

The silver moonlight shone through the patchwork of stained glass and cast a kaleidoscope of cool colors across the city. High above, the Phoenixes glowed dimly as they slept in their hanging cages that dropped like pendants over the towers and domes below. They walked quickly through the quiet streets, the clap of Speilton's boots, and clank of Beati's talons echoing in the hushed city. Once again, Speilton was struck with the artificial beauty of Civitas Levi, with all of its ornate artistry and architectural splendor. If such a city had existed in Liolia, it surely would have been the greatest wonder of that world. A vast expanse of towers and cathedrals and domed halls were all enveloped within a massive cage of seamlessly crafted gold columns that stretched to the heavens then back down again. But in all of its perfection, it lacked that most basic of qualities: the error of human craftsmanship. The city had been built by the magic of the ancient Phoenixes of the Order and the Wizards of a time long ago, and with that magic they had lost the comforting touch of labor and toil as well as the grandeur and pride that comes from the creation of such a city by the hands of its people. Magic may have bent gold beams into a wondrous grid of arches, but it had also left the city feeling cold and false, as if merely a still wet painting that could be wiped away with a simple brush of the hand.

When Speilton had returned to Caelum, he hadn't been given the chance to once again look upon Civitas Levi, for by the time he had awoken from his journey's slumber, he had already been carried off to his room. He hadn't been surprised, for the Phoenixes had told him such imprisonment would occur if he ever returned to their land. It seemed silly to him at first that such beings of peace were so quick to incarcerate deviants, but he had quickly realized that such reactions had always been fundamental to their civilization. A world of such purity could only exist when all evil or rebellion was contained or removed. Such beliefs had led the Phoenixes to banish those of their kind born to the element of darkness. Perhaps it had been this same policy that kept storms from forming and endangering their land.

"How much further?" Speilton whispered to Beati, beginning to grow concerned that the young Phoenix truly knew his way.

"Not far. They had to confine Prowl in one of their strongest cells. It should be right up…"

They rounded a corner to see two figures emerge from the shadows. One had hair of gold that appeared to emit a slight glow as it swayed in the wind, and the other was a creature the size of a large dog that pranced along beside the first. Speilton ran toward the figures, catching the golden-haired woman by surprise. He embraced her, then quickly released to catch the small four-legged creature that hopped excitedly into his arms. Prowl pawed at him in excitement, flapping her small wings and snorting sparks of blue flames as Speilton turned back to Aurum. "Speilton," she began, but Speilton interrupted.

"Thank you, Aurum," he said in a voice just above a whisper. "I know this must've been dangerous for you."

"It was the least I could do," she smiled. "I know your journey must have been difficult. And Speilton, I am so sorry for your loss."

She took Speilton's hand, and he nodded graciously. "It's alright. Thank you. I just...was never really given the opportunity to know him. The short time we were given together, I was almost always angry with him. And now he's gone, after following us into battle. And we lost many others as well, but it was necessary that we went. We had to see for ourselves the threat we were up against."

"And now you intend to go back?" she questioned, fear evident in her eyes.

"Yes," Speilton said simply. "I know it must sound insane to you."

"You do understand the danger of such a journey?" she asked.

"Of course, I do."

"They won't let you return to Caelum. If they are able to get ahold of you again, they will put you in the deepest dungeon they can find and ensure you are incapable of escaping again."

"I know."

"And I won't be able to help you again. Neither will your mother."

Speilton nodded and smiled. "I was worried she would throw my message away. But I assume she was the one who brought you into this."

"Yes, she knew I would be more capable of freeing than she was. And I think she knew how ready I would be to help."

Speilton laid a reassuring hand on her shoulder and smiled. "I thank you again. I know you have risked a great deal being here, but I promise you it is for a good purpose."

"What do you intend to do in Liolia?" Aurum asked.

"I think there is something there that can help us, that can help Liolia."

"So, you still haven't given up on that world."

"Given up? How could I?"

"I know it's your home. I know how much you care about it – how important it is to you. But, here… here there is no Retsinis. No evil. Here, you could start something new."

"But here isn't real. It's not…home. There's nothing for me here."

"I'm here," Aurum responded, and her amber gaze was so pure, so penetrating, that Speilton was forced to turn away.

"I know. And I'm sorry. I didn't mean–"

"I know what you meant," Aurum assured him. "I know you have to go back, if there is any chance of saving Liolia. I just hope you understand the consequences."

"I do understand," Speilton responded. "But I also know what the consequences will be if I do nothing."

Aurum nodded and gave a small smile. "Then I truly hope it – whatever it is you think you will find there – will work."

"Thank you, Aurum," Speilton smiled, turning back to Prowl. "Now, do you know anywhere we can find her some food. She'll need to be fed to get her back to flying size."

"Right this way," Aurum ushered them down the street, her golden hair and gown flowing behind her as it reflected the soft flickers of light from the moon and Phoenixes above them.

Prowl and Beati kept pace with them, nearly equal in their height. When Beati hopped and beat his wings to keep from falling behind, Prowl extended her leathery wings as well, brandishing their greater reach with a quiet pride. Aurum eventually ducked down an alley and pulled a bag from the shadows. In it were rolls of bread and what appeared to be a pie. "Here, eat this," she whispered, offering the food to Prowl who quickly snatched it up and swallowed with only the slightest chewing. "And here Speilton. You must be hungry as well. I've seen what little they were feeding you."

Speilton looked at the muffin she held out to him but shook his head. "I'm fine. Prowl needs it now more than I do."

As Prowl dove her blue-scaled snout into the pie, her growth became evident. The larger she grew, the farther down her neck had to reach to eat from the ground. Her bites were larger as well. After another loaf of bread and two muffins, she was the size of a bear, and following a large melon and a few potatoes, she stood nearly seven feet at her shoulder. Once again feeling the power of her full size, Prowl sat back on her haunches and stretched out her wings so that they filled the great cobblestone streets. Speilton patted her neck, struck as always with the beauty of his dragon, with her royal blue scales sparkling in the multi-colored moonlight.

"Oh, there is something else you will likely need," Aurum said as she stepped further down the alley, emerging with a second bag, stretched wide by some large object inside. Speilton first pulled out a chainmail overshirt with long loose sleeves that clinked as he held it up to the slight light. "I found this armor. I thought it may fit," Aurum explained as Speilton slipped it on over his undershirt.

Next, he found a padded vest that fell down nearly to his knees that he slipped on over the chainmail. "And now your weapons," Aurum announced.

Speilton pulled forth his sword with its hilt pale like bone. He unsheathed it from its scabbard and observed the shiny steel of the curved Versipellis blade, before putting it back and strapping the belt around his waist. Then he pulled his wand out of the bag and felt the power of the object in his hand. Slipping the wand into his belt, he pulled out the last weapon that he only knew to be there by the weight and round shape of the bag. It was his shield, which appeared nearly invisible in the dark, save for a slight shimmer and a few hair-wide cracks that had formed from years of battle. Attaching the shield to a longer strap, he threw it over his shoulder so that the translucent disk sat on his back. "How'd you secure these?" Speilton asked.

"My position with the Order of the Bow has many benefits," Aurum said wryly. "Accessing the storage rooms was only a mild challenge."

"Quite impressive. Now what do we do?" Speilton whispered.

"The gates into the city are guarded," Aurum explained. "If they see you, they'll stop you and put you back in your cell."

"So, we have a different plan!" Beati announced. "There's a second way out."

"We opened a pane in the glass near the top of the city. I can show you," Aurum said.

"Then we fly out to the hills where the portal is located," Speilton continued,

"Yes, yes, and then I will activate it for you!" Beati said.

"And then, at dawn, you'll leave," Aurum finished with a small smile.

"What about you?" Speilton asked. "When I go, what will you do?"

"I guess I'll just try to feign innocence and go back to helping your mother negotiate with the Order for the release of the Liolians."

"Your brother," Speilton said, "Senkrad. He is with them. He came with us when we returned. I'm not sure if you —"

"I know," Aurum smiled. "I had heard, but I have yet to see him."

"They have him in a cell as well? But this is his first time in Caelum. He is not guilty of the rebellion that the rest of us partook in."

"Yes, that may be true, but he is the nephew of Retsinis. Senkrad fought by his side for many years. And hc, like the rest of the Wodahs, are creatures of darkness – born of ash and smoke."

"But you're his sister, and yet you serve the Order?"

"And I look human in every way. The preservation of peace and goodness is much more about perception that truth. Just as they banished the Phoenixes of Darkness, so too did they imprison the Wodahs."

"I am so sorry. I know it must be hard to be kept away after all this time without him."

"Yes, it has been so long since we were last together," Aurum stared off solemnly, her mind quite evidently wandering off to memories of her old life in Caloria. "But still, I try to reason with the Order. Your mother has been a strong ally in the campaign, as well as your friend, Onaclov, I believe he is named."

"Lord of the Lavalands?"

"Yes, and all of those funny little dwarves."

"So, he and the dwarves escaped imprisonment. It's good to see some of us are still on the outside."

"They are all free as of now, but with the great commotion that those dwarves have been causing I wouldn't be surprised if they too are locked away as well," Aurum laughed, and it made Speilton happy to see her smile.

"Well, if you are able to free them – your brother and my siblings – let them know I am sorry for leaving. But make sure they know what I'm doing is important."

"I'm sure they will understand. They all want what you want as well," Aurum said.

"We best get going," Beati chirped, his eyes looking off to the distant horizon. "It appears morning is almost here."

The fear of the journey ahead of Speilton was suddenly coupled with his realization that he would once again be leaving Aurum. For a second, he nearly thought he may be capable of staying and giving up the fight. He had done his fair share for Liolia, surely someone else would step up this time. *But Rilly spoke only to you,* Speilton reminded himself. *Only you can do this.*

Like that, the pleasant warmth of such a dream of peace and inaction was crushed, leaving only icy nerves. "We should get going," he said, pulling himself aboard Prowl's back.

He reached down, clasping Aurum by the forearm, and pulled her aboard behind him. Then Beati flapped up and nestled in the gold fabric between Aurum's arms. "Let's go, Prowl."

The blue dragon paced forward a few steps, her claws clattering on the stone street, before she pushed off and pumped her wings, taking the three passengers up into the night air of the city. They soared higher and higher until they were able to look down upon even the tallest of towers in Civitas Levi. All around them were the dangling cages of the Phoenixes, glowing in a multitude of colors. "Up there," Aurum said, pointing to a small opening at the top of the dome where the gold rim of the structure's cap met a glass pane. "Prowl should be able to fit through that."

Prowl saw the gap and began propelling herself forward and up. With one last thrust of her wings, Prowl shot up through the dome, breaking out into the open air. Free from the city at last, the dragon glided forward on her massive wings, floating on the cool early morning air. Speilton looked all about from their vantage point. To the south, or what appeared south if Caelum followed such compass orientations, was the dark sea that stretched as far as the eye could see and possibly on forever. Far to the north was the distant silhouette of dark, jagged mountains, like a row of fangs rising up from the soil. The lands to the west were those of rolling hills, within which the portal was hidden, and beyond them were great fields of tall grass and grain that rippled in the moonlight like wide bodies of water themselves. A winding stream cut a silvery path through the land, with small clusters of red and blue flowers nestled in the folds of its banks. Straight below was the grove of silver trees, growing whether by magic or pure coincidence of nature in perfect concentric circles, whose fruit healed all wounds, but condemned those who ate it to be tied to the land from which it grew. And then to the east was a great forest, and beyond it was a horizon slowly warming with the approaching dawn.

"It looks to be a beautiful sunset," Aurum observed.

"They're always beautiful here," Speilton said.

"Yet, they just really aren't the same as those I remember in Liolia."

Speilton nodded his head and smiled as she held tight to him, and they stared off to the horizon.

Prowl began her descent as the horizon took on the first shades of pink. Gracefully, Prowl landed amongst the green hills, and it took only a moment for them to find the small metal disk in the ground with a star emblem carved into it that served as the marker for the portal. And then the party waited for the sun to finally rise enough so as to touch the horizon.

"If they find out that you helped me, what do you think they'll do?" Speilton asked.

Aurum stared off at the impending sunset and smiled. "Who knows? Probably lock me away with the rest of your people."

"If you're with them, who will fight for their release?"

"Your mother still will. That's why she didn't come tonight. She knew I could free you better than she could, and there was no need for us both to risk it."

"Well, I thank you again. I mean it. I know how much you've risked coming here tonight. And I'm sorry I have to leave —"

"Don't be. I expected nothing less from you."

Suddenly, against the distant glow of the approaching sun, a small dark shadow seared through the air like a bolt. "What is that?" Speilton asked, his hand moving to the wand at his hip.

As the black shape crashed into one of the highest glass panes of Civitas Levi, three more shapes appeared out of the early morning darkness to the north.

"Phoenixes," Aurum muttered. "They're Phoenixes of Darkness."

The three shapes that had followed entered the city through the shattered panel created by the first, and then a horde of others appeared behind them. A flock of the dark Phoenixes swarmed the top of the city's walls, and then funneled in through the opening. Through the multicolored windows, they could see the birds descending upon the city like a cloud of smoke sinking instead of rising.

"They're under attack," Speilton said, jumping once again on Prowl's back. "We need to do something"

"No," Aurum grabbed him before he could urge Prowl forward. "Sunrise is almost here, and if they see you, they'll put you right back in jail."

"Maybe if I help them now, they'll forgive me," Speilton proposed.

"Perhaps, but even if they release you, they won't let you leave. They'll take back your weapons and keep you from ever going back to Liolia."

Speilton watched the mayhem gripping the city, and the horns erupt in alert. He wanted to help but knew that Aurum was right. This was his one chance to escape, and there were thousands of lives at stake. He sat back and reluctantly put his wand away.

"The sun!" Beati chirped. "It's there!"

"Aurum, you must be careful," Speilton said. "Promise me you'll look out for yourself."

"Of course," Aurum assured him. "I don't know why they have attacked, but it doesn't look like there are enough of them to do any considerable damage."

"Still, just…be careful…please," Speilton said, becoming anxious as the sun rose higher and his time grew shorter.

"You know I will. I have survived this far," Aurum took his hand again.

"Come, King Speilton! Time is short," Beati cried, standing above the star symbol carved into the metal disk lying flush with the tall green grass.

Speilton dropped down from Prowl's back and walked beside Beati. He looked back at Civitas Levi, now alight with an army of Phoenixes glowing as pinpricks of every color as they dashed around the cage-like city in battle with the Phoenixes of Darkness. Beati pecked at the symbol, and Speilton reached down and touched it as well. "Beati, are you coming with us? We'll need you to get back to Liolia," Speilton said.

"I'm sorry, but I don't think I should leave. So far, the Phoenixes don't know I was here, but if I left they would know I freed you."

"Now that the city is awake they'll likely find you anyways," Speilton said.

"Not if you leave now," Aurum said. "Quick, Beati, take to the hills and I'll follow you."

"Then you will have to use the portal to meet us at Mt. Flig. I don't know how long it will take – possibly weeks. But with the way time works it should only be a few days for you here."

"I will check to see if you have made it to the mountain as often as I can," Beati said.

"Thank you," Speilton smiled at the little bird.

As the winds began to swirl and the air became warped, Speilton turned back to Aurum. He opened his mouth to say something, but she cut him off. "Just go already," she said as she pushed Speilton back into the portal, and he was pulled into the void of rushing colors that soon faded to black.

LAZAR'S INTERROGATION
~ 3 ~

"Like we've told you," Usus exclaimed, slumping tiredly in his chair, "we have no idea why he left."

"But we can confirm there was no way he was in league with those Phoenixes of Darkness," Millites added sternly.

The King sat forward in his chair, glaring at the proud Phoenix he knew to be Lazar. Millites and Usus sat opposite the perched bird, with a table separating the Liolians from the Phoenixes. Dark circles beneath Millites' eyes showed he had not been sleeping much the past few weeks.

"So, the two of you see nothing peculiar with the fact that Speilton, your brother," the Phoenix addressed Millites individually, "broke free from his prison the same night that the dark Phoenixes attacked?"

"Peculiar, yes," Usus agreed, "but merely coincidence. Now, there is the possibility that they broke in so as to take Speilton hostage. Why they would do that, I have no idea. Then again, I wouldn't understand any of their reasons for doing anything. I didn't even know there were dark Phoenixes out there until you brought us in here."

"We have already ruled out the possibility of this being a hostage situation," the Phoenix said. "When our guards were alerted in the early morning, two of them reported seeing Speilton leaving with his dragon through the portal in the hills beyond the city."

"So, he went back to Liolia?" Millites asked stone-faced.

"It would seem so," Lazar nodded.

"And why would the dark Phoenixes possibly want to send Speilton back to Liolia?" Usus asked. "You claim that this being a coincidence is too improbable, yet you propose a narrative that is even more outrageous."

"The Phoenixes of Darkness are a mysterious group," Lazar spoke simply. "The attack on Civitas Levi was an irrational attack in itself, and even more so if it was only, as you believe, a random attack and not part of a larger plot. You see, they attacked with a substantial force, but clearly not enough to do any real damage. They would have known they were outnumbered, yet they came all the same. And then, after only a few minutes they retreated to the mountains."

"It was a foolish attack then," Millites said. "Appears to me like they have poor strategic planning."

"They've had nothing but time to plan such an attack for years, decades even. Yet this is the first they have done so. I only seek to answer why," the Phoenix explained with fabricated cordiality.

"We get that," Usus leaned forward, wielding an equal air of false pleasantness. "We really do. And we're telling you that your theories are in fact incorrect. We don't know why, or how Speilton escaped, but we can assure that he was not working with these Phoenixes of Darkness."

"How can you be so sure of that?" the Phoenix asked. "You mean to tell me that Speilton has never hidden anything from you? That he has been nothing but transparent all of these years?"

He addressed Millites alone once again, who narrowed his eyes and glared at the table.

"What are you insinuating?" Usus demanded.

"King Millites here knows exactly of what I speak," Lazar pulled his beak into a smile.

Millites looked up and clenched his jaw. "Yes, you're right. Speilton did keep the news of the Versipellis from us. I do not know why, and I'm not dismissing his actions. But there is a difference between keeping secrets and collaborating with the enemy."

"But what if the two were one in the same?" Lazar asked. "What if he kept these secrets because of his collusion with the enemy?"

"That's insane," Millites seethed.

"And what evidence do you have to prove that? The first time the two of you and your people came here, it was because Speilton had led your men into a trap. You all would have died if not for the gracious assistance of the Order of the Bow. Then again he led your men into a battle fully knowing that the Versipellis were present in the castle in Nuquam."

"They were merely mistakes," Usus spoke. "We all decided to attack the castle. It was not his decision alone."

"Then what of his relationship with Aurum? The niece of Retsinis himself."

"Estranged niece, I believe," Usus interjected. "And yes, it appears they are friends. What does that prove?"

"Well, she was the one to set him free," the Phoenix said. "At dawn, our guards saw her with Speilton and his dragon before they went through the portal."

"That's your answer then, isn't it? It was Aurum that freed him, not the Phoenixes of Darkness," Usus exclaimed, throwing his hands in the air and slumping back in his chair.

"It's not that simple. Aurum had incredible access to different guarded areas in the city due to her service to the Order of the Bow. The dark Phoenixes would have needed her to free Speilton anyway."

"Then interrogate her!" Usus said, growing more and more impatient as Millites clenched his fists and looked down at the table.

"That's the problem," the Phoenix said. "We cannot find her. She left with the dark Phoenixes. Only the small Phoenix that activated the portal escaped, but he, so far, has been resistant to talk much. I believe he knows very little about the larger plot as it is."

"So, you jump to the conclusion that she is also working with them for some reason, along with Speilton?" Usus questioned.

"It makes sense, considering the way events occurred."

"You don't know Speilton like we do," asserted Usus.

"Well it appears you didn't know him as well as you thought you did," responded the Phoenix coyly.

Millites slammed his fists on the table, and the two Phoenixes guarding the door fluttered their wings in preparation. "We have told you all we know. If there is nothing else you want, then send us back to our cells."

"There is something else," Lazar continued. "One of our strongest reasons for believing Aurum is in league with the dark Phoenixes is her relationship to Retsinis. When the dark Phoenixes returned to the mountains, we sent our own Phoenixes after them. But, when they got there…"

"Retsinis," Millites' gaze turned to fear. "Retsinis is here?"

"We are not sure of that," the Phoenix said hurriedly. "The truth is that they couldn't find anything. The mountains were wreathed in darkness and storm. But, the Order of the Bow believes…well they have some grounds to hypothesize that maybe…that another portal has been opened."

"There are other portals here in Caelum?" Usus asked. "Besides the one just outside the city."

"There are many mysteries throughout this world," the Phoenix responded diplomatically. "We do not believe there to be any others than the one outside Civitas Levi…but –"

"The Phoenixes of Darkness could have found one," Millites finished for him.

The Phoenix nodded his feathered head on his long swan-like neck. "It is not outside the realm of possibility that they may have found their own means to enter Liolia."

"You know what this means don't you?" Millites said sternly. "You know what Retsinis will do to this world if he can in fact come here with his armies?"

"The danger of this situation is not lost on us," the Phoenix responded.

"So, you will raise an army?" Millites asked. "You'll mobilize the Phoenixes to resist Retsinis and his forces? Let me tell you, even if you have every Phoenix fighting, it will not be –"

"We will not," Lazar responded.

"Excuse me?" Usus jumped in.

"We will not militarize our people. It is against our ways to engage in warfare."

"You must be kidding," Usus laughed. "You were quick to attack when we attempted to take back our weapons the first time we were here."

28

"It was a matter of last resort," Lazar responded. "Then, we had no army. Now we do."

The two were silent as they soaked in the implications of the Phoenix's statement. Millites sat upright in his chair and looked apathetically at Lazar. "You mean to send us and our men out to fight them?"

"It would mean your freedom," the Phoenix reminded him.

"No," Millites said his body rigid and poised, "it would mean our death."

"Again, we are still unsure that Retsinis has in fact formed ties with the dark Phoenixes. This may in fact be no more than a ruse."

"And if it's not? If Retsinis and his armies, and the Versipellis, and the Daerds and everything else he commands has made it into Caelum, then what?" Usus asked.

"That will be determined once their presence can be confirmed. As of right now, we only intend to send you on an investigative campaign."

"'Investigative campaign'," Usus repeated shaking his head. "That sounds nice doesn't it? One moment you are claiming that our friend, his brother, our King, is none other than a conspirator with Retsinis, and now you send our army – what's left of it, that is – to face down an enemy force larger than any Liolia has ever seen."

"I see it as a chance to prove yourselves. If Speilton has sided with the enemy, this is your chance to prove you too have not turned to their side. If he is innocent, as you claim, then your actions should speak for themselves."

"No," Millites responded. "No, we will not help. We fought Retsinis and his armies for decades, and you and your Order never came to help us. Now he is Caelum's problem."

"You still believe you can return to Liolia? That is can still be saved? Liolia is dead, and Caelum is all that is left. If this is Caelum's problem, then it is your problem as well. And as far as I've seen, you are not afraid to take up arms."

"So, it's fear?" Usus said. "That's what keeps you from fighting, even when you know it's right?"

"I didn't mean to imply that. We do not fight because that is not the way to achieve peace."

"Then don't fight them. Go...embrace them all if that's what you think secures peace."

The Phoenix shook his head and looked back at the guards at the door. "I believe our time is us," then looking back at Usus and Millites said, "I do hope you will reconsider our offer. It would be quite a waste for you all to live out the rest of your days in those cells."

"It would be an even greater waste for you all to be massacred by Retsinis and his men without the least bit of resistance," Usus smiled as the guards approached to take them back to their cells. "I think we'll be a bit safer in our cells when his army comes marching."

THROUGH THE LAND OF FROST
~ 4 ~

A gust of frigid air shook Speilton awake. He turned over to his side and tucked his knees to his chest as he shuddered against the torrent of ice and frozen rain that barraged his meager armor and thin cloth pants. Speilton fumbled for his wand and conjured a wave of flames against the onslaught of the torrential snow. There was a burst of heat, and then a sizzle of steam as the fire and ice collided. It was enough to energize Speilton and bring him to his feet. He looked across the frozen tundra blurred by the descending sheets of ice and found Prowl lying on her back only a dozen feet away, her legs kicking lazily up at the sky as if trying to paw away the cold. Speilton stumbled over to her, crouching down against the roaring wind to push the blue dragon, now only the size of a large dog. Prowl grunted, then sprang quickly to her feet, looking confusedly at the blue and white world around them.

"We're here," Speilton called against the roaring wind as he surveyed the land around them, trying to identify some features that would give him a bearing. "We're in the Icelands – that's for sure, but in this blizzard, I can't see much of anything."

Prowl shook, throwing the frost that had built up on her wings into the wind. As she turned to look around her, ice pattered against her snout. She snarled and exhaled a stream of blue flames that lit up the white ground around them before sizzling out.

"There!" Speilton said, pointing at a hazy outline of tall, looming feature in the distance. "It looks like some kind of mountain. We may be able to find a place to stay for the night."

At this moment, it was impossible to tell the time of day. The sun was masked by a thick veil of grey clouds, and the constant snow gave the impression of an endless white plain as far as the eye could see. Speilton hugged his shirt and vest tight, and clutching his wand tightly, he started off towards the mountain with Prowl close at his heels. Every few seconds, when the bitter cold was too unbearable, Speilton would let out a blaze of flames. But as the magic consumed more and more of his energy, the periods in between his fire grew longer and longer.

The walking was monotonous. After a few hours and only a couple of miles covered, it became obvious that the shape was not a mountain but a glacier, rising high above the flat tundra with hanging icy walls. Upon reaching the edge of the glacier, they realized they wouldn't be able to ascend its walls, at least not without any food or warmth. Instead they nestled into a crevice in the side of the icy embankment where they were sheltered from the wind and waited as the grey clouds turned to black and the white of the Icelands turned blue, then dissolved into the dark of the night sky.

Sometime in the night, the snow stopped. There was a stillness to the landscape interrupted every so often by the roar of the wind against the glacier walls. By the time the sun rose again, Prowl was the size of a coyote. She had taken advantage of her shrunken size by curling up in Speilton's lap where she could further avoid the ever-present wind. But now it was time for them to walk again, this time assisted by the enhanced visibility that the clear weather had granted them. The pair started off south along the edge of the glacier.

Speilton's bones ached as if ice had built up in his joints. His breaths were shaky and his eyes stung against the cold. He wondered why they hadn't had the luck of arriving in Liolia somewhere warm. Even the volatile, molten landscape of the Lavalands with its black cliffs of jagged stone and its perpetual dome of smoke would've been better than here. However, he had to constantly console himself that this was for the best, especially considering how close he was to the land to which he intended to journey.

At about midday, Speilton looked back behind him at the glacier they had already passed to see the ghostly shape of structures on the opposite side of the tall icy walls he had just left behind. It was a town, nestled beside the glacier as if bracing against the frigid wind. To the south was a near endless expanse of ice, but to go to the village would mean doubling back around and heading northwest. As Speilton stood weighing his options, Prowl rolled up into a ball to rest.

"We need food," Speilton muttered, more to himself than the sleeping dragon, "but there's a good chance the village is empty."

Another gust of wind caused Speilton to shudder, and he realized if he continued south without any supplies they may not make it across the icy plain.

"Come on," he said, nudging Prowl with the toe of his boot.

The dragon began to get up, and then collapsed back to the ice indignantly.

"There's food ahead!" Speilton said hopefully.

Prowl raised her head, gave the village another look, then rose to her feet and began to follow. They walked back toward the towering white cliffs.

To the far west, another range of icy mountains became visible, cradling the village in a small valley. Along the edge of the far mountains they saw what looked like a small group of some type of tundra mountain goat, but the pair were too drained and too far away to pursue the animals. As they approached the village, they saw the goats ascend the icy slopes of the mountains on invisible switchbacks. "There seems to be a path that way," Speilton said pointing to the mountains. "Up the mountain may be our best way out of here."

Prowl continued on north, her attention set solely on the village for the time being.

As night began to fall, causing the glassy ice of the tundra to sparkle like a field of stars, they arrived on the outskirts of the village. Even from outside the buildings, Speilton could tell there was no one living inside. The many buildings stood gaunt and hollow. While the hard stone and permafrost walls of the structures remained standing, many of the wooden roofs had collapsed under the buildup of ice and snow.

"This was a great village once," Speilton mused as they came upon the first buildings.

The thick doors were bolted shut, but the high slopes of snow against the entrances showed no one had entered or left in quite some time. They walked down the main street, with only small uncovered patches showing that a cobblestone path lay beneath the thick snow. The town was expansive, more of a city in size. Intricate statues and squares lay around nearly every corner with tall bell towers and high-ceilinged gathering halls rising above the stout maze of houses and stores. Each building appeared oversized and solid, obviously once accommodating the giants that lived in this region. "What is this place?" Speilton pondered.

He couldn't remember hearing of a city of this size outside their regional capital, the Castle of the Giants. It was rare for the giants to live in large groups, as they normally stuck to isolated towns of small clans. For so many to be living in the shadow of one glacial mountain was unheard of, unless...

Speilton quickly turned back to the towering walls of the glacier. The icy blue and white striped cliffs met the flat tundra along the edge of the city, but Speilton realized there was something hidden in the crevices of the glacier. He began to jog with the last of his energy further north through the city, his eyes fixed on the tall walls. He passed through abandoned markets and squares until finally he could see it. Set deep within the walls of the glacier, facing up to the north, were the massive stone walls of a giant fortress, built into the massive icy structure. "This is it!" Speilton exclaimed to Prowl who had finally caught up, "The stronghold of the giants - Ettonsfast. I've only heard about it in legends!"

Speilton continued through the village, heading toward the stone fortress. Suddenly, he burst out of the rows of buildings onto a flat plain at the doorstep of Ettonsfast, and his heart fell. He had found the citizens of the city.

The hundreds of yards of flat ice were littered with the massive, twisted bodies of the giants. Spears and flags of the men stood erect out of the ground like the tombstones of the fallen whose bodies had been frozen and preserved under a film of frost. The smooth ice had been churned up into a rugged battlefield, blackened by fires. Looking up at the massive stone walls of the fortress, Speilton realized with certainty that the giants had lost this day. The two stone doors, nearly forty feet in height, had been blown open and leaned flimsily against the entryway. Massive holes had been blasted into the battlements of the wall, and only one of the two large bear statues that had stood guard on either side of the fortress still remained. The other lay in a broken heap at the foot of Ettonsfast with the bodies of the fallen soldiers.

Then Speilton saw the other corpses mixed in with the giants. They were hideous monsters, each different from the others. "Retsinis was here," Speilton spat as a whimpering Prowl nuzzled his leg. "If the giants fell here, then there is no hope that any survived elsewhere. This was once their hold – an impenetrable fortress where they fended off the Calorians for the centuries of warfare."

Speilton looked across the field of death and ice at gaping faces and frozen outstretched arms of giants and Nuquamese. He wondered how many of Retsinis's possessed soldiers had once been giants in life before his sword struck them down and possessed their spirits, turning them into these hideous beasts. The lonely howl of the wind through the icy figures and frosted war banners was the only sound. Speilton looked once more at the towering walls of Ettonsfast and the solitary stone bear standing guard over the fallen. Then he nudged Prowl and turned back to the city.

After melting the snow embankment of one of the few undamaged buildings, Speilton threw his shoulder into the door and thrust it open. While, the grey brick walls gave shelter from the wind, no warmth could be found inside the long-abandoned chamber of a room. He quickly went to the fireplace and stirred up a fire. Prowl curled up against the edge of the flames, yawned once, and then fell asleep. Speilton found no food in the cupboards, but in the next house over, he found a slab of some unknown meat preserved in the ice and two thin fish.

He thawed the meat over the fire, and Prowl ate her fish while it was still raw. The food was enough to allow her to grow to the size of a large hound. While his fish cooked, Speilton found a large fur jacket from some dark-haired animal that he cut down with a knife to a human size. Prowl began to nuzzle the remaining slab of meat, but Speilton stopped her. "We have to save that for later," Speilton said. "There's a long journey ahead."

Finishing his fish, Speilton lay down next to Prowl and closed his eyes, letting the heat of his new fur coat and the fire lull him to sleep.

In the morning Speilton rummaged through a few more houses and found a pair of thicker pants, four more fish, and some loaves of bread and frozen carrots that must have been brought down to the city from the Plains to the north. He ascended the bell tower to see above the maze of stone and ice buildings. Straight south in the direction he had ventured the day before was an open stretch of white ice as far as the eye could see. Gusts of wind blew the dusty snow powder into the air where it rose and danced like some ancient spirit before dissolving into the bright haze. The tundra seemed endless, yet Speilton knew that far enough in that direction was Caloria. From the bell tower, he could see the far mountains to the southwest and what appeared to be the footpath that the mountain goats had taken the day before. "That's the way," he said, pointing to Prowl.

The dragon peered up at him quizzically, and he realized he hadn't told the dragon where they were headed. "We're heading back, just like Rilly told us to. Back to where this all began."

He fed the dragon again, bringing her up to a rideable size, and loaded her back with a saddle and sacks filled with the food he had scavenged. From an old blanket, Speilton tore off a piece of thick wool and wrapped it around his head and face to protect against the frigid wind that lashed at his skin like an icy whip. With Speilton on her back, Prowl took to the air, flying southwest towards the distant mountains ... towards Kal.

ATTACK ON CIVITAS LEVI
~ 5 ~

Metus heard the tremulous clap off to the North before he saw the dark shapes approaching.

"Did...did you just hear thunder?" he asked a Phoenix hopping down the street beside him.

The bird tilted its small head on its long slender neck. "It does not thunder here."

Metus tried to peer between the towering buildings around him towards where the sound had come from. "Well, thanks for your help," Metus said distantly, beginning to walk off through the streets, his eyes searching the horizon.

He raced to the end of the street, but his view was obstructed by the towers of a cathedral. The faun darted into the nearest building, his hooved feet clattering against the cobblestone alleys. Once he found a staircase he ascended the steps, constantly checking through the windows to see if he was high enough above the other buildings. Finally, he came out upon a balcony and could see through the massive multicolored glass panels of the dome that two black shapes were racing through the air towards the city. They appeared like birds but larger than any man, and as they flew, they left a trail of smoke that coiled off from their bodies.

"What are they?" Metus wondered aloud, but there was no one else around him to answer.

Suddenly there was a splinter of lightning on the horizon and a few seconds later he heard the faint thud of thunder. The distant mountains were darkening, and a storm appeared to be brewing around their peaks. This was obviously where the two shapes had started their flight. They emerged out of the thickening clouds like physical manifestations of the darkness.

Metus leaned over the balcony to peer down into the streets below, where Phoenix and human alike walked casually about without noticing the impending threat. "There! Look! To the north! Something approaches!"

A few beings stopped and looked up first to the faun high above and then to the distant area he pointed towards. As the black creatures grew nearer, Metus began to make out great black wings, sailing forth with ease on high currents of air. Another boom rocked the sky with enough force to cause the very buildings beneath the gold and glass dome to tremble. All throughout the city, Metus saw things begin falling. Flags and banners tipped and billowed down to the ground. Stacks of fruits and vegetables toppled and rushed out across the streets. And from above, roof tiles slid out of place and cascaded down where they shattered against the street.

Now there was commotion in the streets, and all around him, Metus saw more people flocking to windows and terraces, looking for the cause of the thunder and finding the two black shapes instead. It suddenly became clear that the approaching creatures were heading for the open panel where the Phoenixes of Darkness had broken in only nights before. With it being day and with the city already on edge from the recent attack, the horn went up almost immediately, and all about Phoenixes were appearing and taking to the sky. With untold speed, the two figures flapped their wide black wings one more time and passed into the city, immediately diving down

40

toward the cluster of Phoenixes that had emerged to buffer them. Suddenly, from beneath the black wings and robes that swayed and rolled like smoke, arms emerged with blades like glaives where hands should be. In the fluid moves of a painter with his brush, the two black creatures dispatched the first of the Phoenixes to reach them, sending them plummeting down in bursts of feathers and whatever elements of which they were composed. The Phoenixes did not outright attack, but circled closer. They were *too* close and the two creatures rushed at those nearest to them in a smear of black cloth and shadow before stabbing forward with arms now long and rigid as pikes, skewing, two, three, four Phoenixes at once before cutting more down with limbs now turned to curved scythes. After suffering these two rapid attacks, the Phoenixes fell back, hovering with greater distance between them and the creatures as they waited to see what their next move would be.

High above the city, the black demons sat, their vulture-like wings – larger than those of any of the multicolored birds around them – flapped and kept them aloft. Their hooded black robes fell far beneath them, fluttering in the soft winds. Suddenly, they began to speak, their voices at once splintering shrieks that threatened to shatter the stained glass of the city, and also deep and trembling like the rolls of thunder that had announced their arrival. As the city listened the creatures announced, "Citizens of Civitas Levi, witness, and fear us. Your days in this paradise are limited, for none escape our wrath. We are the Versipellis, killers of worlds, harbingers of destruction, bearers of death, and we have named this land as our next victim. You can send forth your greatest challengers, or hide away in your golden

city, but the result shall be the same. This land will be laid to waste, fields burned, towers torn down, buildings ground into rubble. Count your days, however few you have left, for when next we return, doom will fly with us."

They rose on their black wings, and a few final Phoenixes leapt between them and the opening, but were cut down with the same ease as their brethren. Then the Versipellis flew out through the open pane from which they had entered and returned on dark wings to the mountains.

Chaos had already gripped the streets when Metus descended the tower and left the building. The Phoenixes dashed through the air, searching for friends, family, or someone capable of giving guidance. Below, the humans, dwarves, and various other Liolians without the blessing of wings scurried frantically through the large alleys that now appeared cramped and looming. In the air was the constant droll of the horns, ceaselessly announcing a danger that the entire city was already well aware of.

Metus did not know where to go in such a situation, and despite the urgency in which others ran, it appeared they did not know either. A dwarf trundled into Metus, and even though Metus was much taller than the bearded man, the dwarf was much more solidly built and knocked him to the side of the street where he ran into a merchant's stand. Metus quickly shuffled to pick up the fruits he had sent scattering across the cobblestone and between his hooves, when suddenly two Phoenixes dropped down from the swarm above and hovered just above him. An apple fell from the cluster between his arms as he looked at the two, one blue and shimmering like the sea, and the other a blinding mirage of multicolored light.

"You are Metus of the Rich Woods, are you not?" the Phoenix of Water asked sternly.

Metus slowly set the fruit down on the abandoned wooden structure and responded quietly, "Yes."

"The Order of the Bow requires your presence. You are to be escorted before them now," spoke the Phoenix of Color.

Metus took a step back, nearly entering the stream of rushing civilians. "What do they want with me?" he stuttered.

"You have been given a particular gift by Caelum, and though graciously given, that gift requires recompense," the blue Phoenix responded flapping closer to the faun.

"What gift?" Metus asked, considering whether he would be able to flee before they could stop him.

"When you first arrived in this land, you had incurred serious injuries which were healed using the magic of this land. However, the cost of such healing has now put you at the service of the Order of the Bow, whom you have to thank for your life."

"At their service?" Metus questioned. "Because I was healed, I can't return to Liolia. Isn't that enough of a price to give?"

"Yes, that is a side-effect of the fruit's healing," the color Phoenix spoke, to which the other Phoenix looked at him in frustration.

"But that is no price to pay at all, for it is lunacy to leave this land as it is," the water Phoenix continued. "The true cost of your healing is fealty to the Order, and constant readiness to serve them when they need you. For you, that time is now."

With this, the two Phoenixes moved in close around Metus, and he didn't even have to ask what would happen if he refused, for he was quickly ushered through the streets and out of the city.

Only an hour later, Metus walked out into a pitch-black room and waited as all around him, shapes slowly began to materialize out of the dark. His furry legs trembled and buckled slightly as before him the shapes of dozens of Phoenixes appeared in a luminescent rainbow of every color, slowly changing from one shade to another as if the elements that they were composed of passed through the flock in continuous waves. Metus reached up to the pendant hanging around his neck that had been given to him by the two Phoenix guards before they had sent him into the tunnel that had led him here. Now, before him, the congress of Caelum's most elite and powerful Phoenixes had emerged, perched in a great tree with twisting branches and plump leaves. He felt the multitude of eyes glaring down at him as the Phoenixes ruffled their feathers and shuffled their feet to ready themselves for the meeting.

"You are Metus, faun of the Rich Woods, are you not?" asked a Phoenix just larger than the already oversized assemblage of Phoenixes.

"Yes, I am Metus," he responded, shrinking slightly beneath their gaze. "Who are you?"

"Who am I?" the voice asked, entertained by the question. "You can call me Círsar, Head Consul of the Order of the Bow. And you were the hand of King Visvires Lux, were you not?"

"King Speilton, yes I was - am! I still am his hand."

"No, I do not believe you are any more," Círsar said softly but surely. "You are aware that King... Speilton, as you call him, did leave this city with the assistance of the Phoenixes of Darkness?"

45

"I had heard that he left, but I hadn't heard there was any reason to think he was working with the Phoenixes," Metus responded, fearful of challenging the beings before him.

"His decision to leave was in itself a violation of the laws of our land, and while we are still attempting to understand his relationship with the dark Phoenixes, he is clearly a traitor to this land. The King is no longer an inhabitant of Caelum, and it is unlikely he will ever return again," spoke the lead Phoenix as Metus remained silent. "This however is extremely fortunate timing, because in that same series of events, we lost a previous servant of ours."

"In the attack?" Metus asked.

"Yes, we lost her in the attack. Aurum, our previous hand, has gone off with the Phoenixes of Darkness, which now puts us in an extremely delicate situation. Our servants are entrusted with a great deal of power and knowledge, as is required for them to serve as our emissaries to the other Liolians. She, just like you, experienced grave injuries before being brought to Caelum, which were only healed by a particularly powerful remedy unique to this land. We gave you your life, now all we ask in return is your service."

"I hardly seem the best choice," Metus spoke sheepishly. "You speak of Speilton as a traitor, yet you look to his hand to be your trusted servant?"

"Well, we believe it to be clear that you were not a part of his plans, as many of our sources indicate you have not had any contact with Speilton since his last return to Caelum, and that you never left the vicinity of your room during the night of his departure."

"Wait, how do you know all of that? Have you been watching us?" Metus asked, juggling both fear and anger.

"Apparently, not well enough," Círsar said, clearly apathetic to either emotion. "Our information on the location of King Speilton that night was less reliable. But now, that is neither here nor there. We have selected you to serve us due to your particular debt to Caelum, as well as your experience with serving other leaders. But most importantly, we have brought you here before us today to fulfill a most complicated, but necessary, task for us."

At these words, the other Phoenixes adjusted themselves and peered down at Metus with even more analytical eyes. It appeared to the faun that they found amusement in his visible signs of distress. The lead Phoenix paused as if waiting for the past conversation to be cleared away so that they could now focus on the true topic of this meeting. Finally, he spoke. "I am sure you witnessed the proclamation made today by the two creatures known as the Versipellis," the Phoenix paused for Metus to nod his head. "Then I am sure you are now aware that there is a very serious and imminent threat to Caelum. To what degree we do not know; nor do we know precisely what enemies we face. What is clear to us is that some force will be needed to combat whatever threat does exist out there. After much deliberation, the Order has decided that Caelum will not to give in to the fear that many so quickly turn to in times of danger, but will hold true to its most ancient of beliefs on the value of peace in the face of adversity."

"Are...are you saying you will not send any force to stop them?" Metus asked, now merely confused.

"Yes. No Phoenix of Caelum will be sent to participate in warfare. However, it is clear to us that the Liolians have long viewed themselves as very separate from the populace of this country. Therefore, in payment for the security given to them by this land and considering their previously demonstrated beliefs on the utility of warfare, we believe it to be their duty to fight whatever forces have arrived in Caelum."

Metus slowly began to understand the implication of the demand being made, and also the excessive hypocrisy. An urge to call out the indifferent egotism of the Phoenixes rose up in Metus, but the horde of eyes peering down at him made any such hopes of a reaction seem childish. "You want the Liolians to go fight the Versipellis and…whatever else is out there?"

"Yes, we believe it to be a reasonable request. We would even forgo their sentences, allowing them to win their freedoms and to rectify their past sins through their service to Caelum and its people."

"But you don't even know what is out there! What if you are just sending them all to their deaths?" Metus asked, fully aware he was negotiating for the lives of thousands of Liolian soldiers.

"We have no reason to believe at this time that there is a sizable threat. All that has been confirmed is that the Versipellis have in fact arrived in Caelum. But we have sent more scouts to survey the mountains to the north. Other messengers have been sent to the many other cities in this land to evacuate if they are in areas we believe could possibly fall under attack. The Liolian armies will be sent to some of these cities to monitor the evacuations and ensure all the citizens of Caelum are able to leave safely."

"And once that has happened, what will the Liolians need to do? You can evacuate the cities, but if the enemies to the north are not stopped, those some evacuees will be hunted down wherever they go. The Versipellis said that—"

"We are well aware of what they said," Círsar interjected. "And yes, we understand that evacuation is only the first step. The actual warfare we will leave to the most capable hands of the Liolian leaders."

Metus was quiet, as he thought for any way to change the Phoenix's mind, but it slowly became clear that regardless of the danger that awaited them, this was the only way. If the Order remained resolute in their desire to refrain from warfare, then the Liolians would have to fight. "You still haven't told me what any of this has to do with me," Metus spoke.

"Of course," the Head Consul of the Phoenixes spoke. "Your job is quite simple really. We need you to speak with the leaders of the Liolians – Millites, Usus, Senkrad, Onaclov – and persuade them to take up arms. You see, we already offered to Millites and Usus the freedom of the Liolians for their service, but they turned us down. The arrival of the Versipellis emphasized the danger of our approaching enemies, and thus the neccssity for the Liolians' cooperation. We believed if we were to tell them about the added threat of the Versipellis here in Caelum, they would continue to reject us, maybe even theorize we were using it as a ploy to win their assistance. But you saw the Versipellis yourself, so you understand the threat. They will trust you. They know you…respect you. You must get them to raise their banners and march their armies out against the Phoenixes of Darkness and the Versipellis…and maybe even King Speilton, or else all of Caelum may fall, and every Liolian here with it."

Metus stood there in the shadow of the great twisted tree and the flock of constantly evolving Phoenixes, and he felt the weight of not one but two worlds on his shoulder. Then he looked the greatest of the Phoenixes in the eye, and said, "I'll do it."

RETURN TO THE BEGINNING
~ 6 ~

"Down there!" Speilton screamed to Prowl over the roar of the air rushing past them.

Seeing the glint of a large body of water in the distance, the dragon altered her direction and began to descend.

It had been years since Speilton had been to Kal, the small forested island where he had been raised. He had always wondered about what had befallen his old home but had never felt the need to return. All that remained of the island and his village of Lorg was death and ash. To go back would've only meant to dwell in the loss and pain of his old life.

However, it seemed he was always fated to return to Kal. In the isolation of his prison cell in Caelum, he had recalled Rilly's final words of advice before he had left Kon Malopy. *Whenever I need to find something, anything*, he had said, *I always go back and start looking at the very beginning.*

Speilton now knew the "beginning" wasn't the Milwarian capital city of Kon Malopy, as he had already walked through the ruins of the massive castle. That meant he must go further back to where his journey truly began.

What lay ahead on the abandoned island of Kal, Speilton knew not. For all he knew Rilly's advice may have been inconsequential, and the only thing he would find among the ruins of his past life would be dust and skeletons. But a certainty moved within Speilton that before him was all the answers he needed.

As the lake came closer into view, Speilton's heart began to pound in his chest. He didn't understand why, since he doubted there were any threats on the island. Even if there were, he would be able to quickly escape on Prowl. It was just the realization that he would be confronting his past after all these years of burying it away that now made him nervous and tensed his body.

The lake came closer into view, a sprawling, flat body of water stretching as far as the eye could see. It seemed untouched, appearing abruptly out of the tens of miles of wilted forest that Prowl had been flying over for hours. The choppy waves down below sparkled with the glint of millions of suns. The closest shore was littered with large boulders that appeared like a wall between the lake and scrappy woods. Speilton was instantly reminded of sailing across the water and crashing into rocks just like those in a boat given to him by the water spirits that lived below the surface of the lake. *King Maerts,* Speilton recalled.

He wondered if the underwater kingdom of the Naiads still stood deep beneath those waves. As Prowl dropped and glided only a few feet above the choppy surface, he knew that trying to find the underwater palace would be impossible. The lake was too large. Prowl could fly over the water for weeks looking for any sign of life or structures under the rough surface, and it wouldn't be guaranteed that anything would be visible.

Instead Speilton fixed his eyes on the gradually materializing shape of an island far out on the near infinite expanse of waves. On that small stretch of land, only a couple miles wide, Speilton had lived the first dozen years of his life. It had once been densely wooded and full of foul creatures that lurked in the shadows. Then, one day, they had been attacked, and his village of Lorg and all the tightly packed trees around it had burned to the ground. Speilton had escaped and never looked back, knowing nothing was left.

Now he could make out the dark, flat form of the island against the blinding glare of the setting sun against the water. Where a thick forest had once stood was now just grey dirt and black, twisted stumps, smoothed from years of wind and rain.

"Down!" Speilton yelled over the rush of wind, and the dragon descended over the waves and then came to a stop on the shore of Kal. Speilton moved slowly, his eyes fixed on the barren land before him. He slid down from the back of the dragon and slowly walked across the rocky soil. The abundance of ash that had once coated the land had been blown away or beaten down into the soil, but when the wind whistled across the land, some lone particles still swirled up into the air. Speilton climbed up the nearest hill and found himself looking out at a wide expanse of open land. The ground was flat for the most part with small black stumps and twisting briars being the only features rising above the ground for as far as Speilton could see. For thirteen years, Speilton had only ever seen the trees, but had never been brave enough to venture out to see the lake. Now, from his vantage point and without the obstruction of the woods, Speilton could just about see clear across the island to the lake on the far side.

He began walking without hardly noticing. Prowl followed slowly behind, sniffing at the ground as if she might find something among the dirt and stone. Speilton was drawn by some instinctive force toward the center of the island. He knew that was where his village had once stood, and as he got closer he began to see indications that he was right. Above the ground, small shapes stood, stretching toward the sky like skeletal arms clawing wildly for help. It was the ruins of the village: fractions of structures made of stone or beams of wood that had somehow avoided the blaze. Even with just a handful of remains, Speilton could tell exactly where he was. He came to the edge of what was once Lorg, and scraped the toe of his boot against the ground, pushing back the ash and dirt to reveal the cobblestone path that had once run through his village as the central street. People had congregated here, bringing food and crafts to sell in the

markets during the day. At night, people had danced for successful hunts or to summon days of plentiful food.

On either side of the cobblestone path were small collections of wood and brick, now blackened and frail. Speilton could still remember how the houses looked when they were standing, and he used these memories to guide him through the ruins. He passed where the large feasting table had once been laid out, then turned a corner once he came to the town square. Eventually he arrived at an empty lot where his house had once stood. Here he had been raised by a woman unrelated to him that he had called mother. She had smuggled him here at his true mother and father's request to this land where he was supposed to be safe from the Calorians. But the Calorians had come, and she had died at their hands.

Speilton paused a moment where his house had once been and looked at the rubble. "I'm here," he whispered, "back where everything began. Now what do I do?"

He waited, still staring down at the ash as if something would leap out at him at any moment, but nothing happened. Still, he was certain this was what he was supposed to do, so he remained.

The sun set an hour later, and Prowl came up and nudged him as if telling him they should start a fire and settle in for the night. Speilton shrugged her away, transfixed on the spot where his house had once been. It got dark after a while, and only in the black of the night did Speilton allow himself to first begin to doubt. Maybe this was the wrong place. Maybe it was the wrong time to come. Maybe Rilly's words, after all, had meant nothing.

Eventually Speilton fell to his knees out of exhaustion, then sat back, still looking at the dirt. The moonlight gave a faint glow to the dark land. Without the sun, the wind was cool, and Speilton shivered. Sometime in the middle of the night, he slumped forward and fell asleep. Prowl finally approached again and wrapped the boy in her wings before falling asleep herself.

In the morning, Speilton laid in the shadow of his dragon's wings for quite a while before finally slipping out and leaving the remains of his old home. He walked down the dust-covered streets, surveying the grey hills around him. All of the old sounds of the village - the birds, the chattering voices, the buzzing of insects – they were all gone. Only the mournful moan of the wind over the barren island remained.

Speilton suddenly found himself in front of what was once another familiar house. The quiet man who had once lived here had been the last person Speilton had seen before leaving Kal. Seconds before he had watched the man die under the collapse of his house, he had told Speilton he was a member of the Wizard Council. It was from this man that Speilton had been given the round blue egg that Prowl burst out of days later. Speilton stood over the empty lot, replaying the scene in his head. Just as he turned to continue through the village, something caught his eye.

In the far corner of where the house had once been, next to a stone the size of a head, there was a slight disturbance in the ash. Speilton walked across the rocky ground, kicking up all types of utensils and plates and trinkets that had been hidden under the packed dust and dirt. He finally came to the small area where some object was emerging above the dirt. Speilton bent down and scraped away the dust to reveal a soft, flat surface. He pulled some more dirt back and dug his fingers along the side to pry the object out of the earth. It was a thick leather-bound book, well preserved even though it appeared to have been buried for years. Speilton opened the book to find empty pages. His heart dropped as he realized this must be some unused journal.

Why am I here? Speilton wondered helplessly as he ran his fingers over the spotless white pages.

"Hello, King Speilton," a voice spoke from a few yards behind.

Speilton leapt and dropped the book. Instinctually, he drew sword and spun on the figure behind him.

"Rilly?" Speilton gasped.

The shadow of a man stood behind Speilton, composed of the dust and rocks of the landscape. If it hadn't been for the voice, Speilton would not have recognized the spirit.

"It has been many years, King Speilton," Rilly said with what may have been a slight smile if he had a more physical form.

"How can you be here?" Speilton asked. "I thought you were tied to the Rich Woods. And when we went to your hut, you weren't there."

"The age of the Rich Woods came to its end when Kon Malopy fell. My spirit was released, as I no longer had a purpose there."

"Then why are you here? There's no one here you can help," Speilton exclaimed.

"There is no one left to help," Rilly said forlornly. "This is where Liolia will make its final measure."

"Here?" Speilton asked, looking around at the empty hills. "There is nothing here but ash and death."

"Oh, but that is not true," Rilly said wryly. "You are here, King Speilton."

Speilton stared quizzically at the spirit, fading into and out of existence. "What are you saying?"

Suddenly Prowl burst forth, snapping at Rilly's form and crashing through the cloud of dust. Realizing she hadn't caught anything, the dragon turned quickly, darting her head around in search of the vanished enemy.

"Prowl!" Speilton cried. "Stop! It's Rilly!"

The dragon looked at Speilton confused as Rilly reformed a few feet away.

"It seems Prowl is as battle-ready as ever," Rilly smiled.

"What did you mean with that comment before?" Speilton questioned, bringing the conversation back. "Why does it matter that I'm here? I'm just one person, but there are thousands of Liolians far from here that need our help."

"I cannot help them," Rilly said, "There is nothing else I can do."

"So what are you saying? You're abandoning the Liolians?" Speilton asked growing frustrated.

"Of course I am not abandoning them, King Speilton. That is why I am here now," Rilly paused a moment and looked down sorrowfully at the ground. "You see, there is only one hope for the Liolians now. For years I have served the kings and queens of Milwaria in the hopes to bring about lasting peace between the countries of Liolia. But I have seen the future, and I know that there is only one path left."

"And which path is that?"

"The path to destruction," Rilly said slowly. "The days of Liolia are over."

"How do you know this?" Speilton snapped back.

"I have seen it, in that book," Rilly responded pointing to the leather book Speilton had just uncovered.

"The Book of Liolia," Speilton whispered, realizing for the first time what he had found.

"It shows the entire history of Liolia – from its creation…to its end."

"And how is it here? The last time I saw it, that book was at your hut in the Rich Woods."

"I brought it here," Rilly explained plainly. "That book and I are bound together – to this world. My powers are merely to be the caretaker of the knowledge that those pages possess. And, just like that book, I am merely a source of wisdom unable to do more than influence others."

"So, is that your excuse for not helping them?" Speilton questioned. "Is that why you've chosen to hide here instead?"

"The knowledge I possess, Speilton Lux, would be wasted on the people of Liolia. There is nothing more I can tell them. At least, nothing I could tell them that they would want to hear."

"So then, why are we here now?"

"You," Rilly said, seemingly regaining a sense of hope, "I can help. You are the last hope for the people of Liolia, and you alone can save them."

Speilton felt his heart pumping hard in his chest. "I…I can't be the only one."

"You are," Rilly responded. "There is a power within you, King Speilton – a power I am sure you have noticed."

"In Nuquam," Speilton admitted quietly, "I…I was able to…"

"You performed many acts that should be far beyond an average man's capabilities. In Nuquam you conjured your element without the assistance of your wand. You were able to wield other elements besides just fire. And…"

"And I saw things…" Speilton interrupted, "scenes…where…where I saw – but they were just images – right?"

"Yes, you did see many things, but I cannot tell you whether they were true or not," Rilly said apologetically.

"But you said you have seen the future? Can't you just look in this book to see?"

"I can see, Speilton Lux, but whether it is true or not means nothing now."

"What do you mean it 'means nothing now'?" Speilton questioned. "I saw my friends and family die! How is that not important?"

"Your actions here, now, will determine the fate of your friends. Knowing the future means nothing if you do not act properly."

"Act properly? What does that mean? What is there for me to do?" Speilton asked, growing desperate.

"You have much to learn, and there is much that I can teach you."

"Much you can teach me for what?" Speilton questioned.

"For the final battle," Rilly said, fixing the two spinning stones that were his eyes on Speilton. "For the Liolians' final stand."

"So, you have seen one last battle?" Speilton asked, a fear spreading through his chest and down to his legs.

60

"Yes, Retsinis's forces from Nuquam will march on the combined forces of Milwaria and Caloria very soon. And Retsinis will make sure he is not fighting alone. Already he and Worc have mobilized the full force of the Daerds, and the witch, Venefica, has prepared the Warlocks for battle."

"Then…then we will go to the Wizards for help!" Speilton proposed.

"In the past, the Wizards would likely have been quick to offer their wands in such a crucial battle. But things have changed. Retsinis has one more ally that has recently revealed itself…"

"The Versipellis," Speilton confirmed.

"You have become acquainted with them already," Rilly said with certainty. "And you have already killed one of them. But the Wizards fear these beings more than anything. In the last battle in Nuquam, they saw the Versipellis in action. Now that they know the evils that the Liolians are up against, it is unlikely that they will lend their assistance."

"The cowards!" Speilton exclaimed. "Well then, we don't need them! We can rally our troops and gather power by other means."

"But you see, you *do* need the Wizards. They know more about the Sword of Power, Ferrum Potestas, that makes Retsinis invulnerable and allows him to turn all those cut by his blade into mindless slaves. In this final battle you will need to kill Retsinis if you hope to be victorious, but only the Wizards can tell you how to achieve this."

"So, it's hopeless then," Speilton exclaimed. "You came here and told me to return to this ash heap just to tell me that all hope was lost."

61

"No, King Speilton," Rilly said patiently, "I believe there is another way."

"And what is this other way?"

"I can teach you, as I said before."

"Teach me?" Speilton asked. "Teach me to do what?"

"To control your powers."

"Ha!" Speilton laughed, slipping into desperation. "I already know how to control my wand, thank you."

"Not just the fire, but all the elements."

Speilton remained silent for a second, his anger giving way to confusion. "But …I can only control one element… unless…"

"The blood that runs through your body contains a power beyond that of any mere mortal. In Nuquam you did things that only a Wizard should be able to do."

"Are you saying …" Speilton's head swam as he tried to comprehend what Rilly was telling him. "Am I a …"

"A Wizard? No, not yet. But I believe you have the potential to become one if you get the proper training."

"And if I train then…"

"Then you will be able to wield the power of all twelve elements. You will be able to use all types of powerful artifacts. And, if the Wizards know there is another capable Wizard here in Liolia…they may return to help."

"So if I can gain these powers, I can get the Wizards to help us?" Speilton asked, a spark of hope forming in his chest.

"Yes, it is possible."

"And I will be able to save Liolia?"

Rilly fell silent here, considering his words carefully. "Well, there is something you must understand. Liolia…this place…it cannot be saved."

"What are you saying?" Speilton questioned as the spark within him fizzled out. "You just said there was one last battle. You said we could kill Retsinis! You said we could win!"

"I said the Liolians will have one final battle," Rilly explained, his words coming slowly as if they were hard to say, "but it will not be for this land. Liolia, the place, is already beyond saving. The darkness that creeps across the land is terminal. But the people! The people can rise above the evil of Retsinis. The people will have to fight one last time. But they will not fight on this land. No, Retsinis has already left Liolia for dead, and they have moved on to the Liolian's last bastion of hope."

"Caelum," Speilton realized, becoming weak.

"Yes," Rilly nodded his ethereal head solemnly. "On the plains of Caelum…the last battle of Liolia shall be fought."

MARCH OF THE LIOLIANS
~ 7 ~

Horses reared as they were pulled through the streets and led back to their riders. The soldiers of Milwaria and Caloria filed out of Civitas Levi and assembled on the plain outside the city. Those horses who no longer had riders and those soldiers who had lost their horses were coupled together, while the infantry troops formed into columns beside them. Standing beside the massive gold structure of the city and among the boundless rolling hills, the remaining troops appeared small and tattered, like a stain amidst an endless vibrant painting.

Millites and Usus flew high above the armies, the king on his dragon, Hunger, and his second in command riding his griffin. From such a height, they were able to watch the parade of freed Liolians as they left the golden gates of the city. Along the way, they were handed weapons according to their rank by the older Liolians that had sought shelter in Caelum long ago and for years had called it home. Tents had been arranged where metal plating, padded leather, and chainmail were being offered, while dwarves and human blacksmiths toiled nearby to add to the inventory of armor. When Millites and Usus swooped low over the crowd, the soldiers cheered, holding their weapons to the skies. Human, dwarf, and Wodahs stood together, garbing themselves in the same gear and sharing conversation as they continued on their path from the mess halls where they had just eaten to their ranks amidst the larger army.

When it appeared that the majority of the men had assembled, and the tents were beginning to be deconstructed and packed up so as to be carried in the wagons with the rest of the army, Millites and Usus landed at the front of their soldiers from Kon Malopy. They surveyed their men, broken into their smaller cohorts, and then they turned to observe both flanks. To the west of the men of Kon Malopy, Onaclov sat upon his horse as black as night once again dressed in his full steel body armor. Behind him were the troops of the Lavalands, composed primarily of the dwarves of Igniaca with their thick armor and heavy weapons. Among their ranks were also the Isoalates, or at least what little remained of them, under the command of Hopi. They clutched spears and bows, and they declined the heavy army of the other soldiers for lighter vests and gauntlets of leather that better suited their swift and explosive style of warfare. Then, to the east, were the Calorians, led by King Senkrad, who sat upon a horse-like beast with a long neck and clawed feet known as a hakesorsee. He and his steed shared midnight-black skin and long white manes, and Senkrad wore only a vest of chainmail and the fur of some great pale beast from Caloria which showed his great looming figure. Behind Senkrad was the army who had once served the Calorian king's uncle, Retsinis, but who had since been freed from their tyrannical ruler. Now they served a just man, standing side by side with the Milwarians who for centuries had been their enemies. As the sun danced in and out of the shade of the city's tall golden columns, the army of Wodahs melted back and forth between their human appearance in the light and their true forms in the shade, and only Senkrad, being of his unique heritage, had the power to retain a single form. Years ago, he had used these skills to appear human, but now he knew who he was and who he wanted to be, and so he appeared constantly in the shadowed form of the Wodahs.

Millites looked back at his knights with spears raised while they sat upon their horses, and at the few remaining flags that flapped in the breeze with the Milwarian crest. Usus had taken notice of them as well, and said, "Looks like our flags have seen too many battles. Some you can't even see the sigil. Those others look about ready to tear free all together."

"I figure it's about time we made some new ones," Millites said. "Times have changed. We're not fighting the Calorians anymore. We're fighting alongside them now."

"Still fighting Retsinis though," Usus countered.

"You know that has yet to be officially confirmed," Millites said.

"'Officially', sure, but do you really believe he has nothing to do with this? Come on, I'd bet nearly anything that we see his horned head again before this is all over," Usus said.

"I'm guessing you're right. But we can still hope," Millites turned away from the soldiers and patted the nose of his dragon whose scales appeared a golden brown shade but had the power to reflect the wide range of the dragon's emotions. "But my point still stands. It is good to see our counties, our people, together."

"Oh, is that the point you were trying to make? See I thought it was just some convoluted way for you to offer up a new flag design or something," Usus laughed.

Millites shook his head. "Always with the jokes."

"You telling me you don't have any new designs? I find that hard to believe," Usus continued, as his griffin below him ruffled its feathers and picked at a wing with its beak.

From the gates of Civitas Levi, a small party was approaching. Two women aboard large horses led the group, nearly identical in appearance and stature except for the two-dozen year difference between them. The first to arrive was Teews, Queen of Milwaria, and beside her rode her mother. Behind them, a company primarily of hands and maids of many types followed, as well as Metus who had trotted along on his goat legs in pace with the horses.

"Our mother has forbidden me to join the army," Teews spoke haughtily to Millites.

The King nodded. "We discussed it just now at breakfast. Teews, it is for the best."

"After all this time, you still want to keep me from fighting? I had thought my contribution in the recent battles in Liolia would be adequate proof that I can hold my own," Teews said now scowling at her brother.

"No one is doubting your fighting skills," Millites said calmly.

"The Wizard Council gave me a wand for a reason, and I doubt it was so that I could sit back waiting miles from the battlefield."

"And you can use that wand to protect the Liolians that are still within the city," Millites said.

"I think I could do that more easily if I were actually with the army."

As their mother led her horse alongside Teews' she said, "And if the army fails, who then will protect us that stay behind?"

"They won't fail," Teews said boldly, "I know we won't."

"I appreciate your trust in us," Millites said, "but Mother is right. We don't know what we will face out there. We have few men and no real knowledge of the terrain. Just look how much land there is between here and the mountains. Whatever forces are out there might somehow slip past us, and if they do, and they reach the city, we'll need someone who can protect our citizens here."

"Then tell one of the others to stay. I'm sure Hopi would be happy to protect the city."

"Hopi's men need him to lead them in battle."

"And why don't our men need me?"

"They do," Millites said with a small smile. "That's why you need to stay here. If the worst does come while we are out there, Liolia will still need a ruler. Even if the army is lost, at least they will still have their queen to guide them."

"And why me?" Teews questioned. "Why don't you stay then?"

Usus chuckled slightly, and then seeing Teews' stern face, he said, "You know your brother here is a warrior through and through. But of the two of you, I believe he has always been the lesser when it comes to leadership."

"The people of Liolia will need someone who can help them recover if the worst is to occur," their mother said.

"And what about Speilton?" Teews asked. "Are we just going to forget about him?"

Millites' jaw clenched. "Speilton made his choice. He has left, and there is no way to contact him now. So, we must go on without him."

"And why don't we leave as well?" Teews asked. "You were the one who said this is not our home. Why don't we leave the Phoenixes to handle whatever evil resides in their land?"

"Because it is our fault that evil is here. The Versipellis have already laid Liolia low, and now they plan to do the same here. If we return, we condemn the Phoenixes to die, and we lose our only refuge from the darkness that still resides in Liolia."

"You're willing to die here?" Teews asked, and the question was sincere.

Millites turned back to his men who stood in position in the rainbow-colored shadow of the golden city beside them. "There are many Liolians here, and as their King, I am compelled to protect them."

"And what of the men in Liolia?" Teews asked. "What do we do about everyone we left behind?"

Millites was quiet and even Usus and his mother turned and awaited his response. Finally, he looked up, regained his austerity, and said, "When our enemies are defeated, we can discuss how best to help the rest of the Liolians."

"Maybe that's why Speilton left," Teews said, offering this slight optimism.

"Maybe," their mother said, but Millites had already turned away and had begun to walk back to his men.

"So, it looks like I really am stuck here," Teews said.

Usus laughed. "In a way you really do have the most important job."

"Oh stop," Teews snapped. "I know he wants to keep me away from the battlefield. I just hope for the sake of all of you that I won't be needed."

"As do I," Usus said with a nod.

"Watch out for him," their mother said to Usus, nodding in Millites' direction.

"I will," Usus said. "But your son can be pretty hard-headed. I'm sure he will look out for himself. He's seen many battles in his life, and he hasn't failed yet."

Millites had been speaking with Metus, and now the two turned back to the small gathering at the front of the Milwarian army. "Why haven't you retrieved your weapons and armor?" Usus asked the faun.

"I'm not allowed to leave," Metus said sheepishly. "The Order forbids it."

"Some Phoenixes approached him just now and told him that as a servant to the Order, he is not allowed to leave the city," Millites explained.

"Ah, good to see I'll have some company," Teews said standing beside the faun.

"Wait a minute," Usus said shaking his head in feigned disappointment. "You're the one who brought us into this whole situation. You convinced us to march out there and now you're just going to be sitting back here in the lavish chambers of the Order?"

Despite catching Usus' sarcasm, Metus still responded apologetically, "I am sorry, your Highnesses, I truly am. I did not think they would need me after I had spoken to you, but it appears my service to them must continue."

"It's okay, Metus," Millites said. "You can assist Teews with maintaining order here while we are away. And, if things go poorly for us, I'm sure my sister will appreciate having you to fight alongside her."

Metus nodded proudly and said, "Of course, my King."

Teews rushed forward and embraced her brother. "Be careful," she said. "And be aware. There's no telling what is out there."

"I will," Millites responded, and when his sister stepped back away, he turned to his mother.

He was still surprised by how foreign she appeared to him, despite her hauntingly similar appearance to his sister. Millites had never known her, at least not well before she had left him at the age of three. Perhaps he didn't want to recognize her, because it would mean forgiving the many years in which she had left him alone to fend for himself and lead a nation. In their short time together in Caelum, he had said very little to his mother. Despite over a decade of stories and adventures to share with her, Millites had never found anything worth saying to bridge the gap that lay between them. Now, as he prepared to leave once more for battle, he still could find no words with which to address his mother. But she appeared to understand, and with sadness in her eyes, she stepped forward first and hugged her son. "I'm sorry," she said quietly, and Millites hugged her back.

The army rode out along a wide road that cut through the hilly range leading north. The Kon Malopy knights rode at the front, followed by the dwarves and Isoalates of the Lavalands and finally the Wodahs of Caloria. Wagons led by horses were scattered amongst the long train of travelers. Millites and Usus rode up and down the line, checking with the other leaders and generals to make sure all was going as planned. Above the men they would race on their winged steeds, garnering cheers from their men, and then they would land and walk beside those with which they wished to speak.

They rode with the company of Onaclov for many miles, and together the men discussed their plans for whatever lay ahead.

"There is a city the Phoenixes said sits in the foothills of those mountains there," Millites explained. "They said it would be a suitable place to station the army."

"And what exactly is it we are expected to do upon reaching the city?" Onaclov asked.

"For the time being, I believe we are to overlook the evacuation of whatever inhabitants still remain in the city."

"How many of these other cities do you think there are?" Usus asked. "I had been under the impression there was just the one, but I guess there was a great deal they were keeping from us."

"I've heard people speak of the other cities out across this land these past few weeks," Onaclov said. "Supposedly there are many, spread out in every direction. I recall some place called Aerindor and another city called Marenta Loras or something, and a few in the Arcanian Woods to the east."

"Ah great," Usus mused. "More lands for us to go save. And what city is it that we are riding to?"

"Esphodale," Millites said.

"Supposedly, there are even more lands far across the sea, but it seems very little is known of those lands," Onaclov continued as his black horse huffed.

"For now, I believe we are only tasked with preserving the peace in the land between those mountains and Civitas Levi," Millites said.

"And how far is that exactly?" Usus questioned. "Judging by their size, I'd estimated them to be only a day's ride out, maybe a little more. But it's been hours now, and we don't appear to be any closer to reaching them."

"From what the Phoenixes told me, we should expect to arrive within four days," Millites explained.

"Four days out, and they still look that tall?" Usus asked.

"The mountains are said to be enormous," Onaclov said. "Over five miles tall from the base of their slope to that highest peak in the middle."

"You seemed to have picked up quite a lot of information on the geography of this world while we were rotting in our cells," Usus laughed.

Onaclov smiled slightly, but his face was still rigid. There was a time not long ago when he had been known across Liolia for his cool and ease under pressure. People had been drawn to his composure and optimism, but the years in which it had appeared the Milwarian Kings and Queen were dead had changed him. Onaclov had been forced to accept the responsibility of leading the survivors of Milwaria, and that experience had quite evidently changed him. His easy-going attitude had been stripped away, leaving a stoic, direct man. "It was quite a lot of time with very little to do. My time with the dwarves has taught me the importance of knowing the terrain, if not for mining and farming then for warfare."

Beside them, the dwarf Ore had ridden up on a short, bristly-haired horse. The others moved their mounts in order to let him join them.

73

"You've done well," Millites said. "I'm sure all the knowledge you have gathered will prove valuable to us in the days to come."

"Thank you, my king," Onaclov nodded slightly upon his horse.

"Not a single dwarf stayed behind, did they?" Usus asked.

"Everyone is accounted for," Ore proclaimed.

"And how many dwarves is that?" Millites asked.

"I believe we are nearly three hundred strong," Onaclov said.

"The official count is two hundred eighty-five," Ore specified. "The Isoalates are an additional fifty-two."

"And any word from the Wodahs?" Millites asked.

"I believe they said there were about four hundred of them as well, but of those only forty or so still have horses or hakesorsees, so it is predominantly infantry," Ore explained.

"We have only three hundred twenty-two," Usus added. "That puts Senkrad in command of the largest force."

"Yes, but our cavalry numbers nearly one hundred armed knights," Millites responded quickly. "And the Kon Malopy and Igniacan troops combine to a greater Milwarian force than a Calorian."

"Millites, we still must consult with Senkrad. We will need every soldier to be working together," Usus said.

"I am aware," Millites said.

"Do you fear him, my king?" Onaclov asked.

"No, I don't fear him," Millites said.

"I do think we must be cautious in trusting them," Ore added. "If it is Retsinis we are fighting, we would do well to prepare for the potential…hesitation of some of the Wodahs."

"Hold on," Usus interjected. "Are you really questioning the loyalty of the Calorians now? It has been years since the war between our people."

"Yes, but only a few years," Onaclov said, "and many of these men once served Retsinis when he was their king."

"When he served as a tyrant," Usus said. "And we freed them from that reign."

"And they replaced him with none other than his own nephew," Ore grumbled.

"Senkrad has already proven himself a worthy ally to Milwaria. They *all* have. Do you not remember that they fought alongside us in the battle down in Nuquam?"

"Look, I am not accusing them of anything," Millites said. "I only believe we should be cautious. We are in an unknown land fighting an unknown enemy. If it is Retsinis that lies before us, things could begin to go downhill quickly. We just need to be sure that we can trust all of our men."

"I think that is wise," Onaclov said, and Ore nodded beside him.

"It's fine to be cautious," Usus conceded, "but we better not lose trust in our allies. We need as many men as we can find, and the last thing we need to do is turn on each other."

The others agreed and the four rode on in silence, all watching the jagged mountains that rose like the fangs of the land itself.

TRAINING ON THE ISLAND OF ASH
~ 8 ~

Before Speilton, the ground began to tremble. Small pebbles shifted slightly as if moved by a slight earthquake. He closed his eyes and focused harder, until his face squinted, and his extended arm shook. Soon the ground was once again calm, and only the sound of the wind could be heard across the barren island. Speilton fell forward, breathing hard. Next to him, ash and rubble were picked up in the wind, and Rilly took form. "You were close, King Speilton."

"Close to what?" Speilton asked haughtily. "We've been working at this for nearly a week now, and you've come no closer to explaining exactly what it is you want me to do."

"You need to concentrate, and attempt to connect with—"

"With all twelve elements," Speilton finished. "I know. But how exactly is one supposed to do that?"

"Only a true Wizard knows," Rilly confessed. "I may be well versed in many forms of magic, but mastery of the elements is something beyond my capacity."

"So, I need to use these powers to receive help from the Wizards, but only the Wizards can tell me how to use the powers?" Speilton summarized.

"It is not impossible to learn on one's own," Rilly said. "Others have achieved it before you."

"It seems pretty clear that I'm incapable of it. How can you even be sure I really do have this power?"

"You said yourself that you have controlled flames without your wand," Rilly said.

76

"Yes, but I've wielded that element for years now."

"That may be so," Rilly said, "but it is still highly unusual for a mere mortal to be able to control elements without the assistance of his wand. You see, the wands, though of great power, are a reduced version of the powers that the Wizards possess. With training, anyone could come to be master of his element with his given wand, but the power still resides entirely within the wand, not the wielder."

"Well, I may be able to control fire without my wand, but that doesn't mean I can control all eleven other elements."

"Oh, but you have," Rilly countered. "When you faced Valzacor, you said you used the Wizard Cigam's staff. Most people would have been incapable of making the staff produce anything at all, but any mortal who was able to use its powers would have been consumed entirely by the weapon's strength. But you survived, and not only that, you defeated Valzacor as well. Admittedly, his guard was likely down, but only because he would have had no reason to expect you to truly be able to use the scepter."

"Well then, I guess I need a Wizard's staff," Speilton said, "but it appears there aren't any sitting around here."

"No, you will not have such luxuries in your training. But that is no reason to fret."

"I don't 'fret'" Speilton said, walking over and picking his wand up from the shoddy camp he had set up amidst the ruins of the town square. "I just think this is all a waste of time. If what you say is true, I've left all of them in Caelum with Retsinis and the Versipellis on their way to destroy that land as well."

"The work you do here will be important," Rilly explained. "It could very well decide the outcome of the war to come."

"If I can get the Wizards to join us?" Speilton asked. "Even if I somehow can control the elements, that doesn't guarantee they will come. And even if they come, they aren't guaranteed to stay and fight. And, in all honesty, the few times I have seen Cigam in combat, he didn't really impress me much with his skills."

"The Wizards are skilled in their magic, but they have much more to offer."

"Yes, they already offered us our share of their enchanted artifacts and look where that got us. We had our three, and I even stole two more by accident. They're all either missing or in the hands of the enemy."

"Not all," Rilly reminded him. "You now have the Book of Liolia."

"Oh, how could I forget? A book I can't use, which can show me everything that will happen. And tell me again why you don't you use it?"

"I cannot use it, my King, because I am a being tied to Liolia. The future you seek to understand will not take place in this land, but in Caelum. Only you can use the book to show you the future of that world."

"*This* is my world," Speilton said. "Not Caelum. I will go back to save the people there, but then we will return to Liolia because this is our home."

Rilly looked down disappointed, and then slowly glided over to the book that sat on a charred log in the small campsite. His image faded into and out of existence as he opened the empty pages of the book and

placed his hand on the faded paper. The pages shimmered, and suddenly a thin wood branch began to sprout from the binding like a tree limb. Rilly plucked off the branch and crossed to the fire that burned low. Prowl, who had been resting beside the fire, raised her head to watch as the spirit hoisted an iron cauldron upon the flames, mixed a concoction in its simmering depths, and then dropped the stick in. Just as Speilton had witnessed years ago when Rilly owned a hut deep in the Rich Woods, a glowing orb rose out of the potion, dripping with the blazing liquid. Hovering in the air, images began to appear across its curved surface.

The first image to appear upon the spherical orb was a landscape of massive trees, congested with vines, and then a fallen tree, far larger than the others with roots exposed and trunk caved in. The scene shifted to the desert where a great palace could just barely be seen rising out of the tall dunes that had consumed it. Sand had laid siege to its great walls, and the central dome had given way. Then there was a black landscape of hard stone and a smoke-filled sky. The multitude of volcanic peaks began to erupt, pouring lava down its slopes and ash into the air, consuming all in its way. Next, he saw a great castle built out of the swirling sea, with waves crashing against its walls. The temple at its center was rocked by a sudden tidal wave. Appearing as if it were made of sand, the castle was wiped into the sea. Then Speilton saw a familiar sight – a great stronghold in a tundra wasteland blanketed in snow. Just as Speilton had witnessed over a week before, nothing moved. Finally, Speilton saw a castle built upon a ring of cliffs overlooking a drained lake bottom. The castle was Kon Malopy, the capital of Milwaria, and Speilton's former home, which now lay in ruins.

"As I said, I can see the future of Liolia, and it is exactly what you see here," Rilly said sadly. "The soul of Liolia itself has already left this place, and soon all the lives of this land will die as well."

"You talk as if Liolia was a living creature," Speilton said.

"Who says it is not? Like all things, it was born, and now what you have just witnessed is in fact its death."

Speilton turned away as the orb receded into the cauldron and the bubbling liquid settled. He walked to the same blackened log and sat beside the *Book of Liolia*. "You believe, if I can harness my powers, I'll be able to use the book just as you did?" Speilton asked.

The dusty head of Rilly nodded as Speilton opened the pages and flipped through. "So I'll be able to see whether or not my visions, the ones I received from the Versipellis, are truly events to come?"

"Yes, if that is what you wish to see," Rilly said.

Speilton set the blank book down. "Then I will keep training, if you can help me."

"It is about the connection," Rilly explained, as Speilton focused beside the slow lapping waves of the lake. "You must understand that which you wish to control."

"And how do I understand water?" Speilton asked, his eyes still firmly closed.

"You cannot tell me you have never had an experience with water. Search your memory and find a moment in which you fully felt the water's power."

"The water's power?" Speilton almost laughed.

"Yes, a moment in which you acted upon water, or water acted upon you."

81

"I almost drowned once," Speilton said, "in this very lake. After being saved, I then had to sail a ship across its waters in a terrible storm."

"Yes, yes, either should work. Especially given your connection to this specific body of water," Rilly said.

"So, I do what? I connect with the water, then what?"

"Then exert your will upon it. The same as you would cup the water in your hands and lift it up to drink, take up the water, but without the use of your body."

"That sounds insane," Speilton said.

"I'm sure many would think so, but then again many are incapable of such a feat."

Speilton sat silently, his eyes closed, and hand held out towards the soft tide. Just like the dust had in the days before, the water began to tremble, as if moved by some creature just below the surface, but then the water smoothed out again. He focused harder, tensing his muscles and shaking in concentration.

"No, no," Rilly spoke. "It is not about physically concentrating. Ease your body, but expand your mind."

Speilton nodded and loosened his body. "Your focus should not be pointed like an arrow, but it should be as wide as the lake before you," Rilly added.

There was silence, and then another tremor in the water. Speilton no longer focused on the water before him, but on the entirety of the lake. He thought of swimming out into the lake the first time to rescue the body of the deer he had shot, and his meeting with the Naiads that lived in the depths of the lake. He also recalled his voyage through the crashing waves. And then he remembered flying over the waves with Prowl and seeing Kal once again after all those years away. The lake was vast, and dark, and cool.

Suddenly, the water began to bubble and a spout rose suddenly out of the lake, erupting like a small fountain that shot into the air and fell back on itself in an endless cycle. "That is it," Rilly exclaimed. "Concentrate now, do not lose that image."

The water continued to rise, until the spout was three feet above the surface, then four, then five.

"Now, push it further," Rilly said. "Control it. Let your mind flow as it does, and guide it as you desire."

Speilton kept his mind on the lake in its vastness, but now he constricted it. He pictured his own body and how diminutive it was beside the lake. Then he imagined the lake being forced to fill such a frame. Before him, the spout of water began to change, dividing its base into two columns, and above that two more until it appeared like a man, with upward rushing water for legs and falling water for arms. Just as the man took shape, Speilton exclaimed with joy, and the fountain pattered down into the water. He had lost the image, and with it, his control on the water. But he was too excited to care.

"Did you see that?" Speilton turned to Rilly, who appeared to smile in his dusty form.

"Well done, my King," Rilly said. "You are clearly well on your way."

"If I can control water, I should be able to control other elements just as easily."

"Well, you do have quite a connection to water. It may not be the same for every element, but yes, in theory you could."

"What more is there to learn? If I can show my ability to control elements, shouldn't that be enough to bring the Wizards here?"

"Well," Rilly said, "controlling the elements and fully wielding them are two separate things. Just like with the individual elemental wands, you can both control that which already exists and create it yourself. When you can summon elements through your own will, I believe you will have show your full capacity to be a Wizard."

Speilton saw the flash of images just as he had the first time, and every other night since. First, he saw his father die, as he always did, stabbed through the chest by the massive black sword in Retsinis's hand. He never saw his father morph into whatever hideous beast the Sword of Power had determined best suited him, because the image had already switched to the one that always followed. Aurum with her hands bound stood before a sea of the beasts in some ruinous city of stone, and standing behind her, with sword in hand, was Retsinis once again. When he swung, there was a new image, this time of his friend Ince, rushing toward him. Words were forming on his lips when a blade emerged from his chest, and he fell forward at Speilton's feet. Then Usus was falling from the sky, then the Head Consul of the Order of the Bow was limp in the toothed-beak of Worc, the King of the Daerds. Then a beaten and broken Millites was impaled by Retsinis, and finally, Speilton himself was stabbed.

And then, like a light upon an endless ocean, a voice spoke amidst the dark scenes and heavy pounding of Speilton's heart. It was the same voice he had heard the first time he'd returned to Liolia, and a few times since. In the long weeks when he had been isolated in his cell, the few arrivals of the voice had been his only companion, yet he had never been told or had even thought to ask to whom the voice belonged.

"They need you," the voice said. "Evil has made its presence known in Caelum."

"I returned here. I found Rilly, and I know now how I can help."

"But you cannot help them from here."

"I know that, but I am not ready. I need more time to learn and train so that I can be effective in the battles to come."

"And what if you return too late? You can help them now, but every day you wait is another second evil grows closer to taking all those you love."

"My dreams," Speilton said. "The scenes I see of my friends and family...and myself, all dying. Are those truly visions of the future, or are they just images the Versipellis gave me?"

"You know how to discover the truth yourself," the voice spoke. "The Book is with you."

"But I can't use the Book of Liolia yet. I haven't mastered the magic yet."

"If it is the truth you seek, the Book will show you."

"It'll show me everything?" Speilton asked. "Even what the future holds for Liolia?"

"Speilton," the voice spoke soothingly. "You must understand now that Liolia's days are limited."

"Even you believe that?" Speilton asked.

"It is not a belief," the voice said. "Sadly, it is reality. The sun is setting on this world, but a new day may dawn in Caelum."

"So I must abandon this world?" Speilton questioned. "What about all the Liolians that are still here?"

"There is room in Caelum for all those who seek it. The Phoenixes are powerful, but they are few. Their realm covers very little of the land there."

"So, I must lead them all there?" Speilton asked. "Every Liolian left in this world? But you said it yourself, evil has entered that world as well."

"Then you must vanquish it, but you cannot do it from here."

"Then what must I do?"

"You have already shown that you know what you must do."

"I have to harness my skills," Speilton said. "And I must return and help my friends in Caelum. And I have to save the rest of the Liolians. But how do I do all of that?"

"You can seek guidance from the Book, but the majority you have the capacity to accomplish yourself. Trust in your abilities Speilton, and remember to fight for the light."

At noon on the fourth day of their northward march, they saw the city of Esphodale on the horizon. Thin spires rose from a rocky plain in between the gradual slope of the mountain to the northwest and a vast forest to the east. The closer the troops came to the city, the stranger it appeared. The towers that composed Esphodale were astonishingly tall, and only ten or so feet wide each. They slowly tapered, coming to a point hundreds of feet in the air, and just below their peaks, many supported large globe-like structures of interconnecting silver bars. They appeared almost like trees, with thin stone trunks of white marble ordained with the round ornamental cages near their tops. It soon became clear these globes served as perches and homes for the Phoenixes that had lived in the city. The strange structures and layout of the city became more sensible when the army encountered the caravan of fleeing inhabitants which was composed nearly entirely of Phoenixes. Very few Liolians had traveled north to this city to settle, and unlike Civitas Levi, the city had not been constructed to accommodate a ground-dwelling people. Each spire was really a lofty nest for the flying creatures, and the few huts peppered throughout the city were the only structures which human beings could enter.

The Liolian army entered into the maze of towers and followed the simple and underused stone streets to help the straggling Phoenixes gather their belongings and join the group of southern-fleeing birds. Hundreds filled the skies, clutching soft bags in their talons as they flew either back above the main road to Civitas Levi or out to one of the cities in the Arcanian Woods. As the Liolians worked and watched over the city, their eyes constantly floated up to the great imposing mountains that loomed above them with their peaks that were impossibly tall.

When the sun set far to the West, the Liolian citizens wandered outside of the now empty city and set up their camps upon the rocky land. The leaders of the armies pitched their tents in a central location amongst their men, and a fire was built between them all. As each finished sorting out their few possessions within their tents, they drifted out and sat upon great slabs of stone around the fire.

Ince was the first to sit, and he was stoking the fire when Millites arrived. Taking a seat beside him, Ince asked, "So what are our plans now? It seems nearly everyone has evacuated the city."

"It's not our decision as to what we do next," Millites muttered. "We're serving the Phoenixes."

Ore had taken a seat beside them now, and his short legs swung in the open air between the boulder he sat on and the ground. "So we are still awaiting word, I presume."

"Yes," Millites confirmed. "We haven't received any further information from Civitas Levi."

"Don't you find that…odd?" Ince asked carefully.

"Of course it is odd," Ore said. "Everything in this land is odd. The fact that they sent us, their former prisoners, to handle their enemies is odd enough."

"Are you worried?" Ince asked.

"It's too early to be worried," Millites said. "We just got here, and things are still peaceful."

"And when will it be a good time to be worried?" asked Senkrad, who had emerged out of the deepening shadows of the tents with only his red eyes, white hair, and pale fur cloak showing in the darkness.

Millites looked up at the towering Wodahs with muscular, bare arms and a pitch-black face that obscured all visible signs of emotion. "Not now. If another day passes without a word, we may be able to assume the Phoenixes did send us here only to endure the force of whatever enemies move in those mountains, but for now this is still just a mission to oversee and protect the evacuation of Esphodale."

"Well, Esphodale has been evacuated, so what do we do now? Shouldn't we be preparing for the worst?" Senkrad asked, seating himself opposite Millites across the fire.

"And what do you think 'the worst' will be?" Ore questioned.

"Like, Millites said, that we've been sent here to take on the enemy at their doorstep."

"If you're asking whether or not we have a battle strategy," Millites said, "the answer is yes. Or, at least, as much of a strategy as is possible given the circumstances."

"What's this strategy?" Senkrad asked.

"I just discussed with Andereer, one of my commanders, the best course of action in case of an attack," Millites explained.

"So, you do not intend to lead an offensive strike?" Ince asked.

"This is not a great location to hold a defensive position," Senkrad added.

"Well clearly," Ore muttered. "But it's not like we have many other options at the moment."

Millites nodded to the dwarf in agreement. "We know very little of the terrain, and what forces we even face. If we were to mount an offensive attack, we would be marching our troops into those mountains, which, as you can imagine, would likely end in catastrophe."

"So, we are just to remain here until they come after us?" Senkrad asked.

"We will remain here until given further orders by the Phoenixes," Millites said. "We can fortify the city-"

"Fortify the city?" Usus said as he emerged into the firelight alongside Onaclov. "Maybe I'm missing something here, but the city has no walls. There's not much to use as fortification."

"Think you're clever, do you?" Millites fired back with the smallest glint of a smile. "What are walls supposed to do to defend against a flying enemy?"

"It's clear the city was designed for the Phoenixes, and not creatures like us," Onaclov said. "It also appears as if it were built without any expectation of ever being under siege."

"And while we know little of our enemy, we are sure that their ranks are composed of Phoenixes of Darkness and those winged Versipellis," Ore continued.

"Then why settle here at all?" Senkrad asked. "It is clearly a poor place to be attacked."

"Because the Phoenixes expect us to remain. If they do send word, we need to be here to receive their message."

"But we're an army of hundreds. Shouldn't they be able to find us regardless of where we go?" Usus asked.

"Where is there to go?" Ore asked. "This land is foreign to us. We could travel east into the forest and seek shelter there, but we do not know what lies within its depths."

"I've seen those woods from the back of Hunger," Millites said. "They stretch as far as the eye can see. Nonetheless, Hopi has taken a small group of Isoalates into the woods to scout out the area. If there is anything close, they will find it."

"I did hear word of at least two great cities within the Arcanian Woods," Ince recalled. "One is supposedly built within a grove of massive trees."

"From Flamane I could see those woods as well," Usus said, "and for all the miles of trees I saw, there were no signs of cities. They must be deep within the forest, and it is likely our army would only grow tired and lost if we ventured into it."

"We should also recognize that all this time we have been assuming that the enemy will be attacking from the mountains to the north," Onaclov said.

"Well, that's where the Versipellis appeared to come from," Senkrad said. "And the Phoenixes said the area was shrouded with some type of magic."

"All I'm saying is that we should consider that it may be a diversion," Onaclov countered. "The woods to the east would be a strategic spot to hide an army. Or those rounded mountains to the west. If they did find a portal with which they are bringing over Retsinis's armies from Liolia, it could be located anywhere."

"The more we discuss our current position," Ore observed, "the less I wish to be in it."

"It is indeed difficult circumstances," Millites nodded. "Which is why Andereer and I agreed that our best course of action would be to wait here until we have a better understanding of the situation, so as not to endanger our soldiers further."

"I'm assuming we decided to camp outside the city instead of within its boundaries so as to be able to better view our surroundings," Ince guessed.

"Yes," Millites nodded. "Our view is greatly diminished within that cluster of towers, but out here we can see further out across the land."

"And from here we've got quite a beautiful view of the mountains," Usus added, and a few of the seated leaders glanced up at the distant silhouette of the rocky peaks.

The short silence that followed was disturbed by Ince, who asked quietly, "Do you really think that Retsinis is here? Do you think he has followed us into this land?"

Millites looked sternly into the fire as the others shifted uneasily on their stone seats. It was Senkrad who answered, saying, "Yes, I do."

"And what makes you so sure of that?" Millites questioned.

"I know Retsinis," Senkrad said somberly, "and I know that if he was given the opportunity to come here, he would do everything it took to destroy this world as well. I think the Phoenixes of Darkness or the Versipellis or someone gave him that opportunity."

"So, is that all there is to Retsinis?" Onaclov asked. "Is he just simply a being that wants to see the destruction of all that is good?"

It was Senkrad who shifted uncomfortably now. "He's…more complicated than that. Retsinis is difficult to understand."

"But you're his kin, are you not?" Ore questioned. "Wouldn't you know better than anyone?"

"I likely do," Senkrad said. "Still, it's not too easy to explain."

"Well, try," Usus said. "If we have to fight him in battle, it will be good to know a little bit more about how he thinks."

"I already know everything I need to know about Retsinis," Millites said. "He's a ruthless tyrant who wants nothing more than to watch all others suffer at his hands. We destroyed him once knowing only that, and we can destroy him again."

"I don't disagree with you," Senkrad said, "on the matter of him being a ruthless tyrant, that is. He truly is a monster, and even when I served him I could see that."

"If you could see that, then why did you serve him?" Ince asked sincerely.

"Because, underneath all that evil and savagery, he was once a Wodahs like any other. Well, I say that but in fact he was very different from an average Wodahs. Stronger, faster, more resilient – superior in every way. Retsinis was a hero to many Wodahs in those days in a time when Wodahs heroes were hard to come by."

"A hero? Like a war hero?" Ore questioned.

"Yes, I do believe he served in the war some when he was young, but he was also something of a folk hero. The Cave of the Magmors –– that cavern near the Evly Forest from which the great beasts of Liolia are born – would give birth to these terrible creatures that

93

used to pillage the land and wreak havoc across Caloria. That was, until Retsinis set off to slay them all. As you may know, the Cave allows only three beasts at a time in Liolia. In those days, all three lived in Caloria. Retsinis hunted and slew each one all alone with only his sword, and after those three had been killed, he killed the three more that were born after. To the Wodahs, he was like a god, and his particular powers to control his appearance in both light and dark made him even more of a divine figure. It was a special gift from his – or I guess I should say, *our* – unique descendance from the bond between human and Wodahs."

"And so, he used those powers to take the throne?" Onaclov asked.

"No," Senkrad admitted. "He never did take the throne. It was always his desire, and he easily could have taken it for himself. But the Wodahs gave the throne to him. They chose him as their leader, and he was swift to accept it. Only once he had ascended to the throne did he became dead-set on taking over Milwaria. You see, he had grown up as an outcast for his particular disposition as the son of a Wodah and a human, so as soon as the people deified him for his ability to dominate the monsters from the Cave of the Magmors, he believed himself to be divine as well. He saw Caloria for what it truly was – a trash heap weathered down after decades of war with Milwaria, and he wanted more. He wanted to end the war and take all of Liolia. He wanted to dominate it just like one of the beasts he had fought in his youth."

"He wanted to end all life in Liolia," Usus said.

"Not exactly," said Senkrad. "As he found out with the Cave, slaying your foes does not ensure victory. Eventually, he saw the beasts from the Cave of the

MagmorsMagmors not as a nuisance, but as a potential strength. He killed the beasts that proved themselves too great a threat to the Calorians, and from their remains he constructed weapons for himself. That's how he came to possess his near impenetrable suit of manticore hide armor. Other beasts, he merely beat down and dominated until they submitted to his will, like his great fire-breathing hound, Dnuoh, or his shape-shifting pet, Doolb. He went to the Archipelago of the Daerds and sparked a mutual agreement with their leader, Worc, who enlisted their multitudes in his army. And other creatures he simply led north to wreak havoc in Milwaria, like the Chimera that attacked in the Jungle of Supin. Luckily, the tiger Burn was able to slip through his grasp and fall under the protection of Ram Imperium back in the day, or he would have had one more of the creatures in his possession."

"So, you see, Retsinis doesn't want to just destroy all those who oppose him. He wants to dominate them. He wants others to submit to his will and swear their fealty to him, so that he can go forth and control more people. Retsinis sees it as his destiny, and now the Sword of Power has given him that capacity to make others serve him, whether they desire to or not."

"Perhaps he doesn't desire only death, as you claim," Millites said. "But nonetheless, he has destroyed Liolia. That world – our home – is in ruins because of him."

"Yes, that is so. However, I believe that is the consequence of his ambition and not the true intention of his actions."

"But it is the Versipellis's intent," Ince chimed in. When others looked at him with confusion, he continued. "Long ago, I stumbled upon the Versipellis in Caloria, and they marked my hand," he showed them his eye-shaped scar. "So, I did a great deal of research on them. There is little officially known, but it appears their goal, upon arriving in a world, is to destroy it. They truly desire only pain and suffering. If they are working alongside Retsinis, then the objectives of our enemies are split."

"I disagree," Millites said. "I think Retsinis wants power, and he doesn't care what it takes to achieve it."

"Destroying the same worlds, he hopes to rule seems hardly sensible," Ince said.

"And when have any of his actions been sensible?" Millites questioned.

"Like I said," Senkrad said. "He is like the rest of us. He has a goal and a plan. He's not just acting out of some feral instinct."

"And what plan do you think he has?" Millites asked. "If you truly know him so well."

"Well," Senkrad thought quietly for a moment. "If he is here in Caelum, as he likely is, he is probably waiting to gather all of his forces. He has thousands of Nuquamese, and the portals only permit so many at a time, and he would want them all here and ready to fight before making a move. But he also likes to strike quickly and strategically, so he rarely sends out all his troops at once. I expect him to strike us soon, but not with everything he's got just yet."

"How can you be so sure?" Onaclov asked. "It seems to me like if he did send us everything, we'd be unable to stand a chance, especially sitting out here like this."

"He wants to be careful how he uses his soldiers, because he doesn't see this as his last battle. Retsinis probably sees our army as only a few leftovers to be wiped away before he takes his men on to new worlds, just waiting to fall under his dominion."

"And you think he could go to these other worlds?" Ore asked.

"Most likely," Millites said quietly, suddenly in agreement with Senkrad. "When Jupit - I mean, my father, explained the way these other worlds and portals work, he said this world we are in now, Caelum, is one of the hardest worlds to reach. If Retsinis has the Versipellis with him, and if he is able to come to this world, he will have no problem finding other worlds to conquer."

Usus shook his head. "Well, that isn't a very reassuring thought," he said.

"No, it is not," Senkrad agreed.

"But only we can stop him," Millites said, "because the Phoenixes have made it clear that they will give no assistance."

"And neither will Speilton, apparently," Usus gave a slight laugh.

"Where do you suppose he is now?" Ore asked.

"I think he's looking for something," Ince said.

"Or maybe it's someone he's trying to find," offered Onaclov.

"Wherever he is," Millites interrupted the hypothesizing, "he cannot help us now. He failed to warn us about the Versipellis, and now we have to handle it without him."

Another silence set in, and then Usus laughed, "So does anyone else remember that time Speilton turned King Senkrad over there into a rat? Because I feel like that is an event worth noting."

Ince and Ore laughed, Millites chuckled, and even Onaclov cracked a smile. "It was deserved at the time," Senkrad nodded with a hidden smile of his own. "I had stolen his identity for some time. I just hadn't expected him to show up after all of those years at the same time."

"Yes, yes," Usus waved his comment away. "But did anyone else notice that Onaclov smiled just now?"

The smile that had formed on Onaclov's face tightened again into a more stoic amusement, as the others laughed. "After all these years" Usus continued, "with so much change, I think the most startling development has been Onaclov's maturity into a stern man incapable of cracking a joke."

"Ah, it appears to be the cost of leadership" Ore laughed deeply.

"It's true though," Ince remarked. "Just think about how far we've come. A centuries-long war was ended, and now nearly all of Liolia is destroyed. We're having to fight here, in a land that isn't our home for a people that aren't our own."

"The enemy is the same though," Senkrad said. "It is still Retsinis and the Versipellis that we face, and all of the legions that follow them."

"But our army that opposes them has changed," Usus said. "We have men that were once mortal enemies who rode here side by side and are prepared to die beside each other against our foes. They already have in the Battle in Nuquam. We've come a long way, and we have overcome much. I believe we can get through this, as well."

"Always the optimist," Ore laughed.

"I agree with Usus," Onaclov said. "When I led the group of Milwarian survivors in the Igniacan

Underbelly, I witnessed firsthand the resolve of the Liolians. All those that had fled from Kon Malopy arrived in the Lavalands with nothing, and yet they persevered."

"And all those Liolians are still trapped there in Liolia," Ince said.

"Well, the bright side is that if Retsinis and his men are here, those still in Liolia are safe," Usus said.

"They aren't safe," Senkrad shook his head forlornly. "Liolia is dying, and soon everything that lives within it will die as well."

"How exactly does that work?" Ince asked.

"After all the death and destruction that has occurred there, the land cannot take anymore. The world will darken, the trees will fall, mountains will crumble, and soon nothing will be left but barren rock and choked skies," Senkrad explained.

"The Wizard Cigam told of similar events happening to other dying worlds he had encountered," Millites nodded his head. "I just never imagined it would happen to Liolia."

"Then we should bring the people here," Ince offered. "If we can stop Retsinis from taking over Caelum, we could bring the rest of Liolia here."

"It is possible, but the Phoenixes will not permit it," Ore grumbled.

"They'll have to, if we save their world," Ince said.

"If," Onaclov said, and there was silence around the fire.

"Where's Henry?" Millites asked. "Henry Swifttongue, where is he?"

"Swifttongue!" Onaclov shouted to a campfire not far from theirs', and the jester came running over to them from the shadows.

"Does the King fancy a song?" Usus asked with a smile.

"I was hoping for a story actually," Millites said to the waiting Swifttongue.

"Any story in particular, my King?" asked the jester.

Millites shook his head and looked into the fire before them. "Something new, if you have one."

"I believe over the years I have told you nearly every story I know."

"Then perhaps an old one then," Ore offered. "If a story becomes old enough it can be like hearing it anew."

"An old story," Swifttongue thought for a moment.

"What about the tale about the town on the River Liv. What was that story called again? The Laughing Town..." Usus thought for a second.

"The Laughing King of Livy," Senkrad said.

"Yes, yes I remember now. The Laughing King of Livy," Ince said.

"I'm sorry, but I do not know that story," Swifttongue admitted.

"I wouldn't expect you to," Senkrad said. "It's an old Calorian tale."

"That's where I heard it," Ince said. "When I was out patrolling Caloria all that time ago, a Wodahs in our group shared the story."

"Well, go on," Ore commanded in his gravelly voice. "Tell the story."

Senkrad looked up across the fire at Millites' set face, then looked away. "I don't believe I shall," Senkrad said. "Besides, I fear I've forgotten most of it already."

"Ince," Millites said. "You should tell it."

"Well," Ince said, sitting up straight on the slab of stone that was his seat. "Let me see if I can remember it correctly. The story takes place long ago, centuries before the founding of the two great countries of Liolia. It was in a time before the mer people had settled beside Liolian shores, and before the hooved folk had sprung up the Rich Woods. It was a time when the beasts and spirits of nature ruled the land, before the first Wodahsian fire had been lit, and perhaps even before the arrival of the elves and dwarves. It was the age of Liolia's first humans, in the first town of man built in a small valley at the River Liv's eastern union with the ocean. It was here that civilization began and with it the foundation of the countries we have today. Surrounding the valley, the mountain walls were tall and treacherous, and there were no trees large enough with which to build boats, so the people of the town wandered very little from their enclosed society. Over time, the valley became overpopulated and crowded, and the people became restless and violent. Rivalries and prejudices drove the people to commit the most horrific acts in those early days of man, until a king suddenly rose and dominated the valley with an iron fist. He demanded the utmost adherence to his decrees and expected complete loyalty to himself and his rule. Out of fear, the people did obey, and the king realized the great scope of his power. The king controlled the valley, and with it the entire known world, and quickly such power turned to venom in his veins. Others looked to him as if he were a deity, and very soon the king believed it as well. He regularly plotted ways in which to exercise his power, at first through lesser seizures of property or particularly difficult demands, but over time the king became more creative. To prove his godliness, he would go into the town square and declare he would commit some divine act, like setting a field of crops on fire, or filling the well with frogs, and then send out his men to carry out his will in the night. In the morning, when the people saw his words made true, they would bow before him in order to seek the favor of this king. All the while, the king would just laugh.

"There was one man, a farmer however, who was skeptical of the king, and believed his acts to be abuses of his position as their leader. The farmer went to confront the king, calling him foul and a fraud, and in outrage, the people of Livy turned on the farmer. Their old ways of violence once again returned, and they would have killed the man if the king had not stopped them. Instead, he promised a different punishment – the king would withhold the rain throughout the growing season, ruining the farmer's harvest and stripping him of his livelihood. The farmer returned to his home, and the citizens waited in anticipation for this great feat they agreed only a god could accomplish.

"Just as the king had promised, the rains never came, and the food withered and died. The citizens were now greatly short on food, for all the crops had died, and not only those of the bold farmer. But instead of being outraged at the king, they offered their loyalty even more passionately. The farmer realized that the people of the village could not be persuaded to believe otherwise, and with his crops all gone, the farmer took his wife, his two grown children and their spouses, and departed into those mountains that had never before seen the faces of men and women before. In Livy, the people called him and his family fools, and to celebrate the departure of the farmer, the king promised that the rains would return.

"And a week later, the rains did return, hard and strong for days on end. At first the people of Livy would dance in the streets as the rains poured down, but after the days without ceasing, the ground turned to mud, and the huts of the village began to leak. The king did not fear, but merely laughed at the struggling citizens as they rushed to keep their homes from flooding. In desperation, the people of Livy took to the waterlogged streets and supplicated before the king, and in between chuckles he vowed that the rains would indeed cease.

"But the next day, the rains continued, and the next day after that. The people often saw the king standing out in the rain, hands held up to the heavens, commanding the rain to stop falling, but laughing all the time. The rains never did obey, and the water ran down the mountain slopes that surrounded them and rushed across the valley. Houses began to cave, and farmlands were washed away, as the River Liv overflowed and consumed the valley. The citizens of Livy looked to their king for help, but now the king was silent. In time, the town of Livy was laid to waste by the water, and all that existed of that first realm of men was washed out into the ocean. And as the citizens were drowned in the flood or the frothing sea, it is said that they could still hear their king laughing."

There was a silence around the campfire for a moment, and then Usus asked, "But if all the citizens of

Livy drowned, how did anyone tell the tale of the king laughing?"

Ince looked around and smiled nervously, "Well, I guess-"

"Because not everyone died," Senkrad spoke up, eyes fixed on the fire. "The farmer lived, and he and his family watched the destruction of Livy from the mountains. And when there was nothing left, they passed on, and headed north. After weeks and months of traveling and living off the land, they settled in between the Icelands and the Jungle of Supin. The farmer's daughter and her husband would travel on and settle in the peninsula of Milwaria, and the farmer's son and his wife went northeast to the Etnidan Mountains on Milwaria's easternmost edge. It was from these two families that the civilization of man descended – all from the farmer who was brave enough to stand up against a tyrant."

"So that's the message of this particular story?" Onaclov asked. "Oppose tyrants?"

"You could interpret it that way, but it's also a tale of moving on," Senkrad said, turning to Ince, the original storyteller. "Leaving old worlds behind to thrive in new ones."

The group sat in silence for quite a while, listening to the crackle of the fire and the wind whistling through the ghost city of towers and the dwindling discussions from the multitude of surrounding campfires. Then Millites rose, and said, "We better get rest. We don't know what is in store for us tomorrow," and the men departed to their tents.

104

THE LAST ANEMOI
~ 10 ~

Speilton only had to focus slightly to bend the flickering flames of the campfire around the hunk of meat on the spit. It had once been a rabbit, one that they had hunted down in the woods across the lake where few animals still dwelled. Prowl had already devoured a deer and now she sat beside Speilton as he cooked his own dinner, watching the skin slowly darken and turn crisp as the flames were led across it.

The form of Rilly materialized and faded away with the gentle breeze across the barren island, and he looked on in silent observance as the sky turned to night. Speilton ate his rabbit beside the fire. Eventually, Speilton looked up at the spirit and asked, "So, what is it like? Being a spirit – something so…immaterial."

"Why do you ask?"

"It's just, in all the time I have known you, I've never asked," Speilton shrugged. "When I first met you, I remember being surprised, because I'd never seen anything like you before, but then so much occurred during that first meeting that the question of what you truly are seemed insignificant. Every other time was the same thing. We only seemed to meet during crucial moments."

"That is the way we were intended to meet," Rilly said. "My only purpose is to advise the Kings and Queens of Liolia on their decisions and journeys."

"I get that," Speilton said, "but what were you before that? I've never seen another creature like you, and surely you weren't born or created merely for the purpose of being some type of advisor."

"No, it was not my original purpose," Rilly said.

"Then what was?"

"I was one of many beings like myself – Anemoi is what they called us - beings of the wind, tied to the land but free to come and go across this world as we pleased."

"And what happened to the other Anemoi?" Speilton asked. "Are there any others still in Liolia?"

"Not really," Rilly appeared to cast his hovering eyes to the ashy ground. "Not anymore. The Anemoi were caretakers of the land, tasked with maintaining Liolia in its infancy."

"I thought that's what the Wizards do," Speilton interrupted.

"Yes, we are similar to them in many ways. But while the Wizards travel from land to land and send the creation of the worlds into motion, we Anemoi have a much more particular and consistent role in each land. We are more of a manifestation of the land itself, with the purpose of tending to the plants and landscapes and beasts until the conscious races arrived."

"The conscious races?" Speilton asked.

"Yes, meaning those creatures capable of language and culture and being able to comprehend their own existence. If memory serves correctly, first came the elves across the Eastern Bridge before it fell into the sea. Then the dwarves rose out of the cavernous homes deep within the ground. In time, the fauns and satyrs and centaurs and nymphs of the forests and water were born as well, reared from the darkest corners of all of Liolia's great woods. And then the humans arrived on their small wooden ships and settled along the River Liv, not far from this island here. They were no more capable than any of the others, but they possessed an ambition that surpassed all other races. In time, they controlled Liolia and erected the great cities that once prospered in this land. The Wodahs were the last great race to be born when the Warlocks brought their fire to the southern lands of the continent, and in time their numbers created a country separate from the other races."

"But none of this explains what happened to the Anemoi," Speilton said.

"Well," Rilly continued. "As the great civilizations arrived in Liolia and took the land for themselves, the Anemoi had no further task to perform. Slowly, our presence was no longer needed, and one by one we faded to that other realm beyond this world."

"What realm is that?" Speilton asked.

"It…is hard to explain," Rilly considered for a second. "I remember the land from long ago."

"You've been there yourself?" Speilton asked.

"It's where I was created," Rilly said, "but I do not believe it is really the same place that they return to after serving in a world."

"What do you mean?" Speilton asked. "Why is it different for them after they have lived in a world?"

"Because, they never really leave. When I said the Anemoi were not really here anymore, I meant just that. Their form is no longer here, and they are no longer able to speak and change their environment as I can, but I have still seen signs of them, my brethren, in this world."

"How do you see them?" Speilton asked. "What do they do?"

"I don't see them, just signs of them as I said. And they never really *do* anything. They normally just… observe."

"Observe?" Speilton asked.

"Yes," Rilly appeared to nod his head. "We Anemoi are natural caretakers and protectors, and even when relieved of the tasks to tend to the land, there are other things which the Anemoi can serve – the inhabitants of Liolia."

"The conscious races?" Speilton asked.

"Yes, the Anemoi still care for the people of Liolia, whether the Liolians know it or not. They act in silence and without form, but they act all the same. The Anemoi are guardians of Liolia's citizens, even after having faded to the land beyond ours."

"What about you?" Speilton asked. "Why haven't you faded like the rest of them?"

"Well, even after the humans and dwarves and elves and creatures of the forest spread over this land and took it under their domains, one Anemoi was still needed to remain."

"Why's that?" Speilton asked.

"Even though each hill and the individual groves no longer needed protectors, the land as a whole did. And that was my task – to preserve all of Liolia."

Speilton looked up at the ghostly image of a man shimmering before him. "You said the Anemoi were manifestations of the land, created to protect the land which they inhabited."

"Yes," Rilly said.

"If you are a manifestation of Liolia as a whole," Speilton thought. "Then you are in a way…"

"Liolia itself," Rilly completed Speilton's idea. "Yes, in many ways that is true. That is another reason I am bound to the Book of Liolia. You see, when you ask me how I know Liolia is dying, it is because I can feel myself dying. I too am fading to that place beyond Liolia."

"And what exactly is this place beyond Liolia?" Speilton asked. "You mean Caelum?"

"No, no," Rilly appeared to smile. "It is beyond even Caelum. It is the land of the one who created the Anemoi, and all the other races that came to Liolia after us."

"This person you speak of, he created humans as well?"

"Yes, all things. It is for him that the Wizards serve."

Speilton looked into the fire and Prowl nudged closer to him in the chill of the night. The voice he had heard in his dreams suddenly came back to him, and he recalled what it had told him.

"So that's how you have the power to read the Book of Liolia?" Speilton asked.

"Yes," Rilly said. "Being the spirit of Liolia has granted me some capabilities with magic."

"But you cannot see the future? You cannot tell me what is to befall my friends?"

"In that regard, I am very much every other being in Liolia. I can see my past, but the future is difficult to read. Only through certain prophecies can I see glimpses of what is to come."

"Then can I look?" Speilton asked. "You said I may be able to."

"Yes, but only once you have attained a certain level of control over your magic."

"Well, I believe I already may have already reached that level," Speilton said.

"What leads you to think that?"

"A voice told me so, in my dreams. I'm not sure who the voice belongs to, but I think you may," Speilton said.

Rilly remained quiet for a time, his form barely visible against the dark sky. Finally, he spoke. "You may try to use the Book, but you must know your view of the future will be limited. I fear what you will do once you have seen what awaits you."

"Why do you fear what I may do?" Speilton asked. "Do you know what I will see?"

"No, my King, I already told you I do not know what awaits. But the future is supposed to remain unknown. To look could spell disaster. It could make you make decisions that you otherwise wouldn't."

"Or I could know what to prepare for in order to make the right decisions," Speilton said.

"It doesn't work quite like that," Rilly attempted to explain. "What you see will come to pass regardless of what you do."

"How can you know that?" Speilton questioned.

"It is just the way the future works," Rilly said.

"I still must know," Speilton said.

"Do what you must. You know where the Book is."

Speilton dropped the small branch he had pulled from the pages of the Book and placed it into the boiling mixture inside the cauldron. From the bubbles, an orb slowly rose, and it shone brightly in the dark of the night. Prowl stood behind Speilton and growled low as images began to take shape on the orb. It took a moment for Speilton to determine what he was seeing.

There was a campfire, with many individuals seated around it. Speilton identified Millites and Usus, and a dwarf that had to be Ore. Onaclov sat beside him, and on his other side was the dark shape of Senkrad. Last, he saw Ince and the jester Swifttongue. Their camp was beside some tall tower-filled city, and further beyond them were the mountains. Suddenly, the scene shifted, and the shape of a standing bird – a crow – appeared on the orb with some small figure before it. Speilton realized it was not just any crow, but Worc, the King of the Daerds, and the figure before him was not tiny but actually the hulking figure of Retsinis who only looked small in contrast with the massive bird. The two were in some rocky, mountainous area and Retsinis appeared to be speaking to the King of the Daerds. Then, Worc shrieked and beat his wings, and all around him the silhouettes of the Daerds appeared. The flock moved over the mountains and out to some a city of spire-like structures that lay in its shadow. As Speilton realized what was happening, the scene changed. He saw an army – the Liolian army – in a valley surrounded by towering cliffs and waterfalls. Speilton watched as they all turned and faced one of the steep plains leading out of the valley where another army was descending like a tidal wave upon them.

Then a familiar scene began to form, and Speilton felt his stomach drop. Aurum stood in front of a vast army of creatures, and behind her stood Retsinis, with sword in hand. The following images were all as familiar. Ince being stabbed as he looked to Speilton for help, Usus falling from the sky, the Head Consul of the

Phoenixes limp in Worc's beak, and then Millites being stabbed through by Retsinis's black-bladed Sword of Power all appeared before Speilton. As the final image materialized, Speilton turned away, and Prowl snarled and blasted the image of Speilton being struck down as well with a stream of dragon-fire which knocked over the cauldron and cast its boiling mixture out onto the ash.

In silence, the two sat and stared out across the midnight landscape of smooth hills and starry skies. The wind blew across the dusty island, and beside them the spilled potion steamed on the ground. If Rilly was watching, he didn't allow his presence to be known, leaving only Speilton and Prowl on the island – the last living inhabitants of Kal.

Speilton rose from the dust and began to walk, and Prowl raised her head and looked worriedly after him, but it was clear he meant to go alone. There were only a few miles to walk from their campsite to any of the surrounding shore, but he walked as far as he could. Across the hills he went, until the simmering coals of their campfire had disappeared in the distance. Finally, he came to a sandy bank where he could look out across the black lake that lay solid and unfractured in the dark of the cloudy night. The king sank to a crouch and placed his fingertips in the water. Then Speilton released the artificial calm that had allowed him to walk so far in silence, and all at once his emotions exploded forward. Rage, fear, helplessness, sorrow, all rushed forward and caused him to tremble. Like dry wood his arms combusted into flames, but it was not only fire he bent to his will. A column of water shot out of the glassy surface of the lake as if from some great leviathan that had leapt into the air. The misty spray of it carried all the way to Speilton on the night air despite the column being a hundred feet out into the body of water; the few droplets of water were not nearly enough to quell the storm that had formed within him. Then the ground began to tremble, then roll, contorting and flowing all around Speilton like rough waves on the ocean. The sand on the beach was picked up in a sudden cyclone of wind that rushed around Speilton with gaining speed and power. From the clouds above, there was a cackle of lightning, and suddenly along the shore, the lake began to frost and freeze.

Power flowed out of Speilton like a scream, until his body could no longer endure the rigid trembling of the exertion, and he fell forward into the cool water. Now, doused in the waves of the lake, the fire that had consumed him was extinguished, the water and air settled, and the ground lay still once again. For a few minutes, Speilton lay there, afloat face-down in the lake that had once almost taken his life. Then he suddenly noticed a sound coming from above water – a voice. He rose back into the air and took a deep breath. As he shook himself dry, he turned back to the shore, where a figure stood in the dark of the night.

"King Speilton," the figure said, stepping closer and offering a hand to help Speilton back onto the shore. "It is I, Cigam."

THE WAR BEGINS
~ 11 ~

Millites was in his tent with Andereer going over battle strategies on a map that a resident of Esphodale had given them, when from the distant hill to the north, a horn blew. The two lunged for their weapons and pushed out of the tent flaps. They looked to where the scout had blown the horn, and at first, they saw nothing but the mountain and the sunset to the west, but then the enemy presented itself. A dark smudge was drifting towards them from the towering peaks that appeared like a coiling cloud of smoke, but Millites had seen that sight enough times over the years to know what it really was. He turned to Andereer and said, "It's the Daerds. Quick, go rouse the army."

His commander took off into the rows of tents where soldiers stood in confusion, halfway through their suppers. "To arms!" Andereer called. "To arms!"

Usus rushed out of his tent as well, and Onaclov and Ore ran up beside them. "The Daerds?" Usus asked, looking at the approaching enemy as well.

"Ah, our worst fears are confirmed," Ore grumbled. "If the Daerds are here, then Retsinis has in fact entered Caelum."

"Do we know if he sends ground troops as well?" Onaclov asked.

"I haven't heard word," Millites said, "and the hills are too tall between here and the mountain to see."

Senkrad walked out of his tent now, holding a massive glaive in one hand. Standing beside the others, he looked up at the flock of Daerds growing closer every second. "It looks like Retsinis wants us to know he is here," Senkrad said. "I doubt there is any infantry."

Hunger flew down through the air and landed roughly next to Millites. The dragon shook its body and his scales turned the dark flaming red of the sunset as he roared at their enemies. "There's only one way to find out," Millites said, pulling himself on the back of his dragon. "Assemble the men out here beside the camp. We'll fight them in the open."

"I do not think that to be wise," Senkrad interjected before Hunger could take off into the sky. "I believe we will be able to fight them better in the protection of the city."

Millites looked down at the Calorian King. "In the city our view of the Daerds will be obstructed. I know you think you know a lot about them, being as you served beside them for many years, but as someone who has fought against those demons for-"

"You're right," Senkrad interrupted him. "I have fought alongside them, and I do understand their methods well. They obey Worc, and in the open field Worc will be able to see us all and lead his army in a way that quickly picks apart our forces. It will be easy for him out here, but in the city his sight will be limited. His army will have to fight on their own judgement, and they too will be able to see very little."

The group looked up at Millites and awaited his response. There was a moment of silence as Millites watched the great cloud of Daerds drift closer and closer, then he finally said, "Assemble the men outside the city, but on the very edge of the towers. We will meet them in the open field where we can see them, and if their forces are too much we can fall back into the city."

Senkrad nodded, and Hunger leapt into the sky, pushing off with his two legs and gliding on webbed wings. Senkrad and Onaclov raced to assemble their armies, and Usus called Flamane to him and flew after Millites. The camp was alight with men rushing to find their armor and weapons and the sounds of metal clashing with metal as they fitted themselves with their necessities for battle. The men filed into their lines on the western side of the city with the infantry grouped behind each corresponding leader and with the cavalry situated on either side. Millites and Usus descended at the front of the knights of Kon Malopy bringing the relieving news that there were no land troops marching against them at the moment. For now, they had only to worry about the Daerds.

The men waited, looking up at the looming shadow of the flock and the setting of the sun, and they gripped their weapons tightly. Most of the warriors had served in the Milwarian Calorian War, and in their service had fought the Daerds on many occasions. Now they faced the same enemy but in a strange new land. The large black crows fluttered forward on their ragged wings, snarling with toothed beaks and bearing their long talons before them. Far below, the humans, dwarves, and Wodahs shifted nervously, realizing how senseless their formation was against the monstrous flying forces.

Millites raised his sword, and cried, "Nock arrows!" and the archers obeyed.

They could hear the Daerds now, with their ruffled feathers and cacophony of caws as they passed over the army and began to circle them, as if the soldiers were already dead and they were just waiting to feast. The flock continued around them in a wide arc, high above the city, and then moved west. It was here that they began to descend, until the great flock obscured the little bit of daylight that the sun had left behind and cast the army in shadow.

"Loose!" Millites commanded as the Daerds surged forward.

Arrows filled the sky, catching the black birds as they dove toward the army. Many caught in the flesh of the Daerds, but many more of the birds were unharmed. "Again! Nock!" Millites commanded, and the archers reloaded.

"Loose!" and more Daerds were plucked out of the sky.

But as the first wave was shot down, more Daerds replaced them building into a massive black cloud of diving birds. "Again!" Millites called, but it was too late.

The Daerds fell upon the army like water crashing on stones below. The soldiers pulled out swords and spears as they swung wildly at any shape that approached them. Millites himself just barely escaped the talons of three Daerds that swooped at him by summoning a beam of light with his wand that cast the creatures aside. The rocky terrain was filled with the sounds of howling men and vicious screeches from the birds. Black feathers were cast across the battlefield, coated in the blood of Liolians and Daerds alike. All hope of observing and strategically combating the enemy was cast aside as the flock in its entirety swarmed the men, attacking from all directions. Some men were grabbed in the claws of the Daerds and carried up into the sky where they were either eaten or thrown out across the land. Others were struck down where they stood, bitten by the toothed beaks or knocked against the stony ground by the massive wings. The violence was random and vicious, with survival more dependent on luck than skill. And yet the Liolians fought on, cutting or shooting down the birds left and right.

Millites urged Hunger into the sky, and the two raced up through the rush of black feathers and then outside of the thick cloud. Here, looking down upon both armies, Millites took on the swarm of Daerds. A few of the birds had seen the king leave the field of battle and set out in pursuit, but lured away from the flock, they were quickly consumed by Hunger's flames or Millites' light. Hunger then dove closer to the thicker swarm of Daerds, attacking them from above while they were focused on the army below them. Great blasts of smoky fire tore through the flock, sending many of the birds spiraling down in a flaming heap of feathers. Millites aimed his wand into the thick of the flock and summoned a great bolt of light that tore through the Daerds, casting some aside and tearing straight through their wings of others.

Usus rose up beside him on his griffin who raked his eagle-clawed feet through any Daerd who approached. Usus flew above the perimeter of the army and had his wand in hand. He summoned massive spikes of rough stone that he launched down to the ground from above. As they fell, they caught dozens of the Daerds, impaling some clean through, and dragged them all down into the rocky ground where they shattered in a crack of stone.

"Be careful!" Millites called to him above the rush of wind and the cries of the Daerds. "Don't let that stone get too close to our army!"

"You know I'm always careful!" Usus called with a smile.

Few people appeared as confident and content in times of battle as Usus, and the grin across his face as he shot down Daerds was testimony to that. The two Milwarian leaders battled the crows from above, and far below they could see the flashes of lava being launched onto the Daerds from Onaclov's wand, walls of dancing

119

colors blinding the Daerd's from Hopi's wand, and rigid spikes of ice from Senkrad's. While the ground was littered with the oily black carcasses of the Daerds, there was still a multitude of the creatures alive and fighting. Their numbers appeared endless, for no matter how many were knocked out of the sky, the great flock still swarmed. From high above, Millites could see that his army was fighting blind, consumed in the shadow of the creatures that attacked from everywhere. He understood what needed to be done, and he grimaced. "We need to go into the city," he called to Usus. "If they fight with their backs to the buildings, they will be better protected from the Daerd's attacks."

"I'll go and give the command," Usus said, and Millites nodded.

As Flamane dove down into the swarm, Millites flew Hunger across the top of the flock so that the two of them could strike down as many Daerds as possible. Then they doubled back west, bringing a whole horde of the crows with them and pulling their attention away from the soldiers below. Already, many of the warriors were falling back into the city leaving only the dead and wounded on the battlefield.

Hunger swooped and dove to avoid the group of Daerds that pursued them. Millites turned on the dragon's back in order to face the spiked birds. The rush of night air was cold against his skin, which kept him alert and focused on the task at hand. Beams of light erupted from his wand, cutting through the Daerds and knocking each out of the sky. Hunger took a hard right and turned his head so as to aim a stream of flames into the Daerds as they attempted to turn as well. Millites was sweating, and he could feel the strain of his magic usage wearing at him, but there were still thousands of the beasts to eliminate before victory could be attainable. He looked down below at the Liolian warriors and saw there were only a few stragglers remaining outside the city. Knowing these last warriors would be easy for the Daerds to pick off, he led Hunger down into the cloud of Daerds to help the last of the Liolians on the battlefield escape. Hunger grabbed one Daerd by the neck, and after sinking his claws into its flesh, he released and pivoted to avoid a second crow. Hunger looked back and breathed flames across the Daerd's back. Millites held his sword in one hand and his wand in the other as he alternated between striking out with the blade and sending beams into attackers.

The final soldiers entered the city of Esphodale, and feeling the worn Hunger shaking beneath him, Millites led the dragon to the top of one of the tall spires. Hunger landed on the rung of a rounded cage that ordained the top of the tower, and then crawled through the gap. Here Millites stepped off the dragon and positioned himself on the most level rung he could find within the dome. The Daerds were already attacking the city, and from his vantage point Millites could look down at the chaos below. He had been right in assuming that the maze of towers limited the soldiers' abilities to see their attackers, as the Daerds flew chaotically through the maze of towers. But the Liolians now stood with their backs to the buildings and fought with at least one side protected. From the inside of the cage, Millites could see the Daerds swarming around him, but the grid of interconnecting gold and silver bars prevented the crows from being able to simply fly through. As the Daerds struggled to squeeze into the structure, Hunger lit them up with fire and Millites shot them down with his light.

One Daerd flew beneath Millites and snapped its beak, nearly taking the king's leg off. But Millites quickly sidestepped and thrust his sword down into the bird's skull. However, the movement threw off the king's balance, and Millites was forced to reach out and hook his arm around the beam below him. Dangling by his elbows, Millites realized his grip was failing, and he would need to hold on with his hands. But both hands were full, one with the sword and the other with the wand. As his elbow slipped, he let go of the sword and grabbed the beam with his free hand. He pulled himself back into the protection of the cage and looked down to see his sword falling hundreds of feet to the ground below.

Suddenly, a shriek cut across the city so loud the cage itself seemed to vibrate. Millites clutched his wand firmly and turned wildly around, knowing that only one beast made a sound like that. Hunger, too, shrunk back beside his rider at the sound, and the two prepared for the creature to present itself. For a monster of his size, the King of the Daerds was able to sneak up on the two rather effectively, because as soon as they noticed Worc approaching, he had already crashed into their cage. The massive Daerd clutched the globe with his large talons and pumped his wings with enough force to cause the stone center of the spire to crack and then crumble all together. Millites was thrown off his feet at the sudden jolt of Worc's attack, and Hunger let out a cry as he leapt forward just in time to grab the king with one foot. As Worc continued to push the cage over, Hunger flew away from the shifting bars, into the center of the sphere and searched wildly for a place to escape the mass of metal bars. He was capable of crawling out of any of the holes in the grid, but now the cage was rolling over and picking up speed. With Millites still clutched beneath him, Hunger darted for an opening, but as he passed through, the cage toppled off of its perch upon the spire, and a beam caught the dragon in the back. Hunger was battered downward, roaring in pain, and Millites slipped from his grip. For a second, they both fell, and Millites reached out for something to grab, but there was nothing around him but open air. Then, Worc shrieked again, and Millites looked above him to see the round cage falling towards him with the massive shape of Worc even further above looking down at the falling king and dragon.

Hunger rolled through the air, finally catching wind beneath his wings, and reached out just barely grabbing the back of Millites' belt with a single talon. The added weight of the king caused them both to fall for a second more, but then Hunger managed to push them away from the falling cage. However, when the dragon looked up, he realized he would not be able to clear the path of the orb, so with a last bit of strength, Hunger swung Millites forward as the edge of a bar crashed down against the dragon's tail end. Millites flew toward a different tower, and despite groping for some type of hold, was not able to get a grip on the smooth stone. He slid down the side of the tower, putting his back against the polished surface. Luckily, the base of the tower curved gradually giving each spire the appearance of having risen out of the ground instead of being built upon it, so as Millites approached the streets below, his fall was braced by the gradual slope. Still, the king crumpled hard into the ground and then rolled out on the cobblestone road upon reaching the floor of the city. He lay there for a moment, catching his breath, before he pulled himself back to his feet. Millites looked at the wreckage around him. Amidst the endless sprawl of stone towers, Daerds wove and attacked, and Liolian warriors rushed past him in the streets. His eyes finally settled on the smashed ruins of the cage with his dragon, now a grey green like moss upon a stone, lying still beside it. Millites rushed to his side, sinking to his knees so that he could take up Hunger's head in his hands. The dragon's eyes fluttered open slightly, to look up at Millites, then he huffed, and the eyes closed again.

The ground shook, and the air was split by another shriek as Worc landed behind the king. After slowly lowering the head of his dragon, he turned to see the monstrous shape of the King of the Daerds looming over him. Millites reached for his wand, but it wasn't there; he had dropped it during his fall from the castle. As he scanned the ruins, his eyes fell on the hilt of the sword he had dropped from high above. Millites reached down and pulled the sword from the wreckage, only to find the blade broken about halfway up. Holding the half-sword in both hands, Millites took a step toward the massive crow peering down at him with apparent glee. Worc twitched his head back and forth and crept closer on his massive feet.

"Come on," Millites said, shaking the broken sword in front of him. "Come on!"

Worc struck with his beak, and Millites was forced to throw himself to the side to avoid the attack. The cobblestone road was smashed to bits where the beak had struck, but Worc seemed hardly to notice. Worc turned and shrieked excitedly, spreading his massive wings as if to envelop the entire city within them. Propped up on one elbow, Millites pointed the blade at the King of the Daerds. Again, Worc crept closer and cocked back his head. This time, before he could strike, a projectile smashed into the side of his head. Worc hesitated, and turned, as a blast of ice was cast across one of his feet. The King of the Daerds turned to this new attacker, and Senkrad ran forward, stopping between Millites and him. He held his glaive in one hand and his ice element wand in the other. Worc roared at the Calorian King, but Senkrad was ready and shot a spray of ice that covered the Daerd's beak, cutting off the cry.

With little struggle, Worc pulled free from the ice around his foot, and he shook his head, slamming his beak against another tower in order to break the ice that enveloped it. Worc stepped forward to attack again when he was struck from behind by a massive column of stone. Flamane swooped down and raked his claws across the top of the crow's head, and Usus launched another stone into the side of Worc's beak. Flamane landed beside the two kings, and as Usus leapt off his back to stand beside Senkrad, the griffin raced over to Hunger and began nuzzling his friend with his beak.

Worc looked down at the men assembled before him and lowered his head to study his opponents, when a smudge of colors suddenly appeared before his eyes. From a side-street, Hopi emerged, holding the color element wand in his one hand. The Isoalate pointed the wand at the King of the Daerds and conjured a mask of colors that lay across the monster's eyes. Now, with his sight obscured, Usus and Senkrad began firing at the beast, battering him with spikes of stone and shards of ice. Worc's thick feathers protected him from most of the attacks, but his cries showed he still felt their impact. Across the city, the other Daerds had stopped their attacks and turned to the echoing cries of their leader. Millites rose to his feet and searched through the rubble until he found his wand as well, and then began assisting the others with fighting Worc back. Finally, the Daerd unfurled his massive black wings and pushed off into the sky, knocking the men down with the wind created by his wings. As Worc rose above the city, the other Daerds took to the sky as well. Their numbers had been shaved down considerably, but a massive flock of them still congregated over the spire of the city. Then Worc turned toward the mountains, and all throughout the city the people cheered.

THE WIZARD'S ADVICE
~ 12 ~

"We, of the Wizard Council," Cigam explained, "do understand your feelings on this matter. Letting go of a home can be very difficult. I, too, lived in Liolia for hundreds of years during my service. But there is no more we can do for this land."

"I understand that," Speilton said as Prowl glided down out of the night sky and landed with a thud beside him. "As much as it pains me to accept it, I understand now that Liolia is dead. What I ask is that you help me save Caelum."

"King Speilton," Cigam said. "You know the laws of the Wizard Council. We are not allowed to interfere in worlds where the Versipellis are present. In fact, that is one of the only reasons I was permitted to come here to speak with you now. The Versipellis have already entered Caelum."

"What about my powers?" Speilton asked. "They mean I am a Wizard, right?"

"Well, it means you *could* be a Wizard, yes."

"Then why won't you help me? I could be one of you. I could help the Wizard Council in the future, but I won't be able to if I'm dead," Speilton said sternly.

"I understand your anger," Cigam said apologetically. "I really do. But *you* must understand that we cannot break the ancient laws which prohibit us from acting. I truly wish I could help you, King Speilton, not only because of your potential, but–"

"No, I understand perfectly well," Speilton said. "The Wizards are just afraid. You know what the Versipellis are capable of, so any time they appear in a world you give up. You don't want to risk losing your own."

"I'm afraid you are mistaken," Cigam said. "Yes, we are afraid of the Versipellis, but when I say there are laws that prevent us from acting, I mean just that. There are greater actors and rules at play here – an entirely different hierarchy, so to speak, beyond just the Wizards and the Versipellis. You see, the Versipellis are beyond our domain. Our job is to combat the Warlocks, and to that end, we are limited."

"And if the Warlocks are in Caelum as well, why won't the Wizard Council send help to stop them?"

"The Warlocks are not bound to the same laws as the Wizard Council. In fact, it is their rejection of our laws that has led them to engage in dark magic. They follow the Versipellis wherever they go, as they have already accepted the darkness of the dream spirits. But to the Wizards, the power of the Versipellis is a terrible temptation, and thus, combating them is beyond our capability and authority."

"If it is your job to combat the Warlocks, then who is the opposite of the Versipellis?" Speilton asked.

"Well, you may not like to hear this," Cigam said. "But it is the job of you all, the citizens of the world, to oppose the Versipellis."

"We're supposed to handle them ourselves?" Speilton asked. "How often are people successful in doing that?"

"May I remind you that you have already eliminated one of the Versipellis," Cigam said with a hopeful smile.

"So, I must kill the two remaining," Speilton said. "That is what you are saying."

"You or some other Liolian, yes," Cigam nodded. "But it cannot be one of the Wizards."

"Then why did you come?" Speilton asked. "Why appear before me at all?"

"Well, for one," Cigam said. "I thought, as a potential Wizard currently training to harness your skills, I owe you the courtesy of recognizing your work. Just now you demonstrated an incredible feat of control over your environment, and all without even a scepter."

"So, do I get one of those?" Speilton asked. "A scepter?"

"No, no sorry," Cigam said amusedly. "We do not grant those until someone has pledged to join the Wizard Council."

"Then, how do I join?" Speilton asked.

"Well, I do not believe you necessarily want to join, considering you, like the rest of the Wizards, would be forbidden from returning to Caelum to help your friends," Cigam explained. "But returning to the initial point I was trying to make. You have incredible power, Speilton, but the magic you just used was used out of rage and fear, not control. A Wizard can control his environment in two ways, either by understanding and working with the elements or exerting force upon them. What you just demonstrated was the latter."

"And what's wrong with that?" Speilton asked.

"Well, for one it is unstable. In the short run, yes, it may prove to be more powerful. But over time, it will wear on you and the environment around you. All worlds, and the elements that compose them, have a way of observing us as individuals, and if they recognize you as someone who uses emotions to dominate the elements around you, they will begin to resist."

"Resist?" Speilton asked.

"Yes, the elements will stop reacting."

"So, you can lose your powers over time?" Speilton asked.

"Not *all* of your powers. There are twelve elements, and it appears that eleven of them will stop reacting, but one will remain."

"Darkness," Speilton guessed.

"Yes," Cigam confirmed. "This is the way of the Warlocks. They have lost their touch with the other elements, and now, they can only use darkness."

"But I have seen the Warlocks use more than just darkness in combat," Speilton said. "The witch, Venefica, would conjure serpents and other things while fighting."

"Well, darkness appears in many forms," Cigam said. "The greatest Warlocks can use darkness in all of its forms, and they are numerous."

"In Caelum," Speilton said, "I will be facing the Warlocks as well, I presume."

"It appears that way," Cigam said sadly. "They have nearly all left Liolia now, and I assume Caelum is their next target."

"And there's nothing you or any of the other Wizards will do to help?" Speilton asked.

"Well, there is nothing we can physically do to help you. But this brings me to my second reason for coming here before you. I have recently gained some new information on Ferrum Potestas."

"Retsinis's sword? You know how to defeat him?" Speilton asked.

"Well, upon further examination of the ancient runes recorded to have been on the sword, we believe there is one way to reverse its effects. As you know, the first to be cut by the wielder of the sword becomes invincible, and since Retsinis cut himself first upon possessing the sword, he is now invincible. However, it appears that the Sword of Power can have its effects removed if all twelve elements are directed upon him at once."

"All twelve elements?" Speilton repeated. "So, if I can manage to wield all twelve at once, then I can counteract his invincibility?"

"No, it can't be just you. The difficult part is that it requires twelve different wielders all directing a singular element upon him," Cigam clarified.

Speilton's heart fell. "Twelve different wielders? If the Wizards can't help, that leaves only the Liolians to use the twelve."

"Yes, but may I remind you that all twelve elements have been given to the citizens of Liolia," Cigam said with a smile.

"But half of those wands are missing. Their owners are all across Liolia, probably dead. And you said twelve wands? That includes darkness, which last time I checked was in the possession of Retsinis," Speilton shook his head. "And the wind element…it's with Ram, and Ram…"

Speilton trailed off, his mind on his old friend and mentor. Ram had fallen prey to Retsinis's Sword of Power, and now the man he had once known was gone.

"Well, if it makes it any better, the way I see it, you only really need eleven. You don't appear to need your wand to summon fire any more, so I advise you let someone else use that while you conjure whichever twelfth element is needed."

Speilton shook his head. "Great, now we only need the other eleven."

"I know it will still be difficult," Cigam said sincerely. "But I see this as great news. It shows that Retsinis is not, in fact, invincible. You can defeat him, and though it will require hard-fought battles and sacrifice and a good deal of luck, it is better than the alternative."

Speilton turned away from the Wizard and sat down on the sand. Prowl laid down beside him and nestled her head beside his knee. There was a silence for a few minutes that made Speilton assume Cigam had left as soundlessly as he'd arrived. Then he felt a hand on his shoulder and looked up to see the Wizard staring out at the lake beside him. Cigam gave a small cough to clear his throat, then said, "We possess an exceptionally rare power, and with that power comes responsibility. The significance of every action to take is amplified. Some crumble under the responsibility and serve only themselves. Others of us do our best to do good for as many people as we can."

"And how do you know which actions are right or wrong?"

"You never really do. It's a daily struggle, every waking hour. We fail often, yet the next day we try all over again. In time it becomes easier, but the temptation to abandon the fight for others and pursue power for oneself is always present. You will come to understand this just as have all Wizards."

"If the Wizards cannot help those plagued by the Versipellis, then I don't believe I want to be a Wizard."

Cigam chuckled. "And that determination to save others no matter the cost would make you an extraordinary Wizard. But at the moment, you have an incredible opportunity to save your friends and family. With your powers, the fate of thousands of lives are in your hands. That is the curse that comes with control over the elements. But from what I've seen, these powers couldn't be in better hands."

"I'm not so sure if I can handle that responsibility."

"No one ever does. Yet you, like so many others before you must step up to the occasion. Life is difficult. It always has been. Even to me, it sometimes appears one long, desperate struggle. But I think that within it – that struggle – there are little moments of light, of good, of peace, that make it all worth it. It reminds you there's something greater at work, something more than just that endless darkness. Those moments are like...like..."

"Like the stars," Speilton finished for him, and the two were silent once again.

In the morning, Rilly materialized once again beside Speilton. For a moment, he watched as the king sorted through the last of his belongings and packed them up with the rest of his camp. Finally, he spoke, "You're leaving?"

"Yes," Speilton said. "I have to return to Caelum, now."

"I should try to stop you," Rilly said, "but I can tell there is no persuading you."

"I saw it, Rilly," Speilton said, stopping his packing to look at the spirit. "I saw the same scenes in that book that I saw in my visions."

"And you think that leaving now will keep those things from happening?" Rilly asked.

"If I go now, knowing what I know, I may be able to save everyone."

"That's not how the future works," Rilly said. "If you saw it in that book, then that is what will happen. You can't change it."

"But how do you know that? How can you be sure that's how it works?"

"What makes you think that isn't how it works?" Rilly asked. "What if everything you saw will occur only because you try to change the future? What if this decision, right now, is part of that same future?"

"I can't allow myself to think like that," Speilton said, turning away from Rilly but not moving to pack anything. "I have to believe that I can stop it. I have to."

"I know," Rilly said. "And for that, you are brave."

Speilton continued looking down at the ground, until Rilly asked, "You know how to return to Caelum?"

"There's a portal at Mt. Flig. I'll head south and find it. There's a Phoenix in Caelum who is supposed to see if I've arrived, and he can let me back in."

"You did well to plan ahead like you did, but you must beware. If Retsinis is entering Caelum, he may be using that portal as well. However, I find that highly unlikely. I assume there is a second portal they have access to at a different location, but I advise you to still exercise caution."

"Of course," Speilton nodded.

He looked out across the barren waste of the island. In his mind he could still picture the trees and huts and old roads and skittering deer. It had only been a few years since it was all burned to the ground, but to Speilton, it felt like a lifetime.

"Why here?" Speilton asked. "Why'd you choose to come back here?"

"As the spirit of Liolia, I have always been bound to the heart of this world. For centuries, that was the woods around Kon Malopy. But now that the old capital is ruins, I had to depart. So, I came here, knowing that you would return," Rilly said.

"Why me?"

"It has always been you Speilton. From years ago, when you still lived on this island, unaware of your throne, or the dangers in Caloria, or even that there was a larger world outside of the village of Lorg, I knew of you, and I knew what you were destined to do. It appears the Wizard Council knew as well, to some extent, since they did bestow that Wand of Fire upon you, when you were still just a boy on the run. I always knew that Liolia's days were limited, but there was still a chance for its people. I knew you were the only one who could save them all."

"What if I can't?" Speilton asked.

"You will," Rilly answered simply. "You have to."

Speilton looked back at Rilly now. The spirit looked at him with the two spinning pebbles that were his eyes, and the small cluster of ash that was his face appeared to be smiling. "When I leave, what will happen to you?"

"Who can say?" Rilly responded. "Perhaps I will fade as well and return to that place where I was born. Maybe I'll still be able to witness this land like my brethren, in silent observance of the centuries and millennia of darkness that will fall upon this land. Or maybe there's some other place, beyond it all, where I will go."

"And you're not afraid? You're the last of your kind. Are you not afraid of disappearing like the rest?"

"That is the way of all creation, King Speilton. Things die, and others are born. The era of the Anemoi has come to pass, as will the ages of many other races. You see, that is the trend of the universe, of time itself. Over the years, everything becomes…simpler. Every day is the last day for something, someone. In Caelum, if enough years are permitted to pass, then the same will happen there. The Phoenixes's numbers are already few. One day the end will come for the dwarves, and Wodahs, and elves and hooved creatures. All that live today will fade into stories, legends, then myth. Yet, somehow, life will go on."

Rilly spoke of the future fading of the races without fear or bias, as if merely explaining the movement of the sun. Speilton searched the shimmering face for some sign of sorrow or worry, but he found none. "Still, I am sorry that your time is coming soon."

He reached down and threw his last supplies into the sack then hoisted it onto Prowl's back. The dragon sparkled in the warm light of the morning, and her blue scales were jarring amidst the endless stretch of gray and brown. Speilton patted the side of Prowl's neck, then stepped away. Finding the covered streets of the town of Lorg, Speilton retraced his once daily walk. He passed all the old stops, the field where they children would play, the one-room schoolhouse, the feasting table, until he finally came to the ruins of his old house. Here he stopped and crouched down. His hand reached out and touched the dust. He concentrated for a moment and closed his eyes. He pictured his old hut with walls of wooden boards and a roof of sod and bark. There was the sound of the ground shifting, grinding, and something pushing through. He continued holding that image in his head and relived all the times he had to fix it, plug up holes, replace old boards.

His eyes opened, and before him a structure sat, assembled of the thick, intertwining trunks of dozens of small trees. At the same height that the roof of his hut had once sat, branches sprouted from the trunks, woven together so as to block off all light from above. Speilton smiled, looked one last time at his old home remade, then began the walk back to Prowl.

All ready to go, he stood beside the dragon with one hand on her back prepared to hoist him up. Rilly watched, a smile spread across his face. "I guess this is goodbye," Speilton said. "Will I see you again?"

"I wish I knew, King Speilton, but only time can tell."

The wind picked up and blew open the Book of Liolia that still sat upon the charred log of their camp. "Take the Book with you," Rilly said.

"There's nothing more I need from it," Speilton said.

"You never know when it may be useful," Rilly said.

Speilton nodded and retrieved the old leather book. After climbing onto Prowl's back, he looked at Rilly one last time. "Thank you," Speilton said, "for everything you have done."

"It is my job to serve Liolia. Thank you for helping me serve that purpose. Good luck, Speilton Lone of Kal," Rilly said, raising a phantom hand.

Prowl turned to the south and began to run, finally spreading her wings as she mounted a hill. She leapt into the sky, and the two flew off over Kal, and then the lake, and finally open fields of tall grass.

That night, Speilton had a dream of a herd of great beasts running across an immense plain. All around them were herders on horseback, leading the hundreds of the beasts over the terrain. As Speilton watched the herders continue over the land, he suddenly realized that they weren't actually on horseback. The rider and the horse were one, connected into one creature. It was the centaurs, and they rode far out on some distant plain guiding a massive drove of buffalo. Suddenly, Speilton realized it wasn't just any plain, as his eye caught on a landmark on the horizon he recalled from years ago.

He awoke just as the sun had begun to rise and turned to Prowl sleeping beside him. "Wake up," he prodded her. "We have to head west."

ACROSS THE PLAINS OF CAELUM
~ 13 ~

"You're telling me that the Order of the Bow purposefully abandoned us here in Esphodale to lure out whatever forces were within the mountains?" Millites questioned.

"Well, I would not say we abandoned you, necessarily," the Phoenix explained calmly. "We had scouts constantly watching the situation."

"You may have been watching, but I don't recall any of your Phoenixes coming to help us in the battle," Millites snapped.

"Well, you know it is not our way to engage in combat," the Phoenix responded.

"Then, what was the point of even observing us? Would your scouts have just watched us all die if it had come to that?"

"But it did not come to that, did it? We were confident in your army's capacity to repel any sudden attack. Besides, we have now confirmed that Retsinis has in fact entered Caelum with at least all of his forces of Daerds, which likely means his Nuquamese army of those turned by Ferrum Potestas have arrived as well."

"I'm so glad we could help you confirm that," Millites rose from the rock he had been sitting on and walked a few strides past the Phoenix to survey the damage of Esphodale in the moonlight as he already had multiple times that night. "We lost many men. One of my commanders, Andereer, was killed in the battle. My dragon, Hunger, was terribly wounded, and easily could have died if we hadn't received help from our friends at the last minute. You and the Order gambled with our lives."

"Yes, I understand there were losses," the Phoenix said plainly, "but it appears our gamble was successful. We now know what we face, more or less, and your army lives to fight another day."

"No," Millites turned back to the Phoenix. "My men are in no shape to continue fighting. They are worn and the injured are many. In the morning, I will lead them out of the city back south. I assume you have medics who can tend to them at Civitas Levi."

"We have a few, but the Order of the Bow specifically demanded that you not return to Civitas Levi," the Phoenix explained.

"What?" Millites growled. "Are we banished now?"

"Not banished, but as long as our enemies are still active in Caelum, you are forbidden to return as not to draw their forces all the way to the capital."

"So my army is supposed to act as some type of buffer?" Millites questioned. "A line of bodies to stop the tide that is coming?"

"You are to meet them in battle in areas not heavily populated. That means you must draw Retsinis's forces away from the cities of the Arcanian Woods and Marenta Loras in the Great Feather Peaks."

"What does that leave us? Just the open plains between the mountains and the coast? We cannot challenge Retsinis's army in the fields. We need a strategic position, and more than that, we need our army rested and healed."

"I doubt there is much time for that," the Phoenix said. "Unless…"

"Unless what?" Millites asked, retaking his seat on the rock in their camp.

"Unless, you lead your army to the west to Lake Vascent. It is located in a valley just south of the Great Feather Peaks."

"Why would we go to some lake?" Millites asked.

"Because it is a sacred spot here in Caelum. The waters there are imbued with a type of healing quality."

"Don't you have some tree or something that already does that?" Millites asked.

"If you are referring to the Silver Tree, then yes, we do have a tree with healing capabilities, as well. But while the Silver Tree is able to bring back even those on the edge of death, Lake Vascent's potency is much less strong. It heals minor injuries but can also refresh your soldiers. Lead them there, have them bathe in the lake and drink from its waters, and they should be returned to their greatest strength."

"How far is this lake?" Millites asked. "And how do we get there?"

When morning broke above the Arcanian Woods to the east, the Liolians tore down their camps and loaded up all their equipment on the wagons. Nearly every man had experienced some injury in the fray, ranging from scuffed knees from fighting on the rocky field beside Esphodale to limbs lost to the beaks and talons of the Daerds. The city itself had incurred a great deal of damage, with multiple towers knocked over into the streets beyond just the one that Millites and Hunger had occupied. Rubble filled every alley, tossed on top of and beside the bodies of many men. The bodies of the Daerds were more numerous though, and because of their great size, they took up a far greater area of the ground. In the first field in which the Liolians had taken their stand, the stone was layered in their black feathers, piled multiple bodies deep in some areas. In the night, their medics and a few volunteers had been tasked with the terrible job of pushing through the massive bodies to recover the dead and dying Liolians that had been left there. The streets were just as bad, clogged with Daerd corpses already attracting flies. Despite the city's immense size, it appeared that someone or something had died in every street and on every corner. Even after an entire night of searching, a few warriors were still missing, but they did not have the time to confirm what they all knew had to be true about their fate. Any medic left behind to search would be a medic lost when Retsinis's army inevitably came to survey the battle as well.

The wagons and men formed their line leading out of the city in a recession along the same road they had taken to reach Esphodale. All about was open prairie of grass so green that many thought their eyes must be deceiving them. The endless sunlight of the day appeared artificial and inappropriate considering the savage fighting that had so recently occurred. But the men carried on their way, constantly checking the mountains over their shoulders for any signs of their enemies returning.

Before nightfall of the first day of their journey, they came to a crossroads where they diverged from their original path for the first time. This road took them west towards the spot on the horizon where the sun was setting. The lake that they sought was said to be a five days' ride from Esphodale, which for many would be five days too long. Throughout the camp that night the

142

screams of the wounded rang out, and many shivered in their tents thinking about the forces that watched them in the mountains mere miles away. A few soldiers considered asking to stop and find shelter to regroup, but they knew to stop would mean to allow their enemy to find and hunt them down. There was nowhere to hide. When the sun rose again, they had lost three more men to worsening injuries from the days before, and the men set out early for another day of marching.

Around noon on their second day, the road led alongside a river nearly two hundred yards across, with quick flowing water that flowed southwest to where they were headed. Like the men, the water appeared to be fleeing the ominous mountains to the north. The Liolian army marched beside it, staring out across the smooth current of the river. Every once and awhile, they would see the flash of something in the water, and then a water Phoenix would emerge and take to the air for a moment before crashing back into the waves. Some thought to warn the Phoenixes of the threat not far away, but in the end, no one said a thing.

Usus remained almost constantly in the sky on the back of Flamane, watching the surrounding hills and ridges for any dangers. Millites was limited to the ground while Hunger recovered from his injuries. The dragon lay upon an open cart pulled by four horses, sleeping most of the day, but he tried on occasion to walk by himself. These few attempts rendered growls and hisses of pain from the dragon, so attempting to fly was not even considered. Millites rode beside his dragon on a horse that had been left without a rider after the battle. When Usus returned to the ground from time to time, he would claim to not mind staying in the air all day, and it regularly appeared to the men below that he was sleeping upon his griffin's back. No one called him out because they understood the difficulty of his job, and they also respected Flamane's ability to identify danger as much as they did Usus's.

Before they stopped again for the night, they came to a spot where the river connected with another river of nearly equal size. They camped along the river's bank that second night. The one benefit of their short stay in Esphodale was that they still had an abundance of food, even though that food was reserved to the entirely vegetarian diet of the Phoenixes. Fruits, vegetables, and grains had composed their diets throughout their journey, along with the few bits of cheese that the Phoenixes had somehow obtained from some distant land where cattle and goats lived. A couple of Liolians had attempted to fish in the river, but either the fish here didn't bite or there were no fish in the waters at all because none were caught.

Millites slept that night outside of his tent on a bedroll next to Hunger. Asleep, the dragon's scales appeared the dark green of the deep forest. Watching the distant fire of their watchman on the hill to the east, Millites pat the hard shell that encased the snout of his dragon, and Hunger growled cozily in his sleep. When the king laid down, he looked up at a night sky so full of stars that it appeared to glow with warm hues of purple. There was not a cloud in the sky above, and there rarely ever appeared to be clouds over Caelum, as if they knew to avoid this artificial land.

In the morning, when Millites awoke, Usus was already circling above the army on Flamane, scouting the horizon. The gear was packed once more, and then the army continued moving west. Upon his horse,

Millites would ride up alongside the other leaders in the army, moving from one to the next. He knew his active presence amongst the army was good for morale, but the journey had made him grow weary. His arm ached from his landing at the base of the tower in Esphodale, and he missed the company of his strategist, Andereer, who had been a loyal advisor for years of warfare. After all his years of service to Milwaria and the preservation of peace in Liolia, he would forever lay in a rocky tomb in a foreign city in a land he had hardly known. It was the same story for all the other fallen – Liolians, human and Wodahs and dwarf alike – and it would be the same for many more before it was all through.

As they marched, the river beside them merged with many other such rivers, creating a vast river plain of interconnecting streams and little islands before the water tapered into a singular path that flowed nearly half a mile wide.

Usus descended in the afternoon and landed beside Millites. He appeared tired, and Flamane breathed heavily through his beaked maw as they walked upon solid ground for the first time in hours. "There's a bridge some ten miles ahead," he reported. "Just over these hills you should be able to see it. I have to say, I've never seen anything like it. It appears to be absolutely massive. Stretches all the way across the river."

"The Bridge of Moraff is what the Phoenix called it," Millites said. "That means the lake should be only about two days away, now."

"Only two more days," Usus said quietly, more to himself than to the king. "That Phoenix, did he say exactly how the waters are supposed to help? You said it heals wounds, gives energy, that sort of thing."

"Yes, he said something like that," Millites said.

"Could it give me a good long rest? That's what I really need. Just some nice sleep."

"You should get rest now," Millites said. "We have other watchmen. We can send them out to scout the hills on horseback. Let Flamane ride in one of the wagons. If there's not one available, he can probably just rest beside Hunger," Millites proposed.

"I think I'm fine. Really, I do. Two more days you said? I can make it two more days."

"Consider it at least," Millites said. "You'll need your energy if…"

He didn't need to finish his statement. Usus nodded and spurred Flamane forward. The griffin strode stiffly and then slowly ascended into the sky.

Less than an hour later, they had reached the top of the hills, and down below they could see the towering shape of the bridge. Tall columns of rounded, dark stone rose thousands of feet into the air on either side of the river. Between the columns, a long arched bridge sprouted smoothly out of the road on one side and spread the half mile across the river where it descended and sloped into the ground again. Even from the many miles between the army and the bridge, they could see that the great columns and pathway were covered in expertly crafted detail that coated the structure like leaves on a tree. The stone had been shaped by some artisan cable of bending stone as smoothly and carefully as a potter with clay. After days of endless plains and river, the Bridge of Moraff was truly a sight to behold.

The men studied the structure as they marched down the far side of the hill, and slowly the bridge revealed more and more of its artistry as they grew closer. Many believed the columns that rose on either end of the bridge rivaled even Kon Malopy's Sky Tower in height.

The Liolians were still absorbed in the splendor of the bridge, when Flamane shrieked high in the air above, and Usus first began to scream his alert. Flying from behind the army, they were unaware of the griffin and the Second-in-Command screeching down toward them until they had nearly landed. When the soldiers turned around, they saw a frantic Usus with eyes wide and face red from shouting, landing hard beside Millites on the back of his griffin. Millites' heart fell at the hasty arrival of his friend.

"They're coming," Usus said, gasping for breath. "There's an army…on the horizon…to the north."

Millites grabbed his friend by the shoulder. "How far are they? How many?'

"I..." Usus gasped. "I couldn't tell. A couple thousand maybe."

"And how far? How much time do we have?"

"They're coming fast…I just saw them now, miles away, but they're closing in. It's like…it's like they're all sprinting or something."

"Is it just ground troops?" Millites asked. "The Daerds or the Phoenixes of Darkness weren't sent?"

Usus shook his head. "I didn't see any. Just the ground troops."

"How much time?" Millites asked again.

Usus thought for a second, clearly panicking. "An hour, maybe. They were moving fast. Well, it appeared some were. They were spread out, some running faster than others I guess."

"An hour," Millites muttered. "We're still two days away."

Senkrad and Onaclov had ridden up beside them on their horses. Just from the look on the two leader's faces, they were able to guess what Usus' news had been. "How long do we have?" Onaclov asked.

"An hour," Millites said.

"Can we outrun them?" Senkrad asked.

"We have too much cargo, and too many wounded," Millites said. "Even if we left behind all nonessentials and took flight this second, we'd only be going to some other place we know nothing of."

"So, what's our move?" Usus asked.

"We take a stand here?" Senkrad offered. "The river can act as a buffer, forcing them to meet us head on."

"Or it could be cage they could corner us in," Onaclov retorted. "The waters are too deep and the current too slow to carry the men away. There's no crossing it, and there's no chance for escaping in it."

"No," Millites said, an idea forming. "But it might just be our salvation all the same. Usus, how far do you say the bridge is?"

"Umm, maybe five miles," Usus stuttered.

"Just over six," a voice declared, and the group turned to see Hopi, leader of the Isoalates, who had ridden up alongside them.

"Lead the men to the bridge," Millites commanded. "Have all the wagons taken across, but assemble the men on this side of the river, just before the bridge."

"So, you do intend to make a stand?" Senkrad asked.

"A stand of sorts. We will need to fend off the approaching army. Enough for our supplies to cross the bridge, then we will send the rest of our men. Usus, the

148

bridge appears to be made of stone, so when the time comes…"

Usus understood and nodded. "I should be able to do it."

"Then we should go as quickly as possible," Millites said. "If all goes well, we'll be able to put the river between ourselves and Retsinis's forces. But it will take the five of us here, the five in possession of the wands, to hold them off. Our men will be tired, so we must protect them."

"Understood," Onaclov said.

"I will go now to give the command," Hopi said.

"Yes, go," Millites said. "And sound the horns. I'm sure Retsinis's army knows where we are anyways."

There was a great commotion as the word was spread throughout the train of warriors and equipment that an army was bearing down on them. Men spurred their horses towards the bridge in a wild dash, while those without horses summoned whatever strength they had left to sprint towards the tall, dark columns. The order of their line had broken, as men spilled out across the grassy plain in a frantic rush to take their positions. Usus circled the fleeing men on the back of Flamane, watching the distant army that covered the hills behind them, growing ever closer in their ravenous pursuit of the Liolians. As they came closer into view, he could confirm that they were in fact the multitudes that composed Retsinis's army. They were the thousands of former Liolians that had been cut by Retsinis's magical blade and had been turned into hideous beasts of every size and shape, united only in their submission to the man who had enslaved them. The terrible creatures seemed absurdly out of place as they tore across the serene landscape without any formation or structure, but even stranger still were the dark clouds collecting on the horizon behind them, as if the army was bringing a storm with them. For a moment, Usus believed it might be the Daerds after all, but a ripple of lightning through the cloud revealed it to be merely thunderheads.

As the first of the Liolians reached the base of the bridge, they stopped, and turned shakily around to face the armies approaching from the east. When the wagons arrived, they were led up the gentle slope of gray stone to begin their passage over the river. There were many gaps in the ranks of the Liolians, left behind by the carnage of the battle days before, but their numbers were still strong. Catching their breath, the men waited, until they saw the first signs of the enemy breaching the hills only miles away. At first, they appeared as only black specks across the green ridges in the distance, but then the shadowy horde washed down the side of the hill, coating it entirely in darkness. Above them, the dark clouds rolled, and the waiting Liolians were suddenly buffeted by gusts of wind. The breeze caused their metal to clatter, as they looked out at an army far larger and far more vicious than themselves.

Millites sat aboard his horse at the front of the army, and he turned to face the hundreds of men collected behind him. "Hold fast!" he called to them. "Be brave here today, and live to see tomorrow!"

Only the wind made noise, as the men remained silent, watching in horror the army approaching. Usus landed and stepped off Flamane to allow him to continue watching the skies. The other leaders had ridden up beside Millites, and he turned to address only them now. "The army that we face were all once

Liolians. There's a chance they can be saved somehow, so we must make every effort to spare as many as we can."

"Do the men know not to kill them, only wound them?" Senkrad asked.

"I believe it is too much to burden them with. They must do what is required to survive. We, however, are more fortunate. With our wands, we can fight more intelligently. We don't need to win this battle, we just need to ensure as many of our men survive as is possible," Millites explained.

"We could all just use our wands," Hopi said. "Each of us can rely on our strengths to keep the Nuquamese back."

"It's difficult to use lava in a way that isn't fatal," Onaclov said.

"Then avoid using it to kill them. Use it more as a…deterrent," Usus offered. "Just throw it down in front of them, and I think they'll have the awareness to avoid it altogether."

"And create a barrier," Onaclov said. "What will the rest of you do?"

"My color element can distract them," Hopi offered. "It does a good job blinding and confusing enemies."

"Yes, that would be perfect," Millites said. "My light can work similarly. And Usus, with stone–"

"Oh, I have many different options," Usus smiled.

"And my ice element can keep them back as well," Senkrad added. "Ice is quite efficient at keeping things stuck in place."

"Then we all know what we must do," Millites said. "Their army may be larger than ours, and they may fight without fear, but we can fight more strategically. It's our only chance if we wish to survive."

ERRANDS FOR THE ORDER
~ 14 ~

Metus stood at the north gate of Civitas Levi, watching as small groups of Phoenixes trickled toward the city in a steady stream. The faun held a piece of parchment loosely in one hand, and a feather quill in the other, but he no longer used them. Instead they hung at his sides while he simply observed Phoenix after Phoenix flee to the walls of Civitas Levi from the various kingdoms across Caelum. The refugees were quite a sight to see in the warm glow of the afternoon sun, as they sailed forward in their V-shaped formations, with streams of their elements tailing behind them and disappearing after only a second after as they moved on. But Metus wasn't watching them. His eyes were on the hilltops that were the horizon, waiting for some beings other than the Phoenixes to come bounding over them.

"Why don't you come on back?" a voice asked behind Metus, startling him. "You've been out here for days."

Teews walked up behind him and leaned against the opposite side of the gate to look out at the hills as well.

"I…well…I have a job."

"Recording how many Phoenixes come through?" Teews asked, nodding towards his quill and parchment. "How's that going?"

"Well, turns out I'm not as good at counting as the Phoenixes had assumed. They said my numbers weren't accurate."

"It's for the best," Teews said. "Let them count their own. The Phoenixes aren't going off to war, so the least they can do is keep their own record of how many refugees they're taking in."

"I didn't mind it," Metus said. "It's been better than the other jobs they've been giving me. At least here, I get this view. But any moment now, they should be sending some Phoenixes to go set me on a new mission."

"Then, you should be resting until they do come," Teews said.

"Yes, I suppose you're right. But…"

"You're waiting for them to come back, too?"

Metus nodded. "It's foolish, I know. Especially considering I know that they are nowhere near Civitas Levi."

"How do you know that?" Teews asked, turning suddenly and approaching. "I haven't heard any news of their whereabouts in days. Did the Order tell you that?"

"I…I can't say."

"They did. And that necklace you're wearing now, I suppose they gave you that, too?"

Metus reached up and fumbled with the small crystal fastened to the thin cord hanging around his neck.

"Yes, I use this to speak to them. Or, at least, to find the location of the tunnel that leads to their chambers."

"So, they've been keeping you updated? And they're keeping the rest of us in the dark? Seems exactly like what they would do. It keeps us under their control."

"I think they only intend to keep the people in the city from being worried."

"You're taking up for them, now?" Teews questioned. "Serving them must really be getting in your head."

"It's not that it's...well, maybe it is that to an extent. I don't know, it's just that, I don't think their intentions are truly nefarious."

"And what makes you say that?"

"They just seem...scared. They're scared about their future. Their society's future. For hundreds of years, it was only them that lived in this world, and with every human and dwarf and Wodahs and faun that they bring to this world, they feel their control slipping away. They see themselves being replaced. And I understand them in a way. I've been here for hours, watching the Phoenixes from across the Kingdom of Caelum flocking to the city, and I realized just how few of them there are. Don't get me wrong, there are thousands. Probably tens of thousands. And they do live for incredibly long times, but still. There are millions in Liolia, at least, there were before Retsinis marched through with his army."

"But why would they fear our coming? We mean them no harm?" Teews asked.

"You know the history of Liolia. It is one of war, for as far back as there has been written records. In fact, past that, to the days of the old orators. Right now, Caloria and Milwaria are united against Retsinis and his slave army from Nuquam. But only a few years ago it was the Milwarians and Calorians in a centuries long war. Before that, there were the Wars for the Rich Woods, between the different human clans, and around that same time were the Dwarf and Elvish Wars. The mers once fought the men and naiads of the Ripples for control of the peninsula. And the centaurs used to be barbaric tribe and raiders, wreaking havoc across the Great Plains."

"What's your point?"

"I guess my point is, that has not been the way of the Phoenixes. Their numbers are not large, but they have also been free from warfare for centuries. They possess a very different outlook on life because of that."

"But that is only because they have quite literally banished all darkness to the mountains on the edge of their world," Teews said.

"Yes, but it has worked, hasn't it? But that's another part of it – the mountains are not the edge of this world. Not in the least. In one of the meeting halls of the Order, I saw a map. Now, it was very crudely drawn, but it showed a vast world, with enormous oceans, and multiple islands and bodies of land. Caelum, this domain of the Phoenixes, is just one small part of that world."

"Then, what do the Phoenixes have to fear? We Liolians can just leave and go off to one of those other lands."

"Maybe, but you've seen this land. There's no life here, save the vegetation and the Phoenixes. I've seen some insects, but no animals in the hills or fish in the sea. What if the other lands are like that?"

"So, you believe we should just take our chances back in the ruins of Liolia?"

"Maybe," Metus said. "Maybe not. I don't know what we should do, and it's not my choice anyway. I just don't believe that the Phoenixes are our enemies. They mean well. They want to protect us, and they always have. That's why we were brought here in the first place. But they also want to defend their own, and I can't blame them for that. I understand their fear."

Teews nodded, and they looked back off at an approaching group of a dozen or so Phoenixes coming from the northeast. Then Teews asked, "You wish you were with the army, don't you?"

"Yes," Metus said.

"Me, too," Teews said. "I have always wished to be with them. All my life I've had to stay back, 'in case something happens', as they tell me. They think they're saving me from the horrors of the battlefield, and for some people, that may truly be the best decision for them. But I've been on the field of battle, and I've waited miles and miles away from it for some word of success or failure. And I would take being on the battlefield every time. Here, we have no power, no agency. All we can do is hope and wait for either our flags to mount the horizon or the enemy's. And you know that if it's the enemy's, there is nothing you can do to stop them from killing every last person in the city."

"I agree," Metus said. "At least on the battlefield, you feel like you have some control."

"So, now that you know the Order of the Bow so well, what do you think they would do if they find that we've run away to join the army?"

"You're trying to flee the city?" Metus asked

"Well, if you know where they are, I can get–"

Two Phoenixes suddenly dropped down in front of Metus and Teews, and they went silent. "Metus," the green Phoenix said, "the Order requests that you find a particular Phoenix who has recently been engaged in some rather strange behavior, and bring him before the Order of the Bow."

Teews turned silently and slipped back into the city while the Phoenixes spoke.

"Why must I talk to the Phoenix? Isn't that your domain?"

"Well, in this particular case, the Phoenix has been seen spending considerable time with Liolians. We would handle it, but the Order believes our presence will cause the Liolians around him to become uneasy and insubordinate."

Metus nodded wearily. "Who is the Phoenix? And where can I find him?"

"His name is Beati, and we believe he is in the Liolians' feasting hall."

"And that building is in that direction, right?" Metus asked, pointing to the southwest.

The Phoenixes shook their heads. "Further East," the green one said.

"Oh, yes, I remember now," Metus said sheepishly. "And, does the Order still want this record I was keeping or…"

"It's been taken care of," the Phoenix said, leaping into the air and flying back into the city, leaving Metus standing there awkwardly with the parchment and quill still held out in his hands.

The banquet hall was a massive building located near the center of the city. It was tall with a pitched roof and hundred-foot columns in front of the tall oak doors. The hall's façade was a thriving with elegant sculptures carved straight out of the stone, surrounded by tall stained-glass windows in as many colors as the walls of Civitas Levi. Five roads met in a plaza before it, with a fountain in its center. Metus climbed the few, short steps and slipped in through the cracked wooden doors and was affronted by an expansive hall with only a few Liolians scattered within. The faun didn't even notice them at first, but instead marveled at the steep walls with their dozens of thin windows letting in slits of rainbow-filtered light. There were more columns inside, spaced out down the long hall, holding up the stone, curved roof, ribbed by carved wooden beams. Statues of Phoenixes overlooked the hall from high above, and what little space on the walls that were not covered by glass or sculptures depicted images of peaceful landscapes through mosaics. At the far end of the room, on a raised platform, was a throne, with smaller chairs on either side. The throne was for a monarch, but the Head Consul of the Order preferred to remain in his hidden chambers.

The former Queen of Milwaria was present in the room, but she sat at one of the long wooden tables at the far end of the room. She was alone, which was quite unusual, save for a single Phoenix perched on the bench beside her. Metus began walking toward them, the sounds of his hooves on the stone floor echoing throughout the near empty hall. Other Liolians dining in the hall – the older individuals saved long before by the Phoenixes and far past the point of being of any use in battle – looked up and watched the faun slowly proceed between the tables, towards the thrones at the front of the room. Herdica noticed him and turned away from the Phoenix with whom she had been speaking. She surveyed Metus as he approached.

"Excuse me," Metus said quietly, feeling the eyes of the dozen or so Liolians on him throughout the room, "would you happen to be the Phoenix known as Beati?"

The Phoenix beside Herdica looked worriedly at the Queen for a moment. He was clearly young, with his feathers disheveled and neck still shorter than many of the others. "Yes," the Phoenix finally said. "I'm Beati."

"Well, I have been instructed by the Order to bring you before them," Metus said, uncomfortably looking back and forth between Beati and Herdica as he spoke.

"And why does the Order wish to speak with him?" Herdica asked sternly.

Her hands crossed regally in her lap exuded composure, but her eyes hinted at a fierceness just below the surface.

"I'm…not sure. They only said that they wanted to speak about some unusual behavior or something of the sort."

"They didn't tell you what behavior exactly they wished to talk about?" Herdica questioned.

"No, they were vague about the specific reasons."

Herdica nodded slowly, clearly thinking. "You were a hand to my son back in Liolia, were you not?" she asked.

"Yes, your highness, I served King Speilton."

"Are you still loyal to him?"

"Of course. He is a good man and a friend."

"Then, I need you to listen carefully," Herdica leaned forward and spoke softly now. "My friend Beati here cannot go to speak with the Order. It is paramount that he avoids them at all cost."

"May I ask why? What is it this Phoenix is doing that is causing the Order to request to speak with him?"

"It's not what he is doing that concerns Círsar and his cronies. It's what he's done, and what he is going to do."

"And what is it he has done?"

"It is probably best if you do not know. But it does concern Speilton, and it is of the utmost importance that the Order not know as well."

"Well, it appears they already know something is happening," Metus said.

"I was afraid they might. One of the Phoenix guards did seem to notice us as we were coming back to Civitas Levi the other night," Herdica said.

"Coming back from what?"

"We can't say! We can't say! Speilton told me I couldn't tell anyone," Beati exclaimed.

"Then, how is it you know?" Metus asked Herdica. "Or were you part of his plan to escape all along?"

Herdica was silent, examining the young faun. After a moment, she said, "We did help Speilton, yes. I tell you that much only because I believe you would've done the same if given the opportunity. And also, because we need your help."

"How can I help?"

"You said the Order of the Bow has begun to notice that we are up to something. They likely have also abandoned their theory that it was the Phoenixes of Darkness that freed Speilton from his prison. That means they suspect us. If Beati goes to speak with them, they will surely discover the truth. We cannot allow that."

"Can Beati not just lie to them?" Metus asked. "He may be able to talk his way out of it."

Herdica smiled sincerely down at the Phoenix beside her. "I am afraid Beati here is much too young, and the Order much too wise for that to happen."

"Then what must I tell them?" Metus asked.

"You must not tell them anything. Beati and I will hide in the tunnels beneath the city. From there, we can sneak out at night to continue our task, but we will have to be much more careful, and attempt it less frequently to ensure we're not caught," Herdica said, more to Beati than Metus.

"Will they find us?" Beati asked.

"They shouldn't," Herdica said. "The Phoenixes rarely go underground, especially in the deeper tunnels now that all the prisoners have been released."

"Can I join you?" Metus asked. "If I don't bring you to the Order, they will surely want to interrogate me."

"No," Herdica said. "I'm sorry, but they would find you."

"They'd find me? How?"

"That necklace around your neck," Herdica said. "That crystal does more than let you find the Order. It lets the Order find you."

Metus looked down at his necklace, then quickly began to pull it up over his curly hair and short horns.

"No!" Herdica said. "Don't! They told you never to take it off, didn't they? That's because the second you take it off they will be alerted. They'll know something is wrong, and they'll send their Phoenixes to find you."

"Then what should I do?" Metus asked, growing scared.

There was a loud bang at the far end of the banquet hall, and every head turned quickly as the door creaked open. Teews stepped through the opening, walking quickly toward the table where Herdica and Beati sat and Metus stood. "Mother," Teews called, indifferent to the way her voice echoed through the quiet hall, "I'm taking that white horse I found in the stables and riding out to join the army."

Herdica did not respond to her daughter, but instead looked back up at Metus. "You need to flee from Civitas Levi."

NOMADS IN CALORIA
~ 15 ~

Miles and miles of muddy wasteland passed beneath them until Speilton finally saw the first signs of the canyon. Years ago, he had crossed the massive split in the ground during his quest to destroy the Inferno of Erif. They had lost a great friend and ally at that gorge – the dryad Ginkerry. She was the first of their company to perish, with the elf Nicholas following after her in the Battle of Skilt. But now, Speilton headed east with Prowl through Caloria to find a different member of their company, one who for years had been missing on a quest in search of his people. His absence had caused Speilton to altogether forget him as a potential ally, but Speilton's dream had made it clear to him how greatly he could help.

From high above Prowl's back, Speilton was able to distinguish the canyon, but for quite a while the land around it was barren. As time passed and they grew closer to the great split in the ground, Speilton began to worry that maybe his dream had in fact been nothing more than just a manifestation of his desires. But there had been something about it that seemed too real, too specific, like it was intended to be a clue or direction of some sort.

Then Speilton saw the distant cloud of dust on the horizon, and a chill ran across his skin as the image from his dream materialized before him. A herd of some great wooly beasts were charging across the vast plain, kicking up the dirt as they charged. Herding the animals were the nomadic centaurs, whooping and calling as they raced around the perimeter of the creatures, leading them parallel to the gorge. Prowl also saw the massive group appear out of the distance, and she began to glide towards them.

As the centaurs noticed the blue dragon descending upon them, they brought the herd to a stop, and drew weapons in preparation for an attack. Speilton forced Prowl to land some distance away from them, and then he dismounted to approach the centaurs on foot. Prowl's defensive, snarling position did not help Speilton's attempted presentation of peaceful intentions, but as the centaurs rode forward in their towering ferocity, he was glad she was prepared in case things took a bad turn.

The centaurs raced up to and around Speilton, with at least twelve of the half-man-half-horse creatures surrounding the king, letting out war cries that Speilton knew were supposed to intimidate him. Instead, Speilton stood firm, strapping his shield to his arm – invisible under the cloudy sky – and laying his hand upon the pommel of his sword. When their rotating formation came to a halt and they lowered their weapons at Speilton, he spoke for the first time. "It is I, King Visvires. I have come to speak with the one who leads your people."

"King Visvires," one of the beings spoke, "is dead."

"I know that is likely what you must believe. But I can confirm that I am in fact alive," Speilton spoke, drawing his wand.

The centaurs pressed forward, rattled by the movement. Speilton continued nonetheless, and from the tip of the wand, he summoned a single flame that fluttered in the wind for a moment. "As you can see, I am the fire-wielding king, and I'm sure you saw Prowl over there, one of only two dragons in Liolia."

There was a moment of muttering as the centaurs turned to each other, conferring on how to proceed. It appeared there were still many who doubted the truth of Speilton's identity. "If you are truly King Visvires, then where have you been all these years?"

"I am not at liberty to discuss that with you, but that is the topic with which I wish to speak with your leader," Speilton explained.

"Excuse our hesitation to trust your story," another centaur said coldly, "but as far as we know, the true King Visvires is dead. We cannot allow you to see the chief until we can confirm you are not merely some deceiver."

"Then take me to Equus, if he has found your people since I last saw him years ago. He knows me and will be able to prove I am no deceiver."

The centaurs looked at each other for a moment, then one finally spoke. "You know Chief Equus?" the centaur asked.

"*Chief* Equus?" Speilton inquired. "I knew he had gone to search for the rest of your people when you all left the desert, but I didn't know…"

"Yes, Equus is our chief now," the centaur affirmed. "We know of his adventure with the Kings and Queen of Milwaria, so if you truly are King Visvires, he should recognize you."

"So, you will take me to him?" Speilton asked.

"We will," the centaur said, "but be wary of the consequences if you turn out to be anyone other than who you claim to be."

Speilton nodded, and as they began to usher him away, Speilton waved to Prowl to follow. The group led the King back to the herd, where a group of the centaurs had left the buffalo and waited with weapons held at the ready. When they met this second group, Speilton was passed to their control while the first group returned to the buffalo herd. Speilton was escorted north over the land freshly trampled by the hooves of the great beasts. He watched the massive, wooly creatures between the trotting legs of the centaurs as they marched. The bison held their heads low, running their dark nostrils over the muddy ground for something to eat. Soon the herd had disappeared behind them, and up ahead, Speilton could see the first signs of some civilization.

They entered a small town, composed of wood and canvas structures and scattered campfires. Small centaur children chased each other through the dirt on shaky legs and wove in between the buildings while the elderly watched and leisurely went about their chores. When Speilton entered their streets with the full escort of the armed centaurs, the inhabitants of the village froze and looked up from their tasks to view the new arrival. Speilton attempted to nod pleasantly to them, but they only gave him quizzical looks in return. Eventually, they reached a larger tent, and the canvas doorway was pushed open and two heavily armed centaurs emerged, followed by a third. The first two, it appeared, were guards, and they were followed by none other than Equus himself.

"Equus!" Speilton called, looking upon his friend for the first time in many years.

The two guards pointed their long halberds at Speilton as he spoke. Equus approached slowly, his eyes narrowed as he studied Speilton's face. The muscular horse legs paced slowly towards Speilton, and then he began to circle him as if a different angle would reveal the truth behind the visitor before him.

"Equus, it's me, Speilton. I know you must be confused, but I can promise you that it is me, and that I come with good intentions. If you would just give me a chance to tell you of what has happened these past few years, I promise I-"

"A few miles west of here," Equus interrupted him, "there is a gorge of substantial size. There, long ago, I crossed with King Speilton in our quest to reach Skilt and end Milwaria's war with Caelum. Something quite important occurred as we attempted to cross."

"Yes," Speilton nodded. "One of our fellow travelers and friends, a dryad named Ginkerry, died as we began to cross. The tree she was bound to in the Rich Woods was consumed by the flames of the Calorians, and so her physical form was destroyed as well. We had to watch as she faded before us."

A knowing smile formed on Equus's lips, and he gave a slight bow of his head. "It appears that it is you, King Speilton. Excuse my apprehension, but I had to make sure. It has been commonly known for many years now that the Kings and Queen of Milwaria were dead."

"I know," Speilton said. "But clearly, we are not."

"The centaurs' numbers are few, and we are not a trusting people. I'm sorry if my men treated you harshly," Equus said, and as he spoke, the centaurs guarding Speilton relaxed a bit.

"They were fine. I understand the hesitation. These are difficult times. But it seems you have done well for yourself."

Equus smiled slightly. "Yes, as you can see, I found the tribe of the centaurs after they departed from their city in the desert. And yes, over the years I was given the chance to lead them. But I believe your story is more pressing at the moment. Please, come inside, and we will talk. And you two," he said, turning to a pair of centaurs that had brought Speilton to the village, "take food out to King Speilton's dragon. I'm sure she's hungry."

After Speilton had told Equus of his many adventures in the years after the end of the Milwarian war with Caloria – from the return of Retsinis to their introduction into Caelum to their second battle in Nuquam to the current state of the Milwarian forces – Equus sat in silence, quietly thinking over the story he had just been told. Eventually, he looked up at Speilton. "It appears," he said carefully, "that you and your men have been through quite a lot these past few years. We understand the threat of Retsinis as well, as we came face-to-face with his army only a couple years ago on the plains of Milwaria. He nearly wiped out our people, but we were able to escape here, and here we have struggled on. But I must ask, why have you have come here? What do my centaurs have to offer you?"

Speilton shifted in the make-shift chair on which he sat in the fire-lit tent of Equus before finally answering. "I request the help of your people."

"If you have come to add more men to your numbers, I am sorry, but I must decline. We have few soldiers left, and they are much needed to protect the rest of my people."

"No, I'm afraid what I request is more than just your warriors. What I have to tell you will be…difficult for you to accept, I am sure, as I too still struggle with accepting it. Before coming here to meet your tribe and to talk to you, I trained with Rilly, the spirit from the Rich Woods that was an advisor to the people of Kon Malopy for many years."

"Training for what?" Equus inquired.

"I was working on developing my skills with magic. It appears I have some higher capabilities with wielding the elements that surpasses just the element assigned to me by the Wizards long ago."

"So, you can wield more than just fire now?" Equus asked.

"Hypothetically, with enough concentration and effort, I should be able to wield them all. With these skills, I was able to summon Cigam back to Liolia after the Wizards fled from the Versipellis. He told me of a way we could defeat Retsinis."

"There is a way?" Equus asked, rising suddenly on his horse legs.

"Yes, but it requires that all twelve of the elements be projected at Retsinis at the same time. Long ago, the element of sand was given to the leader of the centaurs. Do you know where—"

But as he spoke, Equus drew the wand from underneath a buffalo hide in the corner of the tent. The centaur observed the smooth wood, and then looked at Speilton. "You need me," Equus said, "to follow you to Caelum?"

"If you are its wielder, then yes, I would," Speilton said apologetically.

"You understand that you ask me to leave my people to fight a war in a world beyond ours?"

"Yes," Speilton said. "But, I don't believe you should leave them. In fact, I believe they should come with you."

Equus did not speak but looked sternly at the king before him.

"I know you must think I'm foolish or even insane for saying this, but this is my second reason for coming. I spoke at length with Rilly about it, and he claimed that Liolia is reaching the end of its life."

"How is that possible?" Equus questioned.

"Rilly compared the world to a living thing. Liolia has grown old, and the damage done by Retsinis was enough to condemn it to death. That is why he and the Versipellis have moved on, and now they threaten the only world left for us."

"You wish for me to relocate my centaurs into a world that is foreign to us all?" Equus asked.

"Not just the centaurs, but the rest of the Liolians. The centaurs are swift, and I believe they can race across Milwaria quicker than anyone else. Rilly told me of many small groups of survivors across Milwaria hidden away, but I believe you and your people can find them all. Then they must be brought to Mt. Flig to the east of Nuquam, where a portal can take them all to Caelum."

Equus again watched the king, and once he had finished speaking, he replied slowly. "We have never had the best relations with the other races."

"These are different times. After the suffering that has been endured here, I believe that all the races will be united under the common Milwarian flag."

"Speilton," Equus said. "The centaurs are no longer in service to Milwaria. We left that country years ago, which is why you find us here, in these uninhabited lands. For centuries the centaurs were neglected in the sandy waste of Milwaria, and with the rulers at Kon Malopy gone, and with the other realms ravaged, the centaurs finally decided it was time to depart and create their own land."

"So, you are saying you will not help me?" Speilton asked.

"I swore long ago that the centaurs would never bow to the rule of the Milwarian monarchy again. Even if we wished to enter Caelum, I could not betray my people like that."

Speilton nodded and looked away out the slight gap in the canvas entryway. "How much longer do you think they'll last?" Speilton asked, turning back to Equus. "The buffalo. I flew for miles and miles across this land, and it's just dirt and mud as far as I could see. The only vegetation is wilted and patchy. Those buffalo won't be able to make it much longer, and when they're dead, what will your people live off of? I doubt there are many other herds out there doing any better."

Equus considered what the king was saying, but he didn't say anything in response.

"I understand why you and your people left, and I'm sorry for the terrible circumstances that have befallen all of you, but I think Caelum is still your best option. You don't have to do it because your king commanded it of you, but as a chief yourself. You should do what's best for your people."

"How do I know what you say is true? What if there is nothing in this other world? What assurances do I have that my people will not just fall once again under the rule of some greater power?"

172

"Caelum is everything I have told you it is. The land is plentiful, and much appears uninhabited. You and your people can do as you desire when this is all over," Speilton assured him. "I ask this of you because it is what I believe is best for your people, and the rest of the Milwarians."

"But," Equus began, looking Speilton in the eyes. "But, there is another reason why you want everyone in Caelum."

Speilton turned away. "But," he continued Equus' statement, "it is also necessary…it's *imperative* that we unite all the wand wielders in Liolia. We must defeat Retsinis, and gathering all the surviving Liolians to rally against him is the only way can do that."

"And what makes you think that the wielders of the wands are still alive?"

"The wielder of a wand can give it to a successor, or if the wielder dies the wand can be taken up by another."

"What if some of the wands have been lost? Long ago the centaurs possessed a ring that could change the state of matter from solid to liquid to even a vapor. But in battle its owner, the former chief, was killed, and the ring was lost."

"We can only hope," Speilton admitted. "I believe the people know the importance of the wands and have taken good care of them over the year."

Equus nodded quietly and looked down at his wand. "You truly believe Liolia is fated to die?"

"I wish it weren't true, but yes, it appears that way."

"So, you are leaving this world behind? Are you saying this is the last time you will look upon Liolia?"

As he spoke, realization hit Speilton that soon, he would be departing from Liolia, with very little chance that he would ever return. He suddenly felt an urge to break out of the tent and look out across the land, however ugly and worn it may appear. A longing for Kon Malopy suddenly washed over him, as he wished to once again walk through its massive halls and peer out from its lofty towers at the city and lake and forest. But he knew that castle was destroyed, laid to ruins just like his first home. He looked the Chief of the Centaurs in the eye, and said, "Yes, it may be. But if somehow all goes right, and we can defeat Retsinis, it will only be one trip through the portal away."

Equus smiled and set down the wand. His hooved feet carried him to the entryway, and he peered out at the village. "In my short time of knowing you, King Speilton, I have understood you to be a trustworthy person. You fought valiantly and selflessly. I trust what you say, and I respect your opinion. For the sake of my people, I will agree to lend my wand and follow you into Caelum to fight, and out of respect for you and all the innocents of your country, I will gather the forces of Milwaria as well."

Speilton spent the night in their village beside Prowl, and when he awoke the next morning, the tents were already being torn down. By the time he finished breakfast, the centaurs had finished packing and had loaded their supplies either onto the backs of the fittest or onto some of the buffalo. Speilton waved from Prowl's back as his blue dragon flew off to the east and the centaurs rode further and further away to the north. Soon, they were out of sight, along with their herd of bison. For days, Speilton and Prowl traveled across the endless muddy prairie of Caloria, spotting the hollowed remains of ghost towns now and again, but rarely did he spot other life. What little life they did encounter came in the form of lone birds or scampering critters far below them. The centaurs had graciously given them food supplies for their journey to Mt. Flig, but looking upon the land below, Speilton began to worry that the tribe would run out of food before they were even able to reach the distant realms of Milwaria.

Speilton had given Equus specific instructions on the different races that were rumored to still be alive in Liolia, as well as the wands that remained with them: the elves of the Jungle of Supin, the giants of the Icelands, the mers of Mermaid Reef, the fauns and satyrs of the Rocks of Tior, the Naiads of the Ripples, the remaining survivors in the Igniacan Underbelly, and the Treeps, dryads, and other woodland creatures of the Rich Woods. He could only hope now that Equus would find them all and lead them to the spot where they could be brought into Caelum. Someone would have to travel back to Liolia to help ferry them through, and Speilton only hoped he'd stay alive long enough to do it himself.

Prowl came to the edge of the land of Nuquam, with its abrupt border delineated by the curtain of fog that choked the land, spreading from the ground up many hundreds of feet in the air. Speilton knew that all types of hideous creatures and dangerous terrain existed within that fog, so Prowl flew alongside it, not daring to get too close. They slept many nights in the shadow of that land of constant fog, and Speilton many times heard – or at least thought he heard – the distant wailing of something deep within its veil.

They eventually saw the first of the mountain peaks that defined the edge of that mysterious and deadly land, and soon the landscape changed from one of empty prairie and old forests, to one of towering highlands and rocky cliffs. Prowl soared high over the land now, rising up with the steep terrain and gliding in between the jagged crags. A mist hung between the mountains here, as if to soften the coarse nature of the land. Finally, Speilton spotted the mountain that rose taller and steeper than all the others, and Prowl flew to a certain spot on its side they had found months ago. At the foot of the dark stone slope, Speilton once again found the slight ledge where a single symbol had been etched. It was the only indication that this mountain possessed a greater significance than just being Liolia's tallest peak. They had found the portal that only Phoenix and man together could open, and now all they needed was a Phoenix.

On that ledge, he and Prowl sat and waited, and slowly wore away at the remaining food supply. After a few days of doing nothing other than waiting and eating, they flew back out of the mountains and searched for something to replenish their reserve. In all of the many trips they took during those days they were never given much time to hunt, as it took many hours to travel to a spot where a few animals or edible plants still existed. They had to return to the ledge before every sunset and sunrise as they were the only times that the portal could be activated. Speilton tried many times to make the portal work by himself, thinking that maybe his magical capabilities would be enough, but the portal never formed. They were forced to continue their wait for a Phoenix who could let them through. While they waited, they practiced their flying maneuvers, with

Speilton guiding Prowl wildly through the sky and between the mountains. When Prowl rested, Speilton practiced his new abilities. He had learned how to shape the objects around him, first raising columns of stone out of the ground and moving them about with his mind. Then he moved on to smaller, more delicate mediums. One day he sculpted the pommel of his Versipellis sword, bending and twisting the round piece of steel at the end of the hilt into the likeness of Prowl's head without laying a finger upon it. Many times, Speilton would rest and stare out across the mountains with their spiny crests and ornamental bodies of mist that concealed a great many secrets lost to time. Other times, Speilton would examine his work in the palm of his hand, and from time to time would notice the white scar still emblazoned on the back of his hand, reminding him of the enemy that awaited him.

For over a week, they lingered on the mountain, until one day, just as they awoke at sunset, a small, red shape appeared before them. Speilton sat up quickly to see a young, round Phoenix looking up at him excitedly. "King Speilton!" Beati chirped. "I hope you haven't been waiting long! I tried to check as often as I could, but then they took—"

"We don't have time," Speilton interrupted, watching the sun rise slowly and mount the horizon. "Quick! We must go now!"

Speilton placed his hand on the small symbol and looked up to the north as Beati situated himself. In that mere second, Speilton held Liolia in his gaze for what he feared to be his last time. Between the gray peaks of the mountains, he thought he could just barely make out the sparkle of some distant lake, probably nestled within a dark Calorian forest of some kind. He knew if he could see further, he would be able to see Kal and the one standing house that he had built. He could maybe even see Rilly. And if he looked further, he would see the Icelands, with its sprawling tundra, and then the Jungle of Supin with its tangle of trees and multitudes of vibrant creatures. Beyond that, further north, he would see the great plains, once home to a number of villages, some quaint, and some sprawling, and then finally, just beyond, he would see the Rich Woods. That forest that Speilton had traveled through and explored countless times still stood with the same beauty and wonder as it always had, and perhaps it always would, long after the sun had set on Liolia for the final time. In those woods were the ruins of what was once once Rilly's Hut, where Speilton had learned of his true identity and had been given a new family. Beyond that was Kon Malopy where he had served as king and lived the greatest years of his life.

But Speilton could not see that far, and as he tried and tried to take it all in one last time, Beati struck the etched symbol with his beak, and Speilton's gaze faded to black.

THE BRIDGE OF MORAFF
~ 16 ~

"Nock arrows!" Millites commanded, and the archers behind him raised their bows and situated the arrows on the strings. The enemy's army had grown close enough that the Nuquamese's' individual forms could be discerned. Due to the apparent differences in their speed, the army was greatly spread out, appearing more like a stampede of wild beasts than any structured fighting force. Millites scanned the army for some sign of an observant, strategic commander – or even worse – Retsinis himself, but they all appeared to be no more than savages lost in a blind bloodlust.

Usus sat aboard Flamane next to Millites, and as Retsinis's army approached, he kept his eyes closed and wand pointed. Suddenly, Usus's eyes flew open, and he smiled deliriously. "There are caves under the ground!" he proclaimed, and Millites looked at him in confusion. "Caves where the groundwater flows!"

Millites began to question him, but it appeared Usus was actively carrying out the plan he had formed, and as Millites called for the archers to loose their arrows, Usus pointed and loosed a trap of his own. As the Nuquamese closed in to only two hundred yards, then a hundred yards, snarling and growling at the Liolians facing them down, the ground they walked upon began to roll and shake. Great fissures splintered across the soil, and then whole chunks began to drop away. Dust was thrown into the air as a whole section of the battlefield sunk down into the ground, taking those first speedy enemies down with it. When the dust settled, a great sinkhole remained, twenty feet deep. Across the hundred yards of its width, Retsinis's army had come to a halt, and now they roared and shrieked across the void that had formed between the armies.

"What did you do?" Millites asked, amazed.

"I collapsed the caves!" Usus announced, his face drained from the effort. "Senkrad! Freeze it over!"

Down below in the sinkhole, the first of creatures from Nuquam had begun to make the climb out, but as they rose back to the ground level, they were suddenly struck back by a wave of ice. Some were caught up in the frost all together and were frozen in place.

There was a massive roar from their attackers, and Millites looked back to the bridge for a moment and asked, "How far have the supplies gotten?"

"Only about halfway," Ince responded, as he pushed up to the front of the army to stand behind the leaders.

"We need to fend them off just a while longer," Millites said. "Then we can begin to send our men across as well."

As they watched, the enemy army began to move once again, sending men left and right around the collapsed ground to attack the Liolians on their flanks.

"We need to split up," Usus said. "Senkrad and I can take the right, and you, Onaclov, and Hopi go to the left."

"No," Millites grabbed him before he could run away. "You've done enough for now. We need your strong for later. Onaclov will go with Senkrad, and you stay back and ready the troops. I'll give the command when it is time for them to cross the bridge as well. Ince, you watch Usus for me. Make sure he saves his energy."

180

"Yes, my King," Ince said and Usus nodded reluctantly, as Millites ran up to Hopi and Onaclov at the front of the Igniacan forces and gave them the order. The leaders split, with Millites and Hopi taking the left flank beside the riverbank, and Senkrad and Onaclov on the right. Situated between them were the Liolian soldiers, staring in fear of the army attempting to surround them. Millites stood beside Hopi, who clutched his wand in his one tanned hand. Reflecting on his struggle to dually wield his sword and wand in the battle in Esphodale, Millites remembered something Cigam had told him years ago when he had first been given his wand. Brandishing his wand in one hand and unsheathing his sword in the other, Millites pressed his wand against the blade. As Millites concentrated, the wooden wand began to shine bright until it appeared to become a bolt of light itself.

"King Millites, there is not much time," Hopi said as the beasts rounded the edge and closed in on them.

Millites didn't respond, but kept pushing the two weapons into each other, until the shining wand began to crumble away and melt into the steel blade. Suddenly, the sword itself erupted with light, and nothing remained of the wooden wand.

"We must act now!" Hopi declared, as he lowered his wand and conjured up a kaleidoscopic smudge of colors that he cast into the faces of the leading monsters.

Just as the first few Nuquamese collapsed, Millites lowered his sword, pointed it at the column of creatures charging at them between the gorge and the river, and summoned a blinding beam of white light that erupted from the glowing blade. It blasted through the enemies, throwing them backwards or knocking them to either side. Those who had merely been struck with the residual blast began crawling around, blinded.

"You can do that?" Hopi asked in surprise. "Why was this never mentioned to me?"

"I thought I'd give it a try," Millites smiled, running forward to take on his enemies.

More Nuquamese from the vast army had taken the place of the fallen, and these rushed the two leaders. They carried crude axes and spears, and some had hammers and blades. But none were capable of fending off the magic conjured by Millites and Hopi. Millites swung his sword, casting arcs and waves of brutal light that threw the creatures to the ground and singed their rough skin. Hopi battled just as hard beside him, filling the battlefield with a disorienting maze of colors and fractured light that led the creatures to stumbling or rushing confusedly into the water or over the edge into the pit. Hundreds of yards on the other edge of the sinkhole, Onaclov and Senkrad fended off the creatures with just as much success. Large mounds of bubbling lava spilled out over the ground, boxing in the creatures so that Senkrad could wash them over in a glaze of glass-like ice. That dark red and black of the oozing lava was a stark contrast against the rigid spikes of ice that formed and threatened to impale any creature that wasn't careful in its movements.

The sinkhole had created the perfect scenario for their battle, forcing the Nuquamese army of thousands to attack in thin lines which the element wielders could easily dispatch. Millites almost laughed with enjoyment at the success of their strategy, when suddenly the sky boomed with the sound of thunder. In the weeks they had been in Caelum, it had not once as much as rained, but now the men looked up to see massive thunderheads rolling towards them, rippling with lightning.

They continued fighting, with Hopi filling the land before them with a wall of swirling colors and manufactured illusions, while Millites picked off the confused monsters with projections of glaring light from his shining blade. Unconscious bodies filled the corridor of land in which they fought, but when they looked up at the main body of the army, they realized they had hardly put a dent into the full force of their enemy. Seeing the immensity of the Nuquamese, the leaders suddenly recognized their own weariness. The magic usage had been draining them, and though they had not even been touched by the creatures, they felt their strength waning. Millites turned to look back at the wagons that had now nearly cleared the bridge. He began to make the command for the army to fall back across the bridge, when an incredible boom of thunder drowned out his voice.

All eyes faced the horizon, where it appeared as if one of the clouds had begun to descend. The black mass began to swirl and elongate, reaching out for another mass of revolving air that rose up from the plain, ripping up the tall grass. Then the cloud and the ground were connected in a swirling vortex of air, and at its base, impervious to the strong winds, was a single figure.

As if fueled by the creation of the tornado, the creatures rushed forth with even more ferocity, knocking into each other as they fought to reach the wielders of the elements. Millites summoned incredible blasts of light, and Hopi brought many of the Nuquam warriors down with his illusions. But for every enemy that fell, another climbed over, until the distance between the leaders and the creatures was no more. It was now that Millites appreciated most the merger of his sword and wand, as he was able to swing the double-handed sword to meet the weapons of the Nuquamese, while also projecting blasts of light that knocked many of them down with each of his swipes. Hopi was less fortunate, as his wounds in battles years before had left him with only one hand with which he now held his wand. As the creatures attacked, Hopi was forced to evade their attacks at every turn, dodging and ducking under their weapons and claws, in order to blow them away with projectiles from his wand.

Far back in the ranks of the observing army, the Isoalates witnessed their leader struggling with the hand-to-hand combat with the enemy and sprang into action, racing to the thin strip of land between the chasm and riverbed and throwing themselves against the waves of the Nuquamese. With bows and spears and tomahawks, they struck down the creatures, carefully treading over the bodies of the creatures already knocked out cold on the ground. Numbering only forty-four including Hopi and Millites, there were just enough of them to form a wall to stop the flow of the monsters. On the other side of the sinkhole, the dwarves had rushed to the aid of Onaclov as well, and with their war hammers and axes, they formed a solid barrier against the tide of attackers.

The Liolian army of knights from Kon Malopy and Wodahs of Caloria had not been given the opportunity to flee across the bridge just yet as Millites had intended because with the leaders distracted on either end, Retsinis's army had begun to pour down into the gorge, where they climbed over the bodies of their fallen brethren just to scale the far wall and emerge before the rest of the Liolian army. The knights of Kon Malopy and the Wodahs had marched up to the edge of the pit, and as the creatures emerged, they prodded or struck them back down into the hole with spears or arrows. All the while, the tornado picked up size and speed, moving toward the chasm and the Liolians beyond it, slowly but surely. The Nuquamese army had parted, creating a corridor for the tornado to pass, and as it grew closer, the winds picked up, whipping through the Liolians and pulling at the various Liolian flags. That single figure remained in front of it, as if ushering out the natural phenomenon as his own creation. When it came closer and Millites was given a moment to look up from the onslaught of enemies to observe the figure, he realized that the twister was not a natural phenomenon at all, but it was in fact the figure's creation.

The figure was a man, a man Millites knew well, with a wand in his hand with which he controlled the winds. "Ram," Millites muttered.

Ram, the former Milwarian general, led the tornado towards the Liolians he had once served. He was now almost indistinguishable, overgrown with a green moss-like substance as if he were made of old cobblestone. With his wand, he controlled the winds, and with it, the weather itself. Retsinis had turned him into one of his own, and now it appeared that Ram had been entrusted with the command of his legions, or at least whatever fraction of them that attacked the Liolians now.

"We need to fall back to the bridge now," Millites screamed to Hopi over the growling of the attacking monsters and the rushing of wind about them.

"I can give a signal," Hopi yelled back.

The Isoalate turned and pointed his wand at the bridge, conjuring a bright spectacle of concentric circles between the two tall towers that stood on either side of the walkway. The warriors that noticed the shape spread the word and began to fall back, with Usus commanding them from the edge of the pit. As they retreated, the monsters began to climb up out of the pit and rush after them, despite Usus' solitary attempts to hold them all back.

"Without the army protecting us from behind," Hopi called to Millites, "Retsinis's men can surround us. We'll be trapped here."

"I know," Millites said, swinging his bright sword into the shaft of an enemy's halberd, chopping it in half before it could be directed at him. "But we have to get them across now before any more of our men die."

The Isoalates fought with ferocity, but some had already been wounded and their fighting had slowed. Millites noticed they were struggling, and called to Hopi, "Have your men fall back with the rest. They need to cross while they have the chance."

"We will not leave our Chief," one of the Isoalates responded.

"I will protect him," Millites said. "If you stay here you will die."

Hopi looked at his people and nodded, and they slowly accepted the command and ran off to join the other Liolians rushing to the bridge. "King Millites," Hopi called, as he cleared away three attacking creatures. "If *we* stay here much longer we too will be overrun."

"It is our job to protect the people of Liolia," Millites responded between deep breaths.

"Yes, but it is also your job to lead. Your people need you alive, or they are as good as dead, as well."

Millites didn't respond, as a horde of creatures charged him and forced him to leap to the edge of the pit to avoid their attacks. Striking out at their sides and summoning a horizontal arc of light with his sword, he knocked the group backward, and reclaimed his safer spot away from the gorge's edge. To Millites' side, Hopi still dodged amidst the rush of creatures, but without the added support from his Isoalates, and with only one hand to fend off the creatures, he looked increasingly tired. Claw marks painted his arm red from where different creatures had made swipes at him. Though he had avoided any major wounds, the usage of his element was clearly taking its toll on his endurance. His tanned skin was faded, his breaths rapid and ragged, and the prism of colors that he conjured had grown smaller and less vivid. Millites looked across the collapsed ground now swarming with the Nuquamese soldiers, to see that Senkrad and Onaclov also appeared to be struggling. Their earlier barriers of molten rock and sharp ice had been overtaken, and they were now backed up dozens of feet, trying to dam up the flow of the creatures while fighting hand-to-hand with those who got through. The Liolian warriors had almost all fled to the Bridge of Moraff, but without their presence to hold back the creatures climbing out of the pit, the Nuquamese army was following. The creatures were wrapping around the element-wielding leaders, rounding the side of the sinkhole to approach them from behind. Millites saw they were surrounded by Retsinis's army on two sides, and by the river and gorge on the others.

"Hopi," Millites called, and the worn Isoalate looked up slowly. "We need to head for the bridge. We have to cut a path through."

Hopi looked behind them as well to see the approaching Nuquamese rushing at them. He sighed, lowered his head for a moment as if in meditation, and then raised his wand against these new enemies. Millites and Hopi charged, channeling their energy into blowing back the first of the creatures to attack them. Upon meeting this surge of Nuquamese, Millites leapt into their ranks, slashing at the legs and arms of the attacking creatures. With every moment of contact between the bright blade and the beasts, a surge of light erupted from the blade, knocking them back with enhanced power. Hopi remained behind Millites, relying on his wand to cast aside multiple creatures or distract them so that Millites could more easily strike them down. They moved a few feet closer to the bridge, but the tangle of creatures was too thick, and it became too difficult to move further into the rush of creatures. This stagnation in their progress toward the bridge gave the original force of creatures they had been fighting the opportunity to catch up to them, and they suddenly found themselves fighting a swarm of creatures from both directions.

There was a splinter of lightning and the clash of thunder, as Ram led the tornado down into the gorge and began to cross himself. In horror, Millites realized that Ram would likely reach the other end of the sinkhole and then continue on to the bridge before he would. The Liolian warriors would have nothing with which to defeat a foe who controlled the weather itself. Fueled now by a ravenous desperation to reach his men before Ram, Millites charged into the horde of Nuquamese, fighting wildly to clear a path. Sweat poured down his face, and he struggled for breath, but his arms still swung with power, and the creatures still fell all around him. But Ram was moving quicker, and his twister was gaining size and power. All about the battlefield, the air was being ripped toward the tornado. Pushing his luck just too far, Millites stabbed forward with his sword at a large, green-scaled creature, but only caught open air. He fell forward, and in that split second, he was swarmed from all around by the creatures. Hopi screamed from behind him, but now that he was the only soldier left standing, he too was knocked down to the ground, struggling desperately to form some type of shield to keep his attackers back.

Suddenly, the monsters around them began to howl, and as the two struck out wildly from the ground, their attackers dispersed, rushing back to the east where the larger force of Retsinis's army waited. Millites and Hopi rose with weapons before them to see the new arrival that had chased their enemies away. Teews rode forward on a white horse with Metus on his own pony beside her. Away from Teews, the creatures fled, as she rode through a path of unconscious Nuquamese, sedated by her magic. Her elemental wand was conjuring a wide wave of light pink and purple mist that she drew into a great spiral around her body. It appeared she had already passed by Onaclov and Senkrad, because they were rushing back to join the others by the bridge, climbing over the many bodies of sleeping creatures that only seconds before had been blocking them from the bridge.

"What are you doing here?" Millites questioned.

"You can scold me later," she said. "We need to get you two out of here."

"Hello, King Millites," Metus said softly as Teews turned her horse and began to gallop toward the bridge.

The horde of Retsinis's army had already begun to charge again, so Millites and Hopi were forced to turn and sprint over the mounds of fallen creatures after Teews. While Teews had been able to knock out most of the creatures that had crossed the chasm of collapsed ground, more were already replacing them, and Millites and Hopi were forced into a footrace to reach the bridge before they did. Up ahead of them was Teews, turned in her saddle so as to fire plumes of her love element at the creatures, and just ahead of her were Onaclov and Senkrad. Millites pointed the sword to the side, summoning a blast of light that took the feet out of a creature running parallel to him and causing another to trip over the first's body. Then the wind began to pick up around them, pulling them back toward the vast army behind them. They looked back to see Ram on their side of the sinkhole now, marshaling his twister toward the leaders. As they ran, the wind pulled them back, forcing them to lean forward just to avoid being sucked into the twister's roaring maw. Millites and Hopi's feet dug into the dirt, but they couldn't move forward any further. Teews looked back, and seeing the two leaders struggle, she turned her horse around, yelling at Metus to keep going to the bridge. On her white horse, Teews charged Ram and the army that was gathered behind him, pointing her wand at her former ally. A purple missile erupted from her wand, but Ram summoned a gust of wind to deflect the attack into the swirl of his tornado. She fired again, this time in a horizontal arc. Ram was unable to block it all this time, but instead redirected the part closest to him, allowing it to strike those behind him instead. Teews came astride Millites and Hopi, her horse fighting against the pull of the wind, and conjured a full wall of her element. The strength of the wind was dulled, and Millites and Hopi were able to run on again. Together, the three of them raced to the edge of the bridge, and began to ascend its slope, Teews' magic protecting them from the wind.

The bridge was smoothly polished and gradually ascended above the rippling current of the river below. Onaclov and Senkrad turned and looked back at the other Liolian leaders, and for a moment it appeared as if they would all make it across. "Usus!" Millites yelled, gasping for breath. "Tell Usus to get ready!"

Far ahead of them, Onaclov nodded and rushed to catch up with the rest of the Liolian forces. Millites and Hopi were terribly worn, their bodies sapped of all energy from the combined effort of their magic and physical combat. They ran now on their last bits of strength, their boots stumbling across the smooth surface of the bridge. Their shoulders tensed knowing that their army followed close behind them, but they were too exhausted to turn around to check if they were gaining on them. Their eyes were focused on the backs of their soldiers up ahead when they first noticed the clouds collecting on the far side of the bridge. Above the army, the winds had picked up, collecting into a vortex slowly beginning to descend upon the soldiers below.

Millites stopped in his tracks and fell to his knees, recognizing what he had to do. Hopi stopped a few paces later, and turned back to his friend. "My King," Hopi said. "We cannot stop here."

"The clouds," Millites stammered. "He'll create another tornado right in the middle of our men. And on the bridge...there's nowhere for them to go."

The sounds of the approaching Nuquamese army grew behind Millites, and Hopi looked past the king with fear clearly present on his face. "We must keep going. Look! Usus is coming. He can destroy the bridge. We just need to catch up with the army."

"Even if he destroys the bridge, Ram can still create the twister. He can still kill all of our men."

Millites rose and turned to face the long path of the bridge where Ram was approaching. The polished stone of the bridge walkway had been too thin for his tornado to follow, so instead he pointed his wand toward the Liolians, creating a new one in their midst. "I have to hold him off," Millites said, and when Hopi reached to stop him, the king charged off.

With both hands gripping the hilt, he raised his bright blade above his head. "Ram!" he screamed, rushing the figure that led the Nuquamese.

The beast that had once been Ram looked at him. More so than most of the other turned Liolians, Ram still appeared somewhat as he had before being cut by Retsinis's blade. But when Millites called his name, he looked at his old friend with a blank stare from dark, lifeless eyes. Ram lowered his wand, forgetting, for a moment, the vortex he had been crafting. Now he pointed the weapon at Millites, who let out a cry as he leapt at the Nuquamese commander. Ram ducked beneath the wild swing of the sword, and quickly responded with a blast of air to Millites' unprotected side. The king was thrown across the slippery stone, landing just shy of the edge of the bridge. Shakily, he rose to his feet, his body sapped of energy. In the distance, he heard the calls of Usus and Onaclov to "come quick", but his attention was taken by the massive army approaching him now, and its leader who he now faced.

Millites stabbed forward with his sword, firing a bolt of golden light at Ram who was able to avoid all but the slightest contact with the attack. Ram was far less tired than the King, and with his wand he conjured a massive gust of wind that sent Millites spinning. He landed hard on his side, dropping his sword in the process. Seeing his foe disarmed, Ram stepped toward Millites, drawing his old sword with a blade of cold, pale steel, and stood above the King. Millites reached weakly for his sword, but it was beyond reach. The rest of the Nuquamese army had arrived, and they came to a stop at the body of Millites.

Ram raised his sword above his head, but the sudden appearance of a glass-like shard of green light caught the blade in midair. Hopi leapt forward, tackling Ram, and pinning him to the ground for a moment. "Go!" he screamed to Millites, pointing his wand in Ram's face.

Millites grabbed his sword and rose to his feet. "Ram!" he screamed, above the growling of the surround Nuquamese. "Listen to me, Ram! I know there is still a part of you that can—"

But as he spoke, one of the creatures stepped forward and grabbed Hopi in a large, taloned hand. The Isoalate turned his wand on the creature, striking its beaked face with a flash of glaring color, but Ram took his opportunity and threw Hopi to the side. The Isoalate rolled, stopping just at the edge of the crowd of Nuquamese, and like a pack of dogs being thrown a bone, they all sprang upon the man.

Hopi screamed, throwing a few off of him with the magic from his wand, but their numbers were too many. Millites pointed his sword, summoned a beam of light, but Ram swung down and knocked the point of his blade into the bridge with his own sword. Millites raised the golden blade just in time to counter a follow up attack from the Nuquamese commander, but when Ram swung a third time, Millites was knocked back down against the stone bridge. All the while, Hopi fought against the savage claws and jaws of the creatures that had surrounded him.

"Really?" a voice sounded, drawing Ram's attention away for only a moment before he was blown back by a sudden stream of purple vapor. "Three times I have to save you?"

With another swing of her wand, she knocked the creatures surrounding Hopi unconscious, and then reached down from her horse to help the Isoalate to his feet. He was bleeding severely, and he held a gash in his side as he stumbled forward. Millites rose and wrapped Hopi's other arm over his shoulder to help him shuffle across the bridge while Teews held back the swarm of Nuquamese. Seeing them approach, Onaclov and Usus rushed forward to help Hopi and Millites. They half-carried the two men away from the Nuquamese, stopping when Usus decided they had gone far enough. They laid Hopi down to rest, and Ince ran up quickly with cloth to quell the bleeding. Usus turned and walked away from the group, into the center of the bridge, and faced the approaching army of Nuquamese. Falling to one knee, he pointed his wand at the bridge. The roars of the Nuquamese grew as they rushed ever closer.

"Come on," Senkrad said. "We haven't any more time."

A crack suddenly split across the bridge, just in front of Usus, then another splintered off from the first, spreading to the other edge of the bridge.

"Destroy it," Millites urged. "Bring it all down if you must."

Usus placed a hand against the stone surface, and the bridge cracked, fracturing outward like ripples spreading out from a dropped rock in a lake. Chunks gave way, falling hundreds of feet and crashing into the water below. The Nuquamese leading the charge didn't appear to notice or maybe didn't care, because they continued running, even when the cracks spread out beneath their feet, and they were cast down into the river. Usus had created a gap in the bridge spanning the fifty or so feet between the leaders and the Nuquamese. Eventually, their attackers realized and came to a halt, teetering on the edge and roaring out across the abyss at the Liolians just out of reach.

Usus rose from the edge and turned back with a smile. "Look at that. Perfectly executed plan," he boasted.

"I don't think we would've made it if Teews hadn't arrived at the last moment," Onaclov said, and Teews grinned proudly.

"We never got the chance to address that," Millites said. "How exactly did you and Metus find us all this way? I thought it was clear that you needed to stay, and the Order wouldn't permit Metus to leave."

"Yes, you did make that very clear," Teews said. "But with Metus's role, he was given a great deal of information on where the army was and where you were headed. So, when we got our chance, we left to intercept the army along the road."

"And who is leading the Liolians we left behind in Civitas Levi?" Millites questioned.

"I believe our mother has that taken care of," Teews said. "I'm sure she can handle the few Liolians left in the city. All that matters now is protecting them."

The conversation was suddenly interrupted by the desperate words of "No, no, you can't do that," from Ince.

Ince kneeled over Hopi, who appeared to be saying something to him that the others could not hear. As they pressed in around and asked what was happening, they could see tears in Ince's dark eyes.

"Hopi, listen to me," he said desperately. "No, Hopi don't. Hopi."

Hopi closed his eyes as Ince held a hand just below the Isoalate's ribs to stop the flow of blood from his side. He shook the Isoalate, but Hopi's eyes didn't open. Then, with careful hands, he held Hopi's one full wrist and waited. The others were silent as Ince set the arm back down and picked up something else that lay beside them in a pool of blood. "He...he gave this to me," Ince said, his eyes glazed with tears. "Just now, he said...he knew he was about to...Hopi is dead."

The others bowed their heads before their fallen friend, as Ince clutched Hopi's Wand of Color in his hands.

MEETING WITH THE ORDER
~ 17 ~

Speilton sat up in a field of bright green grass. He scanned the land around him and found Prowl asleep a few feet away, lying with the tip of one of her wings dragging in the small stream that snaked through the hills, rolling over small pebbles.

Beati was already awake, and he hopped over to Speilton as he rose to his feet. "King Speilton!" he chirped. "We made it! How was your journey to Liolia?"

Suddenly, there appeared from over the hills a massive flock of Phoenixes. Speilton picked up his shield that shone brightly under the sunlight and strapped his sword belt around his waist. The Phoenixes descended and surrounded Speilton and Beati. When Prowl yawned and opened her eyes, they had circled her as well. One Phoenix, who Speilton identified as the Order of the Bow's emissary, Lazar, spoke with authority, proclaiming, "King Speilton of Milwaria, you are to be detained for your continued illegal activities and suspected act of treachery towards the people of Caelum."

"If I were you, I wouldn't throw me back in your dungeons," Speilton said, raising his empty hands in a sign of peace.

"And why is that?" Lazar questioned.

"Because I know something that I'm sure the Order of the Bow would greatly value regarding the enemies that march here as we speak," Speilton said, and Lazar narrowed his eyes at him.

"I find it difficult to trust a man who has already committed multiple acts of treason against our people

and who may very likely be working with our enemy."

"You do understand the threat that Retsinis and his army presents, do you not?" Speilton asked. "You can bury me beneath the city if you want, but I doubt the Order of the Bow will be very forgiving if you lock away the one person who knows how to defeat Retsinis."

The Phoenix continued glaring at Speilton, but the slightest sense of surprise formed on his avian face. Finally, he turned to the other Phoenixes and said, "We will take him to the Order, then they can decide what to do with him."

There was only darkness for a few seconds, and then Speilton slowly began to see shapes appearing out of the constant black. A massive tree came into view and sparkling throughout its long branches was the ebbing glow of dozens of Phoenixes in every possible color. As Speilton focused his eyes on the shining birds, their shades changed, randomly but smoothly, as their bodies took on the form of a different element every few seconds. They spoke to each other in hushed voices, showing no interest in the King that stood before them. Then, from somewhere in the sky above, a Phoenix larger than all of them descended, pumping his wings to allow it to slowly and gracefully land on a tree limb in the middle of the flock. Once this Phoenix, Círsar, had settled himself, the other Phoenixes fell silent and viewed Speilton for the first time with expectant looks.

"King Visvires," the Head Consul of the Order began, "I am sure you are well aware of the explicit law in this land which you have now broken twice."

"I acknowledge that," Speilton nodded. "But my reason for returning to Liolia was important, and I have learned what I went to seek. I am sorry for disobeying your laws, but I promise you that I am not a traitor to this world."

"Oh, I am well aware," Círsar said. "I never suspected that you had turned to Retsinis's side."

"Then why do your people believe that I did?" Speilton questioned.

"They have their suspicions, and I did not tell them otherwise. You did betray our land by leaving, so I allowed them to believe whatever they liked about you."

"Well, I guess it doesn't matter now. I never intended to abandon your people or my own people, but it was necessary for me to gather what I needed."

"And what was this that you needed to gather?" the lead Phoenix asked.

"Information on how to defeat the enemy forces that march on this land as we speak," Speilton said.

"So you know how to kill Retsinis?" Círsar asked with reservation.

"I do," Speilton said. "It is not easy, but it is possible. The power given to him by Ferrum Potestas, the power that makes him invincible and capable of enslaving all those who he cuts with his blade, can be broken."

"How?" asked the Phoenix sternly.

"Twelve different elemental wands with twelve different wielders all directing their magic at Retsinis at once."

"And what makes you think that will work?" the Phoenix questioned.

"I spoke with a Wizard who says that they have gleaned the method from some of their ancient records on the Sword of Power. The Wizards will not assist us in this fight, since the Versipellis are here, but they did meet me in Liolia."

"And that is why you left?" the Phoenix asked.

"One of the reasons why," Speilton nodded. "There was other information I went to gather."

"So, these twelve wands," the Phoenix spoke, "how many of them are in Caelum at the moment?"

"I have the Wand of Fire, Millites has light, Teews has love, Usus has stone, Onaclov has lava, Senkrad has ice, and Hopi has color. That makes seven I believe."

"Actually, I do not believe Hopi still possesses the Wand of Color," Círsar said, "as I recently received word that he has passed away."

Speilton tensed up with shock. "Hopi is dead? Here in your prisons?"

"He is no longer in our prisons," Círsar said simply. "He, with the rest of the Liolian soldiers, have headed north to challenge Retsinis's men in battle."

"They left?" Speilton questioned. "How? You released them?"

"We sent them to combat the forces that you are all responsible for drawing to this land. They have already met them in battle twice, and it appears there were some casualties."

"You sent them to fight while you sat here?" Speilton seethed. "Their numbers are few, and if all of Retsinis's troops are here, they're impossibly outnumbered. How many Phoenixes did you send to fight with them?"

The tree full of Phoenixes chuckled slightly, and their leader appeared to smile as he explained, "No Phoenixes were sent. Our way is not to fight in open battle. War is the way of your people, not mine."

Speilton's mouth fell open, and he bristled with fury. "They are fighting alone? They do not even know this land, yet you have condemned them to *die* for this land?"

"They were happy to oblige. I freed them from their much-deserved imprisonment. The least they could do was continue their warfare with the Nuquamese."

Speilton was furious, and he felt the sudden desire to leave these pompous Phoenixes at once to join the army, but he stopped himself and said, "If you wish us to fight, then there is one thing you must do."

"I do not believe you are in any position to give demands," the Phoenix said with a wry smile.

"As the protector of your people, I believe I have earned the right to make some demands."

"No, you are not our protector. Your brother and sister and army, *they* are our protectors, but you are not. You are our prisoner, as you disobeyed our laws multiple times."

"Fine," Speilton said. "I may not be your protector, but I will tell you all the same. Other Liolians are coming – all of them. The other element wands and their wielders will be arriving in Caelum, and I warn you not to get in their way because they are the only ones capable of saving you and your people."

"Are you trying to threaten us?" Círsar questioned.

"No, I am merely helping to save you from the real threat," Speilton said with a smile of fake cordiality.

Círsar shook his head and growled, "I believe our conversation here is over. I hope you enjoy your cell."

Speilton nodded as the room around him faded and the caucus of Phoenixes turned back to their hushed chatter.

When Speilton could see once again, he was back in the long hallway, surrounded once again by the group of six Phoenixes that had escorted him to the Order only minutes before. The Phoenix behind Speilton prodded him forward, and they began walking down the near endless hall. "So, I'm to be led straight to the dungeons, am I?" Speilton asked.

"That is the Order's command," one Phoenix confirmed.

"What will happen to the small Phoenix that helped me, Beati?" asked Speilton.

"He has been detained, but he is young and foolish so after some…attitude adjustment he may be allowed to leave once again," a pink and purple Phoenix said.

"And what of my dragon? Is she being taken care of?"

A green Phoenix said, "She has been detained in a cell."

"What happened with the book I brought back with me? It must be handled carefully."

"Enough questions," the first Phoenix snapped.

"And how are the Liolians doing in battle?" Speilton continued. "The Order said there has been some news about their battles so far."

"I heard they lost many in the first battle, but in the second, they only…" but the blue Phoenix who was speaking was quickly cut off by the glare of the pink love Phoenix.

"That information is not for you to know. The Order would not wish you to, and for your own sake it is likely best if you remain in the dark."

"Tell me if they're safe at least," Speilton said. "Those are my men, and my friends, and family. At least tell me if they're somewhere safe."

The others turned to the pink Phoenix who did not regard them, and so the blue Phoenix felt comfortable to say, "At the moment they are. They have arrived at a safe location, a holy space with healing waters. But King Retsinis and his army still pursues them."

"That's enough," the love Phoenix said.

"Am I allowed to speak to someone?" Speilton asked. "Some liaison from the Order. There's a young woman, Aurum, who serves them."

"We know of Aurum," a green Phoenix said. "But she's no longer here."

"The dark Phoenixes," the water Phoenix continued, "they took her at the same time you left."

"To the mountains? Where Retsinis's army is camped?" Speilton asked.

"Where else?" the Phoenix of Water said.

"That's enough!" the pink Phoenix said. "He has been given enough information."

They had reached the staircase that led up out of the tunnel into a field beside the city. "Yes," Speilton said, "I believe I have."

As they began to climb the stairs, Speilton closed his eyes and raised his hand ever so slightly. Recognizing something was happening, the pink Phoenix began to bark an order, but he was suddenly dispersed into a shimmering wave of pink mist. Speilton controlled the cloud he had just created, and projected it at the other Phoenixes, choking them with the vapor one after the other. In the sweet comfort of the thick sedative, the other Phoenixes fell to the ground in a sudden and deep slumber. Once the other five were unconscious, Speilton released his control of the pink mist, and the Phoenix reformed from its many particles. As soon as the pink Phoenix retook his shape, Speilton raised the ground around it, encasing the bird within a cage of soil and grass. Speilton turned and ran off toward the city, and behind him he could hear the Phoenix clawing at the dirt from within. He knew he had only bought himself a few minutes.

It was nighttime as he approached the softly-glowing multicolored city. Seeing the southern gate slightly off to the left, Speilton ran towards it through the tall grass. When he came close to the arched entryway, Speilton sank in between the blades, watching the guards posed on either side. Concentrating again, he took control of the gray stone Phoenix, and turned it into a horizontal column of rock that struck the Phoenix beside him in the side of the skull, knocking it unconscious. Speilton kept his focus on the stone pillar on the ground as he ran through the open gate. Only once he was safely inside the city did he release the Phoenix, allowing it to return to its Phoenix form again and wonder about what had just occurred.

Speilton slipped down a side street, then raced through a courtyard, and then down another street. He emerged in a large square that appeared familiar, and he thought hard about where Prowl had been kept the last time they were detained in the city. Choosing one of the streets, he ran off, trying to keep his boots from clapping too loudly against the cobblestone. Civitas Levi was quiet and still, incredibly tranquil considering the forces to the north marching to slaughter them all. Speilton turned down another street, suddenly spotting the top of a tower over the rooftops of the buildings around him that he remembered had been close to the stables. There were no guards within the city, and it seemed there was no need for them. Many of the street merchants had gone so far as to leave their supplies and merchandise outside, and it did not appear as if anyone considered taking advantage of the situation.

There was not much time, and Speilton could feel the pressure of the situation building. They had taken Aurum, and though Speilton tried to push the image from his mind, he could not help but think of the prophecy he had seen first in his dreams and then in the Book of Liolia. Speilton had no idea how much time he had to save Aurum from that fate, but for now he could only focus on the trials at hand. First, he needed his weapons and his dragon, and both were somewhere here in the city. Then he could consider all of his family and friends that needed his help.

Speilton rounded a corner and found himself on a familiar street. Running past the quiet buildings where he had met Aurum and Prowl many nights before, he finally came to the stables where they had held her. He stepped through a doorway and trod lightly through a dark room. There was a second door behind this one that he pushed open, and inside he was startled to see firelight.

"Who goes there?" a voice called as Speilton hurriedly stepped back into the shadow.

Peering through the cracked doorway, Speilton could see the voice belonged to an old man with thinning hair and scraggly beard. He appeared to be a former Liolian who had found shelter in this land. Speilton stepped forward into the firelight of the torch the old man held and raised both hands in the air to show he was unarmed. "I've come to free an animal from these stables," Speilton explained, finally able to view the room he had just entered.

The stables were magnificent, a massive room with elegantly carved wooden arches and gates enclosing dozens of horses. As Speilton spoke, there was the sound of rustling chains in the far corner of the stable, and suddenly Prowl's blue head appeared out between the iron bars of her pen. She growled in excitement hearing Speilton's voice.

"That's the steed you wish to free?" the man asked worriedly.

"She is," Speilton said testing his luck by stepping forward. "She's mine."

"But that dragon there belongs to…" the man's eyes grew wide. "My King."

The man fell to a knee before Speilton.

"I need your help," Speilton said, walking over to where Prowl was being kept. "Can you unlock the chains that they have used to bind my dragon?"

"Why, yes. Yes, I can, my King," the old man said, searching his belt for the ring of keys.

"Great, thank you. Also, I need to know how to get into the armory located a few blocks from here."

"The armory, my King?" the man asked with a quizzical look.

"Yes, that large building where they store the confiscated Liolian weapons - whatever it is called," Speilton explained.

"Oh, yes I know of the place you speak," the man said, opening the gate to Prowl's pin and timidly stepping forward with one hand gripping a key and the other held out to calm the great dragon.

"Good," Speilton said. "You see, there are some weapons inside that I need to retrieve, but I wasn't sure what forces they have guarding it."

"I believe it is just two Phoenixes most days, or maybe three. They stand inside the entrance hall."

"Just three?" Speilton asked. "Do you know what type of Phoenixes they are?"

The white bearded man had unchained two of Prowl's legs when he said, "If memory serves correctly, their guards trade off fairly regularly. There are new Phoenixes there most days. See, my job is only to tend to the stables, so I have little knowledge of how they operate there."

"That's fine," Speilton said. "I only wished to know what I would have to face to get in."

"I'm sorry, my King," the old man said, finally freeing Prowl from the shackles. "I wish there was more I could do."

Prowl rose up onto her hind legs to arch her back and stretch out her wings. "You have done more than you can know. What is your name?" Speilton asked.

"Baramu, my King."

"Baramu, I thank you," Speilton said, turning away from the old man and leading Prowl back through the two sets of doors and out onto the streets once again.

Prowl strode proudly at Speilton's side as they navigated through the city to that building where Speilton and his men had attacked and retaken their weapons months before. When they neared the domed building with large columns that Speilton knew was the Phoenix's location for hiding foreign weapons, he jumped aboard Prowl's back, and the dragon flew up into the night air, landing silently upon the roof. Not long ago, Speilton had tried to break through the glass domed roof and had been arrested, but now, he felt he had a better chance of getting in undetected. Stepping off of Prowl's back, he concentrated on the glass, picturing the transparent substance as the individual pieces of sand he knew composed it. As he placed his hand against the surface, it appeared to quiver but nothing changed. Speilton searched for some connection to the sand, but nothing came to mind. He had been in the desert only a few brief times, so he was struggling to fully exert control over the material with which he had so little association.

His arm shook, and his frustration suddenly turned to rage as thoughts of the danger his friends and family faced clouded his mind. He couldn't connect with the glass, but he could dominate it, and as he exerted his force upon it, the entire dome began to shake. The air picked up around him, and his skin glowed red hot. But before the glass could break, Prowl knocked Speilton over with her snout. Speilton whipped around in anger, but his fury dissipated as he saw his dragon breathing her blue flames across the smooth surface. The glass turned orange under the heat of the flames, and slowly began to fall away, falling down through open air in globs and cooling before it shattered in small pops against the floor below. Soon the hole was large enough for Prowl to fit through. Speilton boarded her, and the two dropped down into the torch-lit room packed with near empty shelves of dusty old weapons.

It took Speilton only a moment to find his weapons, situated near the front of the room laid neatly next to each other. He fastened his sword belt around his waist, shoved his wand into the belt, and felt for his now invisible shield which he threw on his back. He still wore the light armor he had taken when leaving Civitas Levi the first time. However, he could not find the Book of Liolia. It appeared that the Phoenixes had taken it with the rest of his supplies somewhere else, but he didn't have the time to search for it.

Finally armed, he walked quietly with Prowl to the front entrance of the building and peeked out through the slight crack between the doors to see three Phoenixes perched with their backs to him, spread out in the half circle hall. One of the Phoenixes appeared pale white with blue-tipped wings and plume atop its head. Speilton concentrated on this guard, a Phoenix of Ice, and used its element. Ice was something he had more memories with, and he was able to project flashes of thick frost from the one Phoenix to the other two, catching them both in a flash freeze before they even had time to recognize what was happening. Speilton rushed through the entrance hall with Prowl right at his heel. Then, he suddenly stopped and turned back into the room. There was a desk in the corner where a record-keeper normally sat during the day, and Speilton treaded carefully over the slippery ice spread across the ground to look inside its drawers. He threw each one open then pushed them back shut until he finally found a folded piece of parchment. Upon unfolding it, he saw it was exactly what he was looking for – a map.

Speilton slipped it inside his belt and ran to Prowl who waited just outside the door. "Come on," Speilton said. "Time to go."

Once again aboard his dragon's back, the two took off into the sky, sailing over the towers and their slumbering inhabitants. The panel through which they had escaped before had been replaced with a new pane of glass, so they were forced to head back to the same gate where Speilton had entered minutes before. Even from high above the streets of the city, Speilton could hear a commotion breaking out. It appeared that one of the Phoenixes which he had knocked unconscious had woken up and was now rallying others to combat the threat within their city.

Prowl dropped low between the buildings, picking up speed as she approached the arched gate out of the city. Both guards turned, and as the Phoenix of Stone began to make a trumpeting sound, Speilton took control of his element, changing his shape into a burst of broken rock. This time, the second Phoenix guard was alert and dodged the debris, flying into the air to carry on the trumpeting alert.

Speilton had no time to dispatch this second Phoenix, and the city was surely already alerted. Instead, Prowl pumped her wings, flying just inches off the ground, and raced past the bird, through the gate, and into the night. Holding on tightly to Prowl's blue scales, Speilton looked back at the bright spots of light within the city that were the Phoenixes moving rapidly. They were rallying to find the escaped prisoners, but Prowl was too fast to be caught. The castle was fading from sight, and with the land covered in midnight darkness, Prowl became impossible to see as she flew north over the hills.

Speilton opened the map and attempted to straighten it against the rush of wind around him. Taking out his wand, Speilton summoned a small flame of light to illuminate the map, and after scanning it quickly, he knew exactly where they needed to go.

"The Fangmaw Mountains," Speilton said. "That's where they're holding Aurum."

THE WATERS OF LAKE VASCENT
~ 18 ~

After crossing the river, the Liolian army continued westward. Hopi's body was brought with them, and that night they set up a pyre with some dead limbs and dried grass. The Liolians laid the Isoalate's body on the pyre and lit it. Then, while the Liolians slept, the Isoalates and some others sat beside the burial fire and watched the flames consume Hopi's body.

Metus crouched on his goat legs for hours, mesmerized by the flames. Although, he had only been on the battlefront for a few hours, he'd already had his first brush with death. Metus had faced danger before, in the Jungle of Supin and in the Battle of Skilt years before. But the enemy they faced now was more vicious than anything he had seen, much less fought. In a way, he was grateful to have stumbled upon the army when he did. He hadn't had to endure the quiet fear of waiting for a battle to begin. When he and Teews had crested the hill and seen the battled raging beside the river, Teews had charged forward, and all he had been able to do was follow. Even in battle, he had little time to truly recognize what he was doing, and he wasn't even sure if he had destroyed any of the Nuquamese in the chaos. A part of him hoped he hadn't. Metus knew that underneath the filth of Ferrum Potestas' magic, the Nuquamese were beings just like Hopi who they had slain so barbarically.

While Metus sat lost in thought, Teews sat down beside him. "Hopi was a good man," Teews said.

Metus nodded.

"How are you feeling?" she asked.

214

"I'm alright...it's just....I'm not as used to the battlefield as most people here."

"Yet you chose to come here, all the same. That took bravery, Metus."

Usus walked up from behind them and sat on the other side of Teews. Metus looked at him and then back at the fire, embarrassed.

"You know, Metus," Usus said, "every soldier here was once new to the battlefield at some point, as well. It's not something you easily get used to. Some never do."

"I'm fine. I think it was just a lot to experience at once. I'm sure I'll be ready next time we have to fight."

"It should be soon," a voice said, and they looked over their shoulders to see Onaclov standing behind them, looking sternly into the fire. "The Nuquamese will be back soon, so we can't afford to wait until morning to start marching again."

"The men need the rest," Usus said. "And Hopi deserves this, at the very least."

"You know," Onaclov said, "the Isoalates believe that every time one of their people die, their soul is reborn in another child. Back in the Lavalands when their numbers were strong and every day brought new deaths and new children, this belief was strong. But now there are only a few dozen men left alive with a handful more elderly and children back in Liolia. I can only wonder whether this belief will die with Hopi."

"There will be new life once this war is over," Teews said.

"The fauns and other folk of the forest have a similar belief," Metus said. "We believe that once one of our kind dies, our souls return to the forest to live on amongst the trees and the brooks and the mountains. And sometimes, you can hear the voices of those who've passed on in the wind through the trees and the trickle of water."

The others smiled at the thought, as they kept watching the flames.

"Did you bring weapons?" Usus finally said after some time had passed.

"I brought my spear. And I have some leather armor," Metus said.

"Anything else?"

"Well, I have my flute, but you're just talking about weapons, aren't you?"

"Yes, just weapons," Usus laughed. "If you wanted training, I would offer to help you, but the real master with the spear isn't me."

Teews smiled. "Yes, that would be me," she said. "And I'd be glad to help you train as well."

"Thank you," Metus said shyly. "That would be very helpful."

"You play the flute?" Onaclov asked suddenly.

"Yes, I used to play often in the Rich Woods. It's been a while, but I still remember."

"Do you know the Tawii song, 'The Dawn Sparrow'?" Onaclov asked. "I believe the Isoalates would appreciate hearing it."

"Oh, I think I remember that. I learned it from a dryad long ago. Let me find my flute…"

The faun ran off and rummaged through his pack as he pulled out the flute that had been his companion for many years. Then, he returned to the campfire and took his seat again. He lifted the wooden rod to his lips, and then began to play the soft tune. The

Isoalates watched him intently for a few minutes, and then their gaze returned to the body of their leader smoldering before them. In time, the song faded, and then there was only silence mixed with the popping of the fire in the night.

Two days after destroying the Bridge of Moraff, the Liolian army reached Lake Vascent. The sprawling prairie through which they had walked, ended suddenly at a mountainous land they were told was called the Great Feather Peaks. These mountains grew steep and narrow, situated above the landscape like the petrified heads and shoulders of some primordial giant race. Thick vegetation covered the tops and the few somewhat level parts of the mountains, and they dominated the land stretching to the far north to the Fangmaw Mountains and far west to lands beyond that which was known. The southernmost reach of the Great Feather Peaks gave way to Lake Vascent, which appeared still and bright at the bottom of a craterous valley, ringed halfway by the peaks to the north and by steep cliffs to the south. The Liolians descended into the valley from the East, marching just between the foothills of one of the mountains and the river which they had followed. Reaching the floor of the valley, they were able to cross to the larger expanse of beach beside the lake by hiking through the shallower waters that trailed away from the base of the river's waterfall. Here, they set up camp, and the men all rushed to throw off their armor and dive into the near transparent waters.

The lake was refreshing, and the men spent hours swimming through its waters. There was a large rock that rose out of the center of the lake like a sentinel, and it became a challenge for the Liolians to swim out to touch its steep walls. Others merely sat back and relaxed, allowing the soothing water to cleanse their bodies while they observed the magnificent valley around them. The natural beauty of the valley was spectacular in its own right, but what stole their attention was the massive sculpture of a Phoenix in flight, carved into the side of a peak that towered over the valley. Two rivers that ran from within the mountains poured down beneath its wings, and the waterfall diverged on many ledges in the cliff walls below, creating a spray of mist that washed over the lake causing the air to shimmer.

The healing powers that the Phoenix had spoken of appeared to be true. As the men bathed, all small scratches and bruises began to heal. Water was gathered and given to the mortally wounded in their tents, and suddenly their injuries appeared less fatal. Even with danger marching against them to the north, the soldiers still shared a feeling of peace.

Despite the high morale, Millites still paced along the shore. He had remained in the water as long as he had deemed necessary to heal his few wounds, and now he had returned to focus on their strategy. Digging through his maps, Millites had begun measuring the distances between their current location and other possible locations for battle when Usus emerged from the water. He grabbed a fleece blanket that lay upon the shore and used it to dry off his damp clothing. "Have you even taken a break yet?" Usus asked the king.

"You saw me walk into the water with the rest of the army," Millites replied absently, continuing his measurements.

218

"That's not what I mean by relax. You may have healed yourself some, but that's very different from actually relaxing," Usus said.

"I stayed in long enough."

"Trust me, the longer you stay in, the better you feel. It puts energy back into you, makes you feel like you got a whole–"

"I said, I stayed in long enough," Millites said.

Usus looked at him for a moment, then walked over to the table where Millites was working. He leaned against it and looked out at the lake. "That rock right there. I think it would make the perfect spot for a castle. I can picture a magnificently large one perched upon the top of it, like Kon Malopy, only grander."

Millites looked up at the massive boulder in the center of the lake as well. "We have a long way to go before we can think about that."

"Yes, but shouldn't we still think about it, all the same. These men, they need something to fight for here. Before, they fought for Kon Malopy and their families inside its walls. But now, Kon Malopy is in ruins, and their families are stuck in another world. What do they have to fight for, if not a future here?"

"Liolia is our home," Millites said, turning back to his maps. "We fight this war so that we can go back home to start again."

Usus nodded and turned around to view the maps as well. "What are you looking at?"

"Someplace for our men to fall back. We're too vulnerable here, and we'll need to find a more strategic location to meet Retsinis's men in battle."

"What about there?" Usus asked, tapping a finger on the map.

"Dry off, will you?" Millites said, pulling the map away and attempting to wipe away the drop of water he left on the parchment. "And that is one of the Phoenix cities within the Great Feather Peaks. I considered that as well, but looking at this terrain, it appears to be an extremely difficult landscape to traverse."

"So we just fall back to Civitas Levi, then," Usus offered. "It's only what? A day or two away?"

"Just about two days, yes," Millites said.

"Well, we know the land is easy to travel across, and we know the Phoenixes have their own troops in reserve."

"The Phoenixes will not help us," Millites said bluntly.

"Well, maybe if they had the proper motivation," Usus said.

"We can't take that risk. Besides, that would lead Retsinis's army straight to the capital of Caelum. If they reach the city, there is nothing left between the Nuquamese and all of the innocents that live there."

"But if we die alone out here, the same will be true," a voice stated, and they looked up to see Senkrad approaching the table.

"I see you took a dip in the water," Usus observed.

The large Wodahs was dressed in all his normal battle gear, but his white mane of hair appeared damp and limp.

"My skin is strong," he said, "much like my uncle's once was. In battle, I received few injuries, but the water helps with more than just wounds to the flesh."

"It does seem to have quite the effect on the soldiers," Usus said. "Being in this place, bathing and drinking these waters, combined with our victory at the

Bridge of Moraff has done a great deal to boost the morale."

"I heard a few men referring to our stand there as the Battle of the Bridge," Senkrad said.

"They have a name for it already?" Usus asked. "The Battle of the Bridge – I like it. Likely, the first Liolian battle with only a single loss."

"That single loss was Hopi," Millites broke in. "And any loss should be considered a grave."

"Come on, you know I didn't mean to imply that. Hopi was a friend of mine, just as he was to you," Usus said kindly.

"He died protecting me," Millites said. "And I couldn't save him."

"You tried your best, and he made his decision. He understood the risk of his actions," Senkrad explained.

"No, that does not..." Millites turned towards Senkrad, then stopped, letting out a deep breath to release his agitated anger. "I...I never thanked you for coming to my aid in Esphodale. I know you understood the risk of those decisions as well."

Senkrad extended a hand to the king. "These are difficult times. We shall be tested greatly, so we must all trust each other, and fight to keep each other alive."

Millites extended his hand as well, and the two kings shook. As they did so, Teews strode forward, already dry from her quick venture into the lake. "What's this?" she asked, walking up to the table. "Looks like a meeting with all the leaders. Good thing I came when I did."

"Well, it's not a formal meeting," Millites began to explain.

"And we thought you'd rather just fix your hair than talk strategy anyways," Usus said with a grin, to which Teews elbowed him in the side in response.

"Actually," she said. "I already braided my hair, if you didn't notice." She spun, showing how her hair was plaited into an intricate braid. "Mother showed me how while I was In Civitas Levi. She said it was how she did hers before going into battle."

"She showed you how to braid your hair for battle?" Millites asked. "So, she helped with sending you here instead of making sure you stayed back in the city."

"Well, she didn't necessarily help me leave, but she definitely didn't do anything to stop me from leaving," Teews smiled. "She knew I wanted to leave and that I could help, and she also knew Metus had information on where the army was headed. She just happened to bring the two of us together at the right moment. And aren't you glad she did?"

"You handled yourself well in battle," Senkrad said. "If not for you, we would have been unable to make it out without a great many casualties, perhaps including your men and brother."

"I don't know, I think I had a second wind coming on there. I'm sure I could've figured some way to save you all," Usus smiled arrogantly.

Teews shook her head and looked down at the map. "So where do we go from here?"

"That's what we were discussing," Millites said.

Teews examined the parchment for a moment and then said, "Civitas Levi. It's the only place we can go."

"That's what I said," Usus declared.

Millites shook his head. "The Phoenixes will not like it. And it would have to be a last stand. There's nowhere else to fall back."

"We can only run so long," Senkrad said. "Either we march against them, or we find a spot where we feel capable of holding them off until the end."

"We can't march against them," Teews said. "I saw their army when Metus and I were riding up, and as large as that force was, I could tell it wasn't all of them."

"How can you be sure?" Millites asked. "We have not truly seen their army in its entirety. That may be everyone that Retsinis has been able to turn so far."

"I don't think so," Teews insisted. "Remember when we fought them back in Liolia? The Nuquamese appeared in all different shapes and sizes. Some had scales or fur or even wings. Some were thin and crouched like animals. But then there were some much larger and, well, slower. Some appeared made of stone or were...large-boned."

"I know what you mean," Millites said.

"Well, I didn't see any of those type – the slower ones that is. They all appeared to be smaller, more agile."

"Faster," Usus said, coming to the realization himself.

"You believe Retsinis sent just his fastest to hunt us down?"

"They were all sprinting after us," Usus said.

"And Retsinis wasn't even leading them. Ram appeared to be in command," Teews added.

"Why would he send just the small group? Why not just mobilize everyone?" Millites asked.

A voice behind them announced, "He doesn't think he has to."

Ince walked up to the table, a piece of parchment in his hands with numbers scribbled across it. "I've done the math myself. We left Civitas Levi with a combined force of one-thousand sixty-five men. After the Battle of Esphodale, we were left with only eight hundred ninety-two. We've lost twelve more since then from injuries. Now, after losing Hopi in the Battle of the Bridge but gaining Teews and Metus, our army is eight hundred eighty-one men strong."

"We've had to fight with fewer before," Senkrad said.

"Yes, but that army we fought yesterday was nearly five, six thousand strong. Would you agree?" Ince said, turning to Usus who he knew had seen it best.

"Over five thousand, yes, that seems about right."

"And that's only a fraction of the full army," Teews said.

"There is also the army of the Daerds to consider," Ince said, pointing out his numbers on his paper as he read them. "I believe we killed nearly half of their army, and if we consider what attacked us at Esphodale to be the full extent of their army, I believe we have at least a thousand more of them to deal with."

"I would estimate there to be more than that," Senkrad said. "In my experience with them, I know their numbers to often be deceiving."

"So how many? One thousand two hundred, one thousand five hundred?"

"Five hundred seemed about right," Senkrad nodded.

"So, one thousand five hundred Daerds. We also have to include the army of Phoenixes of Darkness in their possession, which judging by the numbers of other

Phoenixes we can probably assume is in the hundreds, if not thousands."

"That is assuming they are truly working alongside Retsinis's army," Millites said.

"Yes, yes," Ince said, frantically juggling all the stipulations in his math. "Retsinis's sword has control of the great beast, the Drakon, and he, or at least one of his men, is also in possession of the ring that controls the sea monster Cetus. And, Retsinis likely has the help of many Warlocks, let's say twenty, thirty, maybe more based on how many they tend to send. Finally, Retsinis also has the help of the Versipellis, who alone, are known to be able to destroy armies, ravage cities, and end worlds."

Ince scribbled something else down with an old quill and then took a step back.

"So, all combined, what does that mean."

"Well," he began. "If we assume Retsinis has just double the number of Nuquamese as we saw the other day, then that puts the entirety of his army at about twelve thousand and fifty, and that is just considering pure numbers. Considering the monsters and...powerful entities fighting for him, their force will be much grander than that."

"And we don't even have one thousand warriors," Millites said.

"And so, I believe that is why he sent only his fastest," Ince continued on his earlier statement. "He knows he doesn't need to send more. His army could easily overwhelm ours."

"Do you think he will send them all?" Usus asked.

"Retsinis underestimated us at the Bridge of Moraff," Senkrad said. "He will not make that mistake again. Right now, his mind is set on larger plans of domination, and he likely does not consider us as a great threat, as Ince said. But he will also ensure that we have no chance of survival. You see, he cares not for the wellbeing of his soldiers. They're his mindless slaves, just as the Wodahs were when he was our king. He cares only to exploit them for greater control. But he also needs them for his future plans, so he will be careful not to waste them. Our best case scenario though, is that we win enough battles to force him to send everything he has."

"Best case scenario," Usus repeated. "That's a bit ironic."

"What he says makes sense," Ince nodded. "Quite terrible news, but likely the truth."

"That means, we have many battles ahead," Millites said. "We must prepare the men to leave as soon as we can."

"To go where?" Teews asked.

"Like you said, we have to return to Civitas Levi."

INTO THE FANGMAW MOUNTAINS
~ 19 ~

What took the army four days to travel, Prowl crossed in little over twenty four hours. She flew high over the rolling landscape, inching closer and closer to the massive mountains on the horizon. As they flew, they saw no signs of the Liolian army nor did they spot the Nuquamese. The landscape, with all of its vibrant grass and trickling streams, appeared devoid of life. Speilton realized for the first time what Rilly had meant when he referred to Caelum as a young world. It appeared pure, but empty, not yet worn and lived-in like Liolia. He suddenly understood why the Phoenixes were so resistant to have the Liolians enter their world; Caelum was not meant for them. They knew that any other group that entered would replace them. The Phoenixes were merely the first inhabitants, tasked with watching over the land just like the Anemoi in Liolia. Just as Rilly said, the Phoenixes knew they would not control the land forever. So they clung to it, afraid of the others who could grow and thrive in the land in which they lived. But if the land was not made for them, for whom was it intended?

They camped just outside the city at sunset, and Speilton slept for a few hours, waking in the middle of the night. He roused Prowl, and the two prepared for the mission ahead. Prowl soared high into the air, past the clouds that dotted the night sky but still not higher than the tallest peak of the Fangmaw Mountain range. It grew hard for Speilton to breath, and he shivered against the icy wind. Below, the green plains faded into a field of navy blue, about the same color of the sky, but the mountains showed their true scale and immensity. Prowl drifted over their foothills, and Speilton looked down amongst the jagged crags and sharp slopes for any sign of life.

And then he found it, a single flickering light far ahead nestled up in a crevice of a western mountain peak in the range. Speilton pointed to it, but Prowl had already noticed as well and had begun flying toward it, keeping her same elevation above the ground. As they grew nearer, it became apparent that it was not just one light but many, small and dim, spread out across a landing between a steep mountain wall and a smaller jagged peak. It was only once they were flying directly above the multitude of smoldering campfires that Speilton realized there was an entire city down below, or what appeared to be at least the ruins of one, built from the same stone as the mountain. Roofless structures, fallen walls, crumbling streets, and lone, half-fallen arches covered a wide expanse of the mountainside, hidden away by the wall of stone that lay between the city and the valley below.

"That must be their camp," Speilton said. "Aurum is down there somewhere, which means Retsinis is likely there, too."

Prowl looked back at him worriedly, and Speilton patted her neck. "I can do this, trust me. Just take me down to the streets and watch from above. You'll know when it's time to come get me."

Reluctantly, Prowl turned her head around, flew a few more feet, and then dropped down through the air. She tucked her wings as the two dove towards the city, and Speilton's stomach flipped as the campfires and stone building rushed toward them with astounding

speed. As they neared it, Prowl unfurled her wings, catching the air and bringing them to an abrupt stop above one quiet street in the city. Speilton slipped down from her back and landed on the street, turning around wildly for a sign of danger. At first, he saw nothing, and then he heard the grunting sound of a creature coming from an alley up ahead. "Go," Speilton whispered to Prowl. "I've got this."

Prowl flew back high into the sky as the creature appeared before Speilton, strolling carelessly through the dark ruins. While he hid in the shadows, Speilton focused on the wall beside the creature's head, ripping a stone brick from the mortar and bringing it hard against the creature's head. The creature grunted, and then fell face-down onto a pile of rubble.

Quickly, Speilton ran and pulled the grotesque creature by its ankles into the darkness. It was clearly one of the Nuquamese – a former Liolian that Retsinis had enslaved and transformed with his sword. With the body reasonably hidden, Speilton began walking down the streets, keeping to the shadows that fell along the sides of the fallen structures. Up ahead, he saw the warm glow of a campfire, and he peered through a half-remaining window to inspect it. The fire flickered between a grouping of rocks, but there was not a soul around it. The emptiness of the city troubled Speilton more than if it had been full and lively. Every step he took seemed to echo, and the untended fires gave the illusion that the city was watched by some ghostly inhabitants.

As he continued looking at the fire, a shape suddenly stood up inside the structure, appearing between Speilton and the light. Speilton's heart stopped, but since the figure was wreathed in shadow, it took him a moment to realize that the creature faced away from Speilton and had yet to notice him. Speilton stepped slowly away from the creature, which had begun to mutter to itself in some strange dialect, and he took off down a side strect. Ahead of him, there was the shape of another solitary creature lying unconscious beside the wall of a building, and as Speilton crept past it, he realized it was sleeping. Speilton continued past and stepped out into another street. Just as he did so, he caught in the corner of his eye a shape moving towards him from up above. He ran to the shadow of a building as a single Phoenix, pure black in color, flew over his head. Speilton breathed a sigh of relief as it continued on its way, and he was able to resumed walking down the streets.

Speilton suddenly noticed a deep sound echoing through the city. It appeared to be coming from some distance away, but as he listened it grew in strength. It was like the wail of children, and the roar of some massive feline, and the bellowing of a horde of trolls. There were clearly multiple creatures all screaming at once, and Speilton suddenly realized what the sound must be. No longer taking care to remain quiet and hidden, he took off running towards the sound. In the dark, the rubble scattered through the streets created constant, unseen obstacles before him, and Speilton was forced to stumble over and through it, growing closer to the source of the cries.

He turned a corner and ran right into a mass of nearly two hundred of the beasts, all roaring to the sky with their heads thrown back. Speilton froze suddenly, overwhelmed by the sheer multitude of the savage creatures, and realizing that none of them were facing him or had noticed his arrival – none save for one. The crowd of howling creatures faced a stone platform with large roaring basins of fire at either end which rose above the sea of their bobbing heads, and upon the platform were two figures. One was Aurum, with her arms bound together behind her, and to her right was Retsinis. Only he had noticed Speilton's arrival, and as Speilton stood immobile, the King of the Nuquamese raised the jagged black sword in his hand and the crowd fell silent. A greedy grin was plastered across his fanged mouth, and he stared at Speilton with his white, milky eyes.

"My children," Retsinis declared in a voice like a hiss and a roll of thunder all at once, "please welcome our old friend."

The creatures turned, and suddenly hundreds of blank, possessed eyes were glaring into his. Speilton couldn't speak, for his body had lost all capacity to move as he watched one of his many dream scenes of death materializing before him. "You arrived just in time," Retsinis announced. "The Versipellis saw you quite a while ago, and it took you so long to arrive here, we were afraid you had gotten lost or turned back."

Speilton still remained silent, his mouth open as if preparing to form words but incapable of carrying them out. Retsinis bared his fangs in another smile. "I assume you know my niece here," he said, laying one hand on Aurum's shoulder.

"Speilton!" Aurum called, and Retsinis looked at her amused. "Get out of here now!"

"Come now, do you know Speilton at all?" Retsinis asked. "Your *friend* here is much too valiant to leave someone behind. No, I don't believe Speilton will leave."

The Nuquamese began to growl and grow restless, creeping closer to Speilton like wolves stalking prey. "Patience, my children," Retsinis said. "You will all feed soon. But first, I want our guest to witness this. I want him to see how he has failed before he meets his end."

Retsinis raised the massive sword high above his head and stared down at Aurum, who looked out at Speilton in desperation. Something in her eyes snapped life back into Speilton's limbs. He raised his hand, focused on the fire flickering in a torch basin a few feet behind Retsinis and pulled a tower of flame from it. As Retsinis swung the sword downward, Speilton brought the fire hard against the side of the Nuquamese King. Flames enveloped Retsinis's body, but the sword did not stop. Ferrum Potestas dropped down through the rush of flames, coming to a halt only when it had struck the stone floor of the platform. Speilton screamed as the fire cleared, and he could once again see Retsinis, now pulling the sword out of the stone with Aurum beside him, untouched by the blade. Speilton's fire had just barely managed to push the sword away from her.

But as he watched, Retsinis lifted the sword again. Speilton pulled his wand from his belt and summoned all his energy into a singular beam of fire that blew straight from his wand and struck Retsinis in the chest. Retsinis stumbled back a foot, then brandished the Sword of Power before him. The fire from Speilton's wand was unable to coil around the blade, but dissipated upon reaching it, as if it were being drawn into the dark steel of the sword.

Realizing his fire was not enough, Speilton closed his eyes and summoned a gust of wind that struck Retsinis in the side. While Retsinis regained his footing, Speilton focused on the rope that bound Aurum to the platform and lit it on fire at the base. "Aurum, run!" he screamed.

The golden-haired girl leapt down from the platform and hurried out into the ruins, but Retsinis seemed unfazed. He remained on the platform and pointed his blade at Speilton. "Now, you may feast," he proclaimed, and the creatures rushed at Speilton.

The king realized that he could not take them all on at once, and many of the creatures were likely to outrun him. As they hissed and began to rush at him, Speilton brought pillars of stone up out of the ground between himself and the creatures. He turned and began to flee, summoning a blast of fire stretching from one side of the street to the other. The creatures climbed over the stone and stopped momentarily at the fire, then began spreading out as they ran parallel to the street, climbing through the ruins of old buildings on either side of the road.

Speilton looked up at the cloudy sky, but he could not see Prowl. He could only hope she had been watching and had gone to retrieve Aurum. Speilton could hold them off, but she was unarmed. He had to give them enough time to find each other. The growling of the monsters picked up as they pursued Speilton. He could hear the decaying city coming to life with the sounds of the Nuquamese all around. The lonely creatures Speilton had seen wandering or sleeping in the city earlier had been awakened, and they now sprang up at the call of their brethren and swarmed after Speilton. As a few stepped out of the rubble ahead of Speilton, he reached out to a stone wall beside them, bringing what remained of the structures on them from above. One escaped the fallen bricks and dove at Speilton, pulling him hard to the ground. He had just enough time to blow it off of him with a sudden eruption of flames from his wand and climb to his feet before the rest of the creatures were upon him.

As he ran, there appeared a figure standing in the street before him. It was a female figure, smaller than the monstrous creatures that pursued him attacking from the buildings on all sides, and she did not rush at him like the others. But he could tell it was also not Aurum. The woman stood her ground as Speilton fled towards her, and then raised one hand with a scepter clutched in her grasp.

Speilton raised his own wand to stop her, but it was already too late. Black tendrils erupted out of the doorway of a dilapidated building to his right, snagging Speilton's arm and ankles and dragging him in. He struggled against them, trying to concentrate on them, but he quickly realized the element of which they were composed. Then, he was already through the doorway and the tentacles released him, leaving him alone inside.

Two and a half of the walls of the old structure still stood, and the gaps in them were sealed by some dark, writhing material that despite appearing like smoke, seemed capable of effectively sealing up the room. The roars of the creatures outside sounded muddled and distant, as if he were hearing it through water. Speilton had seen the substance before; it was darkness.

He rose to his feet and checked hurriedly for some gap in the black element that would allow him to escape but could find none. Then, through the roiling material, the woman appeared, robed in a similar black material that seemed almost as if she were made of the substance. It was only her pale white skin that gave her away, white and smooth as alabaster.

"Speilton," the woman said. "It has been a while hasn't it?"

"Venefica," Speilton said with a slight nod. "Why'd you bring me here?"

"I thought it was a good time for a chat," she said simply, pacing slowly around the room. "Especially, seeing as you don't look to have much longer to live."

"Chat? About what?" Speilton asked calmly.

"The Warlocks and I have heard about your newly discovered abilities," she said, her lips coiling into a thin smile. "You killed Valzacor, you know."

"Yes, so I heard."

"Never one of my favorites. Too pretentious, really, with the whole title and such. And what a terrible title it was. The 'Inhaler'! Sounds as if it were chosen by a child. But *you* – I think – you would make a very nice Warlock," she said with a confident gaze, as if she were picking an apple to purchase from a market.

"I've been told I have potential as a Wizard," Speilton said levelly.

"A Wizard? And who told you that? Cigam?" she laughed. "He would say that. I believe they are really desperate for new members."

"And the Warlocks aren't?" Speilton questioned.

"There are always more who would happily join us. We don't have to dig as they do."

"Then what is this? Are you telling me you brought me in here for any reason other than trying to recruit me?"

Venefica stopped for a second and sized Speilton up. From the shoulder straps of her black dress, two long, black coils descended, wrapping themselves slowly around her pale arms like serpents. "You caught me," she said as the black coils reached the palms of her hands and opened black, snake-like mouths. "It's not really a recruitment though as much as it is a proposal, or...an attempt to make you consider an alternative view."

"The Warlocks live only to use their powers for evil. They murder thousands, *millions*, in an attempt to end worlds."

"Is that what Cigam told you as well?" she asked. "If that is the case then we really would be no different than the Versipellis. But I would personally say the Versipellis are much more gifted at the whole ending worlds ordeal than we are."

"If that's not the truth, then what is?"

"I like to think we are just...misunderstood. We strive for knowledge, *all* knowledge, and even that which the Wizards have deemed as illicit. The Wizards banished us all from their Council, and so we were forced to continue on our magic outside of their control. That, of course, made us a threat."

"The magic you practice has done great harm," Speilton said.

"In some cases, yes, that is true. But in others, it has been extraordinary. We created those magical flames that give life to Wodahs. *We* created that, a new race – new life!"

"Life that was then enslaved by tyrants."

"I never said it was good life," she smiled. "But my point still stands. We are not the couriers of evil that you think us to be."

"Then, why do you fight alongside Retsinis and the Versipellis now?" Speilton questioned.

"We fight alongside none but our fellow Warlocks. We are very...familial like that. The Warlocks gave me a people when the Wizards denied me from their council. And so, I say to you again, in my opinion, you would be an incredible Warlock."

The black snakes whose heads rested in either of her hands looked at Speilton, and suddenly their eyes began to glow, soft and silver, right into Speilton's. He had begun to say something, but now found he had lost the words. For some reason, he began to really consider Venefica's words. "Come on, you know as well as I do that the Wizard Council is corrupt. They fight for good, yet they have abandoned you here out of fear. The Warlocks wish only to combat them and show them for who they really are."

Speilton began to nod his head, shocked by his own actions. He wanted to agree with her, but he couldn't explain why. Her argument made sense, and he too thirsted for knowledge, or so he liked to think. He stepped towards her, and began to say, "yes, yes I think–" when suddenly one of the walls of darkness was blown in by a sudden burst of fire.

Both Venefica and Speilton were knocked to the ground as Prowl burst into the room. On her back was Aurum. Speilton rose quickly, and suddenly realized that his recent thoughts had not been his own. He knew of Venefica's propensity to charm and persuade with her dark magic, and now he understood her powers. Speilton leapt onto Prowl's back, and Aurum hugged him from behind.

As Prowl dashed into the air, Venefica looked up with her constant smile and shouted after Speilton, "Another time, then?"

Prowl flew into the air, and all throughout the city below the creatures rushed, crawling over each other in search of their prey. Speilton looked everywhere below for a sign of Retsinis, but he saw nothing besides the blanket of Nuquamese that scurried throughout every street.

"You came for me," Aurum said, holding onto Speilton both to stay stable on Prowl's back and to find comfort.

"The Phoenixes told me what happened after I left – how the Phoenixes of Darkness had taken you, so I knew I had to try," Speilton said.

"Speilton, you are kind, but foolish. It was all a trap. They only wanted you. And you nearly gave yourself right to them."

A gust of wind rocked Prowl from the side, and she struggled for a moment to regain her composure. Suddenly, black shapes flew at them out of the night sky.

"Watch out!" Speilton shouted, and Prowl rolled to the side just in time to avoid them as they zipped through the air.

"It was the Phoenixes of Darkness that let Retsinis and his armies into Caelum," Aurum said. "Speilton, I've seen their numbers. Any one of his armies would be a challenge to defeat by themselves."

"Well I have some tricks of my own now. Retsinis is unaware of my new powers."

"Then that's even more reason for you to have stayed away," Aurum said. "But I guess it's too late for – look out!"

Three more dived at them from the side, and despite Prowl's attempt to drop below their attack, one caught her wing, throwing the dragon sideways. As she fell, a swarm of them rose up, diving into Prowl and clawing against her scales with their material darkness. The dragon wailed as Speilton struggled to conjure a shield of fire around them. Undeterred by the flames, the Phoenixes continued their attacks, pelting the dragon in rushes of their prickly, ravenous substance. Prowl had fallen to only a few feet above the tops of the buildings when one Phoenix struck Speilton from the side. He slipped from Prowl's back, and as he reached to grab Aurum's hand, he missed. Speilton fell a few feet, summoning a slight gust of wind to ease his fall but landing hard against the rocky ground all the same. Speilton had landed in what appeared to be an old square courtyard where the streets all met. The buildings facing the square were surprisingly still intact for the most part, with stone walls and narrow windows peering down at the scene unfurling. Prowl fell through the air, landing with Aurum in the far corner of the same square. Speilton ran towards them when he heard the sounds of approaching Nuquamese. At first, they came from behind him, but then he heard the sound from the streets to his right, and then those to his left. The courtyard was dark, with only the cloud-filtered moonlight trickling down on it, but from the ends of all the streets around him he could see the glow of torchlights approaching, and the roars of the Nuquamese swelled.

He reached Prowl's side and helped Aurum to her feet. "Are you okay?" he asked, and she nodded.

"Prowl, how are you?" he asked, crouching over the dragon.

There was a loud thud behind Speilton, and he turned to see someone walking toward them out of the shadows after leaping from the top of one of the gaunt structures bordering the square. The figure was large and muscular with head stooped and a longsword in one hand. It was the sword that Speilton recognized first because of the way it shone pale and cool, even in the dim light.

"Ram?" Speilton asked as a sudden gust of wind threw him off his feet.

He crashed into a segment of a stone wall and quickly rose back to his feet. "Ram, stop!"

But another gust had already caught him in the chest, throwing him backwards into a wooden structure that collapsed on top of him after the impact. Speilton pushed it off and climbed back to his feet once again, facing the man approaching across the square. "Ram! It's me, Speilton. You know me!"

The warm flickering light of the approaching Nuquamese better showed Ram's appearance now, and Speilton could see the moss-like substance that covered his body. His skin was pale and grey, appearing rough as stone. Ram approached slowly, watching him with hollow eyes.

"Don't make me do this," Speilton said. "I don't want to-"

Another gust lifted Speilton off of his feet and threw him down hard into the rocks. The sounds of the Nuquamese were loud now, bearing down on them from all around. "Aurum," Speilton called, rising to his feet once again. "How is she? Can Prowl fly?"

"She's badly injured, Speilton," Aurum called. "I'm not sure if she can."

Speilton began to panic. The Nuquamese were almost here, and they were trapped high on the side of a distant mountain. Speilton aimed his wand at the street beside him, ducking under another blast of air from Ram. Pointing at each street in turn, Speilton combusted them all into flame, fashioning a wall of fire around the courtyard where they stood. Ram saw the fire boxing him in just as the Nuquamese reached it. A few tried to press through, but the flames singed their bodies, causing the masses to stop and wail all around the near empty courtyard.

With the creatures kept at bay for the moment, Speilton approached Ram. "Remember me?" Speilton said. "Remember everything we went through together?"

Ram summoned another blast of air, but Speilton was ready now. He concentrated and diverted the gust before it reached him. If Ram was impressed, he didn't show it. "I know there is still a part of you in there," Speilton said. "I know you can hear me."

Once again, Ram responded with another attack from his wand. Speilton tried to stop this one, but it was too strong and quick, and he was brought hard into the ground. This time, when Speilton climbed to his feet, he didn't hesitate before rushing at the former Liolian general, his sword drawn. As the distance between the two shrunk, Ram, too, raised his sword, and their blades clashed. The crowd of watching Nuquamese cheered all around them as Speilton and his old friend dueled.

The two had sparred often back in the day, and Speilton knew the man's style well, but it hadn't been until the first time they had truly fought each other – back when Ram was first turned by Retsinis – that he understood how powerful of a fighter Ram really was. Ram fought with incredible strength, using the length of his sword, Spirit, to his advantage. Speilton recognized his style had changed. He fought more aggressively, swiping at Speilton with furious blows and rarely taking stances that best defended his body. Perhaps, it was due to his changed mindset, with the magic that had poisoned his brain forcing him to act as a singular body in a greater collective and not as an individual bent on survival. Or perhaps he somehow understood that Speilton was never going to make any attack that would seriously wound him. Even if he wanted to, Speilton found very few opportunities to do so, as he was forced into a largely defensive stance. Ram moved forward with every attack, and Speilton could do nothing more than step backwards with equal speed. He tried to fight spryly yet carefully, since he knew any stumble or unsteady balance on the rocks scattered across the courtyard could lead to his demise.

Suddenly, the roars of the Nuquamese picked up even louder, and Speilton turned to see that they had begun to spill into the square through a gap in one of the stone buildings. Aurum looked up from Prowl's side and called to Speilton. "Speilton! A weapon! Throw me something!"

Ram's blade clashed with his own, and Speilton pushed against it to knock Ram back a few feet. He knew he couldn't throw the sword in such close combat, so his hand moved to his wand. "Here!" he yelled, tossing it through the air as the creatures sprinted at the unarmed Aurum.

She reached up and caught the wand with both hands. "You're the wielder of fire now!" Speilton called.

Aurum lowered the weapon at the approaching creatures, and at first nothing happened. The closest one, a monster with large bulging eyes and a wide jaw with prickly teeth, leapt at her, when a sudden eruption of flames engulfed its body. The other creatures were also thrown to the ground where they thrashed and rolled to extinguish the fire.

Speilton almost laughed as Aurum exclaimed with excitement, but Ram attacked again, thrusting his sword at Speilton. He parried and stepped to the side, his eyes falling on the wand at Ram's hip. In that moment, Speilton remembered what Rilly had said about the twelve elements. Retsinis had one, as did Ram, and Speilton could only make up for a lack of one of the wands. He knew he couldn't take darkness from Retsinis, so it had to be Ram's.

The next time Ram attacked, Speilton ducked beneath the swing and reached out for the wand. His fingers had just barely grazed the wooden handle of it when Ram turned, taking the wand out of range. Ram loomed over Speilton's undefended body. Recognizing his error, Speilton attempted to throw the sword between himself and Ram's sudden attack, but he could only do so much. A fiery pain lit up Speilton's side as Ram swung down at him. Speilton rolled over to his side, clutching the bleeding wound, and Ram approached to attack again. "Please! Ram!" Speilton screamed as Ram raised his blade over him.

A ball of blue flames blew into Ram, causing him to stumble backwards. Prowl struggled forward, clearly limping but snarling with ferocity all the same. Aurum was once again situated on her back, firing a constant stream of fire at the Nuquamese as they approached, and Speilton could tell the magic was already taking a toll on her. When Ram took a step back, Prowl breathed out another jet of fire that ignited the mass on Ram's body. As he staggered away, beating at the flames, Prowl pumped her wings, rising slightly into the air. She reached down, took Speilton in her claws, and slowly began to rise. Speilton screamed, first in pain, and then for Prowl to turn back to get Ram's wand, but a volley of arrows forced Prowl to stay her course.

The blue dragon bellowed as they rose above the streets of the city. All around, the dark shapes of Phoenixes swarmed, but Aurum kept the fire coming, creating a buffer that kept them all at bay. As a first time user of magic, the effort had drained her as she struggled to keep her eyes open, but she pushed through. Prowl kept her wings flapping, however erratically or painfully, and slowly they drifted out of the city into the open air beyond the mountains. Speilton was twisted in pain, blood seeping from his side and dripping down over the stones of the mountain as they flew.

When Aurum could spot no more of the dark Phoenixes, she slipped the wand into her own belt and then fell unconscious on Prowl's back. The dragon fought on, groaning with every strain of her wings, slowly descending towards the plains below. As dawn broke, they neared a stream, and there Prowl first set Speilton down in the grass before landing roughly along the shore of the trickling water.

THE WARLOCKS' STAND
~ 20 ~

The men had left the water and were drying upon the beach when the first horn blew. Onaclov rode quickly through the camp on his black horse, stopping at Millites's tent just as the King was stepping outside. "They're coming," Onaclov said. "Our scout posted at the top of the valley saw them coming from the east."

"How much time?" Millites asked.

"Not enough to escape the valley before they arrive," Onaclov said.

Millites looked to his men as they rushed to collect their armor and weapons. "Retsinis's men will have the high ground," Millites said.

"We can try to use that to our advantage," Onaclov said. "The walls into the valley are steep, so they will be forced to march in only a few at a time."

"That may save us for a moment. We must keep the Nuquamese at bay long enough for our army to retreat from the valley. Quick, prepare the men," Millites ordered rushing away through the crowd.

The horns blared, and the sound of clashing armor and weapons rang throughout the valley as the men prepared themselves. Millites reached Hunger, whose scales were still a light green as he slept. He patted the dragon's snout. "How are you? Can you fly?"

Hunger slowly rose off the ground and stood back on his two legs. The dragon spread his wings and flapped slowly to test his joints. After a moment of grimacing, Hunger fell back onto his clawed wings.

"Alright, you need to rest," Millites said, "but if I need you, make sure to be ready."

Hunger gave a small purring growl as Millites ran back to his tent. "Assemble on the beach north of the camp!" Millites called loudly, and the men around him passed on the message. He reached his tent and pulled on his chainmail undershirt, strapped on his sword belt, and then pulled on his gauntlets. Finally, he pulled on his red cape and his golden helmet decorated to appear like the face of the lion. When he stepped out of the tent, the army had nearly all assembled. Millites ran to the front of the men and stood beside Usus who rode on the back of Flamane.

"Onaclov sent some of the Isoalates to the walls to the south to try to find a path out," Usus informed him.

"Good," Millites said, watching the cliffs in front of them. "We need to figure out how to stop them long enough to escape."

"I guess we'll have to think on our feet, then," Usus said. "You think this is it? Is this when Retsinis sends everything?"

"Seems like we're about to find out," Millites said.

There was the sound of a distant roar echoing from high above them. The men strained their eyes to see if they could spot any of the creatures above, but their enemy was hidden. Chills went down their spines as the screeching and bellowing sounds of thousands of Nuquamese reverberated in the valley, giving the illusion that they were attacking from all directions.

Then the first enemy appeared on the edge of the cliffs above, and as soon as it appeared, hundreds more followed. In only a moment, the cliffs in front of and to the right of the army were covered by the creatures, holding their weapons high and screaming at the Liolians below. The men quaked at the enormity of the army. Then, above the army, a dark cloud appeared that at first they assumed to be the Daerds, but soon revealed itself to be something else. Millites quickly conjured a large dome of light that encapsulated the entirety of his army as thousands of arrows pattered down above them, shattering as they struck the glowing element.

After all the arrows had landed, Millites allowed the shield to dissipate, and the fragments of arrows fell down upon the army like soft rain. "What are they waiting for?" Usus asked.

"I'm not sure," Millites muttered.

The king turned back to the army behind him. "Ince!" he called "Teews! Up here, quick."

Ince shuffled out of the crowd of Liolian soldiers and Teews approached from her position behind the army. "So I prove myself in battle once and suddenly I'm promoted to the head of the army? Looks like I should've snuck to the frontlines a long time ago," she said.

"You're here now, and you are a capable fighter," Millites said. "We need you."

Teews smiled and pulled out her wand in one hand and clutched her spear in the other. "Now, we wait?" Teews asked.

"Now, we wait," Millites said.

A second cloud drifted over the valley, but this one was neither arrows nor Daerds. As it dropped down towards the army, it was clear that they were birds, but much smaller in size than the massive crows of Worc's flock. The closer they approached, the larger they appeared to get, their bodies elongating into trails of dark matter, as if they were becoming black spears. "Brace!" Millites called, and the warriors raised their shields.

Millites attempted again to create a dome of light, but when the Phoenixes of Darkness struck against it, the shield splintered and gave way. The Phoenixes descended upon the army, blowing through their ranks in torrents of pure darkness. Warriors fell to the ground, their bodies being torn and scratched by the terrible element, writhing in pain. While they struggled to fight an enemy that appeared incapable of being harmed by blades, the Nuquamese above had begun to descend the steep switchbacks.

"Regain formation!" Millites screamed as the dark Phoenixes rose to strike again. "Ince! I need you to slow down the Nuquamese! Use your wand!"

A look of fear crossed over Ince's face, but he nodded anyway. Metus ran out of the crowd and said, "I'll go with you."

"Take Onaclov, as well," Millites commanded. "Have him use his lava to block the switchbacks."

Metus and Ince ran off to get Onaclov, and the three proceeded through the stream at the base of the waterfall to reach the spot where the trail met the valley floor.

"Teews," Millites began to say, but she finished his command before he could.

"Next time the Phoenixes come through, I'll summon a cloud to choke them out."

"Right," Millites nodded.

The Dark Phoenixes descended upon them again, this time striking first at the back of their army and racing to the front. As they wove between the soldiers, throwing them down and clawing at those they passed, they were unaware of the creeping purple mist that hung above the army until they rose again. By then, it was too late, and the Phoenixes of Darkness suddenly appeared dizzy. Many from the flock fell out of the sky, crashing in the water or the stretch of grass between the army and the waterfall. The Liolians cheered as the Phoenixes of Darkness rose again, hovering now with hesitation to attack.

Another volley of arrows was fired from the cliffs above them, and again Millites was able to conjure a shield to break the projectiles before they reached the army. But when he let his shield fall again, there were five individuals standing before the army, appearing seemingly out of nowhere.

Millites stepped forward as the five approached slowly. They were dressed all in black, and all human in appearance. In their center, leading the rest forward, was Venefica. "Hello, Millites," she called.

Senkrad, Usus, and Teews all strode up to Millites' side, their wands raised.

"It appears our paths have crossed again," she mused. "I'm not sure you have met my friends here before. They're fellow Warlocks, as you have likely guessed."

The other four smiled hungrily, holding scepters with much more power than the wands of the Liolians. Millites looked back at the army assembled behind them and raised a hand. "Hold your position!" he commanded. "We will handle this."

"That's for the best," Venefica said with a smile. "Wouldn't want any of them to get hurt."

It was Teews who attacked first, summoning a jet of her element at Venefica, who merely brushed the attack away with a wave of her dark magic. She responded with a sudden strike from her own wand, that Usus blocked with a wall of stone he pulled suddenly up from the ground. He then thrust his wand forward, sending the stone hurtling at the five Warlocks assembled before them. At the same time, Millites fired a beam of light into the face of one Warlock. The stones were blocked by all but the one that Millites had blinded, who took the full force of a head-sized rock to the chest. When he fell, the numbers were even, with four wielders of darkness facing down the four Liolians.

Just north, Ince and Onaclov were using their own wands to hold the charging Nuquamese at bay. In the few days that Ince had been in possession of Hopi's old wand of color, he had quickly developed his skills. From the base of the cliffs, he summoned blasts of the element into the descending creatures, blinding them as they raced down the narrow path. Many lost their footing and fell, obstructing the path for those behind them, while others simply stepped over the edge and fell to the next switchback below. Onaclov used his lava to cover the path with molten stone. The thick, fiery sludge coated sections of the path, forcing the approaching creatures to find another way to climb around or to face the fatal element. Their work had slowed the attack substantially, but they suddenly realized it had worked too well. The Nuquamese saw the trail was nearly impassable, so they looked for alternative ways into the valley.

Metus was the first to notice, while the other two were distracted using their magic. "They're climbing down the cliff walls!" the faun cried, pointing to a less steep spot further north where many of the monsters were already clinging to the cliff face.

"Ince," Onaclov said. "You go hold them off over there. I can handle the switchbacks."

Ince nodded, and after knocking one more off, he ran toward the spot below the descending Nuquamese.

"Metus," Onaclov turned now to the faun. "Go with him. He may need your help. The slope is steep, but the fall alone may not be enough to injure all the Nuquamese."

"I understand," he said, joining Ince.

Further south in the valley, the Warlocks fought viciously with the four Liolian element wielders. After the first of the five Warlocks had been struck down, the Warlocks adopted an offensive strategy, no longer playing with their enemies but attacking them with everything they had. Usus had conjured stone barriers to protect the four while Millites combatted the darkness with burning blasts of light. Teews's clouds of her element fared less effective against these much more capable magic wielders, as did Senkrad's ice. The two grew close to striking the Warlocks with their elements, but their enemies were ready now. Darkness spun around them as if the element itself was its own sentient creature. Tentacles lashed out from Venefica's cyclone, breaking through their defenses and grabbing them sporadically by the arms and legs, tossing them off balance. In a similar manner, the other Warlocks summoned massive attacks, creating what appeared to be a large, charging bull one moment and then some ferocious clawed being the next. Most of these conjured creatures broke against either walls of stone or conjured domes of light, but some pushed through, just barely grazing the four Liolians as they ducked away. The substantial difference in the power of the magic wielders caused Millites, Teews, Usus, and Senkrad to fight nearly entirely defensively.

It was Senkrad who turned the tide suddenly, with a quick dagger of ice that he launched from his wand just as one Warlock summoned what appeared like a black hound with fangs. Senkrad's shard struck the Warlock in the hip as the conjured hound of darkness leapt at the Calorian King. At the last moment, Teews blasted the demon dog apart, and the explosion of darkness threw Senkrad onto his back.

As the Warlock clutched the chunk of ice in her hip, Millites directed a beam of light into her chest, throwing her far back into the foam of the thundering waterfall.

Now Venefica opposed them with only two of her Warlocks, but she showed no sign of worry. Her attacks became more fierce, as the swirl of darkness around her began to creep outward from her body, spreading like roots from a fallen tree. It quickly became obvious that she was attempting to spread her magic around them, encapsulating them within her cage of darkness. Now, as the four Liolians defended the attacks of the other two Warlocks, they were also forced to begin attacking the growing field of darkness. Millites fired at Venefica's heart, but another Warlock choked out the beam of light and returned with a quick strike of some winged, clawed creature. Usus drove a spike of stone through its neck, breaking it apart. But Usus's move left him unprotected, and a moment later a lunging serpent

of darkness caught him in the side and wrapped around his body.

Teews rushed to him, destroying the serpent with her element, when suddenly she too was knocked down by another strike from the Warlocks. Senkrad and Millites ran to their two fallen comrades, defending their bodies while they struggled to stand. The wall of expanding darkness had grown above them and now was descending, forming a half dome over them. Millites and Senkrad fought furiously to hold back the onslaught from the Warlocks, until Millites was grabbed by a single tendril of darkness that pulled him to the ground. Realizing he was the last standing Liolian, Senkrad summoned a massive shield, and used all of his strength to continue feeding the ice barrier as the darkness surged against it on the other side.

Suddenly, the creeping black barrier of Venefica's darkness began to erode in the center, opening up in various different spots like a piece of paper being burned by a flame underneath. Then, through the openings, lava poured down, falling upon one Warlock and just missing another. Venefica turned to see her fellow Warlock writhing beneath the thick magma, and she let her darkness disperse all around her.

Millites turned to his men and screamed, "Cavalry! Charge!" as Onaclov, Ince, and Metus ran forward from behind the Warlocks in their own charge. The two remaining Warlocks looked up in fright as the Milwarian knights charged on their horses with spears lowered. As they stepped away from the rush of hooves and shouting warriors, they ran into Onaclov and Ince firing waves of their elements. Venefica was quicker to think than her comrade, and she summoned a column of darkness that whisked her high out of the valley to the cliffs above while the other Warlock lashed out in an attack of darkness that missed any of its targets. After the horses had trampled the Warlock beneath their storm of hooves, the cavalry came to a stop.

Millites, Usus, and Teews climbed to their feet amidst the rearing horse and pushed back to the front of the army where Onaclov, Ince, and Metus stood waiting. Upon seeing their faces, it became clear that their friends hadn't been running to come to their aid, but they were actually fleeing from something beyond.

To the north, a vast army of Nuquamese were charging, their numbers having spilled over the edge of the valley and filled the valley floor. "We tried our best to hold them off," Ince said. "But there were just too many."

Millites nodded, holding his sword in both hands and facing the distant roar of the Nuquamese.

"What do we do now?" Metus asked. "We can't fight them all."

"Onaclov," Millites said, "find the Isoalates. Figure out the best way to escape. But before we can do that, we'll have to fight."

The water of Lake Vascent suddenly began to bubble and froth to the West of the waiting Milwarian army. For a moment, the attention of the men was pulled away from the charging Nuquamese to the strange occurrence in the middle of the lake. "Oh no," Onaclov whispered, just a moment before a massive green tentacle broke through the surface of the lake. A second tentacle followed, looming high over the lake with water cascading down from it. Then a head pushed up from the depths of the water, large and fanged with gills and fins protruding from its scaly skin. The creature opened its gaping mouth and lifted enormous, muscular arms. High up on its shoulder was a singular Nuquamese creature, who appeared minuscule in contrast with a creature of such size.

"Cetus," Onaclov muttered, as the sea creature turned to the Liolian army that stood upon the banks of the lake.

CHAOS IN THE VALLEY
~ 21 ~

The valley had just come into Speilton's view when Cetus emerged from the shimmering blue lake. Prowl growled under the strain of their flight, but Speilton patted her neck and urged her on. "We're almost there. We're almost there."

Aurum clung on to him as they tore through the sky. Below them, the vast Nuquamese army covered the hillside, pushing each other toward the northern mouth of the valley in their struggle to attack the Liolians below. They had no reason to expect an adversary to be approaching them from behind, especially one they had assumed to be on the verge of death. Yet Prowl flew all the same. Speilton reached out with his mind, and as they sailed lower over the hills, he pulled up great chunks of the ground, digging up the soil below the army as if it were being uprooted by the shovel of some unseen giant. The Nuquamese were tossed to the side, creating greater disorder in their ranks but only incapacitating a small percentage of their total force. But this section of the army was not the real threat. The Nuquamese moved slowly, so for now these atop the cliffs couldn't impact any Liolians like those that had already scaled down into the valley.

Cetus had turned toward the Liolians and reached out one long, tentacled arm, and the Liolian forces broke rank. No battle strategy could defend against such a creature, so the men fled to the higher ground beneath the cliffs a bit further from the sea monster's reach. Speilton watched from above as the Nuquamese rushed at the Liolians, and the few element wielders conjured their magic to hold both the army and the sea monster at bay. Then a flock of the Phoenixes of Darkness descended upon the army, sending the warriors into a further state of chaos. Speilton closed his eyes.

"We need to get down there," Aurum said. "The soldiers cannot defend against the Phoenixes of Darkness when they take their elemental form, especially now that they have the Nuquamese to worry about on the ground."

Speilton said nothing, but he closed his eyes and raised his hand ever so slightly.

The sand on the beach between the two armies began to churn, getting picked up into the air. The Nuquamese didn't seem to notice, until the wind blew hard into their faces, blinding some and knocking others down. The charge began to falter, as those behind the firsts ran into them and stumbled, but then they regrouped and continued toward the Liolians. But the wind didn't stop either. As the creatures rushed forward, the wind beat against them, until suddenly the ground beneath their feet began to roll and quake. Speilton kept his eyes closed as he forced the dirt and sand and grass to writhe beneath the army of Nuquamese.

"You're doing that?" Aurum asked, shocked, but Speilton didn't respond. "That's the powers you were speaking about?"

While Speilton held back the Nuquamese, Cetus attacked, swiping his massive hand through the nearest of the Liolians. The great creature waded closer to the shore. Speilton opened his eyes and once again assessed the situation below. Prowl growled in protest, wanting to land, but Speilton reassured her. "Just a little longer. Then we'll land."

"Speilton, the Phoenixes. Can you control darkness as well?" Aurum asked.

The Phoenixes of Darkness dove again, tearing through the Liolian army and striking down the soldiers. This time, when they rose into the sky, Speilton concentrated on them.

Training with Rilly in Kal, he had worked for weeks on controlling the different elements, finding time to focus on each element. All that time, he had never attempted to control darkness. He didn't know why, but perhaps it had frightened him to try to manipulate something so vile. He had only known Retsinis and the Warlocks to wield darkness, yet it was not an element unique to them. In fact, darkness appeared the most present element of them all, especially in a land as empty and desolate as Kal. It was only now, as the Liolians faced their destruction from enemies from all around, that he tried for the first time. Usually, it was difficult to find a connection to exert control on an element for the first time, but as soon as he reached out to take control of the Phoenixes of Darkness, he found they bent quickly to his will. He shredded the whole flock at once from their winged forms, reducing them to a smear of contorted black, and pulled the great cloud of darkness rapidly through the air. Cetus was too busy reaching for the fleeing Liolians to notice the darkness until it had struck him in the side of the head. When he reached to block the attack, it had consumed his face. Cetus stumbled back, crashing through the now choppy water as his head became engulfed with the black element.

Speilton slumped forward on Prowl's back, and it was only Aurum's hold on him that kept him from falling. The attack had quite suddenly drained him of what little energy he had had. "Prowl," he stammered, his vision growing fuzzy. "Land now."

The dragon began to descend, and as Speilton watched, the Nuquamese army climbed over his attempted impediment and rushed at the Liolians. Speilton's head dropped for a second, and when Aurum shook him back awake, the two armies had met, with the six element wielding Liolians leading the way.

Such a noble effort, a whispering, seething voice said. *You wielded the darkness with such ease, and such skill, yet it appears it is all for naught.*

Speilton knew from whom the voice – or more accurately, voices – came, and he felt a sudden chill as he looked sluggishly around him.

Did you think that because you saved the girl, you could stop everything else we showed you from happening? Do you think you can change the future – change destiny? Come now Speilton, you are not a fool. Even in your visions you never saw the girl die. You know her scene was always different. The Book of Liolia only showed her captured, but it never showed the blade truly striking home. Unlike Ince. Unlike your brother. Unlike you.

"Where are you?" Speilton muttered back, pulling his sword free in one weak hand.

The scar on the back of his hand began to burn.

We are everywhere, Speilton. Can you not see us?

"Speilton?" Aurum asked, nudging him. "Who were you talking to? Speilton?"

But as she grabbed him by the shoulders to keep him conscious, he pitched limply to the side, slipping out of her grasp and off of Prowl's back. The dragon let out a cry and dove after him, grabbing him by the ankle with one clawed foot just as he crashed into the water of Lake Vascent.

Prowl pulled Speilton into the air and flew over the waves, laying him out on the sand of the shore and collapsing into the sand a few feet past. They had landed on the beach beside the Liolian camp, just south of where the army was engaged in battle with the Nuquamese. For the moment, they had peace. Aurum rushed off of Prowl and shook Speilton where he lay drenched beside the river. He responded with a small mutter but didn't open his eyes, so she grabbed him by the legs and pulled him back into the lake. The waves were stronger than normal with the thrashing of Cetus further in the waters, but she still lay Speilton in the shallow along the shore. "Prowl," she called. "You, too. Just lie in the water. It will help heal your wounds. Quickly, we don't have much time."

Prowl rose sluggishly and waded into the water, plopping into the lake with a huff. Once they were both in, Aurum walked into the waves. She looked back to shore and was startled to see four men staring at them. It took her a moment to recognize who they were. "You are the Isoalates of the Tawii tribe, are you not?" she asked, her hand on her wand.

"We have found a pass out of the valley," one said. "Just there, beyond the two boulders there is a place where the army can escape."

"Go tell Millites or Onaclov or Senkrad," she said. "I can protect them here."

The four Isoalates nodded and began to run toward the fighting not far from them.

It was clear that the Nuquamese forces that attacked them now were the entirety of their army. No longer were the creatures only the quickest and the thinnest, but now in their midst were lumbering creatures with thick skin or creatures composed of substances other than flesh. Throughout their army, certain creatures towered over the others, seeming to indicate they had once been giants before falling to Retsinis's blade. The dark magic of Ferrum Potestas had only made them larger and more difficult for a human, dwarf, or Wodah to wound, much less kill. As the terrible creatures attacked, the Liolians fought valiantly. Upon their horses, the Milwarian knights charged into their ranks, cutting through the first of the charging Nuquamese before falling to the heart of their armies so as not to become consumed within the near endless expanse of the creatures. The Wodahs charged aboard their own cavalry, the Hakesorsees, who snapped at the creatures with their low-hanging heads on their long necks. The dwarves supported the left flank, armored in stiff pieces of steel and wielding hammers and axes that brought down a Nuquamese with each swing. Even when a quicker creature was able to evade their weapons and leap upon them, the dwarves would grin as their enemies attempted to claw through their thick plates and chainmail. With another swing from their weapons, they were rid of the creatures and back on their feet.

And in front of all of them were their leaders. Millites carved through the Nuquamese with his bright white blazing sword, while Senkrad swung a massive glaive at the attacking creatures. Teews fought within a thick cloud of her purple element, causing most of the creatures that rushed at her to sink to the ground. The ones that were able to push through met the end of her spear. Onaclov fought beside Ore, bathing the land in his fiery red lava while the dwarf struck down those that fled. Usus circled overhead on the back of Flamane, holding his curved khopesh blade in one hand and his wand in the other. He alternated between contorting the ground beneath the Nuquamese and descending upon them to let Flamane grab one in his claws and toss it into the air to crash down upon others. Ince fought alongside them, despite never having been the ruler of anyone. His own desire to help had led Hopi to bestow his wand upon him, and so Ince fought with the weapon to the best of his ability. He was unable to conjure such complicated arrangements of color as Hopi or even Selppir had before him, but he tried his best with his very little training. All around him, the creatures were stumbling away, blinded or confused by the element.

Though the Liolians fought bravely, their enemy continued to pour into the valley. As they began to sweat and struggle for breath, they met fresh enemies eager for their share of the fight. When the Isoalates finally pushed to the front of the army and screamed to Millites over the sound of clashing blades and screams of pain that they had found a way out, he almost sighed with relief. When they told him that they had seen King Speilton land just a few hundred yards away, Millites whooped with joy. "So it *was* him we saw attack Cetus! He's returned!"

"Speilton has returned?" Teews questioned loudly as she fought not far from him.

Millites nodded, then looked around him. Finally, his eyes found Metus, who fought awkwardly with his own spear. "Metus, fall back to the camp. Find Speilton and help him out of the valley."

The faun looked up surprised, but instead of asking questions he said, "Yes, my king," and hurried away.

"You," Millites called, having to pause a moment to duck beneath the swing of an axe from a tall, root-covered creature, "Isoalates! Go to Onaclov and Senkrad, and tell them what you told me. Have them begin to have their men fall back."

In the lake, Cetus had finally broken free of the darkness, and the Phoenixes were reforming out of the black element. Cetus roared, exciting the Nuquamese and causing the Liolians' blood to run cold. The great tentacles of the sea creature writhed in the glassy water, pulling Cetus through the waves toward the army on the shore. He brought an enormous arm down in the middle of the Liolian army, crushing soldiers outright and knocking many others aside. The tangle of tendrils that grew where fingers should be lashed out across the grass and sand.

Millites cut through the army, heading west to the lake. He reached the wall of dwarves with the mound of fallen Nuquamese before them and ran behind them, finally coming to the shore. Cetus loomed over the king and looked down at him and snarled. A mist blew off of the enormous scaly skin of Cetus and washed over Millites as he faced the creature. Millites raised his sword and pointed it at the Nuquamese still perched on the sea monster's shoulder. He was a tiny spot on the massive creature, but Millites knew that it was the bearer of the ring that controlled the great beast of the water. He summoned a blast of white-hot light at the creature, but from such a distance, the light missed, catching Cetus in the shoulder instead. The sea monster roared and turned away from Millites's view, reaching with his other tentacled hand to grab the King. As the great hand swung down toward Millites, he raised his blade and shot a vertical beam of light into the grotesque palm. Cetus barely appeared to notice, pushing hard against the beam, until it appeared the light was breaking through the scaly skin. Millites screamed as he put all of his effort into his blast of light, and the rays broke through the top of Cetus hand, skewering it.

Cetus reared, but did not retreat. Instead he reached out with his other hand, raking it sideways across the beach to swat Millites. The king saw it coming, and began to sprint away from it, but the hand was too large. He dove, but the tentacles that sprouted from the palm reached out like fanged mouths and grabbed his body.

Millites thought quickly and encased his body in a glowing projection of light that formed around him in the shape of a lion. The lion avatar singed Cetus' serpentine appendages, forcing him to withdraw his hand for a moment. Millites allowed it to fade, just as Onaclov ran up to him. "Millites," he said, "where is Hunger? Can he fly?"

"He's back in the camp," Millites said.

"I couldn't get Usus's attention, but I need to get up there," he pointed to Cetus' shoulder. "I need to take back the ring."

"Hunger may be able to fly, but he's still wounded."

"I'll take whatever I can get. We can't defeat Cetus as long as he is under the control of the Nuquamese."

"Go find him," Millites said. "He can get you there. Just…be careful with him."

"Of course," Onaclov nodded as he ran back to the camp.

Metus finally reached Speilton and Aurum laying in the waves of the lake. Aurum rose as Metus waded into the water on his goat legs and stopped alongside Speilton.

"King Speilton," Metus said, shaking him. "You have to get up. We're about to fall back to the cliffs and get out of the valley."

"I'm not sure what is happening to him," Aurum said. "I thought the water would help."

"Was that him who controlled the Phoenixes of Darkness?" Metus asked. "It may just be that the effort sapped all of his energy, but I have never seen him like this."

"He can apparently control all of the elements now," Aurum explained.

Metus was surprised but had no time to question further. "We need to get him out of the water. When the army falls back, the Nuquamese will follow, and if he's still lying here when that happens…"

Aurum understood. She trudged through the waves and rustled Prowl awake. "Prowl, it's time to go."

The blue dragon raised her head from the surface of the water and looked at the two armies growing closer to them. Then she spotted Hunger leaping into the air with Onaclov on his back. "Help me get Speilton," Aurum said to Metus, and the two grabbed him and began pulling him out of the water.

Speilton suddenly opened his eyes and pulled out of their grasp. He rushed out of the water with surprising speed and collapsed on the shore. "They're here," he stammered, looking up at the camp as two pillars of a dark substance descended before him. From the dark wisps of matter, two cloaked figures formed, with large black wings where arms should be and skeletal faces concealed within the shadow of their hoods. "That's the Versipellis," Metus whispered in surprise, as Speilton drew his sword.

"Prowl," Speilton said, still facing the two black phantoms, "take Metus and Aurum out of here. I have to handle this alone."

"Speilton!" Aurum shouted. "We're not leaving you–"

"Prowl!" Speilton shouted. "Now!"

Aurum lunged toward Speilton, but Prowl lifted the golden-haired girl onto her back gently with her teeth. While Prowl was distracted, Metus ran up next to Speilton. "I'm not leaving," the faun persisted. "You don't have to do this alone."

Speilton turned to the faun. "This is my battle. I'm responsible for the destruction they cause."

He summoned a gust of wind that blew Metus backwards to Prowl's feet. The dragon looked worriedly at her owner, but Speilton nodded to her, and she grabbed the faun in the claws of her front legs and began to fly away.

Speilton Lux, alone once again, the Versipellis said in their echoing voice that came from everywhere and nowhere at once.

"You chose me with the Curse of the Verse," Speilton said. "Now you have to deal with me."

Suddenly, Metus pulled free of Prowl's grasp and fell the few feet to the ground. He ran up to Speilton's side as the first of the Versipellis lunged at him. The black cloak of the dream spirit melted away, revealing the hideous corpse-like body that lay beneath. The wings, too, had shed their glossy black feathers and beneath were the long boney arms with machetes where hands should have been. Speilton raised his own blade, taken from their slain brother, and blocked the Versipellis's attack. "Metus," Speilton said, parrying a second attack, "You need to leave. You can't fight them."

"Neither can you," Metus persisted.

The faun raised his spear and rushed at the second Versipellis who appeared to smile at the attack. "Metus! No!" Speilton cried, but the spear had already been blocked by the Versipellis. When the creature raised his other bladed arm to strike Metus, Speilton's heart froze, but Metus leapt away from the blade just as it came down where the faun's head had been. The Versipellis that Speilton was fighting attacked again, so Speilton was forced to let Metus fend for himself while he tried to stay alive.

Further inland, the first of the Liolians were falling back through the camp. As they ran, they collected what few things they could carry, but they left the vast majority of their supplies. Their eyes were divided between viewing the army of Nuquamese that rushed after them, and Onaclov and Hunger who raced through the air, pursued by the flock of Phoenixes. Hunger was clearly worn, and his flight was rigid and slow, but he was able to evade the vicious attacks of the flock of black birds. Every time the dark green scaled dragon approached Cetus, the sea monster would raise its mighty arms and try to swat the much smaller creature from the sky. Finally, Hunger was able to slip past the reach of Cetus and buzz by the monster's head. A great plume of smoky flame burst from Hunger's mouth and danced across the monster's neck as Onaclov leapt from the dragon's back. The soldiers watched

Onaclov hurtle through the air, landing on the shoulder of the beast right beside the Nuquamese that controlled it. They were too far away to see the fight that went down, but they could see that there was a struggle, and then suddenly both men slipped off the slick scales and hurtled toward the lake. Hunger was preoccupied evading the flock of Phoenixes that pursued him, and he noticed Onaclov too late. The leader of the Lavalands and the Nuquamese soldier crashed into the lake. But Cetus didn't move, suddenly abandoning all intentions to attack, and instead, he just observed the warring armies below with a distant fascination.

With Cetus seemingly no longer a threat, the men had only to worry about the thousands of Nuquamese pouring after them. That was, until they noticed Speilton and Metus fighting the two Versipellis. Speilton controlled the land around him to combat the creatures, summoning gusts of wind and sending columns of flames at the skeletal creatures wreathed in decaying cloth. The eye roved across the Versipellis's body, twitching erratically to take in its environment while also carefully avoiding every one of Speilton's attacks. As he used his powers, the Versipellis increased its own to compete. The Versipellis were natural shapeshifters, and as Speilton fought, it made good use of this skill. Speilton drove his sword, but the dream spirit dropped below the blade, crouching into the shape of a dark panther and lunging at Speilton. The black claws gripped the front of Speilton's chainmail shirt, and suddenly the claws were transformed back into the Versipellis's blades. Speilton released a surge of fire from his body that blew the Versipellis away just before the blades could sink into his chest.

When Speilton dove forward in a follow up attack, the Versipellis leapt into the air, its wings formed to carry the cloaked creature out of Speilton's reach. It was not out of the reach of Speilton's powers, however, and he summoned a great gust of wind to pull the Versipellis down to the ground. As it fell, it took on the shape of some large, horned beast, entirely Dark with the exception of the single white eye on its forehead. Just before it landed on Speilton, the king scrambled away, swinging his sword around at the last moment to cut into the side of the creature. But his blade had missed the Versipellis's eye, so when it retook its ghostly, robed form, no damage was done to it.

This time, the Versipellis didn't attack. It floated just above the ground, a few feet away, watching Speilton with its bulging eye. "Come on," Speilton challenged the creature. "Fight me."

Fighting you now is foolish, Speilton. We have no intention to kill you just yet. There's so much more we need from you first.

"What do you mean?" Speilton questioned. "You mean the Curse? What is it you want from me? And what do you want from Ince, and the boy, Nigal?"

Oh, telling you our plans would be incredibly counterproductive, the Versipellis sneered. *And it also appears that you have made quite a mistake. Many mistakes, it appears.*

"Speilton!" Metus' voice came. "Help!"

Speilton looked over to see Metus disarmed beneath the foot of the second Versipellis. The dream spirit he had been fighting loomed over the faun, his bladed arm cocked back to strike. "Metus," Speilton breathed, but as he ran to his friend, the Versipellis he had been fighting vanished, leaving only a slight aura of smoke.

270

Ince ran to him out of the camp. "King Speilton," Ince said. "The men are—"

But Speilton didn't hear what he said next. His heart stopped, as he saw another of his visions materializing before his eyes. Time seemed to slow as the vanished Versipellis began to take shape behind the unsuspecting Ince. The man with curly black hair looked at him confused, saying something that Speilton couldn't hear over the pounding of his heartbeat in his ears. He took one last glance at Metus, who was struggling to reach for his spear, and then he thrust his hand toward Ince and concentrated. Just as the Versipellis took shape behind him, Speilton pulled a column of stone out of the ground, blowing apart the dream spirit before it could run its blade through Ince and knocking the man forward onto the ground. Speilton ran to Ince and helped him to his feet quickly.

"Are you okay? It didn't touch you?" Speilton asked frantically.

Ince wasn't listening, his eyes were wide with fright as he looked past Speilton at something that left him speechless. Speilton followed his gaze and saw Metus, alone now in the grass where he had fallen, his stomach red with blood. "No," Speilton muttered. "No, no, Metus!"

Speilton ran to where the faun lay, his eyes wide with fright and his skin pale. Speilton sank beside him, pressing one hand on the deep wound in his abdomen and holding Metus' wooly-haired head in the other. "Speilton," Metus whimpered. "I couldn't fight it. I'm...I'm sorry...I should have listened. You were...you were…"

Speilton quieted him, feeling tears forming in his eyes. "No, no it's okay. You were doing what you thought was right. I'm sorry I didn't..."

"Was I brave?" Metus asked, his eyes losing their focus.

"Yes," Speilton said. "Yes, you were very brave. I could not have asked for a braver..."

But Metus' eyes had closed, and his body had gone still, and Speilton couldn't finish his sentence. Rage blossomed inside of him, growing and expanding until his body shuddered. He set Metus down carefully and clenched his fists. When he rose to his feet, the sand was already spinning around him. The water of the lake became choppy and fire began to catch on the grass of the valley. "Where are you?" Speilton roared.

Quite terrible are the consequences when one tries to change fate, spoke the voice of the Versipellis, but as Speilton spun around, he couldn't find from where the voice came. *You may have saved Ince for now, but you have paid the price. Go on your way now, Speilton Lux, you have much ahead of you.*

"No," Speilton fumed. "We end this now!"

The ground beneath Speilton's feet began to crack and quake. He felt the power building within him as he reached out to his environment and forced it into submission. Speilton closed his eyes, and relied on his control of the land to view the battlefield. The Nuquamese had reached the camp now, and many were charging after him on the shore, but the Versipellis were nowhere to be found.

Something grabbed Speilton by the arm and yanked him backwards. He struggled to pull away for a moment when another pair of hands grabbed his other arm. When he opened his eyes, he saw it was Millites and Usus dragging him backwards with Ince just ahead of them. "What are you doing?" he questioned.

"We need to go," Millites said. "The Nuquamese are right behind us."

Speilton pulled against them "No, wait! Metus! We can't leave him here."

As the words left his mouth, a horde of Nuquamese rushed toward the three men, running around the body of the faun. Speilton kept struggling until Metus could no longer be seen in the swarm of thousands of terrible creatures. Finally, he stopped resisting, and allowed himself to be dragged a few feet before turning and running himself. The Liolian army was only slightly ahead of them, and all around the Nuquamese were in pursuit. Speilton ran on the little bit of energy left, rushing to the path ahead where the Liolians were already climbing out of the valley. Behind, he could hear the snarling of the Nuquamese growing closer and just as it appeared they had nearly caught up to the three leaders of Milwaria, Prowl dove out of the sky, rushing over their heads and lighting up the closest of the creatures. Prowl's blue flames were coupled with the orange flames from Aurum's wand, and combined they ignited dozens of the monsters, allowing Speilton, Millites, and Usus to rejoin the army. Aurum and Prowl continued lighting up the Nuquamese, sending the creatures running for the clear waters of Lake Vascent. When all of the Liolians had reached the path out of the valley, Usus summoned a tall obstruction of sheer stone at the base of the switchbacks, blocking out the multitudes of Nuquamese who could do nothing other than growl at their enemies.

The valley was now filled with Retsinis's army, with even more of their troops still perched up on the cliffs far to the north. As the Liolians fled, Cetus watched with his vacant glare, and chiseled high up in the rock face of the southernmost of the Great Feather Peaks, the sculpture of the massive Phoenix observed them all with stone eyes.

THE MASTER OF THE STORM
~ 22 ~

"All twelve elements?" Millites questioned.

"All twelve," Speilton said.

With their long strides, the two dragons with the Milwarian Kings on their backs set the pace for the fleeing Liolian army. The escape from the valley of Lake Vascent had given them only a few miles head start while the Nuquamese struggled to climb out of the valley before they could set out in pursuit. The Liolian scouts claimed that they were gaining quickly.

"And now with your new…" Millites searched for a moment for the right word, "powers, you can make up for one missing element?"

"Yes, so I gave my fire wand to Aurum," Speilton said.

"Do you think that is wise?" Millites asked. "I mean, does she have much fighting experience?"

"She was able to protect herself well with it the past few days. I think she's a good choice."

Millites was about to respond but decided not to press the matter any further. Instead he said, "So you make up for just one. That means we have to take either Retsinis's wand or Ram's, and we have to find every other wand scattered across Liolia."

"I already have that partially covered," Speilton explained. "While I was in Caloria, I found Equus, who's the Chief of the Centaurs, now."

"Seems like he's done well for himself," Millites said.

"Yes, but their situation appears dire. Even as nomadic people, they are unable to find any land with which to amply support their people. Liolia is just dying, and—"

"I know, you've mentioned that already," Millites interrupted. "But what do the centaurs have to do with the wands?"

"Well, as we speak, Equus and the centaurs are racing across Liolia trying to locate the remaining civilizations and bastions of life. I have given them instructions to bring them all to the edge of the great mountains in the far southeast of Liolia. And then they only have to wait."

"Wait? Wait for what? For us to bring them here?"

Speilton was prepared for his hostility at the idea. "Millites, I think it is the only way. We need the wands to kill Retsinis, and Retsinis is here. We could bring just the leaders or whoever possesses the wands now, but then we'd just be condemning all the rest of the Liolians to die there."

"What makes you so sure they would all die if left in Liolia?"

"I know you don't want to hear this. Trust me, I don't even want to consider it, but I saw it to be true. Liolia's time has come. The land is all waste now."

"You said you arrived first in the Icelands, then went to Kal to train. Then you found the centaurs. That means you stayed in Caloria that entire time, and Caloria has always been a wasteland. How can you be so sure the rest of Liolia is the same?"

"It was just…it's hard to explain, but it was different. And Rilly, he was sure of it."

~The War for Caelum~

Millites scowled and looked off at the rolling hills ahead of them. "Even if you were to go back to Liolia to bring them here, we cannot be sure that the centaurs will actually be able to find everyone in time, if they even can at all. To travel that far and search so many places could take months if not years. I know the time between our worlds is confusing and time moves much more rapidly there than here, but that's an incredible risk. If you go, you might have to wait in the mountains for a considerable amount of time for something that may or may not even arrive. Is that something you want to risk?"

"Well," Speilton had to tread carefully now, "I was actually thinking you might be the one to go."

Millites looked sternly at his brother for a moment but didn't say a word as he considered Speilton's rationale. "Look," Speilton said, explaining himself, "I know it will be difficult, and it is not a decision I can make for you. It will have to be one of us, or Teews, since I think the people will only leave Liolia if they are following one of their leaders. But with my powers, I believe that the army needs me now, more than ever."

"And they didn't need you before?" Millites questioned. "You didn't seem to have any second thoughts about leaving a few weeks ago, but now you decide it is in the best interest of the army."

"I'm sorry," Speilton said. "I know how you must feel, but I do believe it is important for me to stay."

"And it's not important that I do?"

"I didn't say that!" Speilton said. "It's just, there are things I know now and things I can do that can help me protect this army."

277

Millites returned to his silence for a moment. Prowl and Hunger looked at each other, both keeping their heads ducked to avoid the argument between their masters.

"You 'know things now'," Millites said, referring to Speilton's last statement. "What do you mean by that? What do you know?"

"I just meant with how to kill Retsinis and things like that," Speilton stammered.

"No, that's not what you meant. You told me, so I know that just as well as you do. You were talking about something else. What do you know now? What did you learn while you were in Liolia? And now that I think about it, there are other parts of your story that don't make sense. You said you went to rescue Aurum and then followed the Nuquamese army here to us, but how did you know where she was being held?"

"It was…it's nothing really," Speilton said.

"It is something Speilton."

"But it's not important."

"I don't care if you don't think it is, it's still important that you tell me," Millites said, and when Speilton was quiet for a moment, he continued. "We're fighting the Versipellis now, a threat you knew about for years and never told anyone else about."

"I'm sorry about that, too, but it wasn't your fight. The Versipellis chose me, so it was my problem to deal with."

"That's not how it works," Millites said. "Things like that are larger than just you. We're all impacted by it, and we can all help you with it."

"Metus died trying to help me," Speilton snapped. "I told him I'd handle it, but he fought anyway, and I watched him die."

278

"Maybe if you had let us help earlier, it all could have been avoided."

Speilton glared at his brother, but after a moment, he just looked away.

"Maybe," Millites continued, "if Metus hadn't stepped in, the Versipellis would've killed you. Metus was smart, and he understood the risk of fighting beside you. But he also wasn't the only man we lost."

"I know," Speilton said, his voice calm, "but I still can't help feeling like if I had just done something different, maybe then he wouldn't have died."

"That's always how it is in battle. I let Onaclov fly with Hunger to attack Cetus knowing that it would likely be suicidal. No one has seen Onaclov since. Tell me that I'm not responsible for that."

Hunger let out a low somber growl beneath him.

"Maybe he swam to shore," Speilton said.

"Well, he's not with our army now, which means that if he did, he swam right up to the Nuquamese."

Speilton shook his head at the thought of his friend meeting such an end.

"Hopi died as well, after coming to rescue me. Nuquamese just tore him apart like animals," Millites said.

"The Order of the Bow told me he had died," Speilton said. "Were you with him when…"

"We were all near him, but I don't think any of us really knew how bad it was. And we were all distracted with collapsing the bridge. But it was quick. He didn't suffer long. Like you, there are things that I wish I could've done differently, but I've faced the fact that I can't change things."

Speilton nodded. "So, I'll ask you again, Speilton, what is it that you know? No more secrets. If we're going to defeat Retsinis, we have to have complete trust – complete transparency."

There were a few seconds of silence, and then Speilton explained. "It was after our most recent battle in Nuquam, when I was fighting the Versipellis. I reached out and grabbed the eye, and it gave me this scar here on the back of my hand. But that wasn't the only thing it gave me. I started having these visions. They were just quick, repeating images, but then I started seeing them at night, in my dreams. I went to Liolia because I remembered something Rilly had told me long ago, and I needed to find answers. I needed to know if these visions were real or not."

"And did you find out?"

"Yes," Speilton said. "I looked into the Book of Liolia, and I saw the same visions there."

"What were the visions?"

"It was these scenes…these scenes of us all dying."

Millites was silent for a moment, then he asked. "All of us? You and me as well?"

"All of us," Speilton said. "Rilly told me they couldn't be changed, but so far I have avoided two of them – Aurum and Ince. Well, technically in the vision, Aurum never really died, just came close to it, so I guess that doesn't really count. But just then, while Metus and I were fighting the Versipellis, I saw the scene of Ince dying taking place before my eyes, but I was able to stop the Versipellis before they could go through with it."

"So, you think these visions can be avoided?"

"Maybe," Speilton said, "but I think it's more complicated than that. You see, when I saved Ince, the

Versipellis killed Metus instead. They said it was the consequence of trying to change fate."

"That's why you want to stay," Millites said. "So, you can try to stop the deaths from happening."

"The least I can do is try."

Millites nodded quietly. His eyes looked up to the horizon, and his mind appeared deep in thought. Finally, he asked, "In your vision, how do I die?"

Speilton thought for a second about whether to tell him, but they were past secrets now. "It's Retsinis. He stabs you during a duel."

"Of course," Millites almost smiled. "Well, if it's Retsinis that does me in, then at least I know I'll be safe in Liolia."

"So, you'll go?" Speilton asked.

"If we can make it work, I'll go. But I'll need a Phoenix to activate the portals."

"Aurum can help with that. At Civitas Levi there will be one she can find for us to use," Speilton explained.

"And this also relies heavily on the portals working perfectly. The Nuquamese are coming quickly after us, so if it takes me weeks or even days to return to Caelum, it may be too late."

"Then you can leave now," Speilton said. "Fly ahead of the army on Hunger, and you can probably reach Civitas Levi in just over a day. Take Aurum with you, and she can help you use the portal by tomorrow at dawn."

"Can you lead the army?" Millites asked, Hunger already showing enthusiasm at the prospect of this new adventure. Hunger's color had grown better, as it appeared that the water of Lake Vascent had allowed him to recover a great deal.

"Of course," Speilton said. "We'll fall back to Civitas Levi and wait. You just find the Liolians and bring them here. Oh and Millites, make sure they come prepared for war."

In the late evening, Millites and Aurum prepared themselves. All that day, Aurum had ridden beside her brother, Senkrad, speaking for the first time in years. But now they were separated once again. Speilton hugged Aurum goodbye, and Teews and Usus came to see them depart. Nightfall came, and the men continued, knowing that to stop meant to let the Nuquamese catch up to them. The soldiers were worn and wounded from their battle at Lake Vascent, but they carried on, forcing their feet to shuffle beneath them. Speilton and Teews rode at the front of the army while Usus took to the sky to watch the lands around them. The dark of the night was made that much bleaker by a sudden mass of thunderheads that moved down from the north, the first true storm clouds the Liolians had seen since arriving in Caelum. Flashes of lightning supplied the only moments of visibility since the clouds had choked out the light of the moon. Onward the Liolians marched in that darkness until they stumbled across a field of grain that revealed itself to be not just a single field but thousands of acres. The stalks stood over four feet in height leaving just the shoulders and heads of the men above their swaying shoots and to completely swallow the dwarves in the endless sea.

The visibility of the enemy decreased as well, as Usus saw the vast Nuquamese army enter the wheat fields in the early morning and disappear in the swaying stalks. Even with the flashes of lightning, it became nearly impossible for him to determine the location of the pursuing monsters in the grain the ebbing and flowing of the wind across the grain. So, the Liolians moved on, blind and growing sluggish as their exhaustion set in. Without the stars above to guide them, many of the Liolians began to wonder if they were even still traveling in the right direction. They had yet to find a true path leading to Civitas Levi, and instead they had been walking in what they deemed to be a general southeast direction. But Speilton was sure they were growing closer. When he closed his eyes and reached out to the land, he could feel the presence of the thousands of Phoenixes ahead. What frightened him was that when he reached out toward the Nuquamese army behind him, he could find nothing. Something shielded them from his view, and he was left just as blind as Usus high above on Flamane.

When morning came, Usus could finally detect the movement of the Nuquamese army, and what he saw terrified him. Perhaps it was merely an illusion with the stalks of grain, but it appeared that Retsinis's army had grown in size. The shadow of their army moving through the fields spread as far as Usus could see to the east and west, and now it appeared that a select group of these creatures had broken off from the core of the army and were racing ahead. In the dark of the night, this group had made up half the distance between them and the Liolians, and every moment they made that distant smaller and smaller. Usus rushed to the army to urge them on, and the men who had already walked through the night gathered a power they didn't know they had to pick up their pace. The longer they marched, the more the soft grain began to wear and whip at their skin. If it had not been for the cool gusts of air created by the storm behind them, the men would have likely collapsed from heat and exhaustion. This wind coupled with the new presence of ocean breeze from the shore they knew lay not much further ahead of them.

Just after midday, the Liolian army emerged out of the sprawling fields of grain and climbed a lush green hill to see the golden dome of Civitas Levi sparkling to the south near the shores of the sea. Many of the Liolians would've leapt with excitement if only they could find the strength within themselves to do so. They began down the other side of the hill, allowing the momentum of the slope to pull them toward the large gates. Flamane flew low over the army, and Usus called out to Speilton from his back. Usus pointed behind the Liolians, and when Speilton turned he saw that the Nuquamese had reached them. The detached unit that had been sent ahead emerged from the grain, and now with their enemies in sight, they rushed with even greater speed at the backs of the Liolians. Speilton turned to look once again at Civitas Levi, still over half a mile away. They weren't all going to be able to make it, and the few that would reach the gates would still be pursued by the Nuquamese, which meant that if the guards at the gates didn't close them in time…

Speilton realized that all this time he had been expecting Civitas Levi to be a refuge for the army, but he hadn't thought that they might not be happy to receive the army they'd sent out to defend them, especially since they had led their enemy right to their walls. Speilton turned Prowl around and called out to Teews to keep going. His sister tried to follow, but Prowl had already leapt in the air and was flying over the Liolian army.

Usus flew beside Speilton, and called out to him, "We're going to hold them off?"

"I have to," Speilton said. "But you need to lead the men onward."

"Teews is leading them. You need my help," Usus insisted as the Nuquamese came into view below.

Flamane crowed in his voice like a screech and a growl, and then dove towards the creatures. Prowl followed, and they all rushed through the air at the attacking Nuquamese. Retsinis's army was almost upon the Liolians, and out of the tall grain it was clear that only the best, most capable of the monsters had been sent. The fastest of their ranks were leaping at the last of the fleeing Liolians when Speilton and Usus summoned the ground up between them, shielding their soldiers from the claws and fangs of the Nuquamese. Prowl and Flamane tore over the heads of the Nuquamese, spinning and dipping to avoid the arrows launched up from the army and the few winged creatures in their midst. From the sky, Speilton and Usus tore up the land beneath them, tossing the army asunder and slowing their pursuit of the Liolians.

A massive gust of wind interrupted their flight, knocking Flamane so hard to the side that he was forced to land in the midst of the Nuquamese, and nearly throwing Prowl out of the air, as well. As the blue dragon righted herself, and Speilton looked down to see where Usus and his griffin had landed, he spotted two figures for the first time. Marching shoulder to shoulder in the heart of this detached unit of Nuquamese soldiers, were Ram and Retsinis. Ram had his wand pointed up at Speilton, and he had no time to brace before he and Prowl were buffeted by a surge of wind that brought them down to the ground the same as Usus. They landed not far from where Usus had taken his stand next to Flamane, fending off the Nuquamese from all around with swings of his khopesh and the shifting ground around him.

Speilton drew his Versipellis blade sword in one hand and held his other hand out as the creatures swarmed him. The first to lunge at him was struck down by Speilton's sword, as was the next that dove at the king. When one leapt at Speilton from behind, Prowl lit it up with blue flames. With a swipe of her finned tale, she took out the legs of three Nuquamese warriors before leaping on them and snatching them up in her jaws. Speilton summoned roots that climbed up the ankles of the creature rushing him, and with a haze of flashing colors he blinded a few more to let Prowl knock them down with her wings. Speilton glanced towards Usus who was still over a few dozen feet away, and then he looked back at the Nuquamese to find the two figures approaching out of the monstrous crowd. Retsinis and Ram had reached them, and Speilton could only watch as they split, with Ram marching off toward Usus and Retsinis striding triumphantly on a direct path to Speilton.

"Usus!" Speilton screamed.

"I see them," Usus called back.

The creatures stopped their attacks, deciding now to rove around the two Liolian leaders like wolves. Speilton held his sword in front of him and muttered to Prowl, "Get out of here. Take to the skies, but stay close."

"Speilton!" Usus screamed again. "I think it's time to go!"

Speilton didn't respond. His eyes were locked on Retsinis as he stepped out of the ring of creatures and held his massive sword out next to him. Usus saw that Speilton was not running, so he held his ground as well as Ram confronted him. The wind swirled around all of them and sprouting out of the tall grain behind the army, more twisters formed, tearing up the land and carrying it into the thundering clouds overhead. The sky cackled with lightning as Speilton and Usus raised their weapons.

"Young Lux," Retsinis said cordially, "I didn't expect to see you fighting again so soon."

Again, Speilton was silent. His mind raced as he watched his opponent. They didn't have all the wands, but perhaps there was another way to stop him. All he knew was that if he didn't stop Retsinis here, there would be nothing to prevent him from marching on Civitas Levi.

"I noticed you've been training," Retsinis said. "Did Cigam finally get out of his dusty old chair, or did he just let that forest spirit do all the work?"

"They both lent their aid. I learned many things from them, not just how to use these powers."

"Oh, they gave you some advice, did they? And now you think you have a chance to defeat me and my army?" Retsinis grinned and bared his fangs. "Tell me, what happens if I kill you here and now? What will all of that great knowledge amount to then?"

"You can't kill me," Speilton said. "The Versipellis won't allow it. And we all know they are the ones that really make the decisions."

Retsinis appeared unfazed by this jab. "I do not pretend to fully understand the ways of the Versipellis, but their strange customs are a small price to pay for the services they provide. I do not know yet what they want with the other two of the cursed, but it appears they are now done with you."

The look of confusion must have been evident on Speilton's face because Retsinis chuckled. "You know what that means, don't you? I can kill you now."

Retsinis stepped forward holding the large black blade in one hand as if it were weightless and swung it down at Speilton. He caught it with his own sword, and the blades hummed as Speilton pushed against the incredible strength of the Dark King. He slipped to the side as Retsinis brought his sword to the ground, and when Speilton struck again, pulled up a column of the ground beneath him launch his body into the air at Retsinis. Again, the blades clashed and Speilton landed, quickly summoning flames from one hand. Retsinis held up Ferrum Potestas, and the fire was swallowed in the dark glean of its blade. Then he angled the sword slightly, and the fire was reflected past Retsinis, over the heads of the Nuquamese, and into the edge of the fields of grain. Speilton stopped his attack, but the fields had already caught fire, and before he could reach out and snuff out the flames, Retsinis rushed him again. The Sword of Power swung over Speilton's head, and as he dodged, he sliced his sword across Retsinis's side. Retsinis appeared not to notice. Speilton slipped his shield – invisible beneath the thundering sky – onto his forearm, and when Retsinis attacked, Speilton surprised him by blocking with what appeared to be no more than his gauntlets, and then stabbed again at Retsinis's side. Realizing that Speilton had a new weapon, Retsinis struck again at Speilton's side, and the blow grinded against the shield. Speilton tried to attack again, but

Retsinis caught Speilton by his forearm with his free hand. As Speilton struggled to pull free, Retsinis hooked the guard of his sword under Speilton's shield and thrust back Speilton's arm. With his arm hyperextended, Speilton was forced to pull free of the shield or else allow his arm to be ripped from its socket. With Speilton's arm still in one hand, Retsinis raised his sword to stab Speilton through, but Speilton slipped out just as the blade drove through where he had been. Retsinis responded with a quick jab that caught Speilton just barely on the shoulder. The attack was enough to throw Speilton on his back, and if he had not summoned a quick blast of wind into Retsinis's chest, he would've been stabbed there on the ground. There was a moment of panic as Speilton reached to his shoulder, trying to feel through the chainmail and padded vest to tell if he had been cut. His heart thudded in his ears as he waited. If even the slightest bit of skin had been cut by the blade, it would be only seconds before he would become one of Retsinis's slaves. But as the moment passed, Speilton realized his armor had taken the blow entirely.

Speilton struggled to his feet and tried to regain his composure as Retsinis rushed at him again. This time, Speilton drew the roots from the grass up into a tangle at Retsinis's feet, but his boots kicked right through this as he swung again. Speilton summoned fire, but Retsinis was now holding his wand and a shield of writhing darkness absorbed it all. When Speilton raised his sword, he realized he did not have enough strength to combat Retsinis's charging attack, but he also had no time to flee. Retsinis brought the Sword of Power down like a hammer, and the Versipellis blade could do little to stop it. The strike ripped the sword from Speilton's hand

and even as he dodged, Speilton could feel the blade cut down his chest. He stumbled backwards landing hard on his back and clutching his wound. Retsinis stepped forward, his large body wreathed in a sky of smoke from the burning fields beyond. Blood had begun to spill from his wound. "No," he muttered, "No, no."

Then Speilton noticed his his sword laying a few feet away, the blade shattered in a jagged curve in the center. On the edge of one of these shards was blood; Speilton's blood. Retsinis's blade hadn't dealt the wound at all, but his own sword had. The pommel in the shape of Prowl's head stared at Speilton.

Retsinis grinned down at him. "I'm very disappointed," the King of the Nuquamese said. "I expected much more from your powers."

The blood ran over Speilton's fingers, but he laid one hand on the ground to steady himself where he lay.

"This is how it ends," Retsinis said. "One day when I have conquered many worlds, I hope you know that I will consider you one of my great enemies. You did nearly defeat me once, not too long ago, but you made a terrible mistake. You didn't kill me."

Retsinis raised his sword, and Speilton summoned flames, but the Dark King was now robed in a darkness that devoured the flames like hungry dogs.

Suddenly, the ground behind Retsinis erupted forth, stabbing up into the air in a pointed column of stone and dirt that cut upward and outward at an angle straight through Retsinis's back and out his chest. The stone stake caught Retsinis where he stood, and he let out a terrible roar as he clawed at the spike running through him. Speilton turned and saw Usus standing only a few feet away, his wand still held out before him and his eyes wide. Before either he or Speilton could say a word, a gust of wind knocked Usus from his feet, throwing him through the air. He eventually crashed hard on the ground at the feet of the Nuquamese buzzing around them.

Ram walked toward Usus, his pale white sword ready in his hand, but Retsinis screamed at him, "Imperium! Come here! Deal with this one first."

Retsinis struggled to break off the stone that held him in place as Ram walked over blankly. The stone spike finally shattered, causing Retsinis to stumble forward with the large chunk of stone still running through his chest. It had not killed him, but the savage look on his face showed that he was in a great deal of pain. Speilton knew the pain wouldn't last long.

"I had hoped to kill you myself," Retsinis said with a regained grin despite actively pushing the stone through his body so that it could fall loose, "but I think this will be quite ironic for your former mentor to be the one to do you in. Besides, I always have your brother to kill."

Ram walked toward Speilton, holding the sword in two hands as if it were an executioner's axe. It still looked very much like the man Speilton had befriended all those years ago, but the blankness in the eyes showed that it was clearly no longer Ram.

"Don't do this," Speilton said. "Ram! Look at me! It's me! It's Speilton!"

Ram continued forward, finally stopping at Speilton's feet.

"You know me! It's Speilton! You don't have to do this!" Speilton screamed. "I know you're in there! I know it can be broken!"

Ram raised his sword, blade down, and Speilton stared up at the sharp point looming above his head. "Ram don't! You don't have to be his slave! You can break free of this!"

The blade came down at Speilton, but Speilton raised his hands and summoned wind that directed the blade into the ground beside him. Before Ram could pull it out again, Speilton kicked Ram in the wrist, freeing his grip on the handle. Ram rushed at Speilton in a sudden fury, but Speilton pulled the blade from the ground and held it out before him. "Ram, look at this sword! You know this sword. You remember when we first found it, not long after the two of us met. It was the blade of one of your old friends who died fighting the Calorians in the Icelands. Ram, you remember Spirit!"

Ram hesitated a moment, and his snarling face appeared to ease. Then the blank expression appeared again, and he dove at Speilton. Though he had the opportunity, Speilton did not strike him, and instead endured the hit and fell back to the ground. They struggled as Ram reached for the sword, and Speilton fought to keep his grip on it. Speilton grabbed one of Ram's moss-covered hands and pried it off of his own. He suddenly noticed something upon it. "Ram look! Your ring! Your brother gave you this ring!"

With some unknown strength Speilton forced the hand in front of Ram's face, and though he fought at first, his gaze finally fell upon the ring on his finger. "That's the Imperium family ring," Speilton said. "Your brother gave it to you before he died. You must remember!"

But Ram had begun to struggle again.

Speilton felt his grip lessening as Spirit was ripped from his hand. Ram sprang to his feet and glared down at Speilton. He raised the blade again, and this time the king knew he would not miss. "Ram," Speilton said, almost in a whisper. "It's Speilton. It's you friend. You promised...you promised me, you would fight alongside me...until the end."

Ram didn't bring the sword down. He stopped for a moment, and his blank eyes suddenly looked up at his own hands held high in the air, either at the ring or the sword or both. A horrible growl came from his mouth as Ram stumbled backwards a step. One of his hands released from the hilt of his sword and gripped the side of his head. When he roared again, it sounded nearly human. Speilton sat up suddenly as Ram shook his head wildly and shut his eyes tight as if enduring some incredible pain. The green and black material that covered his skin began to fall from him and the winds picked up into a terrible vortex, laced with the ash and sparks of the fire still burning in the field of grain.

Retsinis had freed himself of the weight of the stone, and already the hole through his chest was healing. The King of the Nuquamese approached his commander with a perplexed look on his face. "What are you doing? I commanded you to kill him!"

Ram's struggle suddenly stopped, and his blank eyes flickered open again, staring down at the grass before him. There was silence as Retsinis and Speilton both watched, and then Ram swung his blade upwards and to his side, arcing through the air and straight through Retsinis's neck. The jaws of the Dark King opened wide as he tried to say something, but then the milky eyes rolled up into the black skull, and the head slid off of the body, plopping to the ground at Ram's feet.

All around them, the Nuquamese began to howl, they leapt in fury and roared at the man who just decapitated their King. Ram did not appear afraid. In fact, for the first time in quite a long time, he appeared himself.

Ram dropped his sword and rushed to Speilton. "Speilton," he said, the moss still falling from his skin, "What have I done?"

"You broke free," Speilton said. "You defeated the dark magic of Ferrum Potestas."

"Are you wounded? Oh no, oh no, what have I done? I remember it all, just barely, as if it were a dream. I hurt so many people."

"That wasn't you. What you did under that sword's spell is not your fault. All that matters is that you're back now."

"You did it, Speilton," Ram said. "For so long I've been trapped like that. And all the things I did…I…I saw it all, and yet I couldn't stop myself."

"You killed Retsinis."

"No, I don't think so," Ram said. "No blade can kill him. He will return."

The creatures were creeping closer now, frothing at the mouth and wailing. Ram stood up quickly and ran to where Usus lay unconscious, using his wand to hold back the creatures trying to surround the Second-in-Command. He dragged Usus beside Speilton, and then retrieved the broken remains of Speilton's sword. "Do you think you can fight?" he asked Speilton.

Speilton rose to his feet, but as he did so his vision blurred, and chest ached. Blood ran down the front of his chainmail, and he would've collapsed if Ram hadn't caught him. "Give me just a moment," Speilton stammered. "I think I can if—"

"Speilton," Ram said, a look of determination set on his face. "Call Prowl. You need to leave."

"Ram," Speilton said, now standing on his own, "what about you?"

Ram smiled at him warmly. "The Liolians need you. There will be another battle before this is over, and you must lead them."

"We need you, too," Speilton said.

"They don't need me," Ram said with a slight laugh. "I'm just an old man, way past my day. At least now, I won't be an enemy."

The first of the Nuquamese leapt at them, and Ram blew them backwards with wind. Speilton shouted to Prowl, and the blue dragon dove out of the sky towards them. When she landed, Ram brought the winds circling around them, tossing the Nuquamese wildly as they tried to charge them. Twisters dropped down from the sky, lifting the creatures in their vortexes. Lightning splintered across the sky as the thunderclouds roared. The fire was growing across the fields, and not even the winds could snuff it out, but the smoke it produced had mixed with Ram's storm, choking the sky over the heads of the Nuquamese army.

Ram lifted Usus onto Prowl's back, then hugged Speilton. "I wish we had more time."

"Come with us," Speilton said, and as the words came out of his mouth, he saw a shape stepping through the cyclone of wind to approach behind Ram.

Speilton began to scream, but the looming figure of Retsinis had already reached Ram, and as the man turned, a blade was stabbed through his body. Retsinis stood behind him, his head reformed upon his body, holding not his own sword but Ram's pale sword. Ram turned, and releasing a cry of rage and pain, he summoned a blast of wind so large and sudden it sounded as if the ground beneath them had been split open. Retsinis was launched backwards, disappearing into the swirling air and dust and smoke, and Ram fell forward. Speilton pulled the blade from his back and caught Ram as he fell forward. In his hand, the former Liolian general still clutched his wand.

"It appears, this is where my journey ends," Ram said, his eyes growing unfocused. "But yours is just beginning."

"Ram," Speilton said, tears falling from his eyes. "I'm sorry. I'm sorry I wanted to—"

"Shhh," Ram shushed him. "It's okay. I knew my time was coming soon. Maybe…maybe I have at least given you time…time to prepare."

"I need your help," Speilton said. "I can't defeat him on my own."

"You made it this far on your own. I know you can win this war as well. Besides, I think it's time I begin a new adventure," Ram said with a smile.

He reached up and placed a hand against Speilton's cheek, and then his eyes drifted over to Prowl's sad eyes above him. Ram nodded his head slightly, and Prowl understood. The blue dragon pumped her wings and began to rise into the swirling wind. Ram dropped his hand and clasped Speilton's for a moment. When it went limp and fell from his grasp, all that was left was Ram's wand in Speilton's hand. Prowl reached down and grabbed the back of Speilton's chainmail in her jaws, lifting him onto her back beside Usus. Speilton was crying as he looked down at Ram as Prowl rose up in the eye of the cyclone around them. The winds began to calm, and the blue dragon flew off through the clouds towards the golden city beside the ocean. Speilton lay upon her back, his eyes blinded by tears, clutching Ram's sword in one hand and his wand in the other.

FINAL PREPARATIONS
~ 23 ~

"The enemy marches upon us as we speak," Speilton said. "My men are tired and battle worn. They have lost friends and family, fighting a war to protect you and your land, and yet you still say you will not help them?"

Círsar peered down at Speilton with eyes that danced between the different elements, and then he observed the other Liolians standing alongside the king. Usus was at Speilton's right, and to his left stood Herdica. Aurum had been waiting at Civitas Levi for the rest of the army to arrive, and as a former hand to the Order, she joined them as well in Círsar's chambers. While the Liolian soldiers slept, these four forced their way into the chambers of the Order.

"We have given you our answer," the Phoenix said. "This is not our war, and we will not betray our oath to preserve the peace."

"And yet the war is occurring on your land, in the city of your people," Aurum said. "This war has been forced upon the Liolians solely because they have nowhere else to flee."

"Can't you see," Usus questioned, "that sometimes preserving the peace requires you to take action to defend your people?"

"That is your way, not ours," the Phoenix said.

"That is the way of all things. Pretending evil does not exist will not bring about peace. Only challenging it and snuffing it out can do that," Speilton said.

"Tell us," the Phoenix said. "What has happened to that faun that served us? I believe his name was Metus."

"You know what happened to him," Speilton spat. "I'm sure your scouts have told you."

"So the faun is dead?"

"You have no right to talk about him!" Teews said, furious.

"Actually, I believe we have every right," Cirsar said. "You see, if the faun had only followed our instructions and stayed loyal to us, he would not have been on the battlefield to die. Yet, it was you, Queen Teews, who convinced him to run off and join your war effort. And it was while protecting you, King Speilton, that the faun was killed. We, on the other hand, meant only to protect him."

Speilton and Teews stared up at the Head Consul with fury in their eyes, but they understood that what Cirsar said was true.

"That's unfair," Usus interjected. "No, I'm sorry, but you do not get to wipe your little bird feet clean of Metus' death. His death was just as much the Order's fault as anyone else here. Metus joined the army because he was brave and couldn't stand by while others died protecting him, which is far more than I can say about the lot of you."

"Your warring ways brought about the faun's death. It may be unfortunate for you to admit, but he was safer here than with you."

"I disagree wholeheartedly," Teews said. "Metus died beside those who cared about him. He knew the risk, and we all did our best to make sure everyone got out alive, but that's not the nature of war. He trusted us more than he would ever trust you. And I don't blame him. You're all just hypocrites, claiming to stand for peace but doing nothing to achieve it."

"And how did his trust in you turn out for him? How did it turn out for your strategist, or the Isoalate Hopi? And how did it turn out for your friend Ram?"

"You speak a lot about matters you don't understand," Speilton said. "And you are quick to criticize our methods of combating evil, yet you have not answered the simplest question. What do you intend to do if the Liolians fail? What happens if our army is defeated, and there is no longer anyone to protect you? You expect to talk Retsinis and the Versipellis out of killing every last one of you?"

"He knows that will not work," Herdica said with a scowl. "They know as well as we do that any attempts to reason with Retsinis and his men will only end with their heads on spikes."

"Our army is here to protect your men, and you don't have the decency to give us aid," Usus spat.

"Don't feign selflessness," the Phoenix said. "We know your true intentions. You only hope to save this land so that you can bring the rest of your Liolians here. You want this land for yourselves. So, don't claim to be fighting for us when it is only yourselves that you serve."

"You know that is not true," Speilton said.

"Then change our minds," Círsar said.

"We intend to," Usus said. "When our seven hundred men march out against an army of twelve thousand, I hope you will see that we don't fight only for ourselves."

Círsar arched his neck and turned away, apparently finished with the conversation. "Good luck," he muttered as all around the room and the large tree within faded into darkness. "I do hope you are all successful in the battle to come."

The four left the tunnel and walked back across the rolling hills to Civitas Levi. The lights of Civitas Levi glowed dully in that early morning darkness. Up on the hills to the north there was a haze of smoke and the distant churning of fire as the grain continued to burn, but there was no sign of the Nuquamese army. The scouts that the Liolians had sent out to inspect came back believing that they were waiting for the rest of Retsinis's forces to come down from the mountains. Senkrad agreed that after failing to destroy the Liolians after so many attempts, Retsinis would not refrain from sending everything he had. Now, the Liolians could only wait, slumbering in their shoddily built camps outside of the city. At first, the guards had opened the doors to Civitas Levi, but once it was clear that the Nuquamese were no longer pursuing them, they sent them back outside the walls. The warriors didn't mind, for the walls of the city felt more like a cage, and at least outside they could see their enemy whenever they decided to approach.

Speilton entered his tent, and Aurum, Usus, and Herdica followed. Inside the dim canvas walls, Speilton leaned against a table to stabilize himself, and Usus collapsed into a pile of furs in the corner. Aurum and Herdica watched them as they struggled to stay awake. Then Senkrad pushed into the tent, followed by Ince.

"Retsinis should be ready to attack any moment now," Senkrad said.

Speilton backed away from the table and fell into a chair, his head slumped forward as sleep threatened to take him.

"Speilton," Ince said, "should we begin to gather the troops? We don't want to be taken by surprise."

"We don't really want to fight at all," Usus muttered, his eyes closed, "and I don't think it will matter much whether our men are in formation or not when that army marches against us."

Teews pushed into the room as well, and seeing her brother and Usus sitting half asleep, she slammed her fist on the table. They both sat up slightly.

"Look here," she commanded. "None of us have had time to sleep these past days. The rest of your men may have been able to grab a few hours of rest, but they're not the ones tasked with leading this army."

"We can't fight if we haven't slept," Usus muttered, but Speilton made a point of standing more surely on his feet.

"Someone, go find Ore," he said, and Ince nodded and rushed out of the room.

"What is our plan?" Herdica asked, approaching her children. "We cannot hope to handle the Nuquamese without a plan."

"There was a plan," Speilton said, "but there isn't one anymore. We can only defeat Retsinis using all twelve elements, and so far we have only seven, counting myself. We needed the other Liolians to complete the twelve, but after Onaclov went down in Lake Vascent we lost the Wand of Lava, which means our plan can't work."

"Unless you take Retsinis's Wand of Darkness," Aurum said.

"And that in itself will be just as hard as killing him," Speilton said. "The point is, we can't win unless we kill Retsinis."

"But Retsinis may not even fight," Senkrad said. "You said Ram wounded him before he…"

"Yes, but he healed quickly from that. His wounds will not encumber him," Speilton said. "But you're right. He may not even fight. He may just let his army deal with us, since I'm sure they're capable of killing us all themselves."

"So, we want Retsinis to fight?" Usus asked.

"Yes," Speilton said, "or we would if we had all the wands. But without them, he is a terrible threat because each person he cuts down with that sword will rise again to join his ranks."

Ince walked into the room with Ore behind him. The dwarf's face was set like chiseled stone, but Speilton knew it was a rigid façade to conceal his sorrow at the loss of his leader and friend in the waters of Lake Vascent.

"Ore, come here," Speilton said.

He held out the twisted wand that had once been Ram's and placed it in Ore's hand. "You're the wielder of wind now," Speilton said. "You might want to train with that a little bit before the war horns blow."

"Yes, my king. Thank you," Ore said with a slight bow.

"We need as many wands as we can possibly find," Speilton said. "They're our only hope of protecting our men."

"Have we considered all of our alternative options?" Senkrad asked. "Is there no chance to escape?"

"There are lands across the sea," Aurum said, "or so they say. But the Phoenixes have built no boats with which to reach them."

"We could fall back to another of the Phoenix cities," Herdica said, "but it would only be delaying the inevitable."

"No, we make our stand here," Speilton said. "We have fled from Retsinis for years. We will not run again."

"I know this sounds naïve," Ince said after a short silence, "but are we sure there is no possibility to reason with them? Is there no hope of any sort of agreement between our people?"

"There is no reasoning with Retsinis," Senkrad said. "This is not a war over land in which some treaty can be arranged. He desires power and domination. He will not settle for anything less than the destruction or enslavement of all the Liolians, and he knows it is easily within his reach now."

"But we must still have some strategy," Teews said. "We have just over seven hundred men, including one hundred mounted knights. There must be some way we can use our numbers and the landscape to our advantage."

"You've seen the landscape," Speilton said. "It's just rolling hills for miles around, and a small creek to the west."

"And the Phoenixes made it clear we are not to fight within the city walls. We must hold the line out here," Usus said.

"That's fine," Senkrad shrugged. "The city is not built for a siege anyway. There's no way to protect Civitas Levi from within. We must put all the children and elderly within the city, and direct Retsinis's troops away from it."

305

"They will be safe in the tunnels," Aurum said. "They run deep beneath the city. It's a good place to hide."

Speilton turned to his mother, "Can you take the civilians down into the tunnels. Barricade them there."

"And do what? Wait for the rest of you to die so that they can come and find us there?" Herdica gave a wise smile. "The civilians in Civitas Levi may not have the training to fight out here on the fields, but they have just as much willingness to protect their people. I think we should take them to the roofs carrying all sorts of supplies with them. Then, if the Nuquamese make it into the city, they can rain fire down upon them."

Teews smiled admiringly at her mother, and Speilton nodded. "Teews, go with her to help."

"No," Teews said outright. "I'll be fighting on the frontlines with you."

"As will I," Aurum said, looking at Teews. "We are the masters of our elements, and the wands are a waste far from the battlefield."

Speilton was hesitant, but he nodded to them as well. Usus resituated himself on the pile of furs. "Well," he said, "it looks like we're all going to die together."

Teews smiled only slightly, trying to conceal her feeling of triumph.

"There is one other alternative that is worth consideration at the very least," Herdica said. "The portal to Liolia lies in the hills not far from here. At sunrise, the Liolians could flee."

"And do what?" Speilton asked. "Hide out in Liolia, waiting for Retsinis to destroy Civitas Levi? If we left, he would only follow us back into Liolia and finish his work."

"It would give you time to regroup," Aurum said.

"There is no regrouping," Speilton said. "This is all we have. Liolia has reached its end, and only death waits for us there. But this land, Caelum, is our last hope at peace. Plus, not everyone is able to leave Caelum."

Aurum nodded with a somber smile.

"So we fight," Senkrad said. "No more retreating."

"We should put all of the wielders of the elements at the front of the army. That way, we can protect the men from any arrows or projectiles they throw at us," Ince offered.

"Ore," Speilton said. "You must lead the dwarves and Isoalates. Ince can go with you. Take our left flank. Senkrad, you will be on the right."

"I'll go with him," Aurum said, looking up at her brother.

"And Teews and Usus, you will be with me in the center. Now Senkrad, have your cavalry positioned to your right, and I'll have the Milwarian cavalry situated on the far left end. When we engage with their army, we can send them across, attacking from the sides of the Nuquamese until they join in the center. If the infantry is able to hold their attention long enough, we may be able to surprise them."

"Even if it works," Usus said, "it will only take out a fraction of their men."

"It's better than no plan," Teews said.

The tent flap was thrown open and a young boy entered, his face ashen. Behind him, there was the dim glow of dawn on the horizon. "My King. My Queen," the page said with short bows. "It appears that the Nuquamese are rallying their army."

"Looks like it's time," Usus said.

"Everyone knows their tasks," Speilton said. "Assemble the men."

Ore and Ince rushed out of the tent, followed quickly by Senkrad. Teews began to walk out of the room, but turned back to Speilton and said, "Don't worry, I'll be careful."

Speilton smiled and said, "It's the Nuquamese that need to worry."

Herdica took Speilton's hand and looked him in the eyes. "You are so much like your father. Brave. Persistent. Dedicated," she said. "He would be proud."

"I hope so," Speilton responded as his mother followed Teews out of the room.

Aurum ran to Speilton and hugged him, releasing him after a moment and saying, "I'll take good care of your wand. Make sure to take care of yourself." Then she left the room as well.

As the war horns blew outside, Usus rose up from his pile in the corner. "I guess this is it," Usus said.

Speilton turned to him, his body feeling weak as he thought about what was to come. "This has to be it. All of this has gone on too long. There have been so many battles I thought would be the end, but now I know for sure. This *will* be the last."

"The end of the War for Caelum," Usus proclaimed with fake gravitas. "The last battle of Liolia."

Speilton almost laughed in bewilderment at the thought that very soon, one way or another, there would be no more fighting. "We've already lost so many people. I can't even count them all over the years. I never thought we'd lose Metus, or Onaclov for that matter. And Ram…"

"It hasn't been easy," Usus agreed. "Too many have been sacrificed, and I'm sure more will be required before it's all through." There was silence as the two considered the gravity of the moment. "But something tells me we just might be able to pull this off," Usus said with a grin. "You can call me insane, but I just have this feeling."

Usus walked to the flap of the tent and called back over his shoulder, "We can talk more after the battle," before stepping out into the bustle of the army.

As the dark outline of the Nuquamese grew atop the hills to the north, the Liolian army assembled in the fields outside of Civitas Levi. The sky had turned a hazy red from the mixture of the approaching dawn and the smoke and flames from the scorched grain that lay behind the Nuquamese. In the cool of the morning, the Liolians waited for their enemy to reveal itself in its entirety. The expanse between the two forces seemed nearly infinite, yet as the black outline of the Nuquamese grew larger and larger on the horizon, stretching as far as could be seen to the east and the west, the Liolians wished only for more distance between them.

The Liolians had abandoned their campsite and armed themselves with every weapon and bit of armor they could find. They were situated between the towering golden frame of Civitas Levi to their right and rolling hills of pastel flowers to their left. Three armies stood side-by-side with their foot-soldiers in the front and the archers behind, and situated outside of them to their left and right flanks were the mounted knights. At the front of the Igniacan fighters was Ore, covered almost entirely in the thick, metal-plated armor of the dwarves, and in his hand he held his war hammer which he had already taken the liberty of combining with his wand.

Now, as he waved the hammer in the air, a gale picked up around him as if the heavy metal were large enough to bend the heavens. Ince stood beside him, garbed in a vest of vibrant beads that the Isoalates had given to him, saying that they possessed incredible strength and flexibility. When Ince used his wand, the colors jumped alive, giving off the illusion that he was in many places at once. To their right were the Milwarian soldiers, holding high the lion banners of their country and their kings. Teews had put on a thick leather tunic and her hair was tied back in the elaborate braid Herdica had shown her. She clutched a spear in one hand and her wand in the other. Next were the Calorians, with their own black banners held high, and at their front was Senkrad. The great hulking Wodahs had on only a light leather vest and the white pelt that matched the color of his hair. In one hand he held his massive glaive with its curved blade situated atop a long wooden pole, and already the grass was becoming frosted as he clutched his wand. Beside him was his sister, wearing a golden dress that had been cut just above the knee, and a breastplate of the same golden color. She held only her wand, but there were two daggers at her waist.

High above them all, Speilton and Usus rode upon their winged creatures. Prowl had just eaten and soared through the sky at her full size, her wings reaching out over twenty yards wide. She roared as she and Flamane circled around each other, and their riders watched the growing numbers of their enemy. Usus had found some discarded pale metal plate armor and a smooth helmet that covered the sides of his face and his nose. Over the armor, he had thrown a tartan tunic with cloth that billowed in the air as he flew on the back of his griffin. Speilton put his padded vest over his chainmail

310

tunic, and had strapped to his belt both the shattered blade of the Versipellis and Ram's sword, Spirit. His shield was lost somewhere far below, and with the sky hazy and not yet lit by the rays of the sun, it remained invisible.

Speilton and Usus watched silently as more and more Nuquamese mounted the horizon, crawling out of the ash of the still-burning grain and joining the thousands of others. Storm crowds thundered above them, rippling with white lighting as if the sky itself was snarling. Before they had assumed the storm that appeared to follow Retsinis's army was merely a creation of Ram's power over the wind, yet even after his passing they remained. It appeared that as evil marched above the pure land of the Phoenixes, the natural darknesses were introduced to the land as well. Beneath the storm clouds something else appeared, drifting out of the smoke-filled sky and growing closer every second. It appeared like a great black fog, rolling across the land and plunging everything below in darkness. Speilton knew exactly what it was.

The flock of Daerds and the Phoenixes of Darkness crept closer, rising and swirling through the air like a manifestation of night. It was this force of thousands that the Nuquamese had been waiting for, and now that they had made their way down from the Fangmaw Mountains of the north, Retsinis would be able to attack in full force. "This is it," Speilton called back to where he thought Usus was flying, but when he turned there was no one there.

He spun around, searching through the air for the golden shape of the griffin and its rider, and then he spotted them, far off to the west, with something black pursuing him. Just as Speilton recognized what it was, Prowl let out a roar and pitched to the side. Speilton was thrown through the air, and as he fell he looked back up to see the second Versipellis, latched onto Prowl in the shape of some large black serpent. Blue flames erupted from Prowl's mouth and ignited the serpent, but the Versipellis merely released and retook its cloaked form.

Speilton plummeted through the sky, realizing with terror that Prowl was too far away to catch him in time. He flipped himself face down as he fell, watching the green grass rapidly approaching him below, and he summoned a gust of wind up from the ground. His speed slowed, but he was still falling, until he suddenly reached the ground with a thud that rattled his bones. For a moment, he could only lie there, and then slowly he stretched out his body and rolled onto his back. The sky above was a soft red, and when he sat up he saw that the sun was just rising over the hills to the east, shining through the multicolored panes of Civitas Levi.

He had landed a few hundred yards in front of the Liolian army, and as Speilton rose to his feet, he heard the terrible roar of the Nuquamese on the hills not far from him now. The great black flock of terrible birds rolled over the heads of the creatures, and as it smothered the sky above Speilton, the Nuquamese roared and charged. The vast army poured down the sides of the hills, covering them in a black tidal wave that consumed everything in its path. Thousands of terrible voices screamed, howled, and bellowed as they raced forward, drawing ever closer as Speilton watched.

Speilton took a deep breath and stared at his enemy spread out infinitely before him. His hand reached down for his wand, but he found Ram's sword instead. He drew Spirit and clutched the broadsword with both hands as his eyes made out the faces of the first of the Nuquamese rushing wildly through the tall grass directly at him. Setting his feet, Speilton summoned flames that spread up his arms and wreathed him in an aura of fire. Then he waited as the Nuquamese grew closer, five hundred yards away, four hundred yards, three hundred, two.

Over the roaring of the Nuquamese, a low rumbling sound came from the hills to the west. Speilton's ears picked up at the sound, but he didn't pay it any mind, until, suddenly, the Nuquamese army slowed their charge, their attention directed off toward the hills. And then they stopped. Their heads were turned to the sound of the rumbling, so Speilton looked as well. Without the roar of the Nuquamese, the sound could be heard much better, and Speilton knew it to be the sound of war horns.

Then a proud creature climbed to the top of the closest hill to the west and rose up on hind legs and let out a terrible shriek that pierced across the land. It was Hunger's shriek, and as the dragon spread out its wings and trumpeted a stream of red-hot flames into the air, a dozen other shapes appeared beside him, and then dozens more, and then it was hundreds. With the golden rays of the sun breaking over the hills and shining on them from the east, the shapes of hundreds of Liolians were emblazoned amongst the hills of flowers where Speilton knew the portal between Liolia and Caelum lay.

On Hunger's back, Millites led the new Liolians down the hill toward Teews, Ore, and Senkrad in front of the Liolians already in formation. Speilton could see centaurs and fauns and satyrs racing on their hooved feet alongside the swift and nimble elves. The mers shuffled across the land on their slippery fins and shimmering into and out of their form were dryads and naiads. Looming over all of them were giants and treeps with massive clubs and hammers in their hands.

Prowl thudded to the ground beside Speilton, and he leapt on her back. Usus had already landed beside Teews at the front of the army and was welcoming the Liolians as they arrived. It appeared the Versipellis had fallen back, as well.

Hunger was a bright golden yellow when Speilton reached them. Millites had already leapt down and hugged Usus and Teews, and then Speilton slipped from Prowl's back and embraced him as well. "Four thousand Liolian warriors," Millites announced. "And thousands more women and children and elderly."

"We must send the civilians inside. Have them find Herdica," Speilton said to a soldier standing close by.

"Equus did exactly as you requested," Millites said. "He found all of the surviving Liolians. Speilton, he found the other wands. All of them."

As Millites spoke, the leaders of the different Milwarian Kingdoms approached them. Equus was at their head with the elemental Wand of Sand in his hand and two scimitars sheathed on his back. Beside him, Speilton identified Whinn, the leader of the mers, who held the Wand of Water. Next to him was a new face, a woman with pale, smooth skin and silvery hair despite her young complexion. From her elegance and artfully crafted armor, Speilton could tell she was an elf, but before he could ask anything further she said, "My name is Cindariel, daughter of Arbustum," and held out the Wand of Vegetation.

"That only leaves one wand," Teews said.

~ *The War for Caelum* ~

There was a thundering sound from the sea far behind them, and the soldiers spun around to see the water roiling near the shore not far away. As they watched, enormous green tentacles erupted from the thrashing waves and crashed down into the beach, pulling forth the scaly abdomen of Cetus. The creature opened its massive jaws and roared, revealing the dark shape of someone situated in its mouth. This figure crawled down from the maw of the sea monster and stood high and proud on its shoulder. Then the figure threw out a stream of lava that crashed down onto the beach far below as if to proclaim who he was from such a distance.

"Onaclov?" Millites whispered in amazement.

"There is your final wand," Speilton declared, turning back to face the Nuquamese.

Their enemy stood still halfway across the plain, and as the sea monster roared, they began to shift uncomfortably. They still didn't show fear, but seemed more to be confused. Speilton knew that if they appeared confused, it was because Retsinis was confused. The moment would pass, and it would only be a matter of time before Retsinis adapted his strategy to combat this new army. But that time would be enough for the Liolians to prepare as well.

Ore and Ince had run over from the head of their troops, as had Senkrad and Aurum. With all eleven of the wand wielders present Speilton said, "Our only chance of defeating this army is to kill Retsinis, but doing so will require all of us. All twelve elements must be directed at Retsinis at once to break the magic of Ferrum Potestas that makes him invulnerable. Everyone must protect themselves and ensure that no matter what, a

Liolian possesses the wands. If anyone sees Retsinis, they must send some kind of signal, and everyone else must make it their mission to reach him. But try not to engage him in combat. We must be quick, and someone must go and tell Onaclov the plan. Does everyone understand?"

The others all said they did, and Speilton smiled.

"We end this today," Millites said.

"Equus, have the centaurs join the cavalry on the right flank," Speilton said. "When the Nuquamese attack, strike them from the side and send them running to the southwest. Cetus can deal with them from there."

The centaur nodded and raced away, his centaurs following after him.

"And have the elves fall back behind our troops to serve as archers," Millites commanded, and Cindariel bowed and raced away on spry legs.

"Whinn, take the mers and the naiads to the left flank near the stream," Teews added.

"Yes, my queen," he bowed as he too ran off.

Speilton turned now to Millites. "Do you want to lead the creatures of the forest?"

"I'll lead all of them and the giants since they are without a leader," Millites said. "The giants and treeps need to be up front to drive a path through the Nuquamese, so we'll form ranks alongside the soldiers of Kon Malopy."

Speilton nodded as Millites ran to gather his troops. Then, bounding down the hill across the plains, Speilton saw a blazing orange creature. When he recognized who it was, the creature was already upon him, nestling his massive furry head against his chest. Speilton ran his hands through Burn's fiery mane, and the massive tiger purred. Prowl ran up behind Speilton and tackled the tiger from the side, growling excitedly as the old friends reunited.

There was a distant howl as the Nuquamese moved forward, picking up speed until they were in a full sprint. High above, the Daerds and Dark Phoenixes dropped low over the battlefield, shifting their flock down to blight out the rising sun on the horizon. The land was thrown into shadow, and the Wodahs skin turned the black shade of night with only their ruby eyes glowing.

Speilton held Ram's sword in his hand and at his side Burn looked and recognized it. A moment of sorrow crossed the tiger's face, and then it snarled, extending its claws and arching its back as it faced the approaching ocean of Nuquamese. Prowl stood at Speilton's other side, her wings poised high in the air with her teeth bared. Teews stood beside Prowl, wrapped in a purple veil of her magic, and Usus sat upon Flamane's back beside Burn. Millites stood at the head of a group of fauns, satyrs, dryads, treeps, and giants, who bellowed back at the Nuquamese. And further to their left and right were the other leaders of every kingdom of Milwaria and Caloria, kingdoms that had never been united in battle before this day.

Senkrad raised his glaive in the air and shouted to his Wodahs, "For Liolia!"

Millites turned with his sword blazing like a bolt of lightning and yelled, "For Liolia!"

Speilton held Spirit high in the air and looked back at the courageous faces behind him.

"For Liolia!"

THE LAST BATTLE
~ 24 ~

The ground trembled beneath their feet as the nearly five thousand Liolians charged through the bright green grass at the army of twelve thousand. Speilton ran on foot, and soon the tiger on his left and his dragon on his right had passed him and were hurtling toward the Nuquamese. Such adrenaline coursed through his veins at the sound of thousands of stomping feet and the voices of every Liolian warrior that the ground before Speilton began to catch on fire and tremble. Teews ran at his side, the pink and purple haze of her element of love forming into the shape of a galloping horse with long flowing mane. Flamane had risen into the air and in place of Usus on the ground was a massive wolf composed of soil and stone that he had animated with his wand. Hunger flew above Millites, blowing balls of flame into the air as if in warning, while Millites lowered his blinding sword at the Nuquamese conjuring a ray of light that tore a corridor through their army dozens of creatures deep. The space between the two armies grew smaller and smaller until the Liolians could see the grotesque faces of the vicious Nuquamese. And then, in a thunderclap that appeared to split Caelum in half, the two sides clashed.

A burst of flames from Aurum's wand blew back the Nuquamese as Usus's stone wolf crashed through the multitudes and snatched them up in its jaws. The ground erupted before Cindariel in a mess of roots that lashed around ten or so Nuquamese, and then Senkrad blasted them with a coat of ice that trapped them in place.

Whinn rushed in a tidal wave that crashed upon the heads of the creatures, and Teews stabbed with her spear, striking one creature and allowing the phantom steed that had enveloped her to continue charging through the Nuquamese, sedating any creature in its way. When Ore swung his great hammer, the winds rushed with it, knocking aside five or six creatures with every swing, as the dwarf roared with glee. When a volley of arrows was launched from some group of archers within the Nuquamese force, Millites summoned a dome of light over the men, and the shafts snapped against it. A prism of dazzling colors blinded the Nuquamese, as Ince dove in and out, striking them with his spear while they lashed out recklessly around him. The giants and treeps marched forward, swinging massive clubs or their own limbs back and forth like scythes as they waded through the monsters. The warriors of Kon Malopy and the Wodahs of Caloria fought the various creatures under Retsinis's command with nothing more than their courage and their swords, shields, spears, halberds, or bows. Behind the charging infantry, the elves fired volley after volley of arrows that rained down upon the Nuquamese. Across the battlefield, there was the sound of thousands of hooves proclaiming the charge of the centaurs and the rest of the Liolian cavalry that drove into the Nuquamese from the sides, striking them down or trampling them as they carved their way through the army. Centaurs, horses, and hakesorsees ran side by side, led by Equus and the two massive blades of sand he had conjured before him to cut down the Nuquamese before they even reached his hooves. Soon, the creatures realized they were sitting in the path of the cavalry charge, and they began to flee to the west, running parallel to the Liolian line. Instead of emerging outside of the conflict, they ran into the stream, where the mers and naiads lay waiting in the shallow current to drive them back. This time, before the Nuquamese could flee again, some force appeared to take command on their movements, pushing them back against the Liolians. It appeared that Retsinis had retaken control over his soldiers by the magic of his sword, tearing them out of their momentary cowardice.

In the center of it all was Speilton, wielding every element at his disposal to cut through Retsinis's army. Flames leapt from the palms of his hands, and the grass snapped like whips around the creatures that crept near him. As he swung Spirit, the ground quaked and split, and the wind buffeted the creatures nearest him. Only minutes before he had been on the verge of sleep, but now all of Caelum moved at his command. Burn pounced upon creatures beside Speilton, dodging in and out of Speilton's magic on nimble feline legs. Prowl fought on the other side, rising up on her webbed wings only to crash down upon the creatures, thrashing her tail and spitting blue flames. Those that slipped past those attacks only fell prey to her gnashing teeth and claws.

High above, there was the clatter of hundreds of cackling birds, and the shadow thrown across the land deepened. The men looked up to see that the Daerds were descending upon them as if the great cloud they had inhabited had suddenly burst. Hundreds of the massive birds dove into the army, raking their claws through the soldiers as they flew through them, or grabbing them and dragging them up into the sky. The elves raised their bows and sent their arrows up into the flock, and though many of the creatures fell, it appeared to make no difference in the winged mass. Spread out amongst the Daerds were the Phoenixes of Darkness, who looked more like black wriggling smears than actual birds as they dashed through the sky in their elemental forms. When they descended upon the Liolians, they merely rushed through the warriors as darkness itself. This vile material was not fatal, but it clawed and bit at everything that came near it, causing the Liolians to fall to the ground and writhe in agony. On Flamane, Usus had risen to fight the birds from the sky, but their huge numbers proved too great for him to fight by himself, and he dropped down to avoid their attention.

Millites gave the command, and the Liolian army shifted, falling back on the left flank to form a sort of curved line shielding the western gate into Civitas Levi. With the mers and spirits of the water attacking from the stream, the Nuquamese army was forced south, approaching the beach and falling into the range of Cetus's thrashing tentacles. The destruction caused by the great sea monster and Onaclov who stood on its shoulder, drew the flock of birds away from the ground troops. Cetus roared as hundreds of black birds swarmed over his body, slashing his slimy scales with their claws and tearing at his fins with toothed beaks. Luckily, many of the Daerds failed to notice the multitude of snapping jaws that protruded from Cetus head and neck like a mane, and many fell prey to them. Onaclov fired into their flock as well, covering groups of the birds in thick magma that tore them from the sky and ignited their feathers. The two fought against the flock until one monstrous black shape flew out of the mass of feathers and talons and swooped towards Onaclov. The King of the Dwarves tried to summon a blast of magma that covered the beaked face of this massive creature, but this bird did not burn, and it was too large to be pulled down by the weight of the molten stone.

Worc sunk its claws into Cetus's shoulders and snapped its beak at Onaclov, who dived away at the last moment and grabbed the inside of one of Cetus's gills to keep from falling down into the water below. Cetus roared as Worc's beak snapped one of his fins instead, and the creature reached up and grabbed the King of the Daerds in one tentacled hand. Worc quickly slipped from his grip, slick as a fish, and dove this time at the sea monster's face, raking his claws across the scaled skin. Cetus swatted at the air as Worc flew forward again, clawing at the monster's neck and the small faces that populated it. The sea monster was wounded, and as it tried to cover its wounds, Worc flew down at Onaclov again. Onaclov let go of the gills, deciding to risk the high plunge into the water rather than die between the massive jaws of Worc, but before he could crash into the water, Worc plucked him from the sky with his large, clawed feet. The talons of the bird held Onaclov tight as Worc flew back over land and out of the reach of Cetus. He was heading towards the golden peak of Civitas Levi to roost and devour his prize, when a stone missile crashed into the side of the bird's head. As Worc turned to look, another projectile caught him in the face, and a shriek exploded from his mouth as a grisly crack formed across his beak. Onaclov slipped from the bird's grip while it wheeled around in the sky, searching for its attacker. But as Onaclov fell, Worc's attacker raced down to catch him. On the back of Flamane, Usus caught Onaclov, and before Worc could find them, the griffin dove to the ground and landed behind the line of soldiers.

Finally upon solid ground, Onaclov explained, "Back in the Battle at Lake Vascent, after the Nuquamese creature and I crashed into the water, I had to dive down to the bottom of the lake to pull the ring that controls Cetus's body. By the time I resurfaced, the army had left, and there were only Nuquamese there, so I hid away in Cetus' mouth and traveled here to the next closest body of water."

"Why do you always choose to hide in the mouth of that creature?" Usus laughed.

"Worked well for me the last time, so it seemed like it would work again," Onaclov said.

"Well, it's extremely fortunate you came when you did. There's a plan, now that we have all twelve elements," Usus said.

"We find Retsinis and summon everyone else to him?" Onaclov guessed.

"Yes...yes that's pretty much it," Usus said. "Sounds like you're ready to go."

"Thank you for the help," Onaclov called, as Usus rose back into the sky aboard his griffin.

Onaclov rushed past the elves and other Milwarian archers standing in the back of the army and reached the front lines. A treep towered over him, kicking multiple creatures away with its thick wooden legs, while fauns and satyrs ran about with knives and spears. The satyr Brutus was on top of one serpentine Nuquamese creature, beating it in the head with a club. When another creature leapt at him from behind, Brutus lowered his horned head and charged it, striking the Nuquamese soldier at the knees. Not far from him, a dozen giants were tearing a path through the enemy, punching and stomping on the Nuquamese while the claws and weapons of the enemy did little more that chafe their thick skin. The dwarves were in formation on the other side of them, arranged shoulder-to-shoulder in their characteristic fighting style so as to appear like steel-armored bricks in a wall. Ore stood at the head of this line, and after clearing whole swaths of Nuquamese with his hammer, he raised it high and the dwarves charged. The Nuquamese that attempted to challenge this wall were trampled under the strength of the dwarves. A pack of hideous creatures, covered in thick white hair from head to toe ran forward and leapt upon the Nuquamese. They were the Nezorfs of the caves in the Icelands. Ince and Teews fought just past these wooly creatures, using the combination of their two magics to painlessly defeat a great many of the Nuquamese. Ince's dance of colors shielded the two from the perception of the Nuquamese while Teews sent them straight to sleep with plumes of her magic.

The Daerds left Cetus and floated over the army, cawing down at the Liolians but not attacking. Instead they flew over them, aiming now for the gleaming city that lay behind their line instead. Before any of the Liolians could react, they had reached the glass panes of Civitas Levi and had begun pecking at the glass to break through.

Suddenly a streak of black matter fell to the ground in the middle of the battlefield, and from the depths of the darkness, Venefica appeared. A giant lumbered towards her and threw a punch, but his fist met a wave of darkness that the witch had pulled from the end of her dress. The giant stumbled backwards, but the darkness still held onto his fist and had begun to climb up it. It bellowed as tendrils of darkness lashed around his legs and tore him down to the ground.

Venefica turned away from the giant and looked now at three Wodahs charging her. With a simple flick of her hand, they were caught up in a web of dark material. With her immediate threats dealt with, she rose above the attacking Liolians with the end of her dress extending and lifting her body high over the ground. From the dark folds of her robe below her, a beast of darkness emerged and charged like a bull through the Liolians. The elves launched a volley of arrows at her, but with a wave of her hand she cast them aside in a veil of darkness. Then she exclaimed and thrust out her hands, and two dozen dark shards were sprayed out across the Liolian army, catching the soldiers like arrows.

Venefica had garnered the attention of the Liolians, but none could figure out how to strike her. Equus ran forward and thrust a column of sand in her direction, but Venefica deflected it with magic of her own. Ore called forth a gale with his hammer, but Venefica appeared unfazed as the wind tore across her. She smiled calmly, reveling in the gaze of so many enemies at once. From the shoulders of her dress, dark serpents coiled around her pale arms. When they reached her palms, she held out her hands and began to speak. "Please, why must we fight?" she asked innocently. "Can't you all see it is futile? Already the Daerds are laying siege to the city you protect. All of those innocents just moments away from death. But it can all be avoided!"

The men slowly began to lower their weapons and look up into the silvery eyes of the serpents in her hands. None of them appeared to be searching for a way to strike the witch anymore. Instead, they listened intently as she continued her speech.

"Lay down your weapons now," Venefica instructed. "End this fighting now. You will be forgiven, and your innocents will be spared. If you continue this fighting, only death will come to you and your people."

A few of the soldiers let their weapons slip from their fingers. Even though her promises were clearly lies, they could think of no action other than to lay down their weapons as she had instructed. They all stared into those silvery serpentine eyes, and none noticed the tendrils of darkness growing across the ground and wrapping around their bodies.

"There you go," Venefica said sweetly as more weapons clattered to the ground and the Nuquamese began to circle.

Hundreds of men had now stopped after catching sight of the witch. Ince and Equus dropped their wands, and Ore's hammer hit the ground with a thunk. The Nuquamese growled with delight and grew closer to the defenseless Liolians, preparing to kill them all. "See, that wasn't too hard. This will all be over very, very soo—"

The witch stopped abruptly as a spear struck her solidly in the chest. Venefica looked down in disbelief at the shaft lodged in her ribs, and then her eyes rolled up in her head. The tall column of darkness that had lifted her into the air dissolved like smoke, and the witch toppled backwards, landing with a thud upon the ground with the spear sticking up into the air. All at once, the Liolian soldiers came out of their trance, and seeing the Nuquamese creatures surrounding them, they lunged for their weapons. Then Teews cut between the soldiers and laid one boot on Venefica to pull her spear from the witch's chest. The Liolians stared in amazement at their queen as she turned around and yelled to them, "You've all had your break. To arms!"

The Liolians turned as the Nuquamese leapt upon them, and the fighting continued around the body of the witch.

Across the battlefield, Speilton and Millites fought alongside each other. The two had waded further into the Nuquamese army than any of the other Liolians, and the bodies piled up around them proved how they had accomplished it. For years the two had fought together, but in this moment, they fought fluidly, cutting down enemies with precise movements. Millites had always been the more capable fighter of the two, but with Speilton's new control over the elements, they were now much more evenly matched. Millites's sword shone bright as he swung it through the air. Great arcs of light were emitted from the blade, slicing down creatures far and wide as if the blade itself were twenty feet long. Speilton relied much more on his magic, pulling up dirt and sand and shaking the air as he fought. Fire scorched the land around him, in part due to Prowl fighting nearby. Speilton's body was wrapped in flame, and Spirit sizzled in his hands as he swung it at any of the Nuquamese that escaped his other attacks.

Behind them, they heard the sound of shattering glass, and when they turned they saw that Worc had smashed into the side of Civitas Levi, breaking a pane to bits. The Daerds were hopping to the opening and pushing past each other to enter the city.

"We have to send someone back to the city now, Speilton," Millites said.

"No," Speilton shouted back. "No, not yet! We can't divide up our men when Retsinis is so close."

"How are you so sure he's close?" Millites questioned, striking down a hairy creature in midair.

"He has to be," Speilton persisted. "I know he's here somewhere. We have to kill him now, before…"

"You said mother is preparing the Liolians within Civitas Levi to protect the city?" Millites called to him.

"That was her plan. I just hope they're ready."

A roar shredded the sky from the hills to the north, echoing down across the battlefield The hairs on Speilton's neck stood up as he realized to whom the roar belonged. He looked to the hills and saw the Drakon, Retsinis's massive, pale wyrm with expansive wings and blind eyes, flying forth towards the army.

Millites looked to Speilton as the winged serpent flew overhead. "If the Drakon is here," Speilton said, "then Retsinis is here."

Already, green mist was pouring from the Drakon's mouth, spilling down off its lower jaw and falling slowly upon the Liolians in great coiling plumes. They had dealt with the Drakon and its powerful magic before, and the sight of the mist was enough to make many turn and flee from the cascading green fog, but there was no escaping it. Ore waved his hammer erratically, summoning wind to blow it clear of the army, but there was too much. Even with Speilton's help, it soon became futile.

As the emerald fog settled down upon the army, Millites called to Speilton, "Be careful. Be alert!" and then he was lost in the mist.

In the constant green, everything became shadows. Speilton tried to limit his breathing, since he knew with every breath he took the magic into his lungs. There was movement all around him, but Speilton couldn't tell whether they were his own soldiers or the enemy. Then he heard the first screams of the Liolian soldiers in the distance, and then it was joined by many more. Speilton spun, his feet shuffling on the torn-up soil of the battlefield. A creature leapt out of the fog, and Speilton turned just in time to cut it down with Spirit. Then a tall figure loomed out of the fog, and Speilton raised his hand to ignite it in fire, only to realize that it was one of his own giants. Speilton lowered his hand, but the giant growled at him and charged. The magic of the Drakon had infected its mind already, and now Speilton appeared like something else to the giant. A gust of wind was summoned to knock the giant sideways while Speilton sprinted off into the mist. He stumbled upon another creature, this one hunched and wrinkled. The creature was crouched with its back to Speilton, but as Speilton approached it turned to reveal a fang-filled mouth dripping with blood. Speilton knew it had been feeding on one of his soldiers. The creature opened it cavernous mouth, revealing rows upon rows of prickly teeth. When it sprang forward, Speilton's fist ignited into flame, caught it in the air, and slammed it down to the dirt.   As soon as the creature went still, another Nuquamese barreled out of the mist, just barely missing Speilton before disappearing again. Speilton ran on, stumbling over the still bodies that littered the battlefield. A Daerd toppled out of the sky, crashing in a heap before Speilton. Just as he climbed over the black body, he saw before him Retsinis driving his sword through Millites.

His heart froze, but he shook his head to clear his mind, and then he looked again. This time, he saw only the bodies of a few warriors, either Liolian or Nuquamese, in front of him. Speilton breathed slowly to calm himself, but he was becoming frantic. More screams were echoing all around him, as all of the Liolians saw their individual greatest fears in the smoke of the Drakon. Speilton continued walking forward in the smoke, and then he saw Ince running to him out of the fog. He opened his mouth, and then a sword stabbed through his chest. Speilton turned away and clenched his fists. "No," he muttered to himself. "It's not real. You saved Ince. He's safe now."

Is he? a voice echoed from somewhere close or somewhere far away.

Speilton pivoted with his sword before him, scanning the land around him. A creature rushed past him and leapt, but a sudden screaming beside Speilton revealed that it had been pursuing a different target. He felt eyes all around him, and he knew the Nuquamese were close. The mist didn't affect them like it affected the Liolians, since their minds weren't their own.

You seem so sure that you can change the future, the voice came again, *but the battle is far from over.*

There was the shadow of something moving beside Speilton, but it faded from view before he could make it out. Then the sound of a flapping cloak came from over his shoulder, but again there was nothing to be found.

"You won't kill Ince," Speilton said, guessing it was the Versipellis who spoke to him. "You still need him. You won't kill the cursed that you have chosen."

After all this time, you still think Ince was one of our chosen? the Versipellis whispered to him. *And why is that? Because we left our mark on his hand?*

Speilton was silent, as he began to question his own reasoning. *You received your scar only recently,* the Versipellis said, *but it means nothing. If you look hard enough,*

I'm sure you'll find many other Liolians we marked with that scar. We enjoy claiming our work.

"If Ince isn't the chosen, then who is?" Speilton questioned.

Speilton, Speilton, the Versipellis sounded disappointed. *We thought you to be smarter than this. Ince and the boy Nigal were never our chosen, but it matters not who the other two were now. Your purpose has been served, and you are of no more use to us.*

"And what was my purpose supposed to be?" Speilton asked.

Is it not clear? the Versipellis asked, sounding amused. *It was always our hope that you would gather all of the Liolians - unite all the Kingdoms under a single flag - and bring them here to us.*

Speilton felt his grip on his sword lessen, as he began to understand.

Like a loyal farmhand, you have led the Liolians right to our blade, and now we can butcher them all, with the Phoenixes of Caelum as well.

"No," Speilton shook his head. "I don't believe you."

Then the thought occurred to Speilton that maybe the Versipellis weren't speaking to him at all. Maybe it was all just hallucinations from the smoke.

You should believe us, the Versipellis responded, and then out of the jade mist they appeared.

Both of the dream spirits materialized before Speilton, floating on their ragged wings with their black cloaks flapping beneath them. The single, bulging eyes of each creature stared at Speilton with a piercing glare, and even when he tried to shake his head, the figures stared on. They were not in his imagination.

331

"We wanted you to know the truth, before you died. We thought you deserved to know as much. This is goodbye Speilton," the Versipellis said reverently. "Oh, and it is too bad about your sword. It does trouble us so to see the blade of our brother broken so callously."

As the Versipellis faded into the mist, a dozen shapes ran forward at Speilton. He raised his sword, but he was too drained from the recent revelation to react in time. The creatures dove on him, and Speilton summoned a burst of flames across his body just before they began tearing through his padded vest and chainmail to his skin. He struggled to climb to his feet, but another creature crashed into him, throwing him back to the ground. When he looked up, he saw the land around him all on fire, with thousands of Liolians running across the battlefield in flames. As another creature lunged onto him, the image of the fire faded and was replaced by an image of himself with a sword through his back. He realized in that moment that if it was truly a vision of things to come, then he was not going to die by the hands of these creatures, and somehow that gave him hope. The wind swirled around him, knocking back the creatures, and as even more of the Nuquamese began rushing at him from all around, he gathered a wave of color around his body to hide his location while he fought them back.

Far across the battlefield, Millites wandered through the mist. His sword glared bright like a torch in the green darkness. Creatures leapt at him from all around, but he was quick to cut them down. He heard them rustling just out of view in every direction, but he couldn't see them.

Millites continued moving forward, striking down beasts as they emerged before him, until he reached a spot where the mist had dissipated a bit. He was on the edge of the field of battle, and his view expanded greatly over the hills to the north. What he saw were thousands more of the Nuquamese hanging back in reserve outside the region where the mist had collected. When he spotted them, they spotted him, and he had just begun to back into the mist once again when something caught his eye. There, just ahead of him surrounded on all sides by his army, marched Retsinis. Millites froze, as the howls of the approaching creatures intensified, and then he raised his sword into the air and fired a bolt of light into the dark sky above. As nearly one hundred of the creatures grew near him, Millites stepped back into the mist where he could better hide himself. There he waited for many minutes, hoping that the others had seen the light through the mist and trying not to wander too far and lose Retsinis's location. While the mist concealed him some, the creatures still found him. As he waited, he fought them back, stabbing left and right as they tore out of the mist until there were piles of the wounded Nuquamese all around him. Millites was frantic, the mist causing his body to tremble and his head to twitch around at every slight noise. The distant screams of the Milwarians echoed in his mind.

Then one creature emerged from the mist that was much larger than any of the others. It did not run wildly like a mindless drone, but walked with purpose, its white eyes set on the king with the glowing sword. Millites felt a chill as Retsinis emerged before him. All at once, he thought of Speilton's command not to engage with Retsinis until the rest of the leaders were there, and he also began to wonder if it was truly the King of the Nuquamese that walked before him or just another hallucination. Then Retsinis raised his sword and brought it down in one mighty swing. Millites pivoted away just in time to avoid the blade, then stumbled over the bodies to put distance between himself and Retsinis.

"Do you smell that?" Retsinis growled. "It smells like fear. This land was already full of it far before my Drakon came and dumped it down upon your men."

"I don't fear you," Millites retorted as Retsinis struck again. This time Millites blocked it with his own blade and slipped forward for a quick strike to Retsinis's side.

"You don't?" Retsinis questioned humorously, the wound seemingly having no effect upon him. "Then what do you fear?"

Retsinis lunged forward again, slicing through Millites's red cape as he ducked away. He quickly followed with a backhand swing that Millites ducked beneath, stabbing Retsinis in the knee before diving away from his next attack. "Do you fear defeat, young Lux?" Retsinis asked. "Or do you fear letting down all your men?"

Ferrum Potestas stabbed towards Millites chest, but he parried it away. "I'm sure you fear the death of so many people under your rule. Or at least the death of all of your friends and family members. I've already killed so many."

It was Millites' turn to go on the offensive, and the King ran forward in a flurry of attacks that Retsinis deflected with apparent ease. "There are also many more I look forward to destroying."

Millites was growing tired with the duel taking every ounce of strength and concentration he had. Retsinis, on the other hand, still smiled and appeared to be enjoying every moment of the fight. "Maybe, you fear what will happen when I cut you with this blade," Retsinis said, putting extra force behind his next attack, as if for emphasis.

Throwing himself out of the way of the blade, Millites summoned a bolt of light at Retsinis, but the Dark King merely held out his sword and let it swallow up all of the magic. Retsinis responded with magic of his own, summoning a wave of darkness that sprung up from the ground. It bit and tore at Millites' legs, pulling him to the dirt.

The green mist had begun to settle down around them as Retsinis stepped over the fallen King of the Milwarians with his sword extended. "Or maybe it's much simpler. Maybe, you just fear death."

"I don't fear death," Millites spat, rising from his knees. "And I don't fear defeat because I know we will be victorious when the sun sets on this day. It's you who should fear."

"Me," Retsinis smiled and narrowed his milky eyes. "I will never die. What do I have to fear?"

Millites pointed his elemental-infused sword at Retsinis, and then his eyes looked over past the King of the Nuquamese as he shouted, "Now!"

From Millites' sword, a beam of light erupted, but as Retsinis raised Ferrum Potestas again to block it, he was hit from behind by a blast of molten lava. He roared and turned to see Onaclov attacking him from behind, when suddenly he was struck from the other side by a blast of ice.

"Hello, Uncle," Senkrad said, emerging from the mist.

Retsinis made a move at his nephew when flames tore across the side of his head, and Aurum stepped out of the mist. He struggled to raise the Sword of Power when vines suddenly leapt up from the ground and pulled his arms down, rendering the weapon useless. Cindariel had arrived as well, and then Ince stepped forward from the mist to summon a pillar of glittering colors that drove into the side of Retsinis like shards of glass. The winds picked up as Ore charged forward, and with a wave of his hammer, brought down a column of air that pinned Retsinis where he stood. Retsinis let out a terrible growl, but he was doused in a jet of Teews's purple love, as his body appeared to lose its strength and rigidity. Sand blasted into Retsinis's back as Equus charged forward, and then the ground quaked as Usus summoned forth another spike of stone that drove through Retsinis's thigh. Retsinis struggled against the attacks from every angle. Then Whinn's water suddenly struck him in the face causing him to choke and thrash all the more intensely.

"We just need one more!" Teews shouted.

"It's Speilton!" Usus called back over the sounds of their streams of magic and the besieged Retsinis at the center.

"Where is he?" Aurum called.

Not far away, Speilton had shed the dozens of Nuquamese creatures that the Versipellis had sent after him, and though his body was torn and aching, he hobbled across the battlefield to where he saw the light. The beasts still pursued him, leaping at him as he raced as quickly as he could towards the sound of Retsinis's cries. And then it came into view on the edge of the mist. He saw the individual elements shining in the green haze, all focusing in on Retsinis like spokes in a wheel, and he could tell there was just one more they needed. He reached out his hand, and focused on the darkness that filled the land around him. The land was rife with it. Darkness filled every crevice and lay under every stone and blade of grass. Speilton felt the connection, and began to channel it into something physical.

And then he felt an even greater darkness from the evil king ahead of him. Speilton tried to pull all of the darkness around him toward himself so that he could use its power, but it was slipping out of his reach, funneling towards Retsinis as if he were a black hole, consuming everything in his path. Speilton realized it wasn't Retsinis that was drawing in the darkness, but the object he held in his hand. His Wand of Darkness was nowhere on him, but its power had been merged with the Sword of Power. In shock, Speilton tried to fire the little darkness he had been able to obtain at Retsinis, but it was already too late. In one concussive blast of the purest darkness, Retsinis summoned a wave of his magic, intensified by the magic of Ferrum Potestas, that blew out from his body and caught each of the wand wielders around him. They were thrown backwards, landing hard amidst the grass and the green mist. Speilton could only watch as they struggled to their feet and searched for their wands. Millites' blade no longer glowed, and Ore's hammer appeared heavy in his hands once again. A sickness gripped Speilton's stomach as he realized what had happened.

Retsinis rose to his feet and held Ferrum Potestas triumphantly in the air. Then he proclaimed what Speilton had already guessed to be true. "The era of your elemental magic is finished. All of the wands have now been destroyed, and soon, all of you will follow."

337

SACRIFICE AND DEATH
~ 25 ~

Retsinis grinned at the shocked leaders of Liolia and slowly raised his arms. From every direction, his Nuquamese appeared, rushing out of the fog or down from the hills where they had been waiting. The creatures surrounded them, snarling and exclaiming with excitement as their king began to back away. "You came so close," Retsinis chided them, "but now the end has been determined. You were all worthy adversaries."

The Drakon emerged out of the mist above them, creeping through the air on leathery wings. Its terrible cry pierced the air as Retsinis departed from the group of stunned Liolians, leaping onto the lowered wing of his Drakon and coasting away on his beast to peacefully observe the battle while his Nuquamese ran forth to finish his work. The Liolians lunged for their weapons, forced to rely solely on the physical swords and spears and hammers they had in their possession to repel the onslaught of beasts. Ince had abandoned his spear long ago, relying only on his wand, but now that it had been reduced to ashes he scrambled across the battlefield in search of something to use. Aurum pulled her knives from their sheathes and backed up next to her brother who swung his massive glaive. Whinn's trident stabbed a creature through, but another leapt onto his side, pulling him to the ground. Ore brought his hammer down, crushing the creature before it could sink its claws any further into the king of the mers, but then, he too was struck down by another of the Nuquamese. From the looming shadow of the Drakon above them, more mist was pouring down upon the soldiers. Then, it turned suddenly and set off on a new course as if it had just been given a new objective by its master. The blind serpent flew off over the Liolians, heading toward Civitas Levi with its multitude of shattered panes where the Daerds had burst in.

Panic began to set in as the former wielders of the eleven wands fought back the growing tide of Nuquamese without their greatest weapons. Speilton's head swam as he stumbled toward them, still unable to come to terms with what had happened.

When Aurum noticed him approaching, she turned to him with a look of terror. "Speilton," she cried. "What does this mean? What do we do now?"

Speilton searched for the right words or for some semblance of hope, but all that escaped his lips was, "It's over. We've already lost."

Flamane burst out of the mist beside them, sinking his teeth into a Nuquamese running up behind Equus and tossing it to the ground. The griffin stopped beside Usus, who after cutting down a scaly, bug-eyed creature with his khopesh laid a hand on Flamane's beak.

"No," Usus said. "I can't accept that."

Usus pulled himself onto Flamane's back and patted the side of the griffin's feathered neck. Flamane reared and clawed at the air with his taloned forelegs, screeching emphatically in support of his owner's statement. When the griffin had returned to all fours, Usus said, "It isn't over. Not yet. As long as we live, Liolia lives."

He spurred the griffin and together they leapt into the sky, the mist swirling as Flamane's golden eagle wings sliced through it. "What is he doing?" Millites questioned, cutting a creature down while watching the two sail up into the air.

Speilton couldn't speak as Usus rose high into the sky which was still dark and red from the dawn shining upon the storm clouds and thicket of Daerds. He was flying after the distant pale shape of the Drakon, and as he did so, he drew the attention of the great flock of demon birds covering the golden city.

"Where's Hunger?" Millites questioned. "Speilton, where's Prowl? We need to stop him."

But their dragons were off somewhere in the fog, so no one could reach the Second-in Command now. Flamane dove below a swarm of the Daerds, then twisted and turned to avoid another group. Usus swung his khopesh, slicing the dark wings of the Daerds as they flew around him. The Daerds slashed at Flamane's sides and neck with their talons, and the shrieking griffin lashed back at them with talons of his own. Soon, they were completely consumed by the black cloud of monstrous birds, and from the ground, the other Liolians could only watch and wait as they continued to contend with the constant flow of Nuquamese all around. The only sign that Usus and Flamane were still alive somewhere deep within the flock was the constant cascade of Daerd bodies that poured down out of the sky, killed somewhere in its depths.

Then the gleam of the golden griffin emerged from the flock of Daerds, tearing through the sky on bent wings, gashes up and down his side. Usus stood on his back, knees crouched, and sword up in the air, ready. It took the Liolians a moment to realize what it was he was preparing to do. The Daerds caught up to Flamane, sinking their claws into the griffin and tearing him from

340

the sky, but they were already close enough. Usus extended his legs and leapt, soaring through the air and landing on the tail of the Drakon. With both hands gripping a spike running down the creature's back, Usus pulled himself up onto its back. Then he turned back to his griffin, but Flamane had gone limp. His griffin looked up at him from the grip of the Daerds and gave one final, mournful cry, then rolled backwards and plummeted down from the sky. Usus paused there for a moment, staring over the edge of the Drakon at his old friend, and then he turned and began sprinting across the serpent's back.

The Drakon had reached Civitas Levi, and its ragged mouth hung over the holes in the glass roof. Green mist poured through the openings into the city already infested with the swooping Daerds. Between the wings of the Drakon, Retsinis turned towards Usus, surprised to have a visitor. The King of the Nuquamese raised his sword as Usus charged across the pale scales of the Drakon and swung as Usus slashed the khopesh across his chest. Retsinis kicked the Second-in-Command back, and Usus fell to the ground.

"No," Millites gasped, far below on the ground as all the leaders turned to watch Retsinis standing over Usus, sword lifted high above his head.

Retsinis plunged the blade down, and Usus rolled quickly to the side. Ferrum Potestas did not catch Usus as Retsinis had planned, but instead stabbed down into a soft spot on the Drakon's back where years ago, during the Battles of Skilt, Millites and Retsinis had blown a hole in the beast's scales. Usus thrust his khopesh forward, driving his blade into Retsinis's neck, and then he laid his hand upon the pommel of the Sword of

Power and thrust the sword further down into the back of the Drakon. Retsinis reached a hand up to the curved blade in his throat and snapped the khopesh in half as his Drakon roared and pitched sideways. With his sword broken, Usus laid his other hand upon the guard of Ferrum Potestas and put his entire weight into driving the black blade deep into the wyrm. The powerful blade slipped through the flesh and spine of the giant winged serpent until it was hilt deep within the creature. Retsinis roared in fury and tore the blade up out of his creature, but the damage was already done. Usus sneered up at the King of the Nuquamese, his own sword in ruins at his feet and his griffin dead far below. The Drakon screeched, its wings thrashing in pain, and then it rolled to its side. As Usus stumbled backwards, Retsinis swung his blade, cutting across Usus' chest. The Second-in-Command kept his feet, trying to remain on the back of the massive serpent, but then it lurched onto its side and the ground fell out beneath Usus. He rolled in the air thrown awkwardly to the side, and then spread out his arms as he fell down down down through the sky.

There were shrieks of disbelief and the leaders watched in horror as Usus plummeted through the sky and the Drakon contorted, its body smashing into the side of Civitas Levi before crumpling to the ground. Arms still extended, Usus fell, his body a tiny shadow juxtaposed against the golden city beside him. He seemed to fall forever, as if at any moment he might catch wind and fly away. Then he disappeared in the crowd of soldiers and the dissipating green mist of the battlefield. The body of the Drakon lay beside him.

With Retsinis's great serpent dead, the green mist was carried off by the wind, revealing the battlefield once again and returning sanity to the Liolian soldiers within it. The sun suddenly broke through the clouds, and unencumbered by the green fog, it shone down upon the army. The Nuquamese roared and shielded their eyes from the glare, and the Liolians looked to the east where Usus' body lay and let the warmth of the sun beat on their face. Something bright caught the corner of Speilton's eye, and he looked to see his shield burning like the sun in the grass close to him from where he had dropped it during his fight with Retsinis the day before. He lifted the shining shield as he strapped it to his arm and looked to the Liolian leaders.

Tears streaked down Teews' face, Ince had begun to cry as well, Onaclov appeared still in shock, and Millites glared with a fury that Speilton had never seen. The Nuquamese were adjusting to the bright sun and beginning to rush forward again. Across the battlefield, the Liolian line had broken, and the ocean of Nuquamese were charging off toward the gates of Civitas Levi. Retsinis had fallen somewhere near the city as well.

"We must fall back to Civitas Levi," Speilton said to the leaders.

"But the wands are destroyed," Senkrad said. "We cannot kill Retsinis. We cannot stop his army."

"That didn't stop Usus from trying," Millites said. "And it shouldn't stop us either."

Teews raised her spear into the air, "To Civitas Levi!" and the others picked up her call, rushing across the plain and rousing the other Liolians to their side. The sun shone radiantly on the Liolians rushing to their leaders, rebuilding their force that had been drawn out and dispersed in the thick mist. The elves had gathered near the outer walls of the city launching volley after volley of their arrows up at the Daerds crawling across the golden dome. A few dozen dwarves who had formed a circular formation amidst a sea of the Nuquamese now ran to Ore and Onaclov. In a column of heavy shields and steel armor, the dwarves marched through their enemies and positioned themselves around their leaders. Cetus roared from the sea and groped across the land with its massive tentacles, catching all the Nuquamese that wandered too closely. Prowl and Burn ran to them out of the thick of the battlefield, and Hunger flew down and landed beside Millites. In their charge across the battlefield all the different races of Liolia joined together and integrated, no longer separated into formation by their kingdoms and creeds. The Nuquamese attacked from all around, but the Liolians were strong in their consolidated force and repelled them all. This regrouped Liolian force swept the battlefield, roaring as they plowed through the Nuquamese and leapt over the fallen that littered the sloping hills.

They reached the walls of the city and struck down the Nuquamese trying to enter the gates ahead of them, reestablishing their line outside the tall, arched entrance way. Millites, Speilton, and Teews pushed through the crowd and came to the spot where the Liolians had gathered around Usus' body. He lay on his back, still, but with a content look frozen upon his face. Millites sank to one knee beside his friend, and Speilton followed him. They lay a hand on the plaid tunic still wrapped around his body, as if searching for any glimmer of life still in him.

It was only after a few moments of silence had passed that they looked up to notice what other creatures had assembled around his body as well. Phoenixes had moved through the crowd and now looked down upon the Second-in-Command of Liolia. They began to shuffle to the side, looking up at something descending above them, and then a massive Phoenix floated down from the sky, beating large, flowing wings. Círsar, Head Consul of the Order of the Bow, landed before them, looking down at Usus with a quizzical look.

Millites rose to his feet and scowled at the Phoenix. "You could've saved him," he spat. "You could've caught him. But you watched and did nothing."

The Phoenix continued staring at Usus. "He had already been cut by the Sword of Power. If we had caught him, he would have only been turned to the side of the King of Nuquam."

"He died protecting your city from the Drakon," Teews said to the Head Consul, "while you cowered inside."

The Phoenix nodded his head slowly, finally looking up from Usus' body. "Perhaps," Círsar said quietly, "we were wrong."

Speilton, Millites, and Teews all watched the Phoenix as Onaclov and Ince pushed through the army to see Usus as well.

"Perhaps," the Phoenix continued, "we were mistaken to assume the Liolians fought only for themselves. This soldier died valiantly and…selflessly. He killed, yes, but he saved thousands by doing so."

"What are you saying?" Speilton questioned.

"What I'm saying…is that I have changed my mind. Perhaps violence is not in itself as great a sin as inaction in the face of evil."

Círsar extended his wings, shimmering as they shifted between the different elements, and then pulled himself up into the air. Following their leader, the other

Phoenixes that were gathered around Usus sprang into the air. The Liolians stepped back and watched as a soft crooning call went out, and Phoenixes from all over Civitas Levi and the surrounding land took to the sky as well. With the Daerds bearing down on them from above and the Nuquamese marching on their city, the Phoenixes had hidden in their shelters or transformed into their elemental form to hide in plain sight, but now that their leader called them, they revealed themselves. Hundreds poured into the sky from every direction, and then there were thousands. From the hills to the south of the castle, other large Phoenixes took to the sky, not composed of singular elements but of every element. These other members of the Order of the Bow assembled behind their Head Consul, and for a moment they appeared to be flying in the V-shaped formation of migrating birds, but then their formation shifted. Phoenixes of the same color and element gathered together into lines, giving the flock the appearance of a floating, glittering rainbow breaking down out of the heavens. But their lines continued to evolve, reassembling until their great flock began to form an image. In the air above the Liolians, the thousands of Phoenixes moved with such precision and in such an arrangement as to appear like one massive Phoenix, rising high into the air above their golden city.

With the colors of eleven elements filling the sky, the other flock of Daerds and Phoenixes of Darkness abandoned their siege of Civitas Levi and rose to meet them. At the head of the great spectral Phoenix, Círsar wheeled around to face the growing black cloud amassed below them and ascending quickly. Then the Head Consul dove, and the thousands of Phoenixes followed. Those larger Phoenixes that composed the Order of the

346

Bow suddenly melted away into golden streaks, tearing through the sky like thunderbolts, crashing through the Daerds and the Dark Phoenixes. As the black flock wheeled around, attempting to recover from the attack, the rest of the Phoenixes met them. The air was riddled with torn feathers of every color and the cackling of the great birds tearing into one another.

For the moment, the city was safe, but with the Drakon dead, it appeared that Retsinis had sent the remaining legions of his army against the Liolians. They poured from the hills like a ceaseless tide and crashed against the Liolian blockade at the gate. With each Liolian standing shoulder to shoulder and every shield held out before them, they held back the Nuquamese forces that struggled to penetrate the city. But they could only protect so much, and the Nuquamese forces still greatly outnumbered them. There were three other gates into the city, and though the tall doors had been shut and secured on each, there was no one manning them. It was obvious they would do little to hold back the Nuquamese.

Millites looked down at Usus' body once more, and then he began to back up to the gate into the city. "Fall back into Civitas Levi!" he called.

Those of the Liolian soldiers once or twice removed from the frontlines began to turn and flee into the city while the Nuquamese still pushed forward. "Speilton!" Millites called to his brother. "Can you hold the Nuquamese off long enough to allow us to close the gates? You still have *your* powers, right?"

"I can do it," Speilton said. "You will lead the men back into the city?"

Millites nodded to him, then added, "Speilton, whatever happens, watch out for yourself. Promise me, for the good of our people, that you will protect yourself."

"You're going after him, aren't you?" Speilton said. "You're going to fight Retsinis."

Millites looked solemnly at him.

"I told you what I saw in the Book of Liolia. You know what happens if you fight him."

"You said yourself that the future you saw can be changed," Millites said. "I have to try. Someone has to fight him."

"Millites," Speilton grabbed his brother's arm as he attempted to run into the city with his men, "no one can kill Retsinis now. Nothing can stop him, not even you."

"But someone has to try, or else we're all already dead," Millites said with a slight smile. "Goodbye, Speilton."

Millites pulled free and disappeared in the rush of retreating Liolians. The Nuquamese were beginning to break through the Liolian line as more and more men fell back into the city, and Speilton rushed at them before they could reach the gates. He closed his eyes and felt his connection with the world around him. The wands had been destroyed, but his power was not contained to that weapon any more. The grass swayed toward him as he moved past the fleeing Liolians and towards the immense army charging forward. Speilton felt the energy and rage of the thousands of creatures belonging to Retsinis that rushed through the tall grass, their boots and clawed feet tearing up the soil beneath them just as their fangs and talons tore through any Liolian in their way. The Liolian line had disappeared, and now nothing remained

between the Nuquamese and the gates of Civitas Levi;
nothing but Speilton.

Arrows tore through the air toward him, but with
a smooth gust of wind he drove their shafts into the
ground behind him. The Nuquamese raced on, growing
closer and closer, and Speilton waited. He felt the ground
rumble with the stomps of so many creatures, and then it
began to rumble at Speilton's own command. He had
just begun to rip a fissure between himself and the
Nuquamese when a volley of bright gold flashes raced
over his head, dropping down and tearing through the
mass of creatures before him. Hundreds of Phoenixes
raked through the Nuquamese army, striking down
creatures with inflictions from all eleven elements that
they represented. Then golden streaks of light crashed
down upon the Nuquamese like falling meteors, as the
Order of the Bow attacked as well. Speilton looked up in
wonderment as the Phoenixes rose again, then doubled
back for a second sweep through the army, their bodies
slipping out of their bird forms and becoming the base
materials that they represented. The Nuquamese looked
up in rage, but there was nothing they could do as the
Phoenixes tore through them again, then rose beyond
their reach once their damage had been done. Then a
black force collided with the Phoenixes as the Dark
Phoenixes once again met them in their aerial combat. It
was now that Speilton realized something he hadn't
before. As they fought, Phoenix bodies were dropping to
the ground. He remembered something that Beati had
told him long ago; that Phoenixes were always reborn
from their ashes into a new element, except when killed
by the element of darkness. That was why the Phoenixes
of Darkness had been banished to the mountains. The

Phoenix bodies Speilton saw falling did not drop away into ash as they were supposed to, but instead remained intact, no different than the bodies of any other slain bird. These Phoenixes would not be reborn.

The Nuquamese rushed forward once more, regaining their force with the preoccupation of the Phoenixes. Once again, Speilton stood alone against them, so now he tore open the ground, forcing them to either attempt leaping over it or fall into its depths. The landscape shook as the crack widened, but it was not wide enough to hold them all back. Some fell or misstepped. But many leapt, and then they were upon Speilton. He drew flames up around him and pulled up a cloud of smashed glass that lay at the foot of the city walls. Winds ripped around him, filled with the debris, as Speilton, robed in flames, fought the Nuquamese.

Then Speilton heard two sounds, one right after the other. The first was the sound of the gate doors slamming shut as all the Liolians slipped inside Civitas Levi. The second was an awful, guttural wailing of some creature from high above. Speilton looked up from his fighting and seized up, watching another of his visions coming true. Worc and the Head Consul of the Order fought in midair, spinning violently as they fell through the sky. Círsar had his massive talons sunken into the flesh of Worc's stomach, but the King of the Daerds had snapped its jaws around the Phoenix's neck. The Head Consul struggled for a moment, screeching again in pain, but finally went limp. Worc's wings stretched out, catching the wind, and bringing the great black bird to the ground not far from Speilton.

Speilton watched in horror as Worc dropped the Phoenix to the ground before him and placed one taloned foot upon it in victory. Círsar was not yet dead, but his light was fading and its constantly changing elements had slowed and begun to dull. Worc stared at Speilton and screeched, baring his toothed beak. Below the talons of the Daerd, the leader of the Phoenixes looked at Speilton as well with a pained expression that may have held sorrow or regret. And then the Phoenix's body faded to gray and crumbled into ash.

A creature lunged at Speilton and as he threw it off him he could feel the ground tremble. Worc had killed the Head Consul of the Phoenixes. Now he was moving forward to slay another leader. Then something else dove out of the sky, something red and billowing a flame of nearly the same red color. Worc looked up as Hunger sunk his claws into the massive neck and blew his smoky flames across the Daerd's face. Worc thrashed and snapped at the dragon, but Hunger had swung out of the way and attacked the other side of Worc's neck. Worc leapt into the air, and Hunger was forced to take wing and flee as the massive bird pursued him.

High above, the Phoenixes continued to fight, but without their leader, their movements seemed more frantic and less precise. The image of the great Phoenix had faded into a squabbling mass, but the Daerds were without their leader as well.

The Liolians were secure within the city, and with the Nuquamese forces momentarily held at bay by the city walls, Speilton searched for an escape. He couldn't hold these creatures off forever, as his body was already worn from such a prolonged use of his magic, but he couldn't flee into the city with the doors bolted shut either. Just a few sections up in the grid of the city walls above the gates, Speilton noticed a glass pane had been shattered. Speilton summoned a fiery wave of destruction that threw back the Nuquamese, giving him a moment to run to the city wall. Then he pulled a column of stone from the ground beneath him, launching him into the air and through the hole. With wind, he caught himself and landed upon a terrace of some tall, marble building. Every color was cast across the city as the light of dawn glittered through the myriad of colored panes of the eastern wall. Speilton took in the beauty of the city, and then began to walk towards the stairs leading from the building. He hadn't noticed the dark shape that had slipped through the broken window behind him. Suddenly, his legs grew weak, and his vision began to fade. He stumbled forward, and then fell in the doorway of the building. As darkness took him, he heard the cackling voice of the Versipellis echoing through his brain.

Hunger fled through the sky, the dark shape of Worc racing behind him. Millites clung to the dragon's back as he dove against the tall golden walls of the city. Worc was close behind and appeared to be exceptionally faster. The massive scale of the King of the Daerds did not encumber it at all, but actually gave it larger wings with which to sail through the sky. Hunger cut upwards quickly as Worc snapped his beak closed where his tail had been, and Millites held on for his life as they flew higher and higher into the sky.

The battlefield appeared small below them, even with the Nuquamese forces still covering the hills and fields on every side of the city. Millites knew the Liolians had split up to guard the four gates of Civitas Levi, and he could only hope that they would be capable of defending them until he could return. He had been within the walls of the city for less than a minute before he and Hunger flew back outside its safety to challenge the King of the Daerds, but in that moment he had been able to observe the thousands of Liolian civilians – the women, children, and elderly untrained or unable to fight – who had collected along the rooftops with makeshift weapons in hand. This final battle required them all if there would be any hope of victory. Millites had no idea how they were going to kill Retsinis now, but he did know that he had to put every enemy that could be killed to death. Hunger lit up with red fury at the sight of the massive Daerd that had killed his mother, Comet, who had been Millites previous dragon. Now, that he had murdered Círsar, Millites knew that it was time for Worc to be dealt with once and for all. It was a desire more easily considered than accomplished.

The dragon and his rider rose past the squabble of Phoenixes and Daerds that filled the sky above the city, and then through the rolling storm clouds that sat thick and pallid, finally entering an empty stratum of open sky. The silence of the altitude would have appeared peaceful if not for the massive black crow flying after them. Worc gained on them, snapping its beak at Hunger's tail. The dragon kicked with his feet, clawing at the massive beak of Worc, and then swung the spiked club that sprouted from the tip of his tail. Worc bent his head to avoid the swing, then snapped his jaws again, catching one of Hunger's feet in his toothed jaws. As Hunger roared in pain, his flight becoming erratic as he struggled to pull away. Millites patted the dragon's neck, frantically reassuring him. In desperation, Hunger blew flames upon the Daerd's face, but fire did nothing to Worc but make him clamp down harder. Again, Hunger lashed out at Worc, and this time the

353

club struck the bird's beak, furthering the crack Usus had already placed in it. Worc released his grip, and shrieked in fury, pursued Hunger through the sky with even more bloodlust.

Millites instructed Hunger to fly horizontally now, heading far to the south away from the land and towards the ocean. He knew that down below, the Daerds would become disoriented without the presence of their king. Worc reached Hunger again and this time flew in feet first. With the talons of one foot, he grabbed the dragon by his back legs, and the other he wrapped around the dragon's neck. Hunger, roared, and Millites dropped low on his dragon's back to avoid being crushed by either foot. Realizing he was safe, Millites drew his sword and stabbed deep into the belly of Worc. Again, Worc roared, and Millites pulled the sword out just to stab again. Hunger struggled out of Worc's grip, struggling forward more weakly now with wings bent in by the King of the Daerd's attack. Then Hunger rose, shooting up into the sky even further than before, further than he had ever attempted to fly. Worc followed, eyes wild with his savage desire for blood. "We can't fly much higher," Millites screamed over the rush of wind around them. "The air is too thin! What's your plan?"

But the dragon continued racing upwards, his wings straining and legs kicking as he climbed higher and higher. The world below appeared to fade to a singular pale blue, with the sea and cloud-covered sky of the battlefield fading into each other. It appeared for a moment as if Hunger would just keep flying, on into whatever lands lay in the heavens. And then the beating of his wings stopped, and the dragon floated upwards on his own momentum, slowing until he reached his peak, and then rolled backwards, gracefully like a diver. Worc was frantically chasing after the dragon, and hadn't even realized Hunger had stopped until the golden-scaled creature finished his backwards roll and leveled off, bringing his spiked tail hurtling down him with the increased power of the roll and gravity. The brutal club dropped like a spiked anvil into the beak of Worc, cracking against the massive bird and shattering the beak to bits. Hunger dropped down into a dive as Worc wailed in a declaration of pain that echoed out across the endless sky for miles around. Only pieces of the once massive beak still remained as Worc dove as well, screeching downward after the dragon who had so horrifically disfigured him. Hunger did not let up, dropping through the sky with wings tucked, allowing him and his rider to cut through the air and hurtle towards the ocean below. Millites felt sick as the expanse of blue suddenly came into focus, and he began to make out the individual whitecaps of the sea below. His eyes stung and watered as the wind beat against them, and he was filled with the sudden fear that they would crash when Hunger's wings shot out. As he caught the wind and lifted them up away from the waves with such force and strain, the dragon bellowed with pain. But even with the pain, Hunger was able to spin onto his back to face Worc as he dove toward him, and – as the great King of the Daerds approached – blow a ball of flames into the exposed flesh where the beak had once been. Worc tried to screech, but fire filled his lungs, blackening his skin and filling his insides. Smokey fire erupted out of the bird's black eye sockets from within. The two massive wings that had once summoned the force of a hurricane twisted wildly to the side as Worc crashed into the waves.

Millites looked back as Worc's body went still upon the waves and slowly began to sink beneath the surface. Hunger didn't look back, but sailed on over the water on weary wings, heading for the distant stretch of land before them.

Speilton awoke in a place that at first seemed foreign, but suddenly became familiar as if he were remembering it from some lost dream from long ago. In fact, that was exactly what the place appeared to be – somewhere from a dream. The steep rocky walls, jagged, stone floor, and grey mottled sky was the same place the Versipellis had taken him during the Battle of Skilt against the Calorians. It was like an arena of sorts, but Speilton knew it to be more accurately a killing field or execution block for the Versipellis. It was a land they had constructed within a dream, and as dream spirits, it was their domain. This was where they drug their slumbering victims to kill them. The last time Speilton had been brought here, it was the Versipellis who had been killed, or at least one of them. Speilton knew from that experience that though the land around him may be only the imaginings of his sleeping mind, the consequences of what happened here had very real effects in the waking world.

"Do you remember this place?" the Versipellis whispered to him from somewhere across the rocky landscape. "You were very lucky here long ago, but way back then, we could not kill you. Even then, we had much greater plans for you."

"Bringing you the Liolians," Speilton said, repeating what they had told them. "And now my curse has ended."

356

"Precisely," the Versipellis whispered excitedly, and all around Speilton felt their gaze upon him.

"So now you're going to kill me," Speilton said plainly, pausing a moment before asking, "Tell me though, when will you kill Retsinis?"

The Versipellis were quite a moment, and then they seethed, "Of what do you speak?"

"Retsinis, he was another of your cursed, was he not?" Speilton questioned, smiling as he realized his guess had been correct. "You didn't just align yourself with Retsinis, you chose him as one of your precious slaves. Why? It appears you have a common goal. Why the need to manipulate him at all?"

"You must think yourself clever, don't you? To answer your question, we are not ones to seek alliances," the Versipellis spoke, no longer feeling the necessity to shroud the truth, "especially not with those as foolish as him. Retsinis desired domination and control. He wanted a kingdom to bow down and worship him – for *all* kingdoms to worship him. What we want is much simpler, more pure, more...primordial. We want only death. We want only darkness. We want this complicated mess of life to return to the cold, empty void from which we were born at the genesis of all things. Retsinis's goal was not our own, but he was a means to an end."

"So, my question stands, when will you kill Retsinis?" Speilton questioned. "If it is death you want, then even Retsinis must die."

"Evil and ego like his is self-destructive in and of itself. When Retsinis dominates this world and leaves nothing but ashes, he will search for something else to conquer. Eventually, years and years from now, he will meet a match, or destroy himself in his own stupidity."

"And you intend to wait that long?"

"Centuries mean nothing to us. We are primeval. When the first light shone out in the infinite dark, we were born to counter it, to extinguish it. All the death and destruction carried out by Retsinis is sufficient to sate our appetite for now. And eventually, we shall succeed in our mission. No life will remain, and we have all the time in the world to wait until that day comes."

"So, you never told Retsinis, I assumed," Speilton said. "If the two of us were chosen, then who is the third?"

"Why do you care so desperately to know, even now, moments from your death?" the Versipellis sneered, but Speilton acted as if he had not heard.

"It was Ram," he guessed. "Ram saved me long ago. Then he went off in search of you. You needed Ram to fall to Retsinis's side to divide up the wands, didn't you?"

The Versipellis sounded as if they were laughing in their ragged, serpentine way. "Ram went after us for your sake, not his own. It was his own actions that led to his demise, but we had no hand in that."

"So, not Ram," Speilton said, his hands firmly wrapped around his sword. "Then who…"

He felt the Versipellis lunging towards him before he saw it. Speilton turned and raised Spirit as the Versipellis materialized behind him and struck wildly with his bladed arms. Speilton ducked as it swiped at his head, and then he thrust forward with his own sword in return. "No," Speilton said, realization dawning on him. "It was Millites all along. You didn't tell Retsinis that he was cursed, nor did you tell Millites. Yet in all that time you never made an attempt to kill him. You knew he would have a role to play, just as I did, but you only

358

needed one of us to know. You tried to drive us apart – to create secrets between us, when all along you were only manipulating us both."

The Versipellis did not respond, but the sudden attack of the second dream spirit from behind confirmed Speilton's beliefs. Their blades clashed against his as Speilton stumbled over the rocky terrain, trying to find a tall surface to place his back against to force them both in front of him. The two appeared like skeletal apparitions, wrapped in moldy cloth and armed with curved blades, and Speilton was forced to wield the elements to hold them back. Stone was one of the few he had at his disposal, along with the sand of the crushed rock below their feet. He attempted to keep one occupied with his magic while dueling the other with Spirit, but fighting two battles at once quickly sapped his energy. Besides, the Versipellis were shape-shifters, and as spikes of stone and blasts of sand were summoned against them, they would quickly transform into some incomprehensible creature out of a nightmare and slip away.

Speilton was growing tired, and his attacks became less consistent. He knew he had to strike their eye, as it was the only place where they felt pain. But every time he tried to run the blade through them, the eye would twitch away, moving to the back of the demons and out of his reach. Then his attacks became desperate, and the Versipellis appeared to grin and take advantage of his sloppiness. One of their blades sliced across his shoulder as another slashed his outer thigh. Speilton fell to one knee with the pain of the attacks, and the Versipellis approached greedily.

"So many times you have slipped from our grasp," the Versipellis muttered, "but never again. Now, you are all alone. Now, you are ours."

An idea occurred to Speilton, and he looked up at the two demons with a sudden confidence. "All these years," Speilton said, "you have lured me into fighting you one-on-one. Now both of you do battle with me. And all this time I have let you keep me isolated. I thought you were a menace only I could destroy, but now I see that was my own pride."

Speilton was reaching out with his mind, outside the walls of the execution arena, to his body sleeping far away in the land of Caelum. And then he wasn't just reaching out for his own body lying there, but the others gathered within the city. He found Teews, and Aurum, and Ince, and Onaclov all scattered across the many fronts of the battle in Civitas Levi, and he called them toward him. Whether they could hear or not, Speilton did not know, but then he let his mind return to the battle at hand. The Versipellis loomed over him, creeping forward with their blades thrust out hungrily before them. Speilton smiled, and before they could strike him, he said, "I'll see you both soon," and then he tore the dreamscape apart in an eruption of stone and fire and dust.

He awoke suddenly back on the terrace of the building.

Hunger finally reached land and crumpled into the sand with a thud, hardly attempting to slow his flight. Millites was thrown from the dragon's back, landing hard on his side. He rose quickly to his feet and pat the snout of his dragon before turning to observe the battle.

~The War for Caelum~

The Phoenixes had scattered and the Daerds now fell upon the city. More warlocks had emerged from the thicket of the Nuquamese army and rained down fury upon the walls of the city. Smoke rose from the buildings, and the great domed structure had been beaten and broken with whole sections falling inwards and leaving the city open to the sky. Millites drew his sword and began to hurry toward the battle, when he noticed two figures ahead of him. They were both large with skin the dark black shade of the night. The larger of the two stood over the other. Fear shot through Millites as he watched Retsinis, with Ferrum Potestas in hand, looming over the body of Senkrad. Smoke seeped from the Wodahs' wounds, and Millites could only watch as a grey substance crawled over the flesh of Senkrad's skin, turning him into another of Retsinis's Nuquamese slaves. It appeared Senkrad had confronted his uncle, and whatever duel had ensued had just reached its conclusion.

Retsinis looked up from his defeated nephew and smiled at Millites. "What impeccable timing," Retsinis said, reaching down and picking up Senkrad's large glaive in his other hand. "I'm beginning to think fate just wants us to keep fighting forever."

Millites brandished his sword before him as Retsinis approached him. Fire burned low in the grass from the warfare that had occurred across this stretch not long before. The two faced each other, Retsinis glaring excitedly, and Millites dragging his sword wearily as he stared down the man who he knew was destined to kill him.

KINGS OF LIGHT, FIRE, AND DARKNESS
~ 26 ~

The Versipellis followed Speilton out of his dream and took shape on the open terrace before him. Speilton sprinted to the stairs, and then began to climb them instead of descending them. He emerged on the open roof of the tower, high above the city, as the Versipellis rose along the battlements on their black wings. Speilton held Spirit before him, and slipped his shield on his arm, invisible in the shade created by the swarm of Daerds outside the city.

"In our world or yours, you still fight alone, Speilton Lux," the Versipellis sneered, their wings melting away as they dropped onto the rooftop in their mummified forms.

"No, this time, I'm not alone."

Behind Speilton, he heard the sound of someone approaching on the marble stairs. He didn't even need to turn. He knew Teews' footsteps. Then there was a clatter of more boots striking the marble.

The eyes of the Versipellis twitched toward the staircase in surprise as Onaclov, Aurum, and Ince emerged next to Teews and stood beside Speilton.

"It looks like you're the outnumbered party now," Speilton smiled.

The Versipellis approached, arms tensed. "We fret not. We have brought legions to their knees before us."

"Yet you allowed a little boy to kill your brother," Teews said. "Doesn't sound too intimidating to me. No offense, Speilton."

~The War for Caelum~

Speilton smiled as the Versipellis flared with anger. There was the sound of beating wings, and then Prowl landed with a thud beside the Liolians, growling at the two dream spirits. The Versipellis eyed the blue dragon, and then they both dropped to all fours and transformed into beasts, one like a boar and the other like a panther as they rushed at the assembled Liolians. When they leaped, they retook their bladed forms. Onaclov swung his axe, and Teews raised her spear as they attacked, and the five Liolians lunged into battle against the two destroyers of worlds.

Retsinis swung Ferrum Potestas down at Millites, but the blade passed cleanly through the air and sunk into the soil. Millites struck his blade on the back of Retsinis's arm. The King of the Nuquamese appeared not to notice. Retsinis struck again with a backhand swipe of the glaive, and though Millites raised his blade to block it, the force knocked him onto his back. Millites rolled backwards as Retsinis stabbed at the ground. Then he sprang back to his feet.

After Retsinis's surge of darkness, Millites was left with only his sword as a weapon. However, Retsinis was only using his physical weapons as well, so Millites realized that whatever surge of power Retsinis had summoned had destroyed his own Wand of Darkness as well. Now the two fought with only their blades, just as they had years ago in the Milwarian Calorian War.

Senkrad began to stir where he had fallen as the two battled, and Millites knew it would only be a matter of time before the Calorian King rose again as one of Retsinis's mindless slaves. Yet there was nothing he could do but continue to fight, as there was no way to escape the Retsinis's attacks. His mind raced as he tried to find a way to kill Retsinis, or at least debilitate him, but he could think of nothing. It took every ounce of his focus to avoid the bite of Retsinis's blade, and so he set his mind only to the task of surviving, hoping that an opportunity would present itself. But a part of him knew that there would never be such an opportunity.

Spirit caught the Versipellis's blade as Prowl dove in and tackled the creature from the side. The dragon snapped her jaws at the eye of the Versipellis, but the demon had transformed into a black serpent and slithered out of her grasp. When the Versipellis formed again, Aurum stood over it, and stabbed at the brittle bones of the spirits with her knives. The Versipellis swung around, striking her in the arm, and started to finish her off when Ince leapt forward and struck the creature in the forearm with the tip of his spear.

The other Versipellis fought back Teews and Onaclov at the same time, quickly dodging the heavy blows of Onaclov's double-sided axe while parrying the quick stabs from Teews's spear. Pride flowed through Speilton as he watched his friends and family fight all around him. While they fought, they would shout to each other, pointing out attacks and letting the others know where they were in the hectic clash of blades. Plumes of fire scorched the stone from Prowl's jaws. The Liolians fought fluidly, dodging in and out of attacks and trusting their friends to protect them from certain strikes while taking opportunities to try and pierce the eyes of the Versipellis. Despite the Versipellis's claim, it appeared they were not used to combatting so many talented warriors at once, and all the transforming and illusions they were capable of performing were not enough to give them the advantage over the Liolians. But the Liolians still couldn't destroy them.

Speilton fought with sword and shield and magic, alternating attacks with Spirit and bursts of flames or wind or shattered glass. The Versipellis fought back like caged animals, lashing wildly at the Liolians as they pressed in around them. Prowl had circled around behind them, and as the demons backed up to the ramparts, she attacked with blue flames and her finned tail. For the moment, the Liolians appeared to have the upper hand, but unlike the Versipellis, they were not invincible. As they tired from their constant combat with the dream spirits, it became apparent that only a moment of confusion or distraction could lead to their destruction.

Senkrad rose, his face contorted beneath a grotesque black mask. Horns curled down from the sides of his head like those of a ram, and his body appeared more animal than humanoid. Millites struck against Retsinis's knee and rushed out of his reach as Senkrad stumbled forward. Now, two enemies were standing against him, one unkillable and the other a friend. Senkrad didn't attack, but merely stood as an observer. It became obvious that Retsinis was commanding him to hold back. He wanted to fight Millites alone. He wanted the victory to be his own.

Retsinis charged, and Millites slipped below the blade. The Dark King was still spry and eager for combat, but Millites was growing weary. He sprinted around Retsinis's attacks, parrying and dodging every powerful swing of Ferrum Potestas, and then pounced forward in an attempt to deal whatever damage he could to the King of the Nuquamese. Every stab and slice healed quickly, but Millites kept attacking, hoping that one strike would get lucky and strike some small fatal spot. Reason told him such hope was foolish; the power of Ferrum Potestas was too strong and too absolute to allow such a flaw to exist. With every attack from Retsinis, the truth of his situation became more evident. Retsinis could not be killed, and the fight would only end with Retsinis's blade driving through him.

Onaclov was the first to be struck down. His heavy axe tore through the smokey shape of the Versipellis and struck into the stone. Teews was stumbling from a close call of her own, and the Versipellis saw the opportunity to strike at the Igniacan leader with its bladed arm. The machete stabbed through a gap in Onaclov's armor at his waist, and then was pulled under his ribcage. He roared, and stumbled backwards, letting the axe slip from his grip. Teews struck forward with her spear, catching the Versipellis between its ribs but causing no harm to the spirit. Her spear became stuck between the rigid bones, and the Versipellis swiped at the shaft of the spear and snapped it, leaving Teews with only a wooden rod in her hands. Turning into a bull, it charged and crashed through Teews, and then wheeled on Prowl who attacked from behind. The dragon sank her claws into the hide of the bull, but then the Versipellis transformed again, sprouting monstrous heads from the tips of each horn that bit into Prowl's side. Prowl reared back and collapsed on the marble floor.

Speilton rushed forward and lit the Versipellis on fire, but as he did so the other spirit turned into a black vulture and grabbed Aurum in its claws, tossing her to the ramparts of the roof. Ince stabbed into the vulture's neck with his spear as Aurum held on desperately to the side of the building, and the Versipellis flew into the air in its cloaked form. Now only Speilton and Ince remained against the two Versipellis.

"You see what happens when you fight alongside your friends?" the Versipellis spoke as the other lunged at Speilton with its blades.

Speilton blocked the strike. The second Versipellis dove down at Ince, who hurriedly battered away the spirit's attacks with his spear. One transformed into a large ape-like creature, and Speilton blew it back with fire and roaring wind. Then, Speilton heard Ince yell out to him and turned around to see his friend rushing toward him. At first, the Versipellis Ince had been battling appeared to be nowhere in sight, but then it materialized behind him. And once again, one of Speilton's visions appeared before his eyes. This time, it happened too quickly for him to react, and the Versipellis's blade stabbed through Ince's chest.

Speilton couldn't make out the words Ince had been screaming, but after Ince fell limply to the ground, he heard the words of the Versipellis. "All that time you thought you could change the future," they said, "but there is no escaping it. You did not save him before, you only delayed the inevitable, and sacrificed your faun friend in doing so."

Speilton felt himself growing weak as all his hopes of survival came crashing down around him. His vision had come true. It could not be avoided, which meant the fate he saw that was to befall Millites and him could not be avoided either. Defeat dulled Speilton's mind and body as he stared down at the dying Ince. The other Versipellis struck at Speilton, and he held out Spirit to block it, but his parry was too weak. The attack knocked Ram's sword from his hands and brought him down to his knees. Speilton sank at the feet of the Versipellis, all motivation fleeing from him. This was how he would die. Millites would die by Retsinis's hand soon if he hadn't already. It was over.

With both of their tormented eyes glaring down at Speilton, the Versipellis raised their swords, when suddenly, a flash of gold crossed the rooftops. One Versipellis shrieked as Aurum dashed past the dream spirit closest to her and slashed her knife across its piercing eye. The cry of pain roused Speilton from his knees, and he quickly reached for the spirit lying before him. Aurum had been tossed to the ground after her attack, but the Versipellis was reeling, its eye twitching crazily across its body. Speilton strode reached high into the sky above and pulled down golden light that shone through the opened roof of the city. Speilton's shield lit up with blinding rays, and the Versipellis's eye squinted against it. The Versipellis was struggling to transform but couldn't decide which form to take. Speilton easily parried away a desperate strike from one bladed arm while slicing through the wing that sprouted from its other side. The eye twitched away from the glare, but the light poured down on them from all around now. Suddenly, the other Versipellis struck from behind, slicing the back of Speilton's hand across the white Versipellis scar, knocking Spirit from his grasp. But as Speilton turned to face this second Versipellis, Teews swung Onaclov's axe into its chest, smashing apart the ribs and throwing the spirit backwards.

Now, it was just Speilton and the wounded Versipellis, which cowered away against the ramparts with its eye red and seeping black blood. Speilton

watched as the eye twisted around, finally staring up at Speilton with fear. Then he pulled his broken Versipellis blade from the sheath at his waist. "This is for Metus," he said, "and for Ince. And for all those innocents in all the worlds slain by your hand." The Versipellis raised his bladed arms in protection, but it was already too late. Speilton leapt forward holding his sword – once part of a Versipellis – and plunged it through steel, bone, and flesh, until it pierced deep into the Versipellis's eye.

The dream spirit contorted. Just as the first Versipellis had years ago, it released a tremulous screech, then began to melt away. The eye blazed with flames, and then dripped with water, and then crumbled away into sand. Aurum rose to her feet and watched in shock as the linen rags and black feathers of the creature faded away, leaving only the black husk of the spirit. The Versipellis stumbled forward as if to attack once more, but the black shape gave way and billowed out across the rooftop, nothing more than ash.

Speilton spun around on the one remaining Versipellis, standing behind the body of Ince, its eye staring horrified at the dust. "Who's alone now?" Speilton questioned, and the Versipellis spread its black wings and rose into the air in response. It stopped for a moment above them, and then carried on, flying high into the air and slipping out of a shattered pane in the walls of Civitas Levi.

Ince stirred on the ground, rolling over onto one shoulder and muttering something with his eyes still squinted shut. Speilton and Aurum ran to him, and Teews ran to Onaclov as he was trying to rise to his feet. Ince rolled onto his back, blood seeping from his chest and back where the blade of the Versipellis had torn through. He was muttering something, and Speilton bent down low next to him to catch the words as they slipped out. "The...the fruit...the fruit of the silver tree," Ince muttered.

"He wants the fruit," Aurum said, looking up at Speilton. "The fruit that heals all wounds. Does he know that it will–"

"Yes," Speilton interrupted it. "He knows that it means he can never leave. We have to act quickly."

"But Speilton," Aurum said, "the grove of the Silver tree is outside the city walls. We'd have to get through Retsinis's forces."

She pointed to the southeast, on the other side of the city. Now that the Versipellis had fled the rooftop, they looked upon the streets of Civitas Levi once again, and what they saw was mayhem. The Daerds poured down from above through the gaping holes left in the golden walls by the attacks of the Warlocks, and the Phoenixes rushed after them. The gates to the east and the north had been knocked open and the Nuquamese forces poured through them. These beasts rushed through the streets, rolling through the Liolian forces that stood in their way. From the rooftops throughout the city, Liolians cast down bricks and shrapnel, but they brought down very few. Instead, they appeared to be drawing the creatures off of the streets and into the towers. Locked doors kept them at bay, but it would only be a matter of time before the creatures burst into the buildings and attacked those on the rooftops, ransacking them just as they did the streets.

"You know where to find the fruit?" Speilton asked Aurum, and she nodded quickly. "Then take Prowl. Sneak into the grove and take the fruit as quickly as you can."

"Are you sure?" Aurum asked. "Prowl seems pretty injured."

The dragon rose to her feet and limped over to where the others had congregated around Ince. "Prowl, can you fly? Ince needs you."

Prowl dropped one wing at Aurum's foot, indicating for her to climb on. "We'll be back soon," Aurum said as Prowl leapt into the air and flew shakily on her wings.

"Speilton," Teews said. "Our people need us down below. The Liolians have no leader, and the Nuquamese are everywhere."

"Where's Millites? I saw him go after Worc, but has he not returned?"

"I haven't seen him," Onaclov said still clutching his wound.

"And Senkrad?" Speilton asked.

"I didn't see him make it into the city," Teews said.

"Then it's just the three of us," Speilton said. "Someone needs to stay with Ince."

"I can stay," Onaclov offered with a grimace. "I won't be of much help fighting anyways."

"Teews, that leaves us to…" Speilton stopped as a voice whispered to him from somewhere far away.

He looked around wildly, recognizing the Versipellis's voice.

"What is it Speilton?" Teews asked. "What do you hear?"

"I am not the only one who fights alone," the voice of the last Versipellis whispered.

"Millites," Speilton realized aloud.

"Millites what?" Teews questioned. "What's happened to Millites, Speilton?"

Speilton looked around the city, but it was too hectic and too large to see anything. Instead, he closed his eyes and felt out across the city for any sign of his brother. He finally found him, not within the city but on the hills to the west, and two other figures stood near him.

"I have to go," Speilton said quickly, feeling that another of his visions was coming to fruition.

"Then let me come as well," Teews demanded.

"Teews, the men need you. They need a leader."

"And you think that's me?"

"It's always been you," Speilton said, looking his sister in the eyes. "You rally the troops in a way that no one else ever has. They trust you, and they will follow you anywhere if you lead them. Go to the streets and prepare them for one last ride against the Nuquamese."

"And what will you do?"

"I'll fight Retsinis," Speilton said, rushing off to the side of the rooftop.

"Wait!" Onaclov called. "Wait! It's Ince. He's… he's…"

When Speilton turned back, he saw that his friend had gone still. Ince's eyes were closed, and his dark skin had become pale. No fruit could bring him back now. Speilton felt the weight of the man's death upon his own shoulders, but he did not wait a moment longer. He leapt from the battlements, allowing his summoned wind to carry him out through the broken window pane. Below him were hundreds of the Nuquamese, all pushing into each other in their attempt to break through the gold walls of the dome. Speilton fell through the air towards them, and then summoned flames across his body. For a moment, he appeared like an eagle, with his extended arms wreathed in fiery wings. Over the Nuquamese forces he glided, and the creatures looked up at him in mixed wonder and fear. He landed on the hillside behind them, and when he took off running he could hear the footsteps of the hundreds of them running after him.

Millites parried and responded with a quick strike to Retsinis's chest. The King of the Nuquamese struck again with his sword, roaring with a wild excitement as Millites scrambled away. He threw the glaive as if it were a harpoon, and Millites' attempted deflection only drove the blade slightly off from its target. The blade stabbed into his shoulder and thrust off his pauldron, and his cape fell loose. He tore off the red fabric and cast it on the ground.

"You tire, young King," Retsinis observed. "Don't worry, when you become one more Nuquamese warrior in my army, you will never tire. You will never know fear."

Millites took deep breaths as he stared at Retsinis. The wind blew gently across the land, and a few rays of sunlight shone out of the thick storm clouds above them. But the darkness of the writhing storm clouds and the cluster of Daerds and Dark Phoenixes was still stifling.

"One day," Millites said, "you will meet your match. It may not be me. It may not be now. But one day, you will know fear as well."

Retsinis smiled a fanged smile and raced forward. Millites raised his sword, and Ferrum Potestas struck hard against the blade, knocking the sword out of his grasp. The King of the Nuquamese stood proudly over him, looking down at the unarmed King of Milwaria. "Go ahead," Millites spat.

Speilton reached the top of a hill and saw his brother just as Retsinis stabbed Ferrum Potestas forward. The blade plunged into Millites' stomach. Speilton screamed, and a fiery rage tore out of him, blowing out across the land. Grass was singed, Senkrad was thrown through the air from where he stood observing, and even Retsinis was knocked off his feet despite being many yards away. When he looked up, Speilton was already upon him. Speilton leapt with Spirit drawn, and drove the blade into Retsinis's chest. The Nuquamese King roared and grabbed Speilton with his massive, clawed hands, Ferrum Potestas having slipped from his grip during Speilton's attack. Speilton pulled out the white blade and stabbed again, summoning flames all around his body as Retsinis attempted to pry him off.

The Nuquamese army reached them, and observing their king, they began to circle. Speilton noticed them but didn't care. A terrible rage coursed through him, and all he was capable of doing was striking Retsinis again and again. Retsinis growled with pain, but each stab wound healed, and he eventually threw Speilton off of him and regained his footing. He reached down for the glaive he had thrown at Millites only a moment before and lifted it high in both hands. The blade glowed red after sitting in the flames of the battlefield, and Retsinis swung it excitedly. "Look at your brother now," he commanded. "Look what the noble King of Milwaria has been reduced to."

Speilton attacked with sword and magic. A wall of color danced between them, allowing Speilton to surprise Retsinis from the side. When the Dark King turned, Speilton summoned a rock spike from the ground just as Usus had done, except this time Retsinis was ready. With one fist he smashed the stone to pieces and charged at Speilton, swinging the red hot blade of the glaive viciously. "He was always the better fighter of the two of you," Retsinis proclaimed. "But even he was not strong enough."

The glaive flashed through the air in a blazing arc, and Speilton caught it with Spirit. Roots sprang up from the ground and lashed around Retsinis's legs and a torrent of wind blew against him, but he was stronger than both. Retsinis pulled free, moving after Speilton with continued vigor. "Your cheap magic tricks are quite amusing," Retsinis said, "but in the end, they will amount to nothing. You can't kill me."

"No one had ever killed a Versipellis before," Speilton responded. "Now I've killed two."

Retsinis paused to look at Speilton a moment with fascination. "Only one of them survives?" he inquired. "They always did appear weak to me – foolish in their desires."

He attacked again, and this time Speilton caught the blade with a column of stone. "Interestingly, they said the same about you," Speilton grinned. "That's why they chose you as one of their cursed."

Retsinis stared quizzically at Speilton now, and then with rage. "You lie," he growled. "The Versipellis serve me. They fight in *my* army."

"No," Speilton shook his head. "They've only been manipulating you all this time. What was it they referred to you as? 'A means to an end'."

"I have done nothing but pursue my own goals. I have conquered two worlds now, with many more awaiting me."

378

"You didn't conquer Liolia," Speilton said. "You killed it. Conquest implies there is still a land left for you to rule. No, Liolia is dead, just as the Versipellis wanted. And someday, you shall be as well…just as the Versipellis desire."

Retsinis roared and rushed him, attacking with strained thrusts and swings no longer intended to spar but to kill. Speilton pulled the land around him and used it to defend himself. But Retsinis's attacks were too strong. The blazing glaive tore through wind and stone alike and smashed hard into the invisible shield on Speilton's forearm. The next strike blew right past Speilton's head, and the following slipped through all his defenses and ran the burning edge of the blade across Speilton's side, cutting straight through his padded vest. But in the wild flurry of attacks, Speilton noticed something very uncharacteristic for Retsinis; he was unbalanced, savage in his decisions. "And to think that all that time, the great King of the Nuquamese was merely a pawn."

When Retsinis leapt at him with glaive raised high above his head, Speilton dropped below the attack, and rose quickly to drive Spirit through the monster's throat. A gurgling sound escaped his lips as Retsinis stumbled backwards, taking the sword with him. While Retsinis struggled to pull the blade out of his neck, Speilton shook the ground with his powers, opening cracks on the hilltop where they fought. Fire shot up through these fissures, and the storm clouds overhead dropped low and circled around the two, blocking out the hundreds of Nuquamese observing the battle. Retsinis finally dislodged the pale blade and snapped the sword over his knee. He cast the pieces of Ram's old sword to the ground, when suddenly, lava bubbled up from the cracks beneath his feet and thickened around him. It was now that Speilton summoned a great wind. He ripped a boulder from the ground and threw it into Retsinis. The Dark King toppled backwards into the pool of magma. His flesh burned as the lava cooled, and Retsinis let out a gurgled cry of pain as his skin festered and blistered. The exertion caused Speilton to feel lightheaded, but he lifted the shards of Spirit's blade with his mind and thrust them down into Retsinis like nails fastening him in a blazing coffin. Lava wrapped around the Dark King, and poured over his face. Retsinis's screaming stopped, and in that silence, Speilton allowed himself to believe that the King of the Nuquamese was truly dead. His body was exhausted, and he fell backwards, letting the winds die around him. He was fading off, and even though the legions of Nuquamese around him screeched and roared as they pressed in, he did not care. All he knew was that his brother lay dead somewhere beside him, and now he too could finally rest.

He wasn't sure if it was the sudden excited tone of the Nuquamese voices or the dark shape rising before him that caused him to snap back awake, but suddenly his eyes flew open wide as Retsinis emerged from the lava, shaking it off his scarred and mangled body. His milky eyes were wild, his lips curled back like some savage beast of the jungle, and his tongue lashed out of his wide, fanged jaws as he leapt through the air at Speilton, clawed hands extended before him like some bird of prey.

Speilton knew he did not have the power to reach out with his magic to control the land around him, and his shield was too small to defend this attack. So he merely watched, a passive observer of his own death.

And it was while he gazed upon the King of the Nuquamese in flight that he noticed the sudden shine of something golden toppling through the air towards him from over Retsinis's shoulder. It flew more quickly than Retsinis, as if propelled or thrown by some incredible strength, and though every ounce of rationality told Speilton to take cover, he felt the urge to reach out for it. Time slowed as Speilton raised his hand for the golden rod hurtling towards him, and the cool metal of the object fell perfectly into his grasp. The looming shape of Retsinis was almost upon him, when the object transformed in the fraction of a second, growing and flattening into a blade – a sword – and then the one Sword of Power.

There was a crack from high above like a clap of thunder as Retsinis's body fell on the blade, that was no longer as black as night but now shone a golden white. Then a beam of light broke through the brewing storm clouds and radiated upon Speilton. It then reflected off of him and coursed through the blade. Retsinis's eyes were thrown back in surprise as a beam of light shot through his body pushing him backwards off of the blade before he could sink his claws into Speilton. Retsinis howled with pain as the light burst from his open mouth, and then his eye sockets. All Speilton could do was hold onto the sword tightly with both hands. The Dark King appeared to be melting away while the beam of light pierced through him, or at least, the skin that encased him was stripped off and cast away into the blinding glare of the light. Ferrum Potestas hummed in Speilton's hands as bit by bit Retsinis was reduced from his terrible hulking incarnation to some withered being. And then, with another clap from the heavens above, the beam of light faded, and Retsinis sank to his knees, now appearing in the Wodahsian form he had possessed long ago. He stood there, awkward and shrunken, eyes wide with fright and bewilderment. The horns like those of a ram that had sprouted from his head had been broken off, and in his meager armor, his one human arm looked pale and thin hanging beside his pitch-black body. From his chest, the tip of an arrow protruded from where Speilton had shot him through the heart years ago. Now, without the magic of Ferrum Potestas to protect him, he fell to his knees. His eyes were fixed on Speilton, wide and confused, and then they suddenly shifted to some other figure approaching to his right. Speilton looked as well, to see a shining figure, radiating golden light walking forward with a sword in hand.

"Fear," the figure said simply, coming to a halt beside Retsinis. "That's what you're feeling."

And then Millites drove his broken sword through Retsinis's chest, and the King of the Nuquamese gasped. Smoke poured out of the wound, and blood dripped down his chest. Retsinis looked up at the shining Millites one last time, then down at Speilton laying only a few feet away with his old sword in hand. Then the Dark King fell forward, and perished as all living things do. The King of the Nuquamese was now no more than a corpse.

"Millites?" Speilton stammered, looking up on the verge of consciousness. "How?"

"Ferrum Potestas," Millites said, his voice clear and triumphant like the sound of ringing brass. "When you knocked Retsinis back, he left the blade still stabbed through me. As I grabbed ahold of it to pull it out of my chest, it changed in my hand. It became a sword of light, just like it is now, and suddenly I was no longer transforming into one of Retsinis's slaves, but something else entirely."

Millites lifted Speilton off the ground and helped him stand. "That means, you're the new master of the Sword of Power," Speilton said, "and if you were the first person it cut, that means you're…"

"Invincible," Millites finished his statement with a smile that showed overwhelming joy.

"And Retsinis…" Speilton began, struggling to keep his feet with his body still sapped of all energy. "You threw me the sword so that I could…"

"So that you could cut him, with the Sword of Light. And it worked!" Millites exclaimed. "The power of the sword counteracted the magic that had made him invincible. The light nullified the dark, leaving Retsinis just as he was before he was cut by the blade. Look! Look at the Nuquamese!"

All around them, the creatures of Retsinis's army were rushing around wildly, no more than feral animals without their master to control them. They seemed to have no interest in Millites or Speilton, or no interest in really anything at all. High above them, the storm clouds had broken, and the light of the midday beat down on them all. In the distance, they saw the western gates of the city open, and Liolian banners emerged from within. The Liolian forces were riding out of Civitas Levi, and the Nuquamese fled as they rode out across the worn and battle-tested land. At the head of the forces they saw Teews riding on a white horse, racing towards them.

"This means…" Speilton began.

"We won," Millites smiled. "We won!"

Still shining with brilliant light, Millites leapt excitedly. Speilton laughed, standing shakily on his legs.

Joy filled his heart, when a thought suddenly blossomed in the back of his mind – a terrible, soul-crushing thought. Millites was distracted by the approaching Liolians, and Speilton was too exhausted to react in time. He could feel the shadow of the last Versipellis forming behind him, and he cried out as the blade stabbed through his spine and out of his chest.

THE DRAGON'S ROAR
~ 27 ~

Speilton was cognoscente of people rushing toward him as he fell backwards beside the dusty robes of the Versipellis. The pain that tore through him was terrible, yet he could hardly feel it. His vision was fading, and his body had gone limp. For some reason, he wasn't even afraid. He was merely present in that moment, just a spectator, watching his final moments alive.

The ground shook as Prowl landed hard on the ground next to him. The blue dragon leapt protectively over Speilton's body, fury building up in the creature until it was released all at once in a terrifying roar that echoed out across the plains and caused every soul to tremble. Even the Versipellis began to back away in fright. As Prowl's roar continued, the few blades of grass before her lit on fire under the heat of her breath, until the hem of the Versipellis's robes caught fire as well. Nuquamese soldiers that had rushed around aimlessly suddenly turned and looked at the dragon with fear in their eyes, and that same fear appeared to be present in the eye of the Versipellis. The dream spirit rose into the air on his black vulture wings and looked down at the Liolians gathered below with its horrific, twitching eye. Then its wings flapped and carried it high into the sunny sky, until it disappeared somewhere in the far distance.

Speilton coughed, struggling for breath as blood welled up in his mouth. The light of the sun was blinding in his eyes, casting a golden gleam across his vision, until he realized it wasn't the sun at all, but a figure crouching over him. "Speilton," he heard his name spoken, but it sounded far away. "I have the fruit. It can heal you but…"

Everything became fuzzy as Speilton began to drift away somewhere beyond the pain. But he fought against it, struggling to stay conscious for just a moment longer. "You can never return," the voice spoke again. "You won't be able to see Liolia again."

It took all of Speilton's effort to nod his head, as Aurum cracked open the scarlet fruit. Prowl walked over to him now, and laid her head on his chest over the wound as Aurum bent over to place the fruit in his mouth. Speilton was only slightly aware of the small seeds being dropped in his mouth. His jaws chewed slowly, and then swallowed. Aurum looked down at him concerned, and then he saw others gathered around – Millites shining like the sun, Teews holding the banner of Milwaria. And then more Liolians stepped into his fading view: Ore, Equus, Whinn, Cindariel, the satyr Brutus, and finally the glowing tiger face of Burn. They all stared into his eyes as the world became dark, and Speilton finally allowed himself to slip away.

A NEW DAY BEGINS
~ 28 ~

Light trickled in through an open window beside his bed. He raised a hand to shield the sun from his waking eyes and rolled over on the cot. His room was small and appeared miraculously untouched by the warfare that had burned through the city. The walls were ornately decorated, and there were arched entrance ways in the walls of the room that led out to a terrace through which even more light poured in. Teews sat in an armchair at the end of his bed, her head resting on a clenched fist while she slept upright. Beneath her feet was Prowl, who's body had shrunk in the aftermath of the war but was still large enough to wrap around the bed like a shield. She slept as well, breathing out small puffs of smoke with each snore.

Speilton sat up and looked around the room, taking in the glitter of the morning light on the architecture. It took him a moment to realize he didn't feel any pain. He lifted the soft tunic he was wearing and saw the thin white scar across his chest where the blade of the Versipellis had stabbed through. The fruit of the Silver Tree had fulfilled its purpose.

Hearing the rustling of his sheets, Prowl opened her eyes and excitedly crawled onto Speilton's bed and lay her head in his lap. Teews' head slipped off of her fist, and she suddenly leapt awake. "Oh, you're up," Teews exclaimed, rushing from the chair and hugging her brother from the side of the bed. "We were worried it was too late. You were still for so long we thought the fruit might not be able to heal you."

"I think I'm better now," Speilton said as Teews finally released him.

"You must be starving!" Teews said. "You slept for nearly a full day."

"I am a little hungry," Speilton admitted. "Where is everyone else?"

"Well," Teews sat down on the edge of the bed as she prepared to explain, "a lot has happened since we brought you here. With Retsinis dead, the Nuquamese were just running around, scared, but still possessed by the magic. The army has tried to corral them all, and the centaurs have helped to herd them so that Millites release the dark magic of Ferrum Potestas. Now that the master of the sword fights for good, his magic counteracts Retsinis's. So far, he's been able to save hundreds of them, maybe thousands by now. The Daerds on the other hand fled off somewhere to the east. There weren't many left, and since Hunger killed Worc, they were leaderless. And when the Nuquamese stopped fighting, the Warlocks realized they couldn't challenge our army alone, even without our magic. We had one final charge and–"

"And you lead them?" Speilton asked proudly.

"Yes," Teews laughed. "Yes, I led the charge. And the Warlocks fled. Then only the Dark Phoenixes remained, and they surrendered. There was talk yesterday of them coming to some type of agreement with the other Phoenixes. I believe they wish to end the banishment of their kind and reintegrate their two people, but I'm not sure if that's official. With the leader of the Order dead now, none of the Phoenixes really know what to do. But Speilton, many, many Phoenixes died. Some were killed by the Daerds, so they will be reborn, but others died from the Dark Phoenixes, which means they are truly gone."

"I know. We lost so many soldiers, as well."

Teews nodded quietly. "It took a lot, but we did it. Caelum is safe, as are the Liolians. Civitas Levi is still somewhat intact. We've already started trying to clean through the wreckage, treat those who are wounded, and collect those that we can't. It'll take some time to restore everything, though."

"I think we'll have plenty of time," Speilton smiled. "And, what of the last Versipellis? Have you–"

"He's gone. Prowl seemed to scare him away. The last one is off somewhere, but I don't think he'll be returning here anytime soon."

Prowl had fallen back to sleep with her head on Speilton, when another figure appeared in the doorway. Aurum suddenly rushed into the room and threw her arms around Speilton. "You're awake!" she shouted.

"Seems I slept through a great deal," Speilton laughed.

"How much do you remember? The fruit of the Silver Tree sometimes has strange effects on those who use it to heal."

"It's coming back to me slowly. I remember fighting the Versipellis in Civitas Levi. I remember destroying one of them. But then Ince...I tried to save him, but…"

"There was nothing you could've done," Teews said. "We were able to kill one of the Versipellis, so Ince did not die in vain."

"Aurum, your brother," Speilton said, "Retsinis cut him down. Did he…"

389

"He's okay," Aurum said with a smile. "Millites was able to counteract the dark magic with Ferrum Potestas just as he did for so many others."

"I remember seeing him turned to one of the Nuquamese, and I remember dueling with Retsinis. And I remember seeing Ferrum Potestas flying through the air, and catching it, and Retsinis transforming back to his original form. Then I remember looking down, and seeing the Versipellis blade protruding from my chest. And then...then I remember seeing you," he said to Aurum, "and Prowl. And you gave me the fruit."

"So you do remember everything," Aurum said. "You passed out not long after that."

"For a while it was hard to tell if the fruit was working," Teews admitted.

"Well I think it's clear now that it accomplished its purpose," Speilton laughed.

"Speilton," Aurum said, "I asked you as I was giving you the fruit, but I must ask again. You do understand what the consumption of the fruit of the Silver Tree means, don't you?"

"I can never leave this land," Speilton nodded, "and I can never see Liolia again. But Liolia was not just a land. The spirit of Liolia lives on in here in Caelum. I'm glad I get to see it, and be present for this new chapter of Liolia. We lost so many that I know would give anything to witness this."

"We did lose many, but we saved so many more," Aurum said.

"Oh, I almost forgot," Teews said. "There's going to be a funeral this afternoon for everyone lost, and a banquet afterwards. All of the Liolians are welcome, and I believe all that are able will be in attendance. And they reopened the portal to Liolia so that they could bring in some animals, so it doesn't look like we'll be having another vegetarian feast."

Speilton lay back in bed and took a deep breath. Strange feelings crept over him that he hadn't felt in a long time: contentment, relief, ease. The war was over. For the first time in years, there was peace.

They began the funeral in the mid-afternoon. The sun had begun to descend, and the sky was darkening to a reddish hue when the Liolians assembled outside of Civitas Levi facing south toward the ocean. On the beach, hundreds of wooden boats sat in a row in the sand, the waves gently lapping against their hulls. Some had been made long ago by the Liolians living in the city, and others were made that day to accommodate the number of deceased. They ranged in size and shape, from canoes to rafts to some single-masted boats, but all were more or less the same size; each just large enough to hold the body of a fallen Liolian. Below the Liolians were small pyres, holding the bodies aloft so that the survivors could bear witness one last time. Thousands had been collected from the battle at Civitas Levi alone, including the Nuquamese which had once been Liolians, and in honor of all the missing bodies left on the battlefields to the north, there was a singular empty boat in the center of all the others.

Though thousands of Liolians gathered around, not a word was spoken as Speilton, Millites, Teews, Senkrad, and Onaclov led the Liolians to the boats, each holding a thin white sheet in their hands. The Liolians walked up to their fallen brethren and carefully laid the sheets over their bodies. Speilton, Millites, and Teews gathered around the simple wooden boat where Usus lay, and Millites pulled forth his curved khopesh and placed it across his chest. Together, they took one final look before pulling the sheet over him. In the boat beside him, Flamane lay, and Prowl and Hunger crouched beside it. Then, they stepped over to Ince, and laid the beaded vest he had been given by the Isoalates over the man's body before covering him as well. They came next to the boat where Ram's body lay, recovered from the hill where he had fallen. Speilton pulled the hilt and half-shattered blade of Spirit, and laid the pale sword on the old man's chest. Burn stood beside the boat and nuzzled her friend one last time before they pulled the sheet over the man's reddish beard and face. Finally, they walked to the empty boat in the center, and Teews handed Speilton the object she had been holding. It was Metus' flute, and Speilton placed it amongst the logs and tinder within the boat.

All around, the other Liolians were doing the same, until the boats each possessed the white silhouette of a Liolian who had passed on from this world. With the bodies properly covered, the surviving Liolians began to push the boats toward the ocean. The boats carved through the wet sand and gentle waves until the water was deep enough for them to float on their own. The tide was going out, but the Liolians kept their hands on the sides of the boats, and pulled them on through the waves until they had waded out to their waists. Then, upon the land, torches were ignited up and down the shoreline and were carried through the waves until they reached those holding the boats steady in the surf. Once every torch had reached the boats, Millites, Speilton, Teews, and Senkrad each lowered a torch into a pyre within a boat, and the other Liolians followed. The boats roared with flames and were pushed off to sea, and the Liolians watched for a few moments before returning to land to sit or crouch in the sand. It was only now that some of the Liolians began to talk, whispering quietly amongst themselves to console those who had lost loved ones. As the sun set and the ocean darkened with the approaching night, the hundreds of boats sailed on, glittering like stars caught on the horizon. Burning ash raced to the heavens, ferrying the physical forms of the Liolians away on the ocean breeze. Somewhere out there, the bodies of Usus and Ram and Ince and hundreds of others were fading away into the flicker of flames, and then mere pinpoints of light on the horizon. Humans, dwarves, Wodahs, Isoalates, elves, centaurs, mers, treeps, fauns, and satyrs, united in their sacrifice for the peace the Liolians could now share, were united one final time in the turning to ash and embers. Then slowly, as the hours went by and night settled in, the lights disappeared one by one, passing over the horizon or crumbling into the sea.

When the lights had all flickered out, and there were only the stars, the Liolians returned to Civitas Levi and entered the massive banquet hall. Situated near the center of the city, the hall had only taken slight damage during the siege, with a single hole blown into the roof in one corner. They gathered around the long, wooden tables, and great platters of food were brought out by the Phoenixes. They ate in the flickering light of the torches posted on the massive stone columns and the soft glow of the chandeliers that hung from the ceiling. They were quiet at first, their mind still entranced by the flames from the funeral, but slowly the great food and warm company raised their spirits and reminded them of everything they had fought for and achieved. At the head of the hall, before the massive mosaic of swooping Phoenixes and brilliant landscapes, the leaders of Liolia sat in plush chairs facing the thousands of feasting Liolians below. Henry Swifttongue leapt up on a table and began weaving stories, and the Liolians around him roared with laughter. At another table, Ore was retelling some event from the battle with incredible enthusiasm, and the dwarves around him leaned in excitedly. Onaclov, sitting next to him, laughed austerely, clutching his bandaged side. His face was still hard and worn, until a young woman came and sat next to him to talk, and his demeanor softened. In the torchlight, the Wodahs appeared like humans, and it became nearly impossible to tell them apart. And at that moment, there was truly no difference between them. Milwarians and Calorians were now one people – the survivors of Liolia. The centaurs crouched beside a table on lifted legs to dine with the giants, and between the two races they consumed more food than any other table, shoveling down cakes and roasted pigs and all sorts of pies and fruits and whole loaves of bread. The satyr Brutus yelled at a mer nearby for allegedly stealing the last slice of pie, but after only a moment the two were laughing and dancing beside the tables. Whinn, the leader of the mers, showed his trident to Cindariel. Herdica spoke with a group of widows and their young children, bringing smiles to their faces. All the while, a constant flock of Phoenixes brought in more food from the makeshift kitchens in the building next door and carried out the empty plates and trays. Food overflowed, and every mug and goblet was filled and refilled to the brim. The Liolians cheered and danced and sang the old songs of Liolia, and Millites, Teews, and Speilton descended from their table and joined them all. Even the stoic Senkrad, freed from Retsinis's dark magic, joined in with the partying after Aurum dragged him down with the others. The banquet lasted late into the night, until slowly, one by one the Liolians slipped away to sleep. Families had been reunited after Millites had returned the Nuquamese to their original forms, so after sharing in the group revelry, they required time alone with each other. Much of the city lay in ruins, but it was vast, and everyone found a place to stay and a bed on which to sleep. Some Liolians merely fell asleep in their chairs at the banquet tables amongst the empty cups and leftover food.

Speilton had slept for a day, and he needed no more sleep that night. He left Prowl where she lay, enormous and sprawled out amidst the tables, and went out into the streets of the city for a walk. The night air was cool, and he could hear the rumble of thunder in the distance, but it didn't worry him. It meant rain was on its way to wash the blood ash from the fields and off the cobblestone streets. The sky was no longer clear as it had been before the war. Ever since the Dark Phoenixes had reached Civitas Levi, clouds drifted across the sky and threatened rain just as they had in Liolia. The grass no longer appeared the brilliant, harsh green that the Liolians had first awoken to see in Caelum. It was duller now, full of shadow and imperfections. But it also appeared real, just like the grass of Liolia. This balanced world, for the first time, appeared like home.

There was the distant sound of singing in the streets from somewhere off in the city where the festivities were still alive. He smiled to himself as he slowly made his way to one particularly impressive tower and entered. It appeared that some people were asleep on the lower levels, but as he climbed the stairs, he was relieved to find it unoccupied. There was a balcony at the top, and he looked out over its edge to take in the sprawling city around him. All throughout were the dim flickers of some still burning torches, but it appeared that most people were asleep. High above, nestled in their cages of steel and wood, the Phoenixes slumbered. Speilton remembered not long ago when their colors filled the sky above the city, but now they were much fewer and less vibrant. With so much of the cage-like walls of the city destroyed, the sky above the city was open to the fresh air of Caelum, allowing Speilton to look out at a field of stars. He was surprised that he knew many of the constellations, though they each appeared slightly off and rearranged. It was a view of the same stars as in Liolia but from a different perspective.

"It is marvelous," a calm voice said beside him, and Speilton recognized the voice instantly.

"Rilly?" he asked, looking into the dark air to make out the glimmer of the Anemoi taking form out of the dust and ash that still blew through the air. "How are you here? I thought you were tied to Liolia."

"As did I," Rilly said warmly, "but it appears I made a mistake. It was not the land I was tied to – the hills and rivers and mountains – but the people. Liolia lives on here in this world, and so it appears that I too was able to live here in Caelum."

"So that means it is truly official," Speilton said. "Liolia is no more."

"No, no quite the opposite," Rilly said. "Liolia has never been more alive. Here, in this world, Liolia is merely awakening to a new day."

"I do hope you are right," Speilton said, looking back out at the city. "I think I'd really like not having to search for another home."

"This world is yours. All of it is untapped potential, boundless land for you and your people."

"And what about the Phoenixes?" Speilton asked. "This is their land after all."

"Speilton, do you remember what I told you about the way in which life tends to…simplify over time?"

"Yes, I remember you mentioning that."

"Well, just as it was the fate of the Anemoi to fade away in time, so is it the fate of the Phoenixes to pass on from this land and leave it for a new people."

"The Liolians?" Speilton asked.

"Yes," Rilly said, "and any other people that find refuge in this world. Caelum is a vast land, with many secrets to uncover. What you have seen is so very little."

"And you believe that, in time, the Phoenixes will die?"

"One day, maybe soon, maybe years and years from now, yes, I believe the Phoenixes will die. Already their numbers have fallen, and many of the inhabitants of the great cities across Caelum have fled to distant lands. The Phoenixes were never meant to rule this land forever, but you shouldn't feel sad. That is the way of all things, and as the years go on, maybe within your lifetime even, you shall see many other races pass on. The dryads and naiads, for instance, can only live so long in this world before the trees and rivers from which they were born in Liolia wither away. Then they too will fade."

"So, will all life die someday?" Speilton asked. "One day, will every race of Liolia pass on as well?"

"Everything must die at some point, but I do believe some things will pass on before others. The giants and mers and hooved folk for instance may pass on before the elves and dwarves and humans, but I think humans will survive them all. They were always the favorite of all His creations."

"His?" Speilton asked.

"Ah, yes, I believe that leads me to my ulterior purpose for coming here this evening," Rilly stated. "King Speilton, you have another guest tonight."

He heard the high popping sound just as Cigam appeared on the balcony behind them with a king but apologetic face. The wizard gave a stiff bow as he approached Speilton. "I wish to congratulate you, King Speilton, on such an incredible victory. My deepest apologies for the Wizard Council's lack of support in your war for Caelum, but we could not be more overjoyed with the outcome."

"Thank you, Cigam," Speilton said. "I assume that your presence here means that the last Versipellis is no longer here in Caelum."

"Yes, we believe the last of the three has chosen a new target with which to wreak terror. He is no longer of any threat to you or your people. That was incredible work, by the way, destroying another of those terrible demons, but it appears one still exists and will exist for some time until another warrior of your prowess can slay him."

"I wish you luck in finding that warrior," Speilton said.

"Well, that is in part why I have come," Cigam admitted. "We had hoped that you might help us find that individual, seeing as you know what it takes to kill the Versipellis."

"You want me to help you?" Speilton asked. "How could I do that?"

"By joining the Wizard Council. By becoming a Wizard. You have the powers Speilton, and the heart to commit to the battle against evil. We could use your talent. You will not have the opportunity to kill the Versipellis here in Caelum, and you can only travel between worlds if you are a Wizard, which means you won't be able to fight them directly either. But, you can prepare others who do have to face him. Additionally, there are many other battles in a multitude of other worlds that could use someone with your skills."

"I ate the fruit," Speilton said, "the fruit that binds me to this land forever."

"Yes, I heard," Cigam said. "However, we at the Council believe that we just might be able to break the magic that binds you here. It would not be easy, and of course, would only be allowed if you did choose to join our Council."

"Thank you for the offer," Speilton said, "but I just finished a war. I'd really enjoy a bit of peace, for at least a little while before I could consider something like that."

"I understand," Cigam smiled. "We at least had to offer. Oh, but before I go, I must ask, has He spoken to you?"

"Has who spoken to me?"

"A voice in your dreams or in moments of difficulty or weakness. A strong voice, that is still somehow soft."

"Yes, actually," Speilton said, thinking back on the voice that had kept him company in jail and in Liolia. "And whose voice is that exactly?"

"It is His voice, the same Him that Rilly was speaking of just now. It is He that we – the Wizards – serve, or at least try our best to serve. He is the light for which we fight – the one who crafted the hills and valleys and oceans of Liolia and the plains and mountains of Caelum."

"He was talking to me?" Speilton asked, suddenly feeling embarrassed to have received such honor without even knowing.

"Why, of course," Cigam smiled. "He speaks to all people and all creatures, just not always as clearly as He did to you."

"He's the one the Wizards serve?" Speilton asked.

"And the one the Versipellis tried to undermine and combat at every turn. We are tasked with carrying out His will as best as we can. But we are all like you – good intentioned, but flawed. Our Council may not be in itself a perfect organization, but we do represent the One who is, and we try our best to pursue it as well. And on top of all of it, we're given some pretty excellent scepters."

"I understand," Speilton nodded slowly. "Maybe – one day – I'll join your Council, but for now I must say that my decision stands. I think I need some time to live in peace to remind me why it's worth fighting for."

"Very insightful," Cigam said pleasantly, backing away from Speilton. "We are always eager to accept a new member, so reach out to us if you change your mind. Rilly knows how to find us."

With another crack, Cigam had vanished, and it was once again just Speilton and Rilly on the balcony.

They were quiet for a few moments, watching the stars and the still city below them. Then Speilton asked, "Will you stay here, near Civitas Levi?"

"I will stay close to the Liolians, whether they decide to live here or move on to some other land to begin again. Who knows, perhaps I'll even make a new hut."

"If you need help, just let me know. I've developed some new methods for building them," Speilton grinned.

Rilly laughed in his light, soft way, and then the two shared the silence of the night and watched the distant rain clouds approach from over the hills.

It was a few days later when the Liolian leaders went for a walk to the beach beside the vast ocean south of Civitas Levi. They walked along that shore, growing nearer the grove of the Silver Tree. They were quiet for a few minutes as they listened to the whistle of the sea breeze and felt the cool air. Onaclov broke the silence. "It is the intention of the dwarves to move on from this land. They wish to explore the lands beyond the Great Feather Peaks in search of a potential home."

Onaclov was still stern, hardened by his years ruling the Milwarians after the ruin caused by Retsinis. Even now, with the war over, he was a rigid man, set on a goal, set on survival. They may have not any more battles to fight, but the battles would always rage in their minds. But his few days of peace seemed to have softened him some, and Speilton could only hope that as the days went by Onaclov would be able to return to the man he was before.

"Well, we wish you luck in your travels," Millites said. "When do you plan to set out?"

"In the coming weeks, once our wounded have returned to health. The dwarves have always been an independent people. They don't much enjoy having to share their land, much less a land as bright and open as Civitas Levi. They are most at home in the darkness beneath the mountains."

"There was a city in the Feather Peaks where the Phoenixes once lived," Herdica said. "Marenta Loras was what it was called. I believe they created towers upon the tops of the mountains, so it may not be suitable for the dwarves, but your people could stay there until they have created a stronghold within the mountains."

"We will look for it," Onaclov said. "Thank you."

"The Wodahs, too, desire a land of their own," Senkrad said. "I do not know where yet, but they are eager to set out and find a place out there in that great beyond."

"I understand," Millites said.

"Cindariel told me as well that the elves are planning to leave as well," Teews added, "most likely for one of those cities in the Arcanian Woods to the east."

"It's for the best," Speilton said. "This entire world is ours now, we might as well disperse and see exactly what we have been given."

"What of the other Liolians?" Onaclov asked. "Where will you go?"

"Lake Vascent," Millites said before the others got the chance. "In the middle of the lake there's that massive rock if you remember. Someone once said that it would make a great place for a castle."

Teews smiled, knowing who he was speaking of. "A new Kon Malopy?"

402

"Something like that," Millites said. "A new home for the humans of Milwaria and all other creatures that wish to come as well. But the castle will take time to build, so the people will need somewhere to stay until it can be completed. Teews, what if they stayed here, under your leadership?"

"Me?" she asked. "Are you sure?"

"Yes," Speilton agreed. "Millites will oversee the construction of the new city, while you lead the people here."

"And when I left the Liolians years ago I relinquished my right to serve as their queen," their mother said. "The people need you, Teews."

"What about you, Speilton?" Teews asked.

"I think I'll pursue a simpler life. I've never had the chance to just exist and wake up every day without a goal or objective. For a time, I need to give it a chance. Then one day, who knows…"

"Well, if you're yearning for the life of a civilian, I guess the only decision you need to make now is which leader you want ruling over you," Millites smiled, and his skin still radiated with the golden light from Ferrum Potestas."

"Why choose one?" he asked with a laugh. "Perhaps I'll just wander, see how life is in each of the future Kingdoms of Caelum."

"The Wodahs would be happy to have you," Senkrad said. "You were the one who saved them from Retsinis, after all."

"As would the dwarves," Onaclov said.

"Sadly, I think we're too crowded here," Teews joked. "Not sure if we have any more room for you…"

They laughed beside the gentle waves of the Ocean.

Millites turned to his brother once they had begun to fall silent again and said, "Just know that no matter where you go in this land, it will be your home."

"And your family will always be here," Herdica said.

The next morning, Speilton awoke early and roused Prowl from where she slept at the foot of his bed. They stepped out into the cool morning air and made their way through the calm streets of the city. Through the few intact glass panes, the glow of the approaching sun could be seen. Speilton held his bow in one hand – the bow once belonging to the elf Nicholas – and he had a quiver of arrows slung over his shoulder. At the gates leading out of Civitas Levi, he and Prowl came across Aurum, leaning against the open doors and observing the hill stretching outward before her. "Where are you two going so early in the morning?" she asked as Speilton and Prowl approached.

"We're going off for a hunt," Speilton said. "Now that the animals have been let into Caelum, we thought it would be a good time."

"So, you're not running away?" she asked with a wry smile.

"Not yet," Speilton said. "For now, I'm here to stay."

"But one day you may?" she asked. "If you ever decide to leave this place behind, just let me know."

Speilton nodded and smiled at the girl with golden hair.

404

"Out across that sea there, they say there are whole other lands, teeming with all types of beasts. Whole other worlds of adventure."

"I'm sure after some years of peace, I'll be ready for another adventure," Speilton said.

Aurum laughed and went on her way back into the city, and Prowl leapt up into the open skies above Civitas Levi. They headed east, towards that place on the horizon where they could just make out that the vast Arcanian Woods began. Speilton looked back at the city glittering in the early morning light behind him. Deep within the walls of the city, Burn slept quietly near Teews who had taken him in after the passing of Ram. Hunger lay beside the bed of Millites, who shined even in his sleep with the power of Ferrum Potestas. Prowl flew on the still morning air, until the brilliant city faded on the horizon, and they arrived at the sea of green trees. Prowl descended on her wide wings, and Speilton slipped down from her back and stepped into the shadow of the wood. A dark canopy of leaves stretched above his head as he trod quietly through the forest. There was the chatter of birds high above, singing the same songs Speilton had listened to years ago in Kal. Amidst the brush, he found the tracks of a deer, and they appeared to be fresh. He had no way of knowing whether it was a Liolian deer or some deer from the far distant lands of Caelum, but it did not matter anymore. Speilton followed them as they wove between the trees, Prowl close behind him, skipping excitedly after Speilton. Then he saw the points of the antlers rising up amongst the trees. The deer was only five yards away.

~*The War for Caelum*~

~THE END~

~The Battles of Liolia~

EPILOGUE

They came down from the north, walking through the shade of the tall, soft trees that echoed with their emptiness in a way that wasn't ominous but pure. Every aspect of the landscape bore the patterns of new life, fresh and untouched. The trees seemed to whisper to the mountains and the brooks with words carried on the wind in excitement at the human eyes observing them all for what may have been the first time.

The boy had often grown tired, and the man had grown accustomed to carrying him on his back from time to time. But as they approached the lake, the boy began to run ahead, weaving between trunks and skipping over brush and roots until the forest reached its edge and gave way to a sparkling lake that spread out before them like the ocean. "Look!" the boy cried, pointing at the island floating in the middle of the dark body of water. The man smiled and nodded to him.

There was a small vessel not much further down the shore, nestled between great boulders where the tide had placed it. It was ancient, with worn wood and many holes, but by nightfall the man had patched it and fashioned a makeshift sail on its mast. That night they slept by a fire, as they had every night of their long journey.

In the morning the man placed the boy in the boat and pushed it into the low tide before pulling himself in as well. The wind caught the sail, and the voices of the trees, and the mountains, and the lake carried them across the gentle waves. As they sailed, the boy peered into the water, desperate to uncover the mysteries of its depths. He thought he saw a face looking up at him from somewhere far below but guessed it had only been his reflection.

They reached the island, and the man secured the boat to the shore. Then he and the boy left the shore and stepped into the thick forest. The boy was ecstatic. He ran and leapt amongst the trees as if they were his friends, and the man laughed upon seeing his joy. They walked deeper and deeper into the forest, filled with the sounds of rustling leaves and creaking limbs and now the laughter of the man and the boy. Then the boy stopped suddenly before something in the middle of the forest and looked at it curiously. The man walked behind him, placing a hand on his shoulder. Amidst a grove of trees, there was a small hut made of woven limbs and tree trunks that was overgrown with ivy and tall grass. A singular edifice in a silent land.

"What is this place, father?" the boy asked, looking up at the man.

The man looked at the house, and then let his eyes wander off towards the trees and brush that stretched in every direction around them. Somewhere, he thought he heard the distant singing of a bird.

"This," the man said, "is Kal."

~The War for Caelum~

~The War for Caelum~

ABOUT THE AUTHOR

Will Mathison is the author and illustrator of *The Battles of Liolia* series. In the 4th grade Will Mathison was inspired to raise funds in honor of his friend's little brother who was diagnosed with Leukemia. Over the following several months, Will wrote and illustrated the story he had been developing in his imagination since reading *The Chronicles of Narnia* in the second grade. In the 5th grade Will completed *The Last of Kal* which is the first of five books in *The Battles of Liolia* series and donated all proceeds to the American Cancer Society's Relay for Life. In the years following, he published three more books in the series: *The Inferno of Erif*, *The Curse of the Verse*, and *The Rise of Nuquam*. So far, Will has been able to raise over $7000 for Relay in honor of Carter and all of those battling cancer.

In High School, Will continued developing and writing short stories, earned the rank of Eagle Scout, and was published in the Huffington Post. He has also spoken at over a dozen schools and community events to motivate other students to find and pursue their passions. Wonderful teachers have encouraged his ability and his love for writing, as well as his little brothers, Charlie and Jack, and their dogs, Lolly and Bailey, who have offered inspiration for several of the characters. Will now attends the University of Georgia where he studies International Affairs and Economics. This book, *The War for Caelum* is the conclusion to the five part series of books, *The Battles of Liolia*.

To learn more about the characters and world of Liolia, please visit www.battlesofliolia.blogspot.com.

~The Battles of Liolia~

Book 1
The Last of Kal

Book 2
The Inferno of Erif

Book 3
The Curse of the Verse

Book 4
The Rise of Nuquam

Book 5
The War for Caelum

Made in the USA
Columbia, SC
08 June 2020